D0436692

DATE DUE

		PRINTED IN U.S.A.

EAGLE VALLEY LIBRARY DISTRICT
P.O. BOX 240   600 BROADWAY
EAGLE, CO 81631   (970) 328-8800

BLACKLIST

BY JERRY LUDWIG

Blacklist
Getting Garbo
Little Boy Lost

BLACKLIST

A NOVEL

JERRY LUDWIG

A TOM DOHERTY ASSOCIATES BOOK

NEW YORK

This is a work of fiction. All of the characters, organizations, and events portrayed in this novel are either products of the author's imagination or are used fictitiously.

BLACKLIST

Copyright © 2014 by Jerry Ludwig

All rights reserved.

A Forge Book
Published by Tom Doherty Associates, LLC
175 Fifth Avenue
New York, NY 10010

www.tor-forge.com

Forge® is a registered trademark of Tom Doherty Associates, LLC.

The Library of Congress Cataloging-in-Publication Data is available upon request.

ISBN 978-0-7653-3539-5 (hardcover)
ISBN 978-1-4668-2218-4 (e-book)

Forge books may be purchased for educational, business, or promotional use. For information on bulk purchases, please contact Macmillan Corporate and Premium Sales Department at 1-800-221-7945, extension 5442, or write specialmarkets@macmillan.com.

First Edition: June 2014

Printed in the United States of America

0 9 8 7 6 5 4 3 2 1

For Eric Bercovici and his family

The **Hollywood blacklist** was the mid-twentieth-century list of screenwriters, actors, directors, musicians, and other U.S. entertainment professionals who were denied employment because of their political beliefs or associations, real or suspected. Artists were barred from work on the basis of their alleged membership or sympathy toward the American Communist Party, based on participation in liberal or humanitarian political causes that enforcers of the blacklist deemed disloyal. Refusal to assist investigations into Communist Party activities, principally by refusing to give the names of others they knew to be similarly involved, was deemed proof of disloyalty. Even during the period of its strictest enforcement, the late 1940s through the late 1950s, the blacklist was rarely made explicit and verifiable, but it caused direct damage to the careers of scores of American artists, often made betrayal of friendship (not to mention principle) the price for a livelihood, and promoted ideological censorship across the entire industry.

—WIKIPEDIA NOTATION

I did what I did because it was the more tolerable of two alternatives that were, either way, painful, even disastrous, and either way wrong for me. That's what a difficult decision means: either way you go, you lose.

—ELIA KAZAN

BOOK ONE

OCTOBER 1959:

HOMECOMING

1

DAVID WEAVER

So I'm sprawled in a lounge chair next to the swimming pool at the Chateau Marmont in Hollywood wondering where Teddy is. Theodore Weaver, my father, best friend, and mentor. A brilliant, witty, extraordinary screenwriter. He died in my arms in Rome four nights ago after he finished editing the movie he'd directed that was to be his comeback achievement. Heart attack at the brutally young age of forty-eight.

Despite the aching loss that permeated me and the feeling of being totally alone in a world where no one gives a damn about me, I somehow made the necessary arrangements to bring him back here for burial. Ending his political exile. But like a lost suitcase, the airlines have misplaced the casket. It went astray when we changed planes in New York. I came on to L.A. and they still don't know where the hell Teddy went. That was three days ago. I feel like strangling someone.

Instead I lean back in the lounge chair and stare at my surroundings. It's late afternoon in October 1959. The pool area is deserted. The sky is smoggy yellow-gray. The Chateau, as everyone calls this place, still looks the same as when I first saw it as a child. A multi-turreted, Mediterranean-style hotel with a carefully cultivated aura of shabby chic. The lobby features overstuffed sofas and languidly turning ceiling fans. It's an oasis of what passes for civility in Hollywood, nestled a couple of hundred yards above the touristy Sunset Strip.

Panorama Studio put us up here for the first couple of weeks when they brought our two families—the Weavers and the Vardians—out from New York in 1937. It's where the studios book the special VIPs until they get acclimated.

Teddy and Leo Vardian were already a red-hot radio writing team—Weaver & Vardian—spoken like a run-on word, two halves that made a dazzling whole. Physically they were a Mutt and Jeff team, bearlike Teddy and foxy little Leo. Two buddies from Brooklyn who had conquered the Big Apple and now were poised for success in Hollywood. All blue skies then.

I get out of the lounge chair and restlessly stroll around the pool, pausing at the deep end to gaze down at my reflection. First time I did this, it was chubby little three-year-old Davey Weaver looking back up at me, innocent happy guy. Now I'm twenty-four, six-two and lean as a long-distance runner, strong as the U.S. Army Ranger I used to be, and if it weren't for my sunglasses I'd be seeing the angriest eyes in the Greater L.A. area. But the shimmering waters of the Chateau pool look the same.

Nothing's changed. Everything's changed. Question is: can things ever change back?

My heels make a hollow clicking sound as I walk across the tiled lobby of the Chateau. Before I reach the desk, the starchy, officious desk clerk I've been pestering shakes his head. No message from the airline.

So I'm still stuck in this surreal limbo. But I realize that much of my anxiety is at being back in the town that I grew up in. Weird, isn't it? So many people dream of coming to Hollywood and I feel like a soldier home from the wars, wary as hell of the reception I'll get.

I start for my room and a guy sitting alone behind a potted plant folds his newspaper and gets up. Tall, tan, lanky, late forties, dressed in a black sharkskin suit without a wrinkle in it. Carrying a gray snap-brim fedora, he's looking more weathered than the last time I saw him. I go down the corridor; so does he. I force myself to stroll, but I'm tensed up by the sight of an old enemy.

I unlock my door and behind me he says:

"Mr. Weaver, my name is McKenna." He flips open a small leather case, shows me a gold badge and an FBI identification card. As if I didn't remember him. The number one figure on my Hollywood Hate Parade. "Can I speak to you for a moment?"

"Sure. Speak."

"Let's go inside."

"Do you have a warrant?"

"Oh, c'mon, kid. Don't be like that."

"I'm not a kid. That was last time."

"Quite a few years. Surprised you remember."

"Some things you never forget."

The last time McKenna appeared on my doorstep was almost a decade ago, in 1951, at our house in upscale Brentwood near the top of Tigertail Road. Mom and Dad had ordered me to never open the door unless I knew who was knocking, but this one time I'd been playing with the dog and the bell rang and I forgot and I swung the door wide and there were two Slim Jims. McKenna did the talking.

"Your father home?"

"N-no," I stammered. "Nobody's home." But they could hear the typing upstairs. They pushed past me and started for the staircase. Later on they signed a sworn affidavit that I invited them in.

"Teddyyyyyyyyyy!" I yelled. It was the first time I'd used his first name. The typing stopped. The two FBI men raced up the stairs. When they reached the second floor and disappeared down the hallway, I saw my father drop off the thick maple tree branch outside the window of his study down onto the lawn. He crouched, like a hunted beast, and looked over at me through the open front door.

I've never forgotten that look.

Then he ran off and they didn't get him that day to serve the pink subpoena for the House Un-American Activities Committee.

The shame that coursed through me that day still remains. It is a frozen instant no son should ever have to experience—the sight of my father stripped of dignity and rendered powerless and all because of my careless blunder. Teddy never blamed me for opening that door, but I never stopped blaming myself.

A nd now here's McKenna at the Chateau. I feel like Rip Van Winkle. Gone from Hollywood nearly ten years. Senator Joe McCarthy, who cowed even President Eisenhower, has died in disgrace. But the Cold War that McCarthy exploited still lives on. Apparently so does the Blacklist.

"What do you say, Mr. Weaver?" McKenna asks. "Can I come in?" So polite, this time. But why the hell should I let him? Then he adds, "I've got some news you'll be interested in. About your father."

"Tell me out here, Slim Jim. I don't want to have to fumigate my room after you're gone."

"My name's not Jim, it's—"

"Brian. Brian McKenna. Says so on your ID, but to us you were all Slim Jim. Dark suits, dark glasses, snap-brim hats, skinny as bird dogs, good manners, bad news."

I lean against the mustard-colored wall outside my closed door. Fold my arms, making myself elaborately comfortable.

Bet I could take this asshole out now if I had to. McKenna pretends he's not annoyed.

"Okay, we can do it out here." Takes practice to make agreeing sound so threatening.

"Guess I should be flattered by your visit," I gibe. "After all those years of being on my father's case, now you're keeping tabs on me."

He probably knows about the screaming match verging on a fistfight that I got into at LAX when the airline people told me they'd lost Teddy.

"You're not a subject of interest to us, Mr. Weaver."

"So why are you here?"

"First of all, I wanted to give you an update. Your dad's casket arrived. You can notify your mortuary to pick it up at the Air America cargo terminal."

"You bastard!" My rage index skyrocketing. "You're still haunting Teddy even after he's *dead*. Fuckin' body snatchers. Shanghaied his casket, moving him from city to city while you go through his pockets and the lining of his coffin, looking for what? An atom bomb? Haven't you turds got any sense of decency?"

Someone clears his throat. "Everything all right, Mr. Weaver?" It's the fussy desk clerk from the lobby. Standing at the end of the hallway.

"Everything's fine," McKenna says, without taking his eyes off me.

"Mr. Weaver?" the clerk repeats.

"Fine," I mutter as I keep the staring contest going with McKenna.

"Just call if you need anything." With a frown, he disappears. McKenna waits until he's gone, then says in that infuriatingly unruffled voice they use, "The airline lost the casket, we helped find it. As a *courtesy*."

"Yeah, you betcha."

"Hey, I'm sorry for your loss. I understand he was a very nice man."

"You mean, for a diabolical Commie menace to the republic, plotting to overthrow the government by force."

"Look, Mr. Weaver—I just gather information. Follow orders. Other people decide how it fits together."

"That's what the war criminals said at Nuremberg."

He ignores that. Just rolls on. "But after all the years of reviewing your father's file, seems to me all he was guilty of was signing some checks and petitions for the wrong causes."

"Are you saying that in an official capacity, Agent McKenna?"

"I'm not here in an official capacity."

"So I asked you before—why are you here?"

"To deliver this."

McKenna hands me a dark blue booklet. There's one like it in my pocket. Been there since the bad times began; Teddy taught me that. Always have it with you so if you have to you can go straight to the airport.

It's a U.S. passport.

I flip it open. Brand new. A photo of Teddy on the first page, taken years ago. Valid from 1959 through 1965.

"This is a joke, right?"

"Your dad applied to the embassy in Paris for a renewal."

"Seven years ago. When they confiscated his old passport."

"Well, it cleared a couple weeks ago," McKenna says.

"Better late than never." He ignores that one, too. So I step up the sarcasm. "Here I thought I was sneaking him in under the radar. But turns out it's all legit. He's got a passport. He's officially welcome again in his own country. With the FBI's thoughtful assistance."

"You've got a bad attitude, Mr. Weaver."

"Gee, I wonder why."

"Probably a problem with authority figures."

"That's what they told me in the Army."

"I was thinking more recently—about your hassle at the L.A. airport."

"No hassle. Only an energetic conversation with some incompetent idiots. Nobody got hurt."

"But your temper scared a few people."

"It's a scary world, haven't you noticed?"

He raises an eyebrow, maybe he's wondering if he can still take me out. Then he gives a small fuck-you shrug and leaves. I enter my room to check for wounds: not only am I okay, I feel exhilarated. Got a little of our own back that time, Teddy. Then I begin to consider why McKenna came. He could have left a phone message about the casket and dropped the passport in the mail. Or even thrown it away. Despite his professed lack of interest in me, Slim Jim is still watching.

2

DAVID

After McKenna leaves, I phone the mortuary and give them instructions. Then I sit alone in my room, the smallest and cheapest one in the hotel, until it's almost dark. I pull the rented Chevy out of the hotel garage and drive west on the Sunset Strip. Still a brassy collage of tackiness and glitz. When our family used to drive along here, my mom would roll down the car window, take a deep breath, and joke: "M-m-m, know what that smell is? Naked ambition." Dad would always laugh. Most of the dinner clubs my parents used to go to with their friends remain. Here and there a new music record shop has replaced an old bookstore, and Dean Martin's neon caricature flashes over a nightclub with a waiting line out front. Since I left, there's been a hot war in Korea to augment the cold one with the Russians, but no sign of any of that here.

I continue on Sunset into Beverly Hills, past the ten-foot hedges protecting the millionaire mansions. Then through elegant Holmby Hills into Westwood just north of UCLA. I'm driving on automatic pilot, as if I'm going home. Guess in a way I am.

When I reach Stone Canyon Road, I turn right and cruise past the classy, secluded Hotel Bel-Air. Deep in the canyon I park in the darkness on the side of the road with a view of the Vardian house. No lights on yet, so I've arrived in time.

The ranch house, designed by trendy local architect Cliff May, still has a friendly look. Simple, deceptively casual lines, soft colors, a place that blends comfortably into the wooded canyon around it. As a child there were two places I thought of as home. "Jana's house" and "Davey's house." We spent so much of our time at one or the other. Wonder if that marvelous tree house out back where we used to play is still there?

Jana and me. Me and Jana. We grew up together. No, that doesn't begin to describe it. Because of the closeness of our families we were inextricably joined. Born only two weeks apart, we learned to walk and talk together. I'm told that, like twins, we had our own private language when we were infants. Our fathers had a pal who was a metal sculptor, and they got him to construct a special double stroller so they could wheel us around Greenwich Village while they worked out story ideas. As kids we played with each other's toys, shared most meals and games, picked each other up when we fell down, laughed and cried together. All to our parents' delight.

Leo Vardian and my dad both came from a Brooklyn neighborhood called East New York-Brownsville, where the New Lots IRT subway line ended. It was an area of cheap duplexes, mom-and-pop stores, still some half-paved streets, a scattering of weed-choked empty lots, and old Dutch cemeteries. Peopled by families of first- and second-generation Jews and Italians.

Teddy's father was Russian and he came to New York as a fifteen-year-old along with his older sister. They both found work in the sweatshops of the garment industry; he eventually became a union organizer. Teddy's mother worked as a custom seamstress. They never made much money, but they were devoted to each other. Rest in peace.

Leo's dad was from Poland and became a plumber; Leo's

mom was the Flatbush High night-school instructor who taught his dad English. Teddy and Leo grew up only a few blocks apart and they were best friends.

I never knew Leo's first wife, Shirley; she died giving birth to Jana. She and Ellie Birnbaum, my pretty mom, also were best friends. The four of them met in Junior High School 149. The two couples were married together in a double wedding and lived across the street from each other in the bohemian, politically progressive Village, while the guys were struggling to establish themselves as writers. They still hadn't made it when Shirley passed away.

In the intense sorrow that followed her death, Leo reportedly fell apart for a while, but my mom filled the void: she became Jana's surrogate mother. She took care of us as if we were both her children. I know how much she enjoyed dressing up Jana. Laughing, Mom used to say it was like playing dolls. Later, when we were almost teenagers and living in L.A., Leo married Vivian Hollenbeck, a snooty New York socialite, who didn't like kids. So Jana still brought all her girl problems to my mom. Teddy, of course, was a second father to Jana. And Leo was that for me, notably during those years when Teddy was away in the war.

So that's how it was. Jana and I always together. Trophy children doted on when we weren't being totally ignored by our parents. Not out of meanness, but they were interested in—and once we reached Hollywood, they were constantly surrounded by—interesting people. And let's face it, they used to say, kids aren't that interesting. So we had to be precocious to get attention, but the rest of the time we could spend amusing ourselves. We invented make-believe worlds, confided every secret, and shared every new discovery.

When we were nine she proposed a scientific experiment. She had heard that methane gas from farts were inflammable, so she borrowed the Ronson lighter on her father's desk and we climbed up into the tree house in the backyard. I dropped my pants and let a big one go—Jana flicked the lighter, both of us braced for an explosive whoosh. And the fart did light up—but only enough to blow out the flame. We both laughed so hard we almost fell out of the tree house.

From the time we were ten we had wheels—bicycles, not cars—and there was no stopping us. We'd pedal to the library or the park where we would stretch out on the grass and gaze up at the clouds, wondering how high is up and whether there are people on other planets. "Not like us," Jana said happily. We bumped shoulders and laughed.

I loved her laugh, it came out almost like a snort. And I adored her gift for sarcasm, except when it was directed at me. In school it often got her into trouble. But she was bold and irrepressible. I remember when we were maybe eleven and had the meanest teacher at Kenter School. Always picking on Jana. We were priming for a district-wide spelling bee. The teacher called on Jana to spell the word assume and use it in a sentence.

"Assume," Jana chanted, "ay-ess-ess-you-em-ee. Assume. Never assume your teacher is smarter than you are." That got her a classroom guffaw and a trip to the principal's office. Her dad didn't punish her, because he and my parents thought it was funny.

Things between Jana and me changed around the time we were thirteen. We became a little shy around each other. I started getting a buzzing feeling when we were together, and she seemed to feel something similar. It was too strange for us to talk about, but Jana found an outlet. She confided in my mom. I would walk into a room where they were having these deep conversations and they'd stop talking. And both smile at me. I really felt left out. When I mentioned it to my dad, he assured me that women just were like that sometimes.

What it was, of course, was hormones kicking in. Mom had

explained all the ramifications to Jana, and she explained them to me. Suitably cautioned; nevertheless, Jana and I began to spend a lot of time up in the tree house where earlier we used to swing on ropes and play Tarzan and Jane. Now we were tentatively embarked on an even more exciting game. We were too young and too scared to do much more than hug and brush lips and dare exploratory gropes. But it was our newest secret and it was thrilling. We were boyfriend and girlfriend. Then our brief interlude of puppy love was interrupted by the House Un-American Activities Committee.

After my dad bailed out the window to avoid the federal process servers, he got to the nearest phone to warn his partner they would probably be knocking on his door next. Teddy and Leo made a beeline for their high-powered lawyer— that's how they always referred to Harry Rains.

Harry calmed them down. Of course, they had reason to be worried, he acknowledged. The Hollywood Ten, comprised of writers, producers, and directors, had recently had their lengthy court appeal rejected and gone off to prison for Contempt of Congress for refusing to answer the sixty-four-dollar question: "Are you now, or have you ever been a member of the Communist Party" and name anyone and everyone they knew who was. Now HUAC was reconvening new hearings. A subpoena was a ticket to the Blacklist.

"So what do we do?" our dads asked.

"Leave it to me," they quoted Harry Rains, who told them to go home and relax. He would handle it. Everything would work out for the best.

We all wanted to believe that. My normally sunny mom— dad always called her "Ellie with the laughing eyes"—had the most difficulty. She was trembling and had to take a sedative that night. But during the next few weeks there were no more knocks on either family's doors.

Then mom had a scary encounter in upscale Vicente Food Market in Brentwood. She was filling her shopping cart and reached for a ripe cantaloupe and someone tried to grab it away from her. It was Lela Rogers, Ginger Rogers's mother. Teddy and Leo had written a hit movie for her daughter. Lela Rogers was one of the Hollywood right-wing activists who used her political contacts in Washington to bring HUAC to town.

"Excuse me," Mom said, "but this melon's mine."

"Whatever happened to share and share alike, you Commie bitch!" Lela Rogers snarled. "You should all go to the electric chair."

She meant like Julius and Ethel Rosenberg, who had been executed recently for stealing A-bomb secrets for Russia. Mom came home in tears.

Again, Harry Rains assured our dads he was working on the matter. But on the afternoon of the Fourth of July, 1950, both our families were at the UCLA baseball diamond for the softball game and picnic sponsored by the Screen Writers Guild. The annual event also celebrated the recognition of the Guild by the major movie studios only a decade before. That had been accomplished after years of stonewalling by the studios. Finally, the writers filed suit with the National Labor Relations Board and the studios were forced by federal court order to negotiate a contract. The directors and actors organized and rode in on the NLRB ruling.

Jana and I were in the bleachers with her stepmom and my mom, cheering for our guys. Bottom of the ninth and their team was ahead by one run, but before the first opposing batter could step up to the plate, the same two Slim Jims—McKenna in the lead again—strolled up to Teddy and Leo in the outfield and served them with HUAC subpoenas. Everyone was silent. Doing it in front of a hundred writers and their families was chilling. A man behind us whispered, "It's like the first roundup of the Jews by the Nazis." The writers in the stands began to hiss and boo the FBI agents. I was scared. Were they going to put handcuffs on Uncle Leo and my dad and drag them off? Then I noticed my mom was shaking, real bad, so I put my arm around her the way I thought Dad would if he were up here.

The FBI agents smiled and doffed their fedoras at the hostile crowd and walked off. Leaving the taint of fear in the air. But after a moment of confusion and murmurs, the home plate umpire shouted "Play ball!" So the game played out. Our team won.

But our family didn't stick around for the picnic. We raced home. Dad showered while Mom packed a suitcase for him. I was crouched in a fetal position on the floor of the landing outside their bedroom listening to them check off the details. Underwear, pajamas, travelers checks, don't forget the reading glasses. As if this were an ordinary business trip, except for the panic in their voices.

My father was making use of the escape plan they had concocted long before. Passport in his back pocket as always. Down the stairs, through the kitchen, into the attached garage. Garage door down, blocking the view from the street, we loaded the suitcase. I climbed into the front seat, my mom got behind the wheel, and my dad, covered by an old blanket, hid on the floorboard of the backseat. We pulled out and drove to the airport, Mom brushing tears from her eyes in order to see the road, me looking behind us through the rear window to see if we were being followed, hoping that when we reached the airport there wouldn't be police waiting or Dad's name on a Stop This Man list. I was scared all the way that a squad car would pull us over.

Sweating, we got to LAX and held our breaths. Dad bought a ticket, and no one stopped him. Plane leaving almost immediately. We raced to the departure gate where Dad hugged me and said, "You're the man around here now. Take care of your mother." I was too upset to ask him what he meant. Exactly how was I supposed to take care of her?

Then he embraced Mom and kissed her, said "I love you, Ellie, see you soon." It was worse than when he went off to the war. She clutched at him, tear-stricken, didn't want to let go, but she had to because the gate was closing. I held Mom's hand, and she gripped my fingers so hard it hurt, but I held on until Dad disappeared from sight. Then we went to the floor-to-ceiling terminal window and watched the plane take off for Mexico City.

I was confused and horrified that after all the overheard conversations during these last years this was actually happening. My father was fleeing the country where he was born, the country he fought for in France, Belgium, and Germany. I was old enough to understand he was leaving rather than appear before HUAC and name names. Betray old friends. But I wasn't old enough to understand how our country had become this way. And why did it have to happen to my family?

We got rid of our house at a loss five weeks later in a distress sale and followed Dad to Mexico. The Vardians saw us off at the airport. Uncle Leo was working around the clock to finish postproduction work on the movie he had just directed. His first A production. While Dad was away in the war, Leo, who had been deferred because of a heart murmur, had climbed the Hollywood ladder and become a hyphenate: writer-director. As soon as he finished editing, they would follow us south of the border—unless Harry Rains was successful in his efforts to quash the subpoenas.

Leo was still hopeful, Jana and I vowed to write to each other every day.

Dad had found us a hacienda in Oaxaca. The town reminded me of Olvera Street in downtown L.A. with all the Mexican craft and clothing stalls and cantinas featuring mariachi musicians and spicy foods. The Mexicans working on Olvera Street all spoke English, and they wore colorful costumes with lots of spangles, as if they were extras in an MGM musical. The citizens of Oaxaca wore simpler clothing and the food was even tastier, but most of them spoke only Spanish. Mom was nervous, as if she had been banished to Mars. Dad promised that when Uncle Leo and his family got here, that would make things better. But the Vardians were delayed. We didn't know why. Dad didn't think the phones were safe enough for us to call Leo. Then he received a call from Harry Rains.

When he hung up the phone, all the color had drained from Dad's face. "What's wrong?" Mom asked, a tremor in her voice. "Leo," he finally managed. "Leo and his family won't be coming."

Leo had decided to go to Washington and testify. It was on the TV news the following night. My mom and dad and I sat there and saw it. Even in Spanish we could decipher the brief report. Leo squirming at a table in front of a microphone facing the Committee. "Hollywood Writer-Director Confesses To Being A Former Communist." Names a half dozen others. The only surefire way to avoid the Blacklist. My parents recognized all the names. I knew several of them from Sunday barbecues. My father's name was not mentioned. He was stoic; mom looked shell shocked.

"Oh my god," she whispered in a stricken voice, "how could Leo have done that?" But instantly she came up with an explanation. The footage was not real, it was doctored, distorted, the way the Hollywood special-effects people can do it. "I'm

sure that's what happened!" She turned to my dad for confir-
mation. He said nothing. It was the closest I'd ever seen him
come to crying.

I was on the verge of crying, too. I kept thinking—will I
ever see Jana again?

I did, but not until eight years later. And then it was totally
unexpected.

Teddy and I were celebrating in the bar of the Ritz hotel in
Paris with a sleazy Italian producer. He was buying the drinks,
a rare gesture of largesse. We were delivering the final draft of
a black-market script we had written for him—I was working
with Teddy, by then in the shadowy world of Blacklisted
writers, serving as a sounding board, helping Teddy plot out
stories, taking a first pass at some of the scenes. Teddy said I
was getting good. We had just been paid the balance of our fee.
As usual, Blacklist rules prevailed: very short money and no
screen credit. The Italian producer left and we were finishing
our drinks before returning to our dinky Left Bank hotel, when
out of the low-lit barroom gloom Jana walked up to us.

My Jana. My heart jumped up into my throat. I had imagined what she might look like now. But my imagination had
failed me. We were both twenty-three and the teenage promise had been fulfilled: she had matured into an absolute
beauty. Tall, slender, lovely figure, dressed in a Givenchy pantsuit. Hardly any makeup, but her face, that face I dreamed
about, was perfection. I was so thunderstruck I couldn't speak.
But she wasn't talking to me or even looking at me.

She said to Teddy, "My father is in the booth over there.
Will you talk to him?" Before Teddy could answer, she added:
"He's dying."

Teddy got up and lumbered across to the booth. Leo was
always a small man, now he was gaunt and shriveled, almost

tiny. Jana and I stayed behind at the bar. I offered her a drink. She asked for a Coke. And we sat there on stools, side by side, watching the two ex-partners and ex-best friends deep in conversation. Leo was doing most of the talking.

I snuck a peek at Jana. "Well, look at you—all grown up."

"You, too." End of subject. She was still staring intently off at the booth. Hadn't really looked at me yet. The flood of things I'd always planned to say to her had dried up. The silence between us extended. Gotta say something.

"What's he dying of?"

"Lung cancer."

I mumbled something I hoped passed for sympathy. She twisted her soda glass on the dark bar and gazed down at it. Still not looking at me.

"Your dad's lost weight, too," she said, "but he looks good."

"Oh yeah," I said, "Teddy's good." Then, trying to keep something going: "Teddy and I are working together now. I'm kind of the *sous-chef* on the scripts we do, Teddy's the master chef."

"When did you start calling him Teddy?"

"A while ago. After I came back from Korea. When we started going to script meetings together, it sounded funny calling him Daddy."

I waited for a response. A comment. None came. Another jumbo silence grew. Teddy and Leo still huddling, Teddy talking now. I shot a glance at Jana; she was holding her breath, obviously concerned about what Teddy might be saying. But the conversation in the booth remained low key. While our conversation here at the bar was nonexistent.

"Remember in the old days," I finally said slowly, sadly, "we'd be able to finish each other's sentences. . . ."

"And now we don't even know how to start one." She didn't say it mean, or sad—just a fact.

Suddenly the meeting was over at the booth. Teddy was rising; Leo got up, too. He looked terrible. Fragile, rickety. They started to shake hands but it became an embrace. Leo desperately clinging, Teddy leaning over and patting his back.

Then Teddy came back toward the bar. Jana rose abruptly, reached over and squeezed my hand. "Nice seeing you." Kissed Teddy gratefully on the cheek and hurried away. My long-hoped-for opportunity to restore contact had evaporated while I dawdled tongue-tied. And she couldn't even bear to look at me even once. Now she was back with Leo, who was swaying, one hand on the side of the booth for balance, waving to me with the other.

Out on the street, while the doorman hailed a taxi for us, I asked Teddy how it went. Teddy stared off. I waited, wanting to know but not wanting to pry. Then Teddy cleared his throat.

"He said, 'I gave them names, Theo—but I didn't give them yours.'"

"You believe him?"

"Would that make what he did to the others okay?" Teddy gave a terrible shrug. "But why berate a dying man?"

Then I got to see my father cry. There were tears slipping down Teddy's cheeks and he pawed them away with his jacket sleeve. I didn't know if he was crying for the fate that had befallen Leo or for what Leo had done. Probably all that and so much more. I put my arm around my father's shoulder and guided him into the taxi.

The headlights turn into the circular driveway of the Vardian house. It's a hunter-green Jaguar, the four-door sedan model. Of course Jana would be driving a roomy car, she's had this claustrophobic thing about narrow spaces since she was a kid. The Jag is probably a birthday or a graduation present to her from Leo. She parks near the front door and the outdoor security lights are triggered. When she comes out of the car I can see her clearly. Casual but expensive sports clothes, suitable for the studio. Running shoes and a Panorama Studio windbreaker. She looks marvelous. Just as she did last night and the night before. This is the person who means more to me than anyone else. I can call to her from my car and she'll turn and I can get out and come across the street and—what will I say?

Suppose I get there and it's the way it was in Paris? Silence. Where there once was a never-ending flow of thoughts and feelings. Suppose that's gone forever. The Blacklist looms like Mount Everest between us. Is it possible to get to the other side? I'm frozen in my car. I've charged up hills under machine-gun fire in Korea and I can't get across this street in Westwood.

So I just watch her in silence again. Until Jana unlocks the front door of the house and disappears inside.

I'm about to turn my engine on when red and blue lights flash and glare in my rearview mirror. Cop car. No, not an LAPD cruiser. Residential security service, the words ARMED RESPONSE visible on the driver's door as it opens. A hefty figure climbs out. Tan uniform and black gunbelt. As he swaggers toward my vehicle, he unsnaps his holster. I keep my hands in plain view on the upper half of the steering wheel. Last thing I need is to be shot by a trigger-happy rent-a-cop.

He taps on my window. Gestures for me to roll it down. He's barrel-chested, with a lifetime of arrogance etched on his florid face. "Can I help you, sir," he challenges.

"Just about to leave."

"Yeah, been watching you from back there. Got business in this neighborhood?"

"A trip down memory lane, officer. Used to know a girl who lived in that house. Wanted to take a look at it again."

"Can I see your driver's license and registration, sir."

"Car's a rental," I say. As I reach slowly into my jacket

pocket, he shifts his hand onto the butt of his .38. So I'm very careful as I bring out a gray folder. He takes it, scans it, then says, "What the hell is this?"

"International driver's license."

Squinting at it—"Issued *where*?"

"Paris."

"Well, well, never seen one of these. You a long way from home, Frenchy."

"I'm not French, I'm an American." He's starting to piss me off.

"But you been livin' in Gay Paree, huh? You a draft dodger?"

"Look, is there a problem, officer?"

"You tell me—we been havin' a rash of burglaries in this area the last couple months." The way he says it, I know it's bullshit.

"Sorry to hear that, but I just arrived in town a couple of days ago."

"Can you prove it?"

"Matter of fact, I can."

Still moving slowly, I produce my passport and point out the arrival date stamped by the custom's officer in New York. He finds the passport even more interesting than the international driver's license.

"Born in New York City. Religion: Jewish." He hands the passport back to me. "Got a local address?"

"Chateau Marmont. In Hollywood."

"Oo-la-la, a shat-tow! I shoulda guessed. Step out of the car, sir."

"*What*?" He's definitely pissing me off.

"You heard me." Drawing his gun. Moving a pace away.

I climb out. He kicks the door shut. "Face the vehicle, hands on the roof." I do it. "Spread your legs." Then he roughly kicks them back so I'm off-balance, leaning against the car. Powerless. At least that's what he thinks.

He frisks me with ham-handed abrasiveness. The black rage
is boiling in me. At the bored, inefficient assholes at the airport,
at pushy, smug Agent McKenna, at myself for not calling out to
Jana, at the world generally—and it's all focusing on this
clown.

The frisk is over, he found nothing, and that frustrates him.
He jabs me viciously in the back with his gun. The demon
within me is rattling the bars of its cage. I struggle to keep it
under control. "Here's my advice to you," he says. "Turn your
cute little rented car around and scoot on back to your shat-
tow and tell all the other fancy New York clipped-dick Jew
boys to stay out of my neighborhood, or—"

Fuck control!

I push off from the car and half-whirl around, smash an
elbow in his abdomen knocking the wind out of him, while
simultaneously slamming a lock onto his gun arm, twisting
hard. Ranger-taught technique. I could easily snap his arm in
this position. But I don't. His gun goes flying and he falls back
onto his butt, like Humpty Dumpty tumbling off the wall. He's
gasping for air and I automatically move into position to finish him off with a kick in the head. But at the final instant I
catch myself. Restore control. Kositchek, the shrink I've been
going to in Rome, taught me that. Anger control, he calls it.
More difficult for me to master than any Ranger technique. I
pick up the revolver and his eyes bug. I let him taste terror for
an instant.

"You dropped this, officer."

Then I flip the chamber open and let the cartridges spill on
the pavement. I toss the gun in his lap.

"Don't bother writing this up. It'll only make you sound
like a schmuck—that's a Jewish word for idiot. Then I'd have
to write up my version of what happened—and anyone who
knows you more than five minutes will believe me. Have a
nice night."

I get in my car and make a U-turn and drive off. As I get back on Sunset, the adrenaline rush is diminishing. I've got the cage door shut again. Been fighting this compulsion to lash out at assholes since the bad days in Mexico.

When I reach the Chateau I'm not hungry or sleepy, so I stretch out on a lounge chair in the near darkness surrounding the pool. Music is wafting from an open window on a rear bungalow, and I can hear Bobby Darin singing "Beyond The Sea." I wonder if Jana likes that as much as I do. We used to have the same taste in music. The underwater lights in the Chateau pool are on and the aquamarine water glows.

In the summer of 1937, when we first came out here, we were only three years old, and Jana and I learned how to swim in this pool. So is that what I'm harkening back to—long ago memories that Jana may have stopped recalling? Has she been married? Nah, I would have heard. Yeah, how? Once we were as close as twins, but that was then. Does she ever think of me? Even if she does, what do I have to offer her? She stayed, I left. Everything that once was ended then.

Yet here I am.

So I ask myself for the zillionth time, why am I really here? I force myself to put it into words:

I want Jana. And I want everything they took away from Teddy. Plus—if, as the adage goes, revenge is a dish best served cold, then I'd like to order a big serving of that icy item on the menu. Is that too much to ask?

3

JANA VARDIAN

I don't know if I'm going to the funeral," I say to my tennis partner Wendy Travers.

She and I play early morning sets several times a week, sometimes with our hosts, Harry and Valerie Rains, on the private court behind their Tara-like mansion in the exclusive Beverly Hills flatlands. We're sitting on the bench toweling off after a fierce workout. Wendy, lithe, raven-haired and gorgeous, is twenty years older than I am, but she's my best friend.

Neither of us have been invited to Teddy Weaver's funeral. But we both saw the two-inch ad in *Variety* announcing the time and place with no contact information.

"I'm kinda scared," I admit to Wendy. "Don't know if I can handle it. Of course, I want to go—for Teddy."

"Just for Teddy?" Wendy nails me. That's the thing about a friend who knows you that well.

"Okay," I concede, "I'm particularly nervous about seeing David."

"Well, it scares the hell out of me, too," she says, "the idea of confronting all those old judgmental faces. But I'm going. Valerie and Harry offered me a ride. Want to come along? Safety in numbers."

David Weaver and I have known Wendy since we were three. She came to the big pool party welcoming our families to Hollywood. She taught us how to swim that day. That was easy for her. She was a water ballet dancer in the Esther Williams "aqua-musicals," those Technicolor romances where all plot complications climaxed in a splashy extravaganza. Since then, Wendy has carved out a career as one of Hollywood's top romantic comedy writers. Twice nominated for the Oscar, her sunny movies have grossed millions for MGM. Harry—who used to be her lawyer, as well as Teddy and Leo's—recently lured her to work at Panorama, where he's head of production now. That's where I work, too, back in the stacks of the research department.

Wendy and I have grown very close these last few years. She's not a mother substitute. Ellie, David's mom, was virtually my mom. Wendy loved her as I did. When I lost Ellie, Wendy never tried to take her place. But we're more than best friends. We share a tangled past.

My father and Wendy were both cooperative witnesses before HUAC. And they each named the other.

My father did it first during the 1951 hearings. Wendy named him a few months later, along with four others. Neither of them named Teddy Weaver. A few months later, I witnessed a shouting confrontation between Wendy and my father outside a Malibu restaurant. It ended in tearful reconciliation. "Friendly" witnesses often could do that with each other. The commonality was that they had succumbed to the same pressures. Those who had been named and Blacklisted were not so forgiving. Reconciliation did not seem possible.

I've never really been able to talk with my father about those days. Whenever the subject came up, he would just rant, and I knew he was trying to assuage his pain. So I stopped bringing it up. But with Wendy I could explore what had happened and try to figure out why. It's been a powerful bond between us. A way for me to understand my damaged dad. And also a safe place for Wendy to share her own pain. As only a pair of outcasts can.

"For three years after I testified," she told me once, "I couldn't bring myself to walk into the studio commissary. I'd get right up to the entrance, but I'd feel so nauseous I couldn't get through the door."

I've experienced those same feelings.

After my father testified, he was ostracized by almost everyone he knew—and so was I. Of course, he made his decision without consulting me, but it totally altered my life. I was a student at Beverly Hills High School and all my friends dropped me; many were literally forbidden by their Liberal parents to have anything to do with me. The other kids, wanting to be cool, almost all joined in. "Your dad is a rat fink," some of them would chant at me in the school yard. I went from being one of the top ten popular girls to being an untouchable piece of shit.

I cried a lot, but my dad's advice when he finally noticed was the bold challenge he'd been issuing to the whole town since he came back from Washington. "Fuck 'em all! You've gotta get over it." But I guess he was stronger than I was. I handled it by getting massively depressed, that's how our family doctor described it, and he prescribed antidepression and anti-anxiety meds. They didn't work.

The only thing that provided relief was eating. I simply could not stop. My doctor asked why I did it, and I told him as honestly as I could that I was hungry. I felt like I was starving, a great gnawing void within me that seemed bottomless. Looking in the mirror was like having a front row seat at a special-effects horror movie. I seemed to be ballooning before my eyes.

Leo said that was why no one had asked me to the senior prom. Then someone did. Sam Kantin was supersmart but a bit goofy-looking at that age. The other girls always mocked him as "The Class Shnook," but when he nervously extended an invitation, I accepted gratefully. Dad had a beautiful dress designed for me that concealed my extra girth, and I waited with unexpected anticipation for my date to show up on prom night. He never did. He stood me up. His father, a warmly regarded Beverly Hills rabbi, wouldn't let him come. As a consolation prize, my father bought me a fire-engine-red Corvette. When I drove around in it, I felt like the whole world was staring at me. A winged chariot ain't so great if there's no one else to ride in it.

I was accepted at USC but begged my father to let me go away to somewhere nobody knew me. Our doctor was my ally—he said I was verging on a nervous breakdown. That's how I got to Northwestern. The distance between Beverly Hills and Chicago helped a lot. I could breathe again. People there had hardly even heard of the Hollywood Ten, and my father's name meant nothing to them. I made a few friends, concentrated on studying—I was a Theater Arts major, to Leo's approval—and slowly lost the weight I'd gained.

Life was looking better. I made the dean's list, lost my virginity to the male lead in a student production of *Our Town* (I played Emily), and was scheduled to direct the next campus show when my father was diagnosed with lung cancer. His wife, the Park Avenue socialite, had divorced him and moved back East. So for the first time in my life he needed me. He pleaded with me to come home. How could I say no?

His chemo treatments were terribly rough—he wasted away and I thought so many times I was about to lose him. He was so vulnerable and, except for Harry Rains, no one came to see him at the Stone Canyon house. It was as if we were the sole occupants of a luxurious leper colony. When he went into remission and his strength returned, his vulnerability also dissolved. His old rages returned, now reinforced by his professional successes. But I knew how much he still needed me, so I stayed on. Where else did I have to go? I finished my course work at USC while tending to the day-to-day details of Leo's life.

Harry and Leo arranged for a job for me at the studio where both of them were. At first I was viewed by my coworkers as what I was—a classic case of nepotism. Driving a spiffy Jaguar onto the lot to perform my menial duties. But I was diligent and discovered I loved doing research, particularly getting lost in the past. I was good at it and was assigned more and more responsibilities. I made some new friends around the lot, had a few inconsequential romances, my confidence gradually rebuilt, but I still felt essentially alone. The memories of the David and Jana times were never far away.

Wendy Travers was my mainstay through those times. But our friendship hasn't been a gloom parade. We go shopping together, play as a doubles team in pro-am tennis tournaments, and go to see old movie revivals at the Nuart Theater. She's had affairs with various guys over the years, none very serious, she claims. For a while now, she's been seeing someone, but she keeps the details private and refers to him as "Mr. Wonderful." It seems like he's nice to her, which I'm glad about.

Of course, I had told her about the Paris meeting between Teddy and Leo and how awkward it was between David and me and how cold he was. I admitted that I was just plain terrified and froze. David had been an inseparable part of me, but times had changed. Perhaps he had become one of them—the school-yard chanters. "Your father's a rat fink." And that's all he could see of me.

"So what do you think, Jana? Are you going to the funeral?"

I think about it for a long moment.

"I don't know," I say. "I don't know how I'm going to feel tomorrow."

BRIAN McKENNA

I'm the guest of honor at a bank robbery. Watching a reen-actment of my glory days from behind the huge Mitchell camera on a movie set.

Three heavily armed gunmen wearing ski masks storm into the bank. They club the security guard and force the customers facedown onto the marble floor. The smallest of the robbers runs swiftly at the row of teller windows. The tellers are sheltered behind a bulletproof shield that almost reaches the ceiling. There's a narrow space left above them. The runner springs off a nearby desk. Like a human cannonball he vaults high, angles his body, clears the barrier, and drops down behind the tellers. He levels his pistol at them as the director calls "Cut!"

I'm sitting in my canvas-backed folding chair with FBI AGENT McKENNA stenciled on it as the director turns to me questioningly. "How was it for you?"

"Just the way the real robbers did it back in my Detroit days," I say.

"Then that's a print," the director announces.

It's the morning of the day after my visit with David Weaver. We're on a jumbo-airplane-hangar-size soundstage at Warner Bros. studio in Burbank. A replica of the bank where I once foiled a daring robbery has been constructed for *The FBI Files* television series. As part of my Bureau duties, I'm the technical advisor on the series and this episode's my baby. I gave them the story. One of the few real ones they've depicted this season. Mostly the producer and the writers make up any old bullshit, and I find some vaguely connected real case, and we slap that file number on the screen to boost the illusion that this is the real stuff. It's just Hollywood hokum.

Besides monitoring the TV series for the Bureau, I also operate out of the Federal Building downtown as liaison with the Hollywood community when they want FBI cooperation on a film or TV project. It all adds up to a cushy, boring, PR backwater job.

J. Edgar Hoover first sent me to Los Angeles thirteen years ago in 1946 to run the Commie-chasing squad. It was a hard-hitting, headline-grabbing mission. A jubilant experience for me. I went after unfriendly witnesses for the House Un-American Activities Committee. We were taking action to curb the spread of International Communism, the same way the Bureau rooted out Nazi spies in America during World War II. At least that's what I told myself at the time.

My powder-puff position now is titled "Special Assignments." It was intended as a reward for a job well done in support of HUAC, but it feels like I've been put out to pasture. I'm forty-seven and worried I will spend the rest of my career with the Bureau stagnating in this velvet trap.

As usual, however, I follow orders. I'm a team player. Even on those occasions when the game gets a little tacky.

Like a few years ago in 1956 when Hoover became obsessively interested in the reported romance between Negro superstar entertainer Sammy Davis, Jr. and platinum blond screen bombshell Kim Novak. He'd be on the phone every day pushing me to put aside Commie chasing for the moment and focus all my energies on digging up the latest dirt about this black-white relationship.

Hoover intimated he was doing a favor for Harry Cohn, who ran Columbia Pictures, where Novak was under contract. A bi-racial love affair could damage her value for Columbia at the box office. Hoover put me on the case. I felt like a garbage picker sifting through trash Dumpsters. Then we hit a development that made it official FBI business.

Gangleader Johnny Roselli reportedly kidnapped Sammy Davis. That's a federal offense, so I pounced—jammed my way into the LAPD's investigation, wound up tangling tails in an ugly fracas with their lead investigator, Ray Alcalay. I hung in there to Hoover's delight. Then, abruptly, it was all over.

Sammy Davis was only missing a matter of hours and when he reappeared he denied being kidnapped. Johnny Roselli was the face of innocence when we questioned him. Word on the street was that during the snatch Sammy Davis had been threatened with death unless he stopped seeing Kim Novak. He dropped her and married a gorgeous Negro dancer very soon after.

Hoover felt the Bureau's presence had been partially responsible for resolving what he called "a clear case of miscegenation," still a crime in several Southern states, but not a federal crime. The experience left me feeling filthy, but sometimes the work went that way. Behind my back some of the other agents then began calling me "Hoover's Hitman."

Nowadays I occasionally overhear the younger agents calling me something even worse: "The Old Guy."

While they reset the lights for the next shot, Chad Halloran sidles up to me. He's the star of *The FBI* series, playing Inspector Stryker. A good-looking, square-jawed Fearless Fosdick type, he projects dignity and decency. The perfect image for the Bureau. Exactly what J. Edgar wanted.

Halloran knows that the Bureau, which means yours truly, had to approve him for the role. So Halloran and I are buddies. Hollywood buddies.

Halloran kneels beside my chair, brow furrowed, asking me how the real case went down. When Detroit was Bank Robbery Central. Back when I was hitting on all cylinders, a genuine G-Man. "What went through your mind, Brian," he wants to know, "when the robbers came out? Did you ever consider letting the bad guys go, because of the hostages?"

"Let 'em go?" I scoff. "My policy is—no one leaves. We settle it here."

Halloran nods, his lips moving, sotto voce, savoring the words: "No one leaves—we settle it here." I know he's going to work those words into the script and say them when they're out on the street shooting that scene tomorrow.

"Agent McKenna," the production assistant interrupts, "phone call."

It's Tom Churillo, calling from Washington. He's one of my long-ago Academy lecturers, who became a good pal. He's up near the top executive ranks in the Bureau now. After we do the how-the-hell-are-you stuff, Churillo gets to the point. The Bureau is forming a special task force to deal with bank robberies on a national basis. "That's how the crooks are operating now, hopscotching across state lines. Detroit this week, San Francisco or Dallas next week. We're almost back to the Dillinger days." Churillo is looking for the right guy to coordinate activities. "Like heading up a super posse," he explains. It's an executive berth with far-reaching powers. Based in D.C. but probably a lot of supervising field work, too. "I thought of you right away."

It's as if Santa Claus is coming down the chimney with the gift I thought would never come. This is the sort of spot I've been dreaming about. A far cry from hectoring deluded

Hollywood writers on their way to the Blacklist. Or vetting
jerky TV scripts. Back to utilizing the crime-fighting expertise
I built in Detroit, and St. Louis before that.

Then Churillo hits me with a big qualifier. There's a problem. "I've been floating your name and getting a lukewarm
response. Good man, everybody says, but isn't he kinda lightweight?"

"I can handle the job, Tom. You know I can."

"Yeah, but I have to convince them. There are other guys
bucking for the slot. They're calling you 'Mr. Hollywood.'
Mac, you have to come up with something flashy to punch up
my recommendation. And you have to do it soon."

So I hang up the phone with mixed feelings of elation at the
possibility of being considered for a perfect assignment—
combined with anxiety that I may not get it. That would be a
heartbreaker. I've got to find a way to make this happen.

5

DAVID

The night before Teddy's funeral, I work very late on his eulogy. I come up with a barn burner of a speech. Placing Teddy in the pantheon of deeply caring Americans— like actors John Garfield, Canada Lee, Philip Loeb, J. Edward Bromberg, Mady Christians, and of course, my own mother— who have died as a result of the Blacklist. I spell out how the anti-union studio moguls, enraged by those activists who forced them to recognize the Guilds, bided their time through World War II and then exacted ruthless revenge by instituting the Blacklist in the name of patriotism. After I finish writing I'm so wired I have trouble sleeping. Up every hour, no dreams that I can hold onto.

Finally, with daylight seeping through the corners of the drapes in my room, I climb wearily out of bed. Today's the day I put my father into the ground. Both my parents are gone now. I've never felt so isolated. Not really connected to anyone in the world. I'm supposed to be the man now. What in the hell does that really mean?

I put on my black suit and drive down to Schwab's, just below Sunset, in search of coffee. Schwab's is a Hollywood institution, a drugstore emporium with a restaurant section that serves as a clubhouse for aspiring showbiz folk. Everyone from Brando to Monroe has hung out in these booths or at the long horseshoe counter.

The place has just opened for the day. I check the newsstand and the front page of the *Los Angeles Times* headlines that NASA has picked the first seven candidates for space travel, and they're going to be called astronauts. I buy copies of the Hollywood trade papers and take my usual seat at the far end of the near-empty counter. Mary Hanlon, the blowsy-friendly waitress, who claims to have been serving a banana split to teenage "Sweater Girl" Lana Turner when she was "discovered sitting right here," automatically brings me black coffee followed by a toasted bagel. After four mornings, I'm a semiregular.

I start scanning the trade papers. A story on page six of *Variety* catches my attention: "Megger Vardian Wraps South Africa Pre-Shoot." "Megger" is trade jargon for "director," dates back to when they used megaphones. Hip-hip-hurrah for Leo, still working. Kicked cancer and riding high. Near the back of the paper, on a page with several obituaries, I see the small ad I ran again today announcing the services for Teddy. Maybe some old industry friends will notice. Maybe someone will come. Maybe Jana reads *Variety*.

When I close the paper, I notice the back page. It's a full page ad. Filled with Teddy's face. A terrific photo I've never seen before. Taken maybe a dozen years ago, glasses pushed up atop his head, laughing. Really catches his warmth, brightness, and humor. Under the photo it says:

THEODORE WEAVER

1911–1959

And then, further down, just one word:

IRREPLACEABLE

No signature or logo or clue as to who bought the ad. I stare long and hard at it. I'm never going to see him alive again. It's a gut-wrenching realization. I'm an orphan. I let my fingertips lightly touch the photo of Teddy.

Then I flip open *Film Bulletin*. Surprisingly, Teddy's name jumps out at me from The Rumor Mill, Joe Shannon's gossip column. The item reads:

"RED REQUIEM: SCUMMUNIST SCRIBE TEDDY WEAVER, WHO WON AN OSCAR (THEY OUGHTA TAKE IT BACK!) AND FLED TO EUROPE (WITH HUAC NIPPING AT HIS HEELS) DIED IN ROME, BUT COMRADE WEAVER GETS HIS LAST WISH. HE'LL BE BURIED IN L.A. TODAY. DON'T FAIL TO MISS IT. . . ."

Maybe no one will come. Maybe nothing really has changed for the better in the nearly ten years I've been away. I leave the rest of my coffee and all of the bagel and start the long drive to Sholom Memorial Park.

When Jana and I were little kids, while our fathers typed scripts in their office at Panorama Studio, we played games on the studio back lot where all the big outdoor standing sets are located. Cowboy and the Lady was a favorite. Always ending at Boot Hill, just above the Western street. There were fake tombstones for Billy the Kid and Jesse James and the Dalton Brothers. Jana would carefully place wildflowers on the grave of her favorite, Calamity Jane.

This muggy hot morning I'm at a real cemetery deep in the parched hills in the north of the San Fernando Valley. But Sholom is well watered and well tended and emerald green. Lots of wide-branched old oak trees shading grass-covered rows of tombstone and monuments. We're gathered at an open grave site for Teddy. His casket is beside it, wrapped in an American flag.

It's an intimate funeral, which is to say not many people
have shown up, about eighteen or twenty. On the drive out I
stopped at an art supply store and bought a chunk of poster
board. Had them glue the page ad from *Variety* onto it. Got
an easel from the cemetery people and propped up the poster
right behind the casket—so Teddy's face is smiling at those
who came.

The mortuary had put me in touch with a pleasant young
rabbi from a West L.A. synagogue who never heard of Teddy
before I met with him yesterday. Now he is reciting Kaddish,
the prayer for the dead. I'm repeating what the rabbi says, using a phonetic version as a crib sheet, because I was never bar
mitzvahed. Neither our family nor the Vardians were much on
practicing Judaism, but today I find the rhythmic incantation
strangely soothing.

And it gives me a chance to case the crowd. An honor
guard of two crisp, decorated U.S. Army soldiers in Class A
uniforms—a staff sergeant and a corporal—stand off to one
side at attention. Another thoughtful arrangement by the
mortuary. In the folding chairs surrounding the casket I notice Mimi Novick, Teddy's and Leo's longtime secretary.
There's Ramon Ortega, who runs the restaurant/bar/hangout
across the street from Panorama. Other mourners look unfamiliar at first glance, but then I imagine away the lines and
wrinkles inflicted by the last decade and see the faces as they
used to be—ebullient and effusive, crowding our living room
at a fund-raiser for defense of the Scottsboro Boys or some
other hot button cause. Where are all the others? The once-
Young Turks, the film-makers and -shakers who were going
to revolutionize Hollywood and save the world. Teddy's old
colleagues and compatriots. Banished from their chosen pro-
fessions as writers, actors, producers, directors, composers,
crew people. Probably dead or relocated—or still too scared
to gather together publicly at a funeral for one of their own.

Apparently it's not all groundless fear, because standing on a knoll overlooking our burial site is Agent McKenna with a young FBI photographer who's snapping pictures of all the attendees with a long-lens camera. As if they're spying on a Mafia convention in Appalachia. Still keeping tabs on these battered survivors of the Blacklist. If I had a grenade, I would lob it at them.

The one person I'm looking for isn't here.

Then I see a sporty MG zip up and park on the road above—and Jana gets out of the passenger seat. She's dressed in a black jersey Chanel suit, white blouse, black pearls. She looks so beautiful, my darling girl. She came to the funeral! Providing me with a graceful opportunity to break the ice. Jana closes the car door and takes off her sunglasses to gaze across at me. Even at this distance, our eyes lock. It's as if we're the only two people here.

Then the driver of the MG emerges and I can't believe it. Jana is with Markie Gunderson, who used to be a running joke between us.

Markie, Jana, and I all attended laid-back woodsie Kenter Canyon grade school in Brentwood until his parents enlisted him in Black-Foxe Military Institute, where I heard he rose through the ranks to become student major. Not surprising. Even back in Kenter school Markie strutted around like he had a field marshal's baton stuck up his ass.

He didn't have any use for us in those days. Markie believed that Jana and I were beneath him because his father was a director and our fathers were only writers. Also, we were what was colloquially known as red diaper babies, meaning children of the left. And the stork had dropped Markie into Hollywood's extreme right wing.

His dad is Rex Gunderson, an award-winning director of old-fashioned, white hat–black hat Westerns and a rabid union hater, who was one of the founding fathers of the Hollywood

Blacklist. Proving I guess that being a son-of-a-bitch doesn't prevent you from being a good director. Maybe it even helps. Hey, I shouldn't be blaming the sins of the father on the son. That would be behaving like the enemy. But I sure wish Jana had shown up today with someone else. What the hell's going on? Is she fucking him? I know she's twenty-four and probably not a virgin, but *Markie Gunderson*?

I give a small nod of recognition to them. Markie barely acknowledges and looks away, but Jana doesn't take her eyes off me. Definitely a good sign. Better than Paris.

Markie guides Jana to back row seats next to Harry Rains and his wife, Valerie Nolan. In the years since I left town, Harry has graduated from high-powered lawyer to production chief at Panorama Studio, while Valerie made the difficult transition from fading movie star to TV superstar. And next to Valerie, greeting Jana warmly, is an attractive woman I don't recognize for a second under the large, ultra-dark Ray-Ban sunglasssses. Then I do. It's Wendy Travers. What the hell is she doing here? She was a family friend, until she elected to retain her career as a top-flight screenwriter by testifying as a "friendly" witness. Making her one of the enemy. I'm surprised to see her here, amid people who suffered while she prospered.

Now my attention shifts back to the rabbi as he launches into some of the biographical details I coached him on yesterday about Teddy and our family. As he speaks, my gaze goes to the tombstone on the adjoining plot. It takes me back to the dark memories of Oaxaca.

The hacienda my father had rented was bigger than our Tigertail house, with a cook and a housekeeper and a gardener, all for much less money than we'd been paying in Brentwood. Which didn't mean we could afford it. I used to lie awake late at night with my door ajar and hear my parents downstairs in the kitchen anxiously talking. They had never been big on savings or investments, so I gathered that even in pesos we were up against it. Dad was only able to get jobs under the table. His name couldn't appear on the screen, of course. He worked day and night, flew back and forth to meet with producers in Mexico City, all for a fraction of what he used to get paid in Hollywood, and sometimes they stiffed him and only gave him a fraction of that fraction. Sometimes nothing. "Damn vultures," I'd hear him raging to Mom, "they know there's nothing I can do about it."

Me? I was despondent. Jana and I had been faithful to our letter-a-day vow—until the night my folks and I saw Leo on TV testifying. The next day I sat down to write Jana, but after at least fifty agonizing attempts I gave up. Just couldn't find the words. If I couldn't write to her about what was really happening, I found it impossible to write to her about anything. We always had tried to share our true, clear feelings. So how could I ignore what Leo had done and pretend it hadn't happened?

I let that day go by without sending a letter, figuring I'll try again tomorrow. Hoping in the meantime a letter would come from Jana. I couldn't understand why Uncle Leo had done it. I wanted to know what Jana thought. She's there, she must know more than we do. But there was no letter from Jana. Soon a week had gone by without our exchanging letters. Then a month. I'd been in daily contact with Jana for all my life and now communication had been broken.

I was in a terrible funk. At the American school in town where I was enrolled, some of the kids were pleasant, but a handful delighted in calling me *Communista* or Hollyweirdo. My grades plummeted; the only class I did well in was Spanish. Somehow I was sponging up the language; my teacher said I had a real ear. But the compliment didn't mean much. I was so caught in my own downward spiral that I didn't notice that my mother was falling apart.

Whenever I looked her way she managed a smile, but I could see it was forced. The familiar glow within her that I'd always known seemed to have gone out. I'd be in the next room and hear her talking and assume it was to me, but when I went closer and asked her, "What?" she'd say, "Oh, nothing, just thinking out loud." Clearly they were dark thoughts.

Overall she was talking less and less, smoking constantly, less careful about her makeup and her clothes. One day when Dad was away I saw her carrying the wastebasket from her bedroom out to the trash, instead of leaving it for the housekeeper. After mom went back inside, I peeked into the trash can and saw a bunch of empty tequila bottles. Emitting the aroma I realized I often detected around her. I put that together with the really long siestas she took every day, plus the frequent black-and-blue marks on her legs. She explained those by making fun of herself: "I'm such a klutz, banging into this oversize furniture." But I'd seen *The Lost Weekend* and knew about alcoholics. I was worried, so although I didn't want to burden my father, considering his workload, I did mention all this to him.

He listened carefully, thanked me for telling him, said he knew she was under a lot of stress and struggling with the relocation, but knew she'd be okay once she adjusted. But he was concerned, too. "We've got to help her all we can, Davey." I translated that into the instruction he'd given to me at the airport when he left us in L.A.: "Take care of your mother."

So I made looking after her my responsibility. Stayed close to the hacienda, except for school. Made sure she ate her meals, even if she just picked at the food. Told her about school, about the vividly colorful vegetation in the surrounding area—so different from New York or California—anything to engage her. She'd offer encouragement if I mentioned a problem, but I was never sure she was really listening. Once I told her a joke and completely muffed the punchline, but she laughed anyway as if I was Bob Hope. I felt like she was slipping away from us.

On a Sunday morning a few weeks later, Teddy went to the airport to discuss changes in a script with the producer he referred to around the house as "The Sleaze Bag." I woke up and went into the kitchen and drank some juice and asked Adela, the cook, where Mom was. She said the señora went out.

Alarm bells rang for me. Mom spoke hardly any Spanish, and she didn't really know anyone in town, so where would she go? I hurried outside and looked up and down the residential palm-tree-lined street—only a few kids playing jump rope, so I walked quickly to the wide boulevard at the corner. Still no sign of her. Traffic going in both directions, but the shops were to the left, so I went that way. Looking in the windows of the shops that were open. Getting increasingly anxious. Midway along the block I heard brassy music playing and people singing. Going into a courtyard, I discovered a narrow whitewashed one-story building with front doors open.

From the outside it sounded like a jam session or a Sunday concert. But inside I saw it was a church service in progress. The congregation was about ninety people on folding chairs, not an empty seat in the house—all singing with the band in an upbeat tribute to "El Señor." For those who didn't know the words, they were being flashed on the wall in Spanish by a slide projector. I realized that the "Señor" they were celebrating was Jesus.

I asked the usherette at the door if she'd seen my mother,

and I showed her the snapshot in my wallet. Long odds, I know, but the usherette nodded, yes, she was here before, but then she went away. Where? The usherette pointed out the door—and I saw a bus wheeze by.

Going strictly by instinct, I ran for the bus. Got on. Then didn't know what to do next. I looked out the windows as we traveled, scanned the passing streets for a sighting of her. But there were few pedestrians, the whitewashed stucco walls with gaily colored doors flashing by. I began to doubt my coming aboard. But feelings of dread and urgency were almost gagging me. I had to find her. The bus rolled on. Where do I get off? Then I thought, where does she know? The Zócolo. The center of Oaxaca, the vast three-block shady square surrounded by sidewalk cafés and souvenir shops. Fountains in the center, people constantly milling about.

So I got off there and began to wander, looking for her, searching the faces at the cafés, getting more and more frightened that I wouldn't find her, sure that something terrible had happened to her—it was getting hot, I was sweating, almost ready to give up, maybe she was back at the hacienda—and then as I shouldered through a line of placard-waving marchers shouting protests about the latest guerilla activities of the Zapatistas, I saw her—sitting on the grass, under a tree, her head buried in her hands, like a child counting to ten at the start of a game of hide-and-seek.

I stood over her and waited for her to look up. When she didn't, I said softly, "Mom, it's Davey. Are you okay?"

She looked up at me, then brought her finger to her lips and said, "Sh-h-h!" Her eyes were wild. She gestured for me to sit down next to her. When I did, I noticed her shoes. They were the same height but my fashion-conscious mother was wearing mismatched shoes. She whispered in my ear, "You've got to be very careful, Davey. He's here, watching us. Stay very close to me, I'll protect you from him."

"From who, Mom?" I looked around and saw only the usual array of locals and tourists.

"From Joe McCarthy," she whispered. "Don't turn your head—he's right over there."

I knew what Joe McCarthy looked like from the TV news and photos in the newspapers—the balding head, beefy face, beady eyes, sneering mouth—but a covert scoping of the area didn't reveal anyone who even vaguely resembled him. "I don't see him," I said, trying to sound reassuring, but a pounding panic was filling my chest.

"He's been following me. Since I first saw him. In the church with the singing. He was hiding in back."

"In back of what?"

"In back of the guitar player. He was playing the mandolin, pretending to be one of the band. Then he got on the bus after me. And followed me here."

It was as if she had struck me—she took my breath away. My mother isn't making sense. She isn't. She isn't making sense. I gasped. Then I put my arm around her. Hoping that I would smell tequila on her breath, but she was cold sober. Just absolutely terrified.

"It's okay, Mom, I think he's gone now. Let's go home."

I meant the hacienda, of course, but tears filled her eyes. "We can't go home, Davey, maybe not ever again—they'll put us in prison. You, too!"

It took a while, I had to coax her, she was like a little girl frightened of the monsters, but I got her back to the hacienda, and when Teddy came home from the airport that evening, Mom was still very upset, and he gave her a sleeping pill so she could get some rest.

On Friday afternoon, August 12, 1951, I came home late after having a fistfight in the yard after school with a big kid whose father was an oil-company executive from Tulsa. He towered over me. But when he called me a Commie-loving Jew bastard I went for him. It was the first time the black rage swept over me. Literally blackness on my peripheral vision, targeting in on an enemy. The big kid kicked the crap out of me, but not before I got in some good licks.

I came home and washed off the blood under my nose, put a couple of Band-Aids on my knuckles and a knee, changed into unmuddied clothes so the sight of me wouldn't upset my mother. But when I went looking for her, the bedroom door was closed and it was quiet inside. Figured she was still napping. Wish, how I wish, I'd gone in then anyway. But instead I went downstairs, and Adela made me a snack. My father was due back from another quick business trip. I ate my snack and watched TV for a long time, then realized Mom still wasn't up. She wasn't supposed to be drinking anymore, she'd promised. But maybe. So. Something made me go upstairs. Listen at her door to hear if she was stirring. Still all quiet. I rapped lightly, not wanting to frighten her, she had become a light sleeper. There was no answer. A flash of foreboding. I rapped louder . . . and louder. Then I cracked the door and looked in.

The curtains were drawn, but in the gloom I could see her in bed. Not exactly lying there. More like sprawled. One arm flung out toward the nightstand. "Mom," I called softly. Advanced into the room. She hadn't moved. I went closer. Looked down. Again said, "Mom." But I think I knew then. Even before I saw the empty bottle of sleeping pills on the nightstand.

I don't know what I thought then. In that exact moment. It seems like my brain just stopped. I kept looking at her. She was so pretty, my mom. I wasn't scared, that came later, after I yelled for help and Adela came upstairs, and after she called for the ambulance and they couldn't revive her. I remember too clearly what I thought at *that* point and so many times since: Why didn't I go into the bedroom when I first came home? Why didn't I do what my father had told me to do: "Take care of your mother."

We only knew a few people in Oaxaca, so my father and I mourned pretty much in private. I kept waiting for him to rebuke me, but he never did. He was as strong as the combat soldier he had been. I tried to copy his strength and failed again. Together we went to the airport when the arrangements had been made to ship her body back to the family plot in L.A. for burial. Neither my father nor I were going along with her. He was concerned he'd be arrested if he set foot in America, and he felt I was too young to face all that alone.

When I saw the cargo hatch of the plane close on Mom's coffin, I began to cry, choking paroxysms of tears, nearing hysteria before my father could calm me enough to get me back into the car.

"It's not your fault, it's not your fault," he kept repeating when I tried to assume the blame. Then whose fault was it?

There's a thing that happens with my left cheek every now and then. It's a small quick twitch, halfway to a wink, but it's involuntary. Just happens. Hugo Kositchek, my shrink in Rome, a transplanted Swiss Jungian, he called it a psychic wince. He was interested in the phenomenon, said it was a bulletin from my subconscious. I never paid much attention. I mean, usually it's just one little tic. Sometimes days or even weeks go by that I don't do it. But here's the first one today. What the hell, if it doesn't happen here at your father's funeral, when would it?

Because it's my turn to speak. The rabbi moves aside and I step up to Teddy's casket. I'm about to take out the pages I struggled over last night. But instead, when I look out over the small crowd, I realize that they already know everything

I've written. It's seared into their psyches. So I leave the pages in my pocket and just begin to talk.

"I can't sleep on planes, but coming here from Rome with Teddy, I got drunk enough over the Atlantic to conk out for a few hours. And I had a dream. Wouldn't you know, it was a scene from a movie, *The Bridge on the River Kwai*. All the POWs are lined up in formation and Sessue Hayakawa, who played the Japanese commandant, is going down the line, asking everyone who they are. When he reaches me, I give him only the basics. Name, rank, and serial number. Sessue Hayakawa squints at me and says, 'Ah, you Teddy's boy.' "

A chuckle starts through the small assemblage. I encourage it with what I hope is a smile. There's a tickle in the back of my throat.

"That's who most of you know me as—been called that my whole life, I'm proud to say. I'm Teddy's boy."

I clear my throat, but the tickle is still there. I look over at the adjoining plot. It's been well kept; we've been paying the maintenance fee for years but didn't know if they were caring for it properly. Now I know. She won't be alone anymore. Teddy and Ellie. Together again.

"And I'm Ellie's boy, too," I croak. My gaze finds Jana in the small crowd; her eyes are waiting for mine. Contact. Maybe there's a chance.

I discover that's all I can say, so I sit down again. Trying to swallow, but the tickle is a lump that won't go down.

DAVID

Peter Zacharias is standing beside the casket now, telling us all how he met Teddy.

"It was in London during the Blitz. I have never seen nights so pitch black—illuminated only by the Nazi high-explosives plunging down from the skies. A dazzling fireworks display, but you didn't want a front seat for that show."

Zacharias—everyone calls him that, as if he's an Old Testament figure—talks like a poet but in a thick Bronx accent. He's still gaunt, big nose, big voice, but his hair has gone snow white since I saw him last.

"I was scrambling like a blind man down a darkened street in Soho in search of the air-raid shelter. When I found it, and plunged through the blackout curtain, it was even darker inside. Not a flicker of light. The thundering of the bombs became louder and louder, as if Goliath was hopscotching toward us. But I wasn't sure there was an 'us' in here. Maybe I was alone. 'Hey, anyone in here?'

"'Just us chickens,' an American guy's voice said from the darkness.

"'Well, whaddayasay?' I called out in relief. Just as a block-buster rocked the shelter. I was scared. But this other guy started to sing:

'Mairzy doats and dozy doats,
And little lamzy divey,
A kiddle-dee-divey-two . . .'

"And I started to laugh. It was that silly song that had been such a hit a few years before. So with the bombs still crashing, I joined in for the final chorus, decoding the gibberish jingle:

'Mares eat oats and does eat oats.
And little lambs eat ivy,
A kid'll eat ivy, too . . .'

"Then the bombers went away and that's when I met Teddy. Turns out we had a lot in common: I was a writer from New York who hated the movies, he was an ex–New Yorker who only hated bad movies. We were both in George Stevens's combat photography unit. Teddy and I were together every day after that. From the D-day invasion to the liberation of Dachau. We shot film of sights that, please God, will never occur again."

Zacharias takes a deep breath, then shrugs.

"What else can I tell you about Teddy? He was a *preemie,* did you know that? Born prematurely, in Kings County Hospital in Brooklyn, weighed only three pounds, twelve ounces. He came through that fine, but he was still premature. In Hollywood, he was a premature union man, a premature anti-Fascist, but old-fashioned enough that when push came to shove, he refused to betray his friends—"

Zacharias looks over at the knoll where Agent McKenna is taking notes.

"—Am I going too fast for you, sonny?"

Then he turns to me. "Duveed," that's what he always called me, "you're entitled to be proud. Your father was a *mensch*." A real person.

Zacharias gazes down at the casket. "Now he's been taken from us at the age of forty-eight—so very premature of you, Teddy." He touches the casket gently. "The war is over, pal. Rest in peace."

I look over at Jana. She's staring straight ahead with that steel-jawed expression she always had when trying to hold back tears. Beside her, Markie looks bored. But on Jana's other side, Wendy Travers is dabbing at her Ray-Ban–concealed eyes with a hanky. Crocodile tears! The bitch is trying to impress anyone who may be looking. I look away.

Zacharias goes back to his seat as the two-man honor guard marches up in stiff precision. The staff sergeant snaps and holds a tight salute as the corporal brings a bugle to his lips and plays "Taps." After the bugler finishes his dirge, the soldiers step up to the casket and, with practiced exactness, fold the flag covering my father's coffin. When it has been reduced to a compact bundle with the stars showing, the sergeant paces to my chair and I take it from him. He salutes me and I snap a return salute automatically. Ranger reflex. My father's funeral service has concluded.

M y duties are not quite over. I'm a one-man reception line. The mourners all throw spades of earth on the coffin and then troop past me for embraces and handshakes. Some of them reintroduce themselves. "Do you remember me? I knew you as a little boy." I see Harry Rains being glad-handed by various people, some of them hugging Valerie Nolan, sharing old fond memories. Wendy Travers stands near them, shunned, isolated by unforgiven history. Nobody pays any attention to Jana or Markie, guess they don't recognize them as adults.

When I look up, Zacharias, with watering eyes, clasps me to his skinny bosom. I squeeze back and he feels almost frail.

"All grown up since the last time I saw ya," he says.

"You still writing?"

"Nah, I'm in the transportation game now." I'm puzzled. He clears it up. "I'm driving a bus." Spoken with a twinkle. "Come see me sometime, I'll let you ride for free. It's an education."

He hands me a business card, and I pocket it without looking at it because Jana and Markie Gunderson are standing in front of me. Actually, Markie has stopped a few paces away. That's it, man, give us a little room.

She tells me how glad she is she spotted the ad in *Variety* or she would have missed this, and I ask where Leo is, and she says her father is on his way back from shooting preproduction footage, otherwise he'd be here. How's his health? She says they removed a lung and hit him with intense doses of radiation and he's in complete remission, doing fine. Then she cuts right through, the way she always did:

"Were you going to call me before you left?"

"Of course I was, sure, I just was—working my way up to it." Nervous laugh escapes me.

But she accepts it, keeps searching my eyes. "Well, let's get together while you're here."

"I'm not leaving for a while." Jeez, sounds like I'm putting her off. "But yeah, let's—I'd like that. Really." Not too much, you'll scare her off.

There's a pause, not awkward though, Jana wants to say something important, I can sense it. And in a shaky voice, "Can't tell you what a shock it was to hear about Teddy." Markie is gazing away, still looking bored. Jana takes a deep breath, then leans closer. "I've been here before to—visit Ellie. Flowers on Mother's Day, that kind of stuff."

Jana looks at the neighboring plot where my mother is buried. At the time, in our absence, Zacharias had handled the minimal arrangements for Teddy and me. I was unaware Jana even knew about this place. Mother's Day. The tic in my cheek fires again.

"Calamity Jane," I whisper. So only Jana can hear, not Markie. Her eyes rivet me again as if seeking to verify my identity. Those remarkable hazel eyes with the gold flecks. I used to think she could peer into my soul. I'm about to say, Jana, it's still *me*! But Markie breaks the moment.

"Hey, Weaver," stepping forward with an outstretched hand to give me a limp-dick handshake. He's my height now, still with a bland round face and a terminally jaded expression. "Sorry about your dad, he was a good writer, my father always said so."

Not before the Committee, when his father pointed an accusing finger at Teddy, but I don't say that. Trying not to confuse what Rex Gunderson did and who Markie is.

"Thanks for coming," I say.

"Had to drive Jana so she wouldn't get lost way out here in the Valley." He grins. Shucks. Jest a-takin' care of the li'l gal.

Jana is holding out a business card to me with the Panorama logo on it. The word "Research" under her name.

"So you're both working for the studio now," I say.

"How'd you know that?" Markie is pleased I'm aware he's an exec in the script development department.

"They sell *Variety* in Rome," I say. Why mention he turned down one of Teddy's black-market scripts six months ago? Nothing personal, there was a phony name on it. And what difference does it make now?

Jana ignores the chitchat. Taps the business card I'm still holding. "You can reach me at the studio—or at home," she says. "Still the same number." Her look says: you remember *that* number.

They move off and I continue receiving condolences from other mourners, but the corner of my eye is still on Jana and

Markie, as he drapes an arm over her shoulder. She doesn't seem to mind, but I sure as hell do. Particularly when Markie's words to her float back to me:

"Some creepy crew turned up here, huh? Looks like the road company of *Mission to Moscow*."

McCarthy is dead, but McCarthyism lives on. My reflex is to go for Markie. But before I can, I hear Jana.

"Shut the fuck up, Markie!" she snaps, shrugging off his arm. "You didn't have to come if you didn't want to." And she stalks away. I'm delighted by her reaction.

Then I look at the next person standing before me. It's Wendy Travers. How can she bring herself to face me? She makes the first move. Taking off her sunglasses, out of some kind of courtesy, I guess, but I see her eyes are red-rimmed. Not crocodile tears after all. For Teddy? Or for herself?

"So very *very* sorry for your loss," she croaks in a choked voice.

What do I say to her? What would Teddy say? I hear my voice: "Thanks for being here." By rote. Flat. She almost flinches, then nods and walks off. Grudgingly, I concede that it took guts—or incredible chutzpah—to come today and brave the hate-filled stares.

Now here are Harry and Valerie. I offer my hand, but Harry ignores it and wraps me in a big *abrazo*. "Sonuvagun, you're not a little boy anymore. Look at Davey," he says to Valerie, "all grown up." Why is everyone so surprised I got taller in ten years?

"Hi, cookie," Valerie says, kissing my cheek and then gazing at me with glistening blue eyes and the smile that launched a thousand close-ups. One of The Great Ladies of the Silver Screen, a box office champ during the 30s and 40s, Valerie has spectacularly managed the segue to her own hit TV series at Harry's studio.

"Harry and I are desolate about Teddy's passing," she says. I remember she never uses the word "death," it spooks her.

The years have been kind to both of them. Valerie's beauty and sweetness are intact, and big Harry, golf-tanned face, waist a bit thicker, but still immaculately tailored by Savile Row, still exudes boundless energy.

"So glad you're here," I say.

"Teddy meant so much to me," Valerie says.

I'm not sure if she's talking personally or professionally. Probably both. In the Progressive days before and during World War II, Valerie Nolan was a flaming liberal. Teddy and Leo also wrote the movie that won her the Oscar.

"Hadda love him." Harry chimes in. "Not that Teddy would ever listen to good advice. Stubborn as a mule." Unlike Leo, who saw the light.

"Water under the bridge," Valerie reminds him.

I glance past them to the road, where Jana has left Markie standing angrily at his MG and joins Wendy at Harry's Rolls-Royce. Markie guns away, the MG burning rubber. Great! Jana didn't go with the guy she came with.

"Let's talk about you," Harry is saying. "What are David Weaver's plans?"

"Well, I've been trying to figure that out."

"No plans? How about working at my studio!"

"Sounds great," I blurt. Too eagerly? Hoping I haven't shot myself in the foot. Jana works at Harry's studio. What could be better?

Harry Rains laughs. That familiar boom of delight. "Let's do lunch. Meet me at my office tomorrow at twelve thirty. We'll decide your future then."

I like the sound of that. Harry is assuming I have a future here. And he's just the man who can make that become a reality.

7

MCKENNA

I'm trying to distract myself, but it's not working. I'm in my cubicle at the Bureau office downtown toying with what is described in the user's manual as a new crime-fighting tool. What I'm really doing is worrying that hot job in D.C. will vanish unless I can glom onto a high-profile case. Prove that I've still got it. I feel like the man who's been notified he won the Irish Sweepstakes but can't find his raffle ticket.

So I fiddle while my future burns. The FBI lab in D.C. knows I'm a gadgeteer, so all their latest gismos wind up on my desk, usually way before anyone knows they exist. A two-way wristwatch radio like Dick Tracy uses, a shotgun microphone that will pick up conversations three hundred yards away, a camera small enough to fit in your tie pin. I get to fool around with them because occasionally I place them—with proper credit to the Bureau, of course—in a movie or on our TV series.

The latest toy they've sent me is this ordinary looking pack of Lucky Strike cigarettes, but tucked inside there's a didn't-know-they-made-them-so-small tape machine, capable of recording up to an hour. I test it out, good tone, while I'm waiting for Willie Pierson, the youngest agent in our shop, to come out of the darkroom down the hall. He's making prints of the photos he shot for me at the Weaver funeral this morning.

Pierson's a good kid, I've taken him under my wing. He's the new generation of agents with masters degrees in political science and criminology from Georgetown. Being a lawyer from anywhere or a meager CPA with an ordinary BA degree was enough once. Now Pierson raps on the doorway of my cubicle. I used to have a spacious office with two large windows facing the street. Back in the HUAC days I had six agents reporting to me. Now I'm a one-man band, with only a small partitioned space and no windows. Wonder how many windows the head of the bank-robbery posse in D.C. rates? I gesture Pierson into my cubicle.

He's carrying a handful of photos. "Hot off the drying rack," he says as he spreads them out on my desk. "Close-up studies of all the toothless tigers."

They're pictures of the mourners. Pierson is still twitting me. It started when the funeral party assembled. As he began snapping away, he snorted skeptically: "This is who the Soviets are relying on to take over the West Coast? They gonna run over us in their wheelchairs?"

"The home office wants an update on who's still around," I told him. "So do a good job. Hoover may be looking at your handiwork."

That's what I'm hoping anyway. The assignment to cover the funeral didn't originate with the home office. The idea was mine. I didn't really expect to find anything new. But the funeral was an excuse to send along a batch of pics and a brief report. Remind Hoover that I'm still alive and on the ball. Every bit counts at this point.

I've already taken some static this afternoon from Bernie Farrell, the L.A. Bureau boss, for requisitioning manpower and equipment without prior authorization. I got off the hook by hinting to Farrell that I received a last-minute order directly from Hoover's office. It used to happen often.

"I particularly like this shot." Pierson picks up one of the funeral photos from the stack. It's of a former MGM story editor who took the Fifth when called to testify. She's aged very badly. Last I heard she was punching a cash register at a checkout stand in Ralphs market in Westwood. "Move over, Tokyo Rose," Pierson adds.

The thing I like about Pierson, sassy attitude and all, is that in a lot of ways he reminds me of myself. When I was a go-for-it young agent and everything seemed so clear. Good guys taking down bad guys. So I ask him what's bothering him? Inviting him to vent. Off the record.

"Far as I know, all those years and dollars spent out here by that Committee of yours and the Bureau didn't add up to diddly-squat. No new legislation ever resulted. No criminal arrests. Just jamming up some jerks who signed the wrong petitions and donated a few bucks to Mickey Mouse causes."

Sounds like me talking to David Weaver at the Chateau the other night. But I can't admit that to the troops. "They gave big bucks to the Party and front organizations," I correct Pierson, "and lent glamour and prestige to subversive activities. When they weren't trying to slip Red propaganda into the movies."

"That still the official Bureau line?" Pierson sniffs.

I used to believe that stuff, why doesn't he?

It was a different world when I first came to L.A. In 1946 the country was on a euphoric post-war high—buying new cars, new houses, the GI Bill turning out hordes of new college graduates—and the Bureau was hard at work combating the new menace: Russia. During World War II we rooted out Fifth-Column Nazis in our midst, now we were tracking Commies. The American people weren't paying any attention. So in conjunction with HUAC we went after Hollywood to dramatize the threat.

Media-event hearings were held in L.A. early in 1947. Friendly studio chiefs Jack Warner, Walt Disney, and Louis B. Mayer testified about subversive elements in the industry, hinting that despite their vigilance, Red propaganda was infiltrating movie screens. The public still didn't care.

Then the hearings shifted to Washington, D.C. and unfriendly writers and directors were summoned to appear. I served most of the subpoenas myself. The activists on the Left voiced warnings of a witch hunt.

When the new hearings convened there was chaos in the Capitol dome. Gavel pounding while shouting witnesses were virtually dragged away. I was in the hearing room for every moment and it was a helluva show. The Hollywood witnesses came off as arrogant, contemptuous, and evasive. Perfect for our purposes. Instantly dubbed The Hollywood Ten, they were cited for Contempt of Congress. This time the public paid fleeting attention.

That's when the Blacklist was born. The moguls who owned the movie studios, frightened by the bad publicity for their industry, fired all of the Hollywood Ten then under contract and set a policy of not hiring anyone who refused to cooperate with the Committee.

The issue moved off the front pages and into the judicial system. The appeal of The Hollywood Ten's convictions slowly worked up to the Supreme Court. That took three years. By then the world had changed again. Winston Churchill, in a famous speech in Fulton, Missouri in 1949, declared that an Iron Curtain had fallen across Europe, dividing east and west. The Russians, with the treasonous connivance of the Rosenbergs, now had the secret of the atom bomb. The federal government invoked prosecutions under the Smith Act outlawing the Communist Party in America. North Korea had invaded South Korea and our soldiers were fighting and dying in the battle against Communism in that distant land. President

Truman, in order to ensure political support for the war in Korea, agreed to a loyalty oath for Americans.

Then the cases of the Hollywood Ten reached the Supreme Court. During the past three years there had been two replacements of so-called liberal justices. The old court might have approved the appeal and reversed the convictions. The new, more conservative court, operating in a wartime era, refused to hear the case. The Hollywood Ten went to prison for six-month sentences. HUAC, with the Bureau acting as its enforcement arm, was back in business.

New hearings began again in 1950, but with First Amendment political privacy rights no longer a possible defense, the only way to avoid answering HUAC's questions—such as naming names—was to claim Fifth Amendment protection against self-incrimination. That kept a witness out of jail—but guaranteed a spot on the Blacklist. Those were the days. Our team had the power and the leverage. We were in high gear.

While Pierson watches, I combine the stack of 8×10s from the funeral with my one-page report. Ready to slip it all into a Classified Material envelope that will go in the overnight pouch to D.C.

The switchboard buzzes me and announces, "Mr. Tolson on line two." I shoo Pierson out and he goes forth to perpetuate the office legend that J. Edgar Hoover and his number two man Clyde Tolson call me every day. But it's been months since I heard from either of them.

The last attaboy I got was on what I privately called Operation Hand Job. When our TV series went on the air there was only one negative review. But it came from Hoover. I received an urgent phone call at home on a Sunday night just seconds after the first episode aired. Clyde Tolson told me, "The Director is very upset." Reason: two of the actors playing FBI agents were seen with their hands in their pockets. Luckily, Chad Halloran wasn't one of them. Mr. Hoover felt it was a slovenly sight and a poor representation of proper Bureau behavior.

The next morning I tore into Warner Bros. like a tornado and demanded that the wardrobe department sew up the pockets on every pair of pants and all jackets worn by an actor portraying an agent. They also reedited a couple of scenes already completed but un-aired to banish the offending sight. Tolson called me again to say Hoover was pleased.

"Brian?" Now Tolson's voice surges through the phone. "Ready for another Special Assignment?"

"Yessir." My ears perking. Sure can use a juicy one!

"You know Harry Rains?"

In the HUAC era, when Harry was a prominent Hollywood attorney, he and I worked hand-in-glove. Convincing his client Leo Vardian to become a friendly witness was a feather in my cap. Oscar-winning directors always made news when they recanted and repented. Elia Kazan had gotten HUAC their biggest headlines, but Leo Vardian was the runner-up. I never understood why cooperating was such a hard sell to so many Left Wingers. Self-destructive behavior baffles me. Like refusing to denounce a cause most of them had long since stopped believing in.

"Yeah, of course I know Harry," I tell Tolson. "Matter of fact, I was with him this morning." I pick up a photo of Harry and Valerie at the funeral for his former client.

"Well, you're about to get to know him even better."

Tolson tells me Harry is up for the chairmanship of one of those do-gooder "are-violent-movies-damaging-our-children?" Blue Ribbon Presidential Panels. Before the White House makes the announcement, they want me to vet Harry Rains. "Keep it quiet. But do a real thorough job."

I promise I will, like if he didn't tell me that I might not?

I could give Harry a clean bill of health right now. Prominent Hollywood player, bulwark of the community, blah-blah-blah. But I know better than to say that. Got to go through the motions and take a week or so to show I'm applying due diligence.

And *this* is Hoover and Tolson's idea of a "Special Assignment"? A dogshit detail. Not what will propel me into that big job I'm after.

8

DAVID

When I arrive at Harry Rains's office at Panorama Studio for our lunch date, his pert, young executive secretary settles me into a chair with the trade papers. "He'll be with you in a few minutes." She's all atwitter. "He's on the phone with the president," she confides.

"Of the company?" Harry's title is Executive Vice President in Charge of Worldwide Production.

"Of the United States," she says.

I'm impressed but not surprised: although he was an ardent FDR and Harry Truman supporter, when the political winds shifted, Harry Rains switched to Dwight Eisenhower, and he raised millions in donations for the "I Like Ike" campaigns in 1952 and 1956.

Through the door I can hear Harry's booming, excited voice. Can't make out what he's saying, but it sounds like good news. In a moment, the phone light on the secretary's console goes off. She buzzes Harry, whispers that I'm here, then tells me to go in.

The palatial corner office has a wall of floor-to-ceiling windows so Harry can look down upon the acres of his domain. He's slouched in an overstuffed easy chair, feet up on the in-layed Spanish tile coffee table, with a dazed smile of delight on his face. He presses a button under the coffee table that automatically closes the door behind me. "Siddown, Davey," he says.

I do—and I wait. Not for long. Harry's bursting to tell someone and that turns out to be me. "Can you keep a secret, kiddo?"

"Absolutely. It's a family specialty." He's so hyped he doesn't even hear the irony in what I said.

"Ike's offered me a job."

"In Washington?"

"In London. U.S. Ambassador to the Court of St. James." He shakes his head in wonder. "Can you believe it? Little Harry from Boyle Heights becomes Ambassador to Great Britain. It's like a fairy tale."

I agree it's incredible and offer congratulations. He says Jim Hagerty, Ike's press secretary, sounded him out a few weeks ago, but Ike just gave Harry the official offer on the phone. "It's under wraps until the White House and State Department do their vetting processes and make the announcement."

"My lips are sealed," I promise.

"Then it's gonna be hard for you to eat lunch. C'mon, let's go to the commissary. We've got a new chef, the food's pretty good."

I really am glad for the honor that's befallen Harry. Just hope he won't be taking off before he can lend me a helping hand.

As we walk out of the executive building and stroll toward the commissary, everyone we pass takes note. Some nod or say hello to Harry, who greets a few of them, keeps moving. I feel like I'm sharing his spotlight—they're all ogling me, wondering who's that with their sun god.

There's a question I've been thinking about so I ask him.

"Harry, did you take that ad on the back of *Variety* yesterday?"

He looks at me and shakes his head. "No, I thought you did. Nice picture of Teddy. So how's it being back?"

"I'm not sure yet. You know that bit in the Bible about being a stranger in a strange land? That's me."

"I know how that is. Hey, why so surprised? You think I was born in a power booth at the Polo Lounge?"

"Weren't you?" I zing him amiably.

We both laugh. My first real laugh since Teddy died. Eases the bad feelings I have about asking Harry Rains for favors, considering Teddy's past history with him.

"Compared to what you've gone through, kiddo, I had it easy—but I remember what it's like to be an outsider in this town. Growing up in Boyle Heights, which is next door to dirt poor, I had to battle my way through some rough neighborhoods just to get to school."

"So how'd you get here?" Always thought Harry was a rich kid—like I used to be.

"Well, after all that rumbling in the streets, I lied about my age and fought Golden Gloves, six KO's in eight bouts. Parlayed that into a full scholarship at USC. They were beefing up their boxing team. I wound up captain of a championship squad. That propelled me through USC law school."

"And the rest is history?"

"Not so fast. When I graduated I took the California Bar exam. Some guys take it five or six times before they pass. I flunked twice, kept my bills paid by working as a process server, took it a third time—dead sure I'd blown it again. A buddy was stationed in San Diego at the Naval Base. He convinced me to come down for a weekend and he'd help me forget my troubles. So I went and drowned my sorrows. Helluva weekend. Came back to discover, lo and behold, I passed the bar! But nobody wanted to hire me. No couth, no connections. So I hung

out my own shingle. In Beverly Hills, though I didn't know a
soul there. Didn't exactly chase ambulances, but you get the
idea. Slim pickings. Until I met Valerie, the love of my life—and
that was the real start of my career."

That part of the story was Hollywood legend. Teddy had
regaled me with it in Paris years later. It was a meet-cute
worthy of a Weaver & Vardian screenplay. Struggling lawyer
Harry has his appendix out, and while he's in the hospital re-
covering he meets another post-surgery patient, a little old lady
who also grew up in Boyle Heights. Now she lived in Malibu as
the housekeeper, cook, and faithful retainer to supernova Valerie Nolan. Valerie came to visit frequently at Cedars, Harry got
to know her, one day she mentioned a legal wrangle she was
having with the Coastal Commission about expanding her
beach house. Harry solved it with a phone call. Soon he had his
first important client. But Harry really came into his own when
HUAC came back to town in 1950.

Valerie Nolan was subpoenaed to testify. The news wasn't
public yet, but she turned to Harry in terror. She had never
actually been a Party member, she was what was categorized
in those days as "a fellow-traveler." But a HUAC subpoena
was enough to turn America's sweetheart into Mata Hari.

In dealing with her problem, Harry made his reputation as a
go-between, shuttling between the Hollywood community and
the Congressional committee. He contacted the head counsel
for HUAC, took him to dinner at Romanoff's, explained that
apart from donating some money to now-unpopular causes,
the worst thing Valerie had done was let a bunch of Lefties hold
a Marxist "study session" that she thought was a reception for
a Stanislavski acting guru. She was away on location in Utah at
the time. HUAC's counsel said, "Great, let her testify about
that." He was figuring HUAC would still get their headline.

But Harry played his hole card: Valerie, then married to a local architect, was three months pregnant. Harry had a sworn affidavit from her doctor to prove it.

"If you put that sweet defenseless woman on the stand and she loses that baby," he warned the HUAC counselor, "your Committee is finished. Public opinion will destroy you." Teddy roared with laughter when he told me how Harry had reenacted this part of the pitch for him. One hand on his heart, the other upraised to the heavens, protecting the best interests of all sides, Harry the Honest Broker.

The subpoena was withdrawn. Never made public. And Valerie was never called to testify.

"And that's the sort of thing I wanted to do for Teddy," Harry told me as we approached the entrance to the commissary. "There's always a way to maneuver around these things. A way to weather the storm. To survive."

Usually, it was the same maneuver. Give names, keep on working. Like Leo. But, hey, I'm listening to Harry's version of those events.

We're seated at the best table in the executive alcove of the Panorama commissary, just off the main dining room, but plainly visible to all. I'm encouraged that Harry is willing to be seen in public with me. He introduces me to everyone who stops by. "Teddy's boy," he always adds. I'm starting to relax, feeling less and less like an interloper. Wendy Travers comes up to the table to kiss Harry's cheek and greet me with a tentative smile.

"Are you coming to work here?" she asks me.

"All the best people are." Harry points proudly at Wendy. "Wooed her away from Metro. She's adapting Jane Austen's *Sense and Sensibility* for us."

"Classy stuff," I say.

She smiles again. But under her smile, there's pain, as if it hurts to look at me. I know what it is, of course.

I hear myself say, "Teddy would have been glad you came yesterday." Who knows? He might have been. Teddy was a bigger man than I am.

"Last chance to say good-bye to an old friend." Then she adds, "Welcome home, David."

I realize she's the first person to say that to me since my return.

While I fish for a response, she touches my shoulder and walks on to the raucous writers' table. The fawning waiter is at Harry's elbow; he orders for both of us.

"So what were we talkin' about, kiddo?"

"How you became head of the studio."

"Oh, yeah. Well, after I solved Valerie's problem, I had a big ticket specialty. Cutting the best deals possible with the Committee. It was a service that benefited a lot of people— including the studios that had huge investments in these film artists. So when the Blacklist finally started to fade, like it has now, the studio owners remembered who pulled their bacon out of the fire, who they could trust—"

"And here you are."

He nods. "So you might say I owe my big break in the business to the Blacklist." Harry looks past me at a man sauntering toward us from the main dining room.

The man is in his mid-forties, whippet-thin, dapper as a duke, sporting a pencil-thin, William Powell–style mustache. But what looks suave on *The Thin Man* comes out sinister on him. He brings a dark rain cloud with him. But Harry gives him a warm smile.

"Hey, kiddo, how'd you like the picture?"

"Good one, Harry. Think you've got a winner. Thanks for setting up the screening. Who's your friend?" I get the feeling he knows the answer.

"This is David Weaver."

"Teddy's boy," he says. "Isn't that what they call you?"

"People who know me."

"I'm Joe Shannon." So this is what the asshole looks like. The Red-baiting columnist who used to smear Teddy—up to and including yesterday. And Shannon relishes the flare of recognition in my eyes.

"You were a household word when I was a kid," I acknowledge. "And you can imagine what that word was."

I hope that's enough to embarrass him, so he'll move on. But it only turns him on. "Guess you're in town to plant your father." What a fucked way to put it! But he rolls on. "Or maybe you're job hunting, planning to stay a while?" He whips out his notebook as if gathering an important item. "So, Harry, the way you and the Prodigal Son are yukking it up together, can I assume you're about to hire him?" I see menace poised in his ballpoint pen.

This turd is used to kicking people without them kicking back. Before I can say or do anything, Harry steps in as an ameliorating referee. "We're just two old friends, gabbing about the past. I've known David since—"

Shannon overrides. Loud enough to be heard by all the neighboring tables. "Harry, if you are thinking of hiring Teddy's boy, well, as a friend I'd advise you strongly to think twice. For the good of the studio and yourself." Looking contemptuously at me again. "The apple never falls far from the rotten tree, I always say."

"C'mon, Joe, no need for that sort of talk," Harry protests, but Shannon isn't listening. He's too busy trying to goad me. Spark a shouting match that will make him look good and me bad. Intrepid Columnist Clashes with Commie's Son. Ain't gonna happen. Not going to allow it. But I do want this pissant to vanish.

So I fold my napkin on the table and slowly rise. I'm way bigger than Shannon. But he stands his ground, hoping I've reached the flashpoint that can make him the talk of the town tomorrow. I put my palms on the white linen table cloth and lean closer to him—and closer—looming over him, putting my face into his and giving him the stink eye.

Then I whisper softly so no one around us can hear. But making sure he gets the threat, "Time for you to go back to your own table, little man."

He drills me with his gaze, but I intensify the stink eye. He blinks first. With a warning glare over his shoulder at Harry, Shannon strolls off to greet a buxom starlet in the main dining room.

I'm relieved I didn't blow my stack. Kept the black rage in check. I sit down again. Harry looks disgusted, but also worried.

"Sorry about that, David," he says. "Guess those ugly days aren't completely over yet."

Then we go on with lunch. Pretending nothing happened. But I know the hiring window at this shop has closed. Harry charms me with colorful tales about Teddy and a few fond memories of me as a child. The distant past is evergreen, but the conversation doesn't get around to my future. Maybe I have none.

MCKENNA

I'm a victim of the Sunday blues, moping around my apartment. Truth is, I'm a bit hungover. I went to a fund-raising dinner at The Beverly Hilton last night. Harry Rains was being presented the Brotherhood and Humanity Award by the National Conference of Christians and Jews. I called Barney Ott, a big gun at Panorama, and promoted a free ticket. Because it was last minute, I could only get one. I was seated between Loretta Young and Fred MacMurray's wife, June Haver, so that was boring but nice. Afterwards Harry asked me to join his coterie for a nightcap next door in Trader Vic's, which told me Harry knows the Bureau is vetting him. One drink led to another and it was after one o'clock when we broke up.

I brew a pot of extra-strong coffee and settle down in the breakfast nook of my apartment to read the Sunday papers. I live in what the local Realtors describe as an upscale apartment house on Wilshire near Westwood. An interior decorator I dated for a while once said my pad looked impersonal. "That's because I'm undercover," I teased her. I never have felt L.A. is home. So what's getting me down today is that the D.C. job is beginning to look like a pipe dream. And I may have to stay here forever.

But that's pushed aside when I flip to the Local News section of the *L.A. Times*. I'm shocked to see a story about a murder in Beverly Hills about twelve last night. It's someone I knew very well. Screenwriter Wendy Travers. She was on her way home from Harry's award dinner—we'd even chatted earlier for a moment at the bar; she was with Busby Berkeley, the choreographer she'd worked with in the old days on the Esther Williams watercade pictures.

As the Beverly Hills cops pieced it together, Wendy was driving alone in her red Ferrari from the Hilton to her house on Kings Road north of the Sunset Strip. There's a stop sign at the top of the hill. She stopped, and apparently an assailant stepped out of the darkness and smashed the driver's window with a hammer or a tire iron. There were shards of glass showered over Wendy and the side of her head was smashed in. Her purse was taken and a diamond necklace she wore. No witnesses. The assumption is, it was a junkie hiding behind a tree who spotted a woman in an expensive car and saw a payday.

I pick up the phone and dial Jerry Borison, the homicide detective quoted in the paper, whom I've worked with in the past. I ask him for more details, but he says that's about it so far. They haven't turned up any real leads. "All her friends seem real broken up; she was a popular gal. How well did you know her?"

"Real well," I say. I let it go at that. But ask him to keep me posted on any new developments. No, nothing professional. Just personal. Clearly it's not a federal case. I hang up the phone and stare out the window at the Sunday drivers passing below on Wilshire.

Wendy and I were closest after I served her with the HUAC subpoena. It was fairly late in the game, the hearings were almost wrapped. Earlier her name had cropped up occasionally. But we tended to go slower in pursuit of pinko women. Especially after playwright Lillian Hellman snookered the

Committee by getting her statement about "I will not cut my principles to fit this year's fashions" onto the public record. Women were too sympathetic and too unpredictable.

Not that Wendy was a die-hard. She had dabbled with Communism as a youngster—her first job in the business at age nineteen was in the mail room at MGM, and she tried to unionize the other workers. She was fired, but came back later after winning local swim championships to be Esther Williams' stand-in—or "swim-in," as she called herself. When that career dried up she became mogul Louis B. Mayer's number one screenwriter. Spinning a string of warmhearted movies for the whole family that were lightweight but consistent box office winners.

By the time I got to her, she was decades away from the Party. "It's one thing," she told me, "to throw yourself off a cliff for what you believe in. But not for what you don't believe in anymore."

But like all the cooperative witnesses, she drew the line at naming others. Or at least she tried to. She wouldn't name anyone who hadn't already been named at least ten times. "Not seven or eight," she insisted, "it has to be *ten*!" That was her way of trying not to hurt people. I went along with her, more or less, but things were murky in those days, so some of the names we got her to give up in the public hearing were more like fours and fives. She adamantly refused to name Teddy Weaver because he was only a two. In any case, the distinction was totally lost to the people on the Left. To them an informer was an informer.

None of that is in the obituary in the *L.A. Times*. The focus is on the Esther Williams days and then the hit movies she wrote, her Oscar nominations and the Golden Globe Award.

There was a man-woman attraction between us back then, but Wendy was too vulnerable and I had made it a rule never to get involved with anyone we were investigating. So it never

· went anywhere, the moment passed with nothing happening, but we have always been glad to see each other whenever our paths crossed.

And now Wendy's dead. A stupid, pointless street crime. A lovely lady. Ambushed for dollars. So some dope-crazed asshole can buy poison to jam into his arm. What kind of screwed up world do we live in?

The phone beside me on the breakfast table rings. I scoop it up thinking it may be Borison calling back with more info. But it's Tom Churillo from his house in Arlington, Virginia.

"Hate to amp up the pressure, buddy." He tells me a hotshot agent from my class at the Bureau training program is making a big push for the job I'm after. "He's just scored a major gun-running bust on the Tex-Mex border." Churillo says he'll hold him off as long as he can, but: "Hurry up, pal, I don't want you to miss this boat."

I tell him I'm hurrying. But so far all I'm doing is treading water. It feels like my life is slipping away.

10

JANA

It's not quite seven thirty on Monday morning when I drive onto the lot, but that's not early for a movie studio. The camera crews report at seven to start rigging the lights on the soundstages for the first setup.

I don't take the usual route to my office. Instead I detour by the writers' building and stop for a moment. The parking area is deserted. Writers never show up until nine. Her name is still there, stenciled in black on the white curbing at the head of her parking space. Wendy Travers. By tomorrow it will be gone. Just like she is.

I cried away all of Sunday after Valerie called with the news.

"We've lost her," she said.

As if saying those words would make the horror easier to accept. But it still seems like a bad B movie. The beautiful, witty, wonderful heroine is unexpectedly killed. Wendy's meaningless death leaves me chilled and despairing.

My father hadn't heard when I picked him up late last night at the airport. He'd been flying fourteen hours from London. At the arrival gate I wept into his shoulder. We drove home and sat in his study and got drunk together, but that didn't take away the pain. He went to sleep, exhausted from the trip; I nodded off for a couple of hours. Then woke up into the immutable awful dawn and decided to go to work.

Panorama's research department is in a white, wooden two-story building dating back to silent-film days. Accounting is downstairs, research upstairs. Now I trudge up the steps and find the lights still dark in every office but mine. When I get there I'm surprised to see Harry Rains sitting on my couch, rimless glasses perched on the tip of his nose like Scrooge's bean-counter Bob Cratchit, perusing a sheaf of legal-size papers. When he sees me he tosses the papers into the attaché case open at his feet and takes off the glasses. His eyes are bloodshot.

"Thought you'd probably be in early," he says softly. "I couldn't sleep either. So howyadoin' kid?"

I know I look like hell, eyes swollen. He doesn't look much better. Immaculately dressed as always, but emitting a marrow-deep sadness. Harry being here is not a rare occurrence, it's unique. In the two years I've been working at Panorama, he has never had occasion to enter the building.

He gestures at the spot next to him on the couch. I sink wearily into the cushions and he clasps both my hands. "There'll never be another one like her," he says.

That chokes me up. All I can do is nod.

"Valerie is too shattered to work today," he says. "But I had to see you." I'm touched that he's come to comfort me. He leans back, sighs heavily, rubs his eyes as if that will erase the images I know we're both thinking. A monster bashing in Wendy's car window, snuffing out her life. When he looks back at me, he attempts a smile.

"Do you know how she became a writer?" he says.

"She was Louis B. Mayer's Scheherazade. He hated to read scripts and he overheard her telling some girls the story of the movie she saw the night before. So he hired her to be his official storyteller."

"Yeah, everybody knows that, but the way she became a screenwriter was, months later, she tells him a story he loves.

He wants to buy it, but who wrote it? Wendy admits she's slipped in a ringer. She wrote it. For a second she was scared he'd can her—and she really liked the job. 'Well, it's not your job anymore,' he says. 'Now you're a screenwriter.' "

He chuckles—and I join him. It makes us both feel a bit better. Then I get a vibe. Like he's softening me up for something.

"Any special reason you stopped by, Harry? I mean, besides . . ."

"Wow, you are one sharp cookie." He reaches down for the legal papers in his attaché case. "This is Wendy's will. I drew it up for her when she was my client. After I took the job here at the studio, I referred her out to Gang, Kopp & Tyre. Last year she had them do a codicil."

"I don't understand. Did she leave me something?"

"Yeah, a few pieces of jewelry she said you admired. She also made you executor of her estate."

It comes as a complete surprise. One that throws me for a loop. "She did that? Why?"

"Because she loved you and trusted you."

"Harry, I'm not a lawyer or a banker, I wouldn't know what to do—"

"Not to worry, Martin Gang and Al Lewis at Citibank can handle the nitty-gritty. All you have to do is look over their shoulders and make sure Wendy's wishes are observed."

He holds out the papers. I hesitate taking them. "You can't say no, Jana, it was what she wanted."

I accept the legal papers. Harry snaps his attaché case shut and rises.

"Sorry to be the one to spring this on you," he says.

"You were very gentle," I say, also rising, and I kiss his cheek. We hug, then he looks carefully at me.

"If there's anything else I can do for you," he says.

"Thanks." He pats my cheek, but as he moves toward the hallway, I call after him. "Harry, there is one thing—"

He pauses in the doorway and looks back. "Tell me."

"Are you going to give David Weaver a job?"

He didn't expect that. "What do you know about that?"

"Wendy told me you mentioned you might when she saw the two of you having lunch." I don't mention that she also told me about that pig Joe Shannon saying vile things to David. Before he can answer, I add:

"You couldn't help Teddy, but you can help David."

He looks at me thoughtfully. "I'll have to think about that."

Then he goes. I sit behind my desk and stare at the papers he gave me. The top page reads "Last Will and Testament of Wendy Diane Travers."

So terribly final. She's gone.

11

DAVID

So I'm stretched out on the bed in my room at the Chateau, staring at the ceiling. The room is tiny to begin with, but it feels as if the walls are closing in. I've spent the last ten days here in Wonderland looking for a job. The people I called are Teddy's old friends and colleagues, those who used to dine and rollick at our family table, who now are in positions to hire me. I can get all these former "uncles" on the phone. My calls are promptly and warmly returned. At least the first time. None of them leads anywhere. I'm getting desperate. I have to find something. The funeral cost more than I expected, so my bankroll has dwindled. Not enough left even for a plane ticket back to Europe. The room here is paid up through the end of the week. After that I could be sleeping on the sand in Santa Monica.

Part of my problem finding a job is timing. The murder of Wendy Travers has cast a pall on the town. Everyone I've talked to winds up dwelling on her death. I'm surprised that I feel the same way. I keep reminding myself that she was one of the enemy. An enabler, an exploiter, a betrayer. Yet what repeatedly seeps into my consciousness are fragments of childhood memories: Wendy was the only one of my parents' friends who really paid attention to Jana and I when we were kids—she taught us how to ride bikes, play tennis, gamboled with us at the rented summer house in Malibu while the adults were busy solving the problems of the world. But then she became a snitch. So is there a moratorium on all that followed because she's dead? What would Teddy say about the irony of a woman who sold out her friends for money and now has been killed by a degenerate thief?

Teddy. It always comes back to him. As if fingering a string of prayer beads, I keep reviewing the past with him. Remembering the good days and the other days in Paris.

When we relocated from Mexico to France, Teddy and I lived in a crumbling fourth-floor walk-up hovel in the Marais neighborhood of Paris, not far from the legendary Père Lachaise Cemetery. He made contact with the Blacklisted writers and directors already there scrambling for a living on the fringes of the French film industry. It was a close-knit community, sharing meals and tips on screen assignments, backing each other up financially and emotionally. Despite the hardships it was an uplifting experience. Some of the exiles had children, so I had some social life. But most of the kids were emotionally shaken up by their expatriation, and I certainly was, too.

But Teddy immediately got in the swing of things. One of the fastest writers in Hollywood, he now had to write three times faster in order to net a pittance. It was as bad as Mexico. Deals based on handshakes, no written contracts, so if you got stiffed there was no recourse.

Teddy went like the wind. "Typing for francs," he called it. Working quickly, he used to say, "This script isn't for reading, it's for writing." He never looked back. But hoping to shake me out of my depression after Oaxaca, he suggested I proof one of the scripts for typos. I also found some gaps in logic and details dangling. With trepidation, I mentioned that to him.

He yelled, "Story conference!"

And he stopped typing and listened to what I had to say and then said the points I raised were good ones. He changed the script. Soon my job expanded. "Why wait until the script's finished to fix the screwups?" he asked. So he began using me as a sounding board while working out sticky story points. And more and more of the suggestions I scribbled in the margins went into the scripts verbatim. I'd never felt so close to him. He valued what I was saying. Soon we were developing scripts from scratch. Both getting our bearings in this new world. He started calling us "The Team of Weaver & Weaver." The closest he ever came to referring to "The Team of Weaver & Vardian."

Then I received a notification from the L.A. Selective Service draft board. I had just turned eighteen, so they hadn't wasted any time. I had been classified 1-A and ordered to stop by the American Embassy. Teddy's passport was expiring shortly so he came along with me.

At the embassy they told me that as I wasn't a student or a conscientious objector, there would be no deferment. They'd prepare a travel voucher to fly me back to Fort Dix, New Jersey for induction.

"You'll be in Korea before you know it," the clerk predicted.

While waiting for my voucher and travel orders, I went down the hall with Teddy to get his passport renewed.

The woman at the desk gave Teddy a form to fill out. When he finished, she ushered us into a small inner office. Not a good sign. A portrait of Eisenhower on the wall was looking down on a bored consul behind his desk. She handed the form along with Teddy's old passport to him.

"Sorry, Mr. Weaver," he said after checking a folder, "according to the Department, your passport is not eligible for renewal."

The old passport still had a few weeks before expiration, but he refused to give it back to Teddy. The best he could offer him was what they were giving me—one-way passage back to the States.

"I'm Blacklisted," Teddy told him, "I won't be able to earn a living there."

The man shrugged. "The Department doesn't recognize there is such a thing as a Blacklist." Then added, "Tell me, Mr. Weaver, do you hate your country so much that you just can't bear the thought of going back?"

That's when I went ape shit. An instant eruption. "This man is a decorated war hero! He was wounded defending his country, you little ass-wipe!" I would have gone over the desk after him if Teddy hadn't pulled me out of there before the Marine guards came.

So that's where we were: I went off to fight for my country while he was unofficially but effectively declared a man without a country. Teddy told me not to worry about him, "I'm a survivor, pal, it'll all work out." But I knew that meant hiding in the shadows, dodging and weaving, begging bureaucrats for green cards and visas. I wanted to kill someone. Soon after, the U.S. Army taught me how it's done.

The phone on the dresser in my room at the Chateau jangles me back into the present. "Yeah," I say listlessly.

"Hey, kiddo"—Harry Rains's voice fills my ear—"had to do a quickie trip to New York, sorry I didn't get back to you sooner. We never really got around to talking about you. Feel like doing another lunch tomorrow?"

Of course I agree. I didn't think I'd ever hear from him again, but he sounds as if we have unfinished business.

Hillcrest Country Club was Hollywood's answer to the L.A. Country Club, which prided itself on rejecting anyone from the film industry. All Jews, and even major movie stars, were undesirables. "We don't accept actors for membership," they told movie hunk Victor Mature, who assured them, "I'm no actor—and I can show you a dozen movies to prove it." They turned him down anyway.

So the Hollywood people, particularly the Jewish comedians, created Hillcrest, on Pico across from 20th Century Fox, for golfers, tennis and pinochle players, with a good restaurant boasting a roundtable where Danny Kaye, George Burns, Jack Benny, Milton Berle, and even Bing Crosby and Bob Hope would frequently laugh it up together.

That's where I'm having lunch today with Harry Rains.

I arrive first and the maitre d' ushers me to Harry's table. In a moment, Harry arrives in golf togs. He's just finished playing the course, suggests we order drinks and steaks. Our drinks appear almost instantly. He holds up his glass as if making a toast.

"Now where were we when we were so rudely interrupted?"

"Harry, it was my fault. I should have kept my mouth shut."

"Shannon was way out of line, kiddo. I called him and told him that." He gestures at the room. "You've been here before, right? Teddy and Leo were members."

I nod. Suddenly understanding why Harry picked Hillcrest for this meal. I thought he was ducking the commissary again because of what had happened. But in Hollywood society this is an even more public endorsement. To make it even clearer, Harry calls over to the comedians' roundtable:

"Hey, you *goniffs*, say hello to David Weaver, Teddy's boy." That gets a rousing response from the group. I wave to them. Then Harry leans closer.

"When we were talking last time, I tried to explain to you how it was. I know you didn't agree with everything I said. I could see it in your eyes. You were thinking, 'Harry the Fixer, persuading decent men to sell out their principles and their friends.' I know that's what Teddy thought."

"He didn't blame you. He felt everyone makes his own decision."

Harry's eyes mist. "Teddy was so very special, I miss him like crazy. He and Leo, they were among my first clients. Valerie introduced us. We were all like family."

He shakes his head as if to clear it. "Do you know what was really at stake back in those days? Behind the scenes in Washington, they were talking about relocation camps for American Commies and their families, just like World War II when they rounded up the Japanese, locked 'em up and threw away the key. I was trying to protect your dad from that. He never could understand that."

Harry leans even closer, sharing a secret.

"We didn't know it at the time, of course, but the Committee never needed any of the names. They'd had undercover agents working as dues collectors for the Party for years and years. So they had the entire Los Angeles membership list way before the hearings began. They just wanted to show us all who's boss. Kiss the ring and they'd let you waltz away."

That stuns me. "The bastards," I mutter angrily.

Harry waves his hand irritably. "Oh hell, it's a dirty chapter in the history books now. But you've gotta put that shit behind you, David. We have to get you started on your life." He starts munching on a breadstick, offers me one. I decline. "What do you want to do, kiddo?"

It's the question I've been waiting for. "I want to write," I say. "I worked with Teddy on eleven screenplays in Paris and Rome. He said I've got the makings of a good writer." I'm about to tell him about the spec screenplay I've been working on, but he's not interested.

"Okay, write. You don't need me for that. Do it on your

own. Studio doesn't have staff writers anymore. I want to give you a job where you can learn."

"Well, on Teddy's last picture, the one he directed, I worked as a production assistant."

"That's what I have in mind. But not on a two-bit Italian flick. On a big movie, a major production with a top film-maker, someone who can show you the ropes. We'll pay you next to nothing, he'll run your ass off, but it's a chance."

"Sounds great." But now I don't know if I should accept it. "Joe Shannon threatened to go after you and the studio if you hired me. I don't want him to make trouble for you."

"Let me worry about that. Shannon runs his column, not my studio." I'm knocked out by Harry. For Hollywood, where cowering before major gossip columnists is a tradition, it's a very brave stance. "There's only one wrinkle in my offer—the director you'd be working for is Leo Vardian."

"Hell no! I'd never work for him! I couldn't. How can you even suggest it?" Then I hear my tone. "Didn't mean to jump down your throat, Harry, but it'd be a total betrayal of Teddy."

"It's a door into the business for you, David. Time to be practical. That's what I always told Teddy. At least give the idea a chance. None of us are the same as we were ten years ago. You've changed, maybe Leo has, too."

I shake my head, but Harry urges. "Look, go see him. Take the meeting, you never know what might happen. Isn't that what Teddy always said?" I remember, it was almost a motto. "I phoned Leo last night. He says he wants to meet with you first. Up at the house."

"Sorry, Harry. I don't think there's anything I can talk to him about. Appreciate your thinking of me."

"You don't have to decide this second, kiddo. Mull it over a bit."

The steaks and salads come and we eat and chat about the old days. Harry tells a couple of very funny new stories about

Teddy in the wild man times. He signs for the meal and we
walk out past the comedians' roundtable.

"Gentlemen," he says, "how goes it?"

Groucho Marx leers at him. "Harry Rains—but he never
pours."

It gets a laugh from the gagsters. But Harry tops him, signal-
ing to the waiter. "In honor of Teddy's boy—the next round is
on me."

They all hold up their glasses. "To Teddy's boy," they chorus.

Wow, that feels good.

W e emerge into the driveway in front of Hillcrest and the
parking attendant races over with the car keys. Harry
tips him ten bucks and leads me the few steps to his car, parked
in the number one spot. The Silver Cloud Rolls-Royce.

"Nice wheels, huh?" he says with pride.

"Yeah. Must be a problem, though, parking it on the streets.
Don't you worry about getting scratched or dinged?"

"If you can afford a Rolls, you don't have to worry. Not
that I ever did. When I was a kid, the first car I had was a
Buick heap; I ran up a helluva score in parking tickets. Parked
in the red zone, the white zone, the yellow zone, it was kind of
a thing with me—gray people park in gray spaces. Part of my
nobody-tells-me-what-to-do attitude. Wasted a lot of bucks I
didn't have on parking fines. But what the hell? Back then I was
concentrating on more important things." He looks at me.
"Kinda like you are now. Think about the offer, will ya, kiddo?"

We hug, he gets in the Rolls and takes off. I find my jalopy
in the self-park section and drive toward the Chateau. Thinking of nothing else but the offer. Even eating in Schwab's and
sleeping in a broom closet, I can't hold out much longer. My
money is running out fast. Not enough for a plane ticket back
to Europe. But—Leo Vardian?

Back in my room, I sprawl on the bed again. The night-stand radio is playing—the Drifters singing "There Goes My Baby" while I continue to turn the proposition around in my head. If I meet with Leo, doesn't mean I have to take the job. What's the harm in talking? If I go up to the house, I might get to see Jana and I can say hello—or good-bye. I decide to flip a coin. Heads I go see Leo, tails I don't. I miss the catch, coin rolls under the bed. So I have to decide for myself.

I dial the number. Harry's perky secretary puts me right through. "Hey, David." Harry sounds as if I'm the call he's been expecting. "What's up, kiddo?"

"Just—I just forgot to say thanks for the lunch."

"My pleasure." He waits. He knows, but he wants me to say it.

I suck in a chestful of air and plunge. I tell him I'm willing to talk to Leo. I'm almost gagging, but Harry is pleased.

"Good decision, kiddo. I knew you'd see the light."

12

DAVID

This time when I drive up to the familiar house on Stone Canyon I don't park across the street in the darkness. I pull right into the circular driveway. My heart's trip-hammering as I ring the bell. I've come ten minutes early. Hoping that Jana will answer the front door.

She does. She's smiling. I'm smiling. Like the old us? Maybe. She looks casual but great, dressed in a maroon tracksuit and spotless sneakers, hair pulled back and secured by a black barrette. Lipstick, no other makeup. This close to her I inhale the lavender soap smell I know so well. My mom used to wear the scent and Jana wanted to be just like her. What I'd like to do is scoop Jana up in my arms and make a run for it. Let's get out of here! But I'm forgetting this is her home.

"Hey, c'mon in," she welcomes me. "He's expecting you."

"Yeah, well, I'm a little early. I don't mind waiting." Particularly if you wait with me. I want to say out loud, "Feels like I've been waiting forever for this moment," but I'm not sure who Jana is anymore.

"You don't have to wait. He's in the study working. You know how that is, when he's writing he loses track of the clock. So he'll think you're right on time."

She leads the way like the lady of the house, which I guess

she has been since Leo got sick. Teddy told me in Paris that he heard Jana's stepmother had divorced Leo years ago.

"How's it feel being back?"

"Little spooky." I don't know if she means back in town or back in this house. The same answer works for both. The house appears almost exactly the way I remember it. But behind the sumptuous sofa in the living room there's now an original Picasso. An agonized distorted face from his Cubist Period. "Place looks pretty much the same," I say.

"More or less," she says. "The studio built a screening room for him out back near the pool, plus a vault to store prints of his movies and the wine collection."

"A loaf of bread, a jug of wine, and your own temperature-controlled golden oldies." That gets another smile from her. So we can still tease about Hollywood's excesses. What else has survived from the happy part of our past?

We stop at the closed door to the study where Teddy and Leo used to work. I can hear rapid-fire typing.

"He's still jet lagged after flying back from Africa," she says softly, "so he might be grumpy. Don't let him scare you."

There's a caring warmth in her voice. "I'm not scared," I say.

She knocks and opens without waiting for a response. Leo Vardian looks up, his hands poised in midair over the keyboard—still the old un-electrified Underwood. He appears startled.

"David's here," she says. She always called me David. Leo takes an unlit pipe from his mouth and gestures me forward. I enter the room where he and Teddy used to make each other laugh while they worked together, and Jana leaves, closing the door behind me.

The study seems unchanged, same books on the shelves, like the Henry Miller novels Jana and I would sneak in and scan for the hot parts. A golden Oscar on a shelf is new, so is the ornate plaque from the National Association of Theatre Owners for one of the Top Ten Grossing Pictures of 1957.

Leo is watching me as I examine the room. Not blinking, no expression, he just gazes steadily at me. He's wearing a khaki safari jacket over a white T-shirt and faded brown slacks. His hair has gone steel gray and he wears it in a crew cut. But even bleary-eyed from jet lag, Leo looks a thousand times better than he did at the Ritz bar in Paris.

I take the client's chair in front of the desk. Multicolored script pages cover the surface of the desk. The wastebasket overflows with crumpled discards; some have missed and litter the floor.

"Burning the midnight oil?" I say. Meetings always began with chitchat, Teddy taught me that. But Leo doesn't reply. I try to think of something else, but nothing comes, and then Leo takes the unlit pipe out of his mouth.

"I'm a rotten stool pigeon son-of-a-bitch. Let's get that over with. I did what I did. I can't take it back. And if you can't get over that, then we've got nothing to talk about."

"Maybe we don't." This could be the world's shortest meeting.

He starts again. "What you and Teddy went through, I could never have handled it—I'm not that strong. Always thought I was, turns out I wasn't."

"What the fuck? Am I supposed to feel sorry for you? Write off what you did as a genetic failure?"

Now I'm braced to get the boot. But he just gazes at me. Then he sets his pipe down next to the typewriter. No tobacco or ash in it, only the taste of an old habit he's been forced to give up. "So where does that leave us?" he says.

"Guess that's what I'm here to find out."

"Okay, I made my bargain with the devil, someday maybe I'll give you details, but what I got in return is the chance to make some movies. That may not seem much in the grand scheme of things. The only way I can justify it is to make good movies, maybe even a great one now and then. Pictures that are real, that hold a mirror up to show us who we really are."

"The classic rationalization of a snitch."

That stops Leo. He studies me again. Leo seems more interested in me now than when I walked in. He leans forward.

"Let me tell you about the job. You know that Jimmy Durante shtick where he's so frustrated and overwhelmed that he throws up his hands and yells—"

"I'm surrounded by assassins!" I finish for him. Teddy and Leo used to do the bit together.

"That's what making a movie for a major studio is like, David. So to buffer me a bit from the shitstorm, I need a slave. But a slave with a mind. Panorama will issue the weekly checks, but whoever takes this job belongs to me. Everyone else on the set is suspect, they work for the studio. I need someone who'll do whatever I ask without question. I'll answer later, if I feel like it." He clamps the pipe between his teeth. "What do you think of that?"

He keeps hitting the ball back to me. So I try to return it harder than he sent it. "Why do you want to consider hiring me?"

"Actually it was Harry's idea. But it interested me. Why do *you* think I'd want to hire you?" It's like being with the shrink in Rome. Ask a question and he turns it around. Leo has spent time on the couch, too.

"You might want me as a walking Band-Aid," I speculate. "Having me around protects a wound. Makes you feel better about yourself."

"Possibility. Or?"

"Could be charity. Pity."

"Not my style. What else?"

"Obligation. Maybe in the dark of night you feel you owe Teddy and this makes up for a little of that." He nods as if claiming advance credit for a good deed he hasn't performed. That rubs me wrong. So I lean forward. "That would make me a pawn in your game."

He toys with his pipe. "You left out one possibility. You and I have a personal history. Having you around might be a reminder of the best part of my life."

"Mine, too," I mutter.

We gaze at each other in silence again. Then he leans back. "You served in Korea, didn't you?" I shrug. "Want to sign on for this campaign?"

The implication being that this mission might be even tougher than Korea? Screw off! To be polite I wait a moment before saying no. During which I glance around the room again. That's when I notice the framed photo half-concealed on one of the upper book shelves. It is the same photo of Teddy that was in the *Variety* ad.

"Nice picture," I say.

"Yeah, isn't it? I took it. That summer we all shared the beach house in Malibu." He's looking at it, a glisten in his eyes. "Except for Jana, I loved that man more than anyone else on earth."

So now I know who took out the memorial ad. "Irreplaceable." To my surprise, when I open my mouth to respond to Leo's offer, I hear myself say, "Okay, I'm in." The face in my mind at that instant is Jana's.

He holds out his hand. I give him mine. "Shaking hands with the devil?" he inquires. A hint of a smile. No laugh. And I realize that's the major difference between the Uncle Leo I once knew and the now-legendary Leo Vardian: there is scarcely any laughter left in this man.

When I close the door and start away down the hall, I can hear the rapid-fire typing begin again.

A s I walk toward the front door I call out Jana's name a few times, but no response. I'd hoped she would be hanging out waiting for the results of the meeting. Invite me into the kitchen for a cup of coffee, we would sit around and talk, fill in some blanks. Maybe she'd agree to marry me. Hey, why not? If you're entertaining a fantasy why not make it the best.

After all, seeing her was the real reason I came. At least that's how I justified it to myself. I don't want to leave without saying good night, but searching the house room by room doesn't seem right. Could she have left? I'm starting to crash when I step outside, and there she is, leaning against my rental car, waiting for me.

"You get the job?" I nod. "Congratulations!" Jana gleefully claps her hands once. "He owes me five bucks."

"For what?"

"He bet he wouldn't hire you."

"Because?"

"He figured you're too soft."

"Not anymore." She's happy I'm going to be working on the same lot where she works. Every weekday. I start to tell her how pleased I am about that—when a car slows to a stop out on the road.

The driver shines a spotlight that catches me in its glare. When the black-tinted side window glides down, I see the face of the fat security patrolman. Attracted by the sight of me and my rental car up here sullying the Vardian driveway. He doesn't see Jana until she steps into the glare and gives him a smiling all's-well wave. He tosses her a two-finger salute. As he starts to roll onward our eyes meet. I give him a mocking half salute. He glowers as he closes his tinted window and continues deeper into the canyon.

I look at Jana again.

She's studying me the way Leo did, as if trying to X-ray my thoughts. "Did you get the condolence card I sent to Mexico when your mom died?"

I could say, "We were moving around a lot," or "A lot of mail got lost." But I don't want any lies between us. "Yeah, I got it. Thanks."

"You didn't respond."

"Couldn't think of anything to say."

"You thought it would be disloyal."

"Interesting word," I say. Part of the HUAC vocabulary.

Even in the moonlight, I see her face redden. "Our families had turned into the Hatfields and McCoys. That had nothing to do with us, David."

"I prefer the Montagues and Capulets. They got to wear flashier costumes." Light and witty is what I was aiming for, but it comes out a putdown. The last thing I wanted. Not when we're finally beginning to talk.

"God," she flares, "I am so tired of this political bullshit. People cutting people down who were their lifetime friends, crossing the street when they see my father, or me, coming. When is it going to end?"

"Poor little rich girl." Damn! It pops out of me, but she would have read it on my face even if I hadn't said it.

"Screw you, Romeo," she says. The wounded look on her face—as if I've betrayed her.

She strides away to her door, opens it, then turns. From that distance I can't see if her eyes are wet, so the quaver in her voice hits me hard: "David, why does everything have to be so complicated?"

She shuts the door. Leaving me feeling frantic.

How did something that should have been such a happy moment erupt into a cluster fuck? I want her so much. Came here to reconnect with her and to turn down the job. But it all worked out backward. Helluva night's work. I've got the job I desperately need but I doubt I can stomach—and I've just blown it again with Jana.

CHAPTER

13

MCKENNA

Basically the only thing I love about L.A. is the trio of family members I have who live here. My sister, Kathleen, is smaller than I am by six inches, as pretty as our mother was, same upturned nose and rosy cheeks. She's also a tougher customer than I'll ever be. She's a public defender in the courthouse in Van Nuys. It's a soul-fracturing job, but she's very good at it. Despite the fact that she's a bleeding-heart liberal and she says I'm on the opposite end of the political spectrum—we had more than a few heated discussions when I was chasing Commies—there is an unbreakable link between us. We know each other's deepest, darkest secrets going back to our tortured childhoods.

She has two sons, Patrick is twelve and Donnie is fifteen, and they're almost my kids. Their father, Vic Donnelly, was a fighter-pilot instructor at El Toro Marine base near L.A. during World War II; that's when he and Kathleen met at a USO dance. After his discharge, they married and he became a building contractor. But the Marines called him back for Korea and he was killed in a dogfight in MIG Alley. I've been taking up the slack in the father department ever since, and glad to do it—cheering the kids at Little League, taking them all to Disneyland, listening to their guy stuff.

This Saturday morning, I've set up an outing for my nephews. A makeup for a family treat that backfired.

A few weeks ago, I had arranged for all of us to attend the West Coast premiere of *The FBI Story*, starring Jimmy Stewart. I'd been tech advisor on the picture and went all out, partly because I had a thing for the sexy script girl and wanted to show her how big a guy I was. I got Warner's all sorts of Bureau cooperation, from helping locate vintage cars and obtaining special permits for the old-timey machine guns, to providing authentic Bureau badges of the film's various eras. Clyde Tolson later told me Hoover got a kick out of that. I went on location to the Midwest and used Bureau muscle to clear away a lot of production complications. Smoothed away irritations with the local cops, sweet-talked some of the merchants who were nervous about even simulated bank robberies on their streets.

In gratitude, Warner's provided four tickets—for me, Kathleen, and the boys—to attend the preem and an A-list afterparty. We all even bought new outfits. The boys were so excited about the movie stars they were going to see. They bragged shamelessly to their friends.

Then two days before the premiere, I got a call from the veep of Warner's publicity telling me he was so sad to report that the theater was overbooked and they had to ask me to give up my seats. "You know how it is," he said, like one pro to another. They would send a messenger to get the tickets. Make it up to me another time.

"Yeah," I said, "I know how it is." Hooray for Hollywood! They never would have done that to me when HUAC was up and running. I hated the boys' shock when I broke the news.

"We're not gonna go?" Patrick said in wide-eyed disbelief.

"Forget it," Donnie gruffly ordered his little brother, trying to conceal his own disappointment, "Uncle Bri did the best he could."

It felt like I'd been hit in the solar plexus with a sledgehammer.

Today I've got a replacement that's a guaranteed winner. I'm taking the boys to the firing range at the L.A. Police Academy where Bureau agents have shooting privileges. The kids are jazzed because, although they've fired .22s at amusement park shooting galleries, this is the real thing. I brought along handguns of varying sizes and kicks—plus a lot of patience for Donnie.

A t first the boys are awed by the long row of outdoor shooting stalls with cops firing away for their yearly qualifying tests. I carefully tell them about range rules. Little Patrick is attentive, but Donnie is impatient to start blasting away. And that's what he does.

Donnie is shooting from the hip the way he's seen gunslingers do it in the movies. Wasting rounds.

"Aim, hold steady, squeeze gently," I repeat again and again. He doesn't want to learn, he just wants to be John Wayne.

Patrick, on the other hand, is soaking up instruction. So when their torso-shaped targets careen toward us for examination, Donnie's outlined man has been spared. Not a scratch on him. The holes are all over the place, most not even within the silhouette. Donnie is embarrassed, more so because his little brother has done well for a first-timer.

"You're a natural," I tell Patrick.

"Were you a natural?" he asks.

"That's what the FBI instructors told me. I'd never had a real gun in my hand 'til then."

"How come I'm not a natural?" Donnie complains.

"First y'gotta listen to what Uncle Brian is telling you," Patrick says.

To change the subject, Donnie asks me to demonstrate how to do it. I use the Army .45, the workhorse of all pistols, and empty the gun. The target comes back to us with all the holes in the heart zone in an area no wider than a man's palm.

"Man, that's real shooting," Patrick says.

"Sure is," Donnie agrees, and he's better after that.

Later, driving in my Mustang back to their house in Sherman Oaks, we stop off at Dairy Queen. We sit at one of the outdoor tables and while Patrick licks the sides of his cone to catch the melting flow of vanilla, he looks at me questioningly.

"Uncle Bri, did you ever shoot anybody, I mean like kill 'em?"

I could give him a phony-baloney answer, but they are not little kids anymore. If I want them to talk straight to me, then I have to do the same.

"Once," I said.

Of course, both boys want to hear. So I tell them.

"It was just after I came to L.A. You guys were real little then. One morning I was in my office downtown and we heard gunshots from only a few blocks away. A sniper—you know what that is?" They both nod. "Well, this crazy man was up in the bell tower of a church with a hostage. He was picking off people walking by in the plaza below."

Their eyes are as big as saucers, but if I started, I ought to finish.

"Several of us G-men joined the cops and we took up positions in the street. I'd brought a long-barrel rifle. But the lunatic in the bell tower," I am now back there in memory, "he was crouching so the wall of the bell tower protected his body. All I could glimpse of him, only for an instant now and then, was a tiny bit of his head, because he was hiding behind the hostage, this scared young girl. He'd peek out for an instant to fire down at one of the cops on the Plaza running to get closer to the tower."

I'm clicking off the vital stats as I saw them then:

"The distance from where I was—about three hundred yards and upward at a steep angle. Slight wind from the north. No sun glare. I asked the ground commander and got the go-ahead to take a shot if I had one. So I squinted and aimed, braced myself rock solid, until I caught a flash of movement. I put one bullet in the shooter's left eye, without nicking the hostage."

The ice cream is running down Patrick's wrist, but he doesn't seem to notice. There is a long silence. Then, Donnie says, "Wow."

Maybe I shouldn't have told them. I read their faces to see if they are frightened. But there's something else there. Respect. So I add:

"The Bureau gave me a special commendation. Signed by J. Edgar Hoover."

"Y'still got it?" Patrick blurts.

"It's around my apartment somewhere."

"Can I have it?"

"What for?"

"My scrapbook," Patrick says.

"Didn't know you had one—what's it about?"

"You," Patrick says.

I am surprised. There hasn't been anything much about me in the papers for so long. The HUAC stuff was all behind the scenes.

"Mom had all these old clippings in a drawer," Patrick says, "from when you used to catch bank robbers and kidnappers. I found 'em and she said I could have 'em."

I'm embarrassed. He's collecting material on me? *I'm* his hero? "Patrick, when I was your age, I had a scrapbook, too. But it got—lost."

Patrick promises me that if I let him paste in the Hoover commendation he'll never lose it. Then Donnie has a question:

"Did it make you feel bad, killing someone?"

"Sometimes that's what you have to do." And I let it go at that. But Patrick isn't done yet:

"My grandpa, your father, he was a cop, too, right?"

"My stepfather. Back in Chicago."

"Did he ever shoot a man in a tower or anything like that?"

"No, he wasn't that kind of cop."

"So what kind of cop was he?" Patrick asks.

How far do I go in this honesty thing? "Hey, guys, gimme a break—isn't that enough for one day?"

They let it go at that. I'm glad they did, because if I was going to be totally honest I'd have to admit that the man in the tower actually was the second man I'd killed.

I'm the second generation in my family to go into law enforcement. If you count my stepfather, which I'd rather not. I was named after my father, Brian McKenna, Sr., who was a third-grade schoolteacher; he died in the Argonne Forest during World War I when I was five and my sister, Kathleen, was three. I remember him as a kind, loving man. Kathleen hardly remembers him at all. My mother, the former Kitty Flaherty, remarried a couple of years later to Declan Collins. He was a big, beefy bruiser, full of smiles when he was courting my mother, but the smiles ended after we became a so-called family. We lived in an old firetrap apartment house on the south side of Chicago. Everyone made noise in that tenement, but the loud and frequent screams were from our place. Nobody ever came to help us. They were all scared to even knock on the door and ask what's going on. Because in addition to being a vicious drunk, Declan Collins was a Chicago police detective.

When he went on the warpath, it always started the same way. We could be at the kitchen table, he'd already had a couple of drinks, and he'd say, "Pass the gravy, Brian *Mc-Kenna*!" He spat my last name as if it was filth. To him it was. A reminder of my real father. Declan had wanted to adopt me and Kathleen and change our names from McKenna to Collins. Mom agreed to the adoption, but refused to alter our last names. She wanted to keep my father's memory alive. That was the last argument she ever won with Declan. We all paid dearly for it.

So back to the gravy. Hearing the hate in his voice would cause my hand to quiver. I'd spill some gravy on the tablecloth, he'd scream at my clumsiness, mom would defend me while mopping up, Declan would be off into his rant: "Sure, the lad's purrrfect, ain't he now? Like his dear departed handsome father, a genius schoolteacher that one was, who could scarce make a living, but better than me, o' course, you all think you're better than me; I'm nothin' but a hardworking slob keepin' the bunch of ya alive!"

By then he'd be breaking dishes, shoving me, slapping mom, Kathleen would be crying, which Declan despised, so he'd grab her by the arm and fling her across the room like a Raggedy Ann doll. Mom would run to her, Declan would go after Mom, and I would move fast as I could to get between them. Pleading and begging never worked, but jumping around like a crazy person and throwing things at him and biting always did. I'd get him to focus his rage on me. I took lumps, but better me than Mom or Kathleen.

As the drunken attacks on us escalated, I was usually so scared I felt like I was going to vomit. Sound in my ears was blurry. Everything looked like it was magnified and moving too fast. Often I'd wet my pants. Then he'd mock me and slam me extra hard. The thing is, I could run, but I couldn't hide. Not in an apartment that small. If I eluded him it made him even angrier.

Declan never hit any of us in the face. There were no swollen lips or black eyes the morning after—the only marks were on my chest and back and ribs and stomach. He once told me that when he was interrogating suspects he did far worse. Guess I was supposed to feel lucky. He was most handy with his leather belt, using the buckle part when teaching me a real lesson, though the lesson was never clear. In junior high when we had to strip for gym, some of the teachers would notice the welts and bruises. If they asked me about it, I'd mumble something about walking into a door or slipping on the stairs. They'd drop it. They didn't want to get involved.

Why didn't anyone want to get involved? That was my huge question during those years. Children and their mother were being beaten. People knew that. It was against the law. Was there no one to protect us? How could they all just ignore it? I dreamed of a defender like the Lone Ranger riding to our rescue. Putting an end to our torment. But no one ever came.

So that's why even as a kid I'd wanted to be in law enforcement. I'd be the one. The supercop who would fight the brutes. Bring bad people to justice. I'd cut stories out of the *Tribune* about the brave exploits of hero cops. Especially Chicago's own Eliot Ness, leader of the incorruptible "Untouchables," the man who had vowed to bring down "Scarface" Al Capone.

Eventually I had so many clippings about Eliot Ness that I started a scrapbook. I'd paste them in when Declan wasn't around and hide it under my mattress. During one of our brawls, I crawled under the bed to get away from him, but he heaved the mattress onto the floor to get at me and discovered the scrapbook.

"*What is this shit?*" he bellowed. "Eliot Fuckin Ness! That prissy, blue-nosed, no-balls faggot! You like *him*? He your idea of a great man?" Declan had me by the neck and was shaking me hard. "Wanna be a faggot like Ness?" Felt like my head was going to fly off. "Say it, you're a little pansy fairy fag. *Say it!*"

He wouldn't stop until I repeated the words, and then he let go of me and tore the scrapbook into pieces and dropped them down the trash chute.

As I got older, he got drunker and meaner. When he chased me around it was more of a stagger. When he caught me, to prevent me from slipping away, he came up with a new idea— manacling me to the living room radiator with his handcuffs. So I wasn't a moving target while he administered punishment. Then, exhausted by his exertion and his liquor, he'd usually black out and fall onto the couch or into bed. Mom would sneak the key to the handcuffs out of his pants and free me.

One night, I was eleven, Declan hooked me up tight and beat me until I was unconscious. To celebrate his victory he dragged Mom and Kathleen to the candy store for ice cream sodas. And that was the first winter night it was cold enough for the building superintendent to send up steam. I woke and my wrist was on fire. The heat from the radiator pipes had inflamed the steel handcuffs. I shrieked. Tugged at the red-hot manacles. Caught! About to shriek again, though knowing that would not bring help. But I suddenly had an inspiration and at the top of my lungs, I screeched *"Fire!"*

That mobilized a neighbor, who called the Fire Department. When they arrived, I sobbed uncontrollably as they sawed me loose and put ointment on my wrist. I heard them say I had third degree burns. Squad car cops were there by then, too, gathering details. I thought, "Saved at last! Declan's finally gonna get his!" But when my family walked in, Declan flashed his detective's badge, conferred with the cops, and they agreed this was just a domestic disturbance and went away. Nothing changed after that, except during the winter months Declan was careful to handcuff me to the heavy legs of the dining room table.

So life went on. Until Halloween a year later.

At twelve, I was too old for trick or treating, but Kathleen was ten and really wanted to go. Mom made me go with her, "You know a girl's not safe alone on these streets at night, what with all the drunks and hooligans." Kath dressed up in her Halloween witch's costume and I put on a Lone Ranger mask and we went knocking on doors in the neighborhood.

There was snow on the ground, and after Kathleen collected a full bag of Tootsie Rolls and Baby Ruths we trudged toward home. An icy wind was blowing. On a dark, deserted street about two blocks from our tenement we saw a man lying facedown in the slush. We turned him over.

"It's Dad!" Kathleen whispered.

Passed out along the route home he took from his favorite speakeasy. We stood there and looked down at him, Declan's eyes flickering but unfocused, drool running from his open mouth.

"We've gotta get him up," she said. "Take him home."

We'd had experience at home picking him up off the floor from a drunken stupor. And he always came awake swinging haymakers at whoever was helping him.

"I got a better idea," I said, thinking of the fantasy I'd been nurturing for so long. I kicked him as hard as I could in the slats. He didn't moan. Just lay there. I was crying. So I gave him the boot again, then turned to Kathleen, tears streaming down her cheeks.

"Your turn!" I shouted. "Go on, you'll never get a chance like this again!"

"I can't!" she wailed. "It's a sin to kick a man when he's down!"

"Not *him*! Do it! You know you want to! *Do it*!"

"No, Brian. No!" she sobbed. "I just can't!"

"Okay, sis," I said. "Let's go."

"Just leave him here?" She was awed by the idea.

"Pretend we came down another street and didn't see him. Coulda happened that way."

"But—"

"The sooner he wakes up, the sooner he comes home—and the sooner it's bad for us again."

So we walked away and left him there, Kathleen and I holding hands. She looked back a couple of times. I didn't. Not even once.

When we got home, Kathleen sorted her candy while Mom made hot chocolate for all of us, then we went to sleep. Without a hint to Mom as to what we'd seen on the street. Declan hadn't come back yet, but that was often his way. He'd come crashing in later. But this time he wasn't there in the morning. Kathleen kept darting glances at me. I read them: should we tell Mom? I'd shake my head, then after breakfast we got a phone call from Provident Hospital. Detective Collins had been found on the pavement and brought there. He was in a coma, being treated for hypothermia and pneumonia.

Mom wanted us to go with her to visit him. I refused—if he was in a coma, why bother? Kathleen went. When they returned Kathleen looked real shaky. We went up on the roof to be alone and I asked her, how'd it go?

"We walked into the ward and he was hooked up to all these tubes and gadgets but his eyes were open. I got scared, 'cuz he seemed to be looking right at me—but when Mom pushed me closer I could see his eyes were totally blank. So

Mom and me sat next to him. She talked to him as if he could hear. I don't think he could."

He died the next morning. Mom asked me to attend the funeral. I did. Not for him. For her. Some of the officers he served with spoke about what a great guy and a great cop he was. I kept my thoughts to myself.

There was a small police pension, and my mother got a job as a secretary in the bursar's office at the University of Chicago, where she and my real father had first met, when he was studying to be a teacher and she was a server in the school cafeteria. With Declan gone, money was still tight, but our lives were so much better. Kathleen and I never discussed what happened on that Halloween night. Not until years later. It was our secret.

My senior year in high school, Mom told me there were funds for me to go to college where she worked. She helped me fill out an application—my grades were very good, and I was a high school track star, so she could arrange for a partial sports scholarship. What really made it possible were the proceeds from an insurance policy paid out on Declan's death. And the money was for Kathleen's education as well.

"Declan would have wanted that," Mom said.

It was a surprise, because he never showed any interest in my going to college and, as for Kathleen, he always said, "Educating a girl is pissing away time and money." Later on, Kathleen graduated from Berkeley Law with honors and became one of the first female public defenders in Los Angeles.

I'd gone to Michigan Law and came back to be an assistant DA in Chicago. Part of the law-enforcement community. Putting away bad guys. But being a prosecutor involved too much politics. I wanted to make a real difference. Only mostly I was convicting poor slobs who had no connections and working with too many cops who mangled the truth, even on the witness stand, to win what they believed was a righteous case. That wasn't justice.

So a pal in the DA's office suggested I try the FBI. The idea pressed a button for me. As a kid I'd cut school to go to the Loop and see Jimmy Cagney three times in *G-Men,* guys keeping America safe with a fedora and a submachine gun. From my first day in the training program it was a perfect fit. Later, working briefly as an intern in J. Edgar Hoover's office confirmed my aspirations: there was great power in the Bureau and great things to be done for the nation.

Years after that, when I was en route to a Bureau assignment in L.A., I stopped off in Chicago to visit my mother. That's when she confided to me that there had been no insurance policy.

"The money that put you kids through colleges, I found it."

"What do you mean—found it?"

"In a metal box hidden away. On a shelf in our bedroom closet. Behind a loose board in the wall. All in cash."

The legacy from my stepfather, the crooked Chicago cop. His share of shakedown money. Corruption stashed in the closet. I was horrified.

"Don't be angry at me for not telling you sooner. I was scared you and Kathleen would never have used the money and gotten an education—and that money didn't pay back a tenth of what he took away from your lives."

But even with the "insurance" money, it had been a battle to get through. Kathleen had slaved away as a waitress all through college and I worked as a night watchman during the school year and as a construction laborer during summers. Now all Kathleen and I had strived for felt tarnished.

"Well," I said, "maybe sometimes from evil comes good." And I hugged my mother. At least the three of us had survived.

After I got settled in L.A., I told Kathleen about our "scholarship fund." She flared up something fierce. "That rotten bastard," she cried, reliving the abuse that the three of us had suffered—realizing that even in death Declan Collins had managed to get us one more time. Our dark secret linked us even closer.

14

DAVID

I t's hot and sticky inside the jungle. Outside Soundstage 18 on the Panorama lot it's a comfortable seventy-two degrees. Inside it's Green Hell, a private world of stifling heat and humidity created at the autocratic behest of Leo Vardian.

No one, except those with duties that require their presence, is allowed inside. Closed Set. Guards posted vigilantly at the few entrance doors. Within these walls of the largest stage on the Panorama lot the jungles of Kenya have been meticulously re-created.

Air conditioners normally run full blast to offset the intense heat generated by the huge arc lights needed to shoot an "outdoor" set indoors. But Leo has forbidden use of air conditioners at any time. Authentic vegetation imported by the ton from Kenya is kept moist by a sprinkler system that keeps all us humans constantly moist, too. No windows on a soundstage and the ventilation isn't great to begin with, so the place has gotten to smell rank. Leo basks in the discomfort. "I don't want the actors to *act* like they're in the jungle," he has decreed, "I want them to *be* in the jungle."

My job is to be within shouting distance of Leo. Usually I'm within arm's reach, but he shouts anyway. Like now. "David, get me the chop-top!"

I race off. Once I leave the brightly lit section where the

next scene is being prepared, I have to be wary of tripping over the python-like power cables that snake across the floor, plus hopscotching the man-made creeks that are part of our jungle, not to mention skidding through the sand and mud we've brought in here to play with. But I'm sure-footed, and I've made this run so many times that I reach the prop man's assembly area in record time. "He wants the chop-top!" The prop man pivots and hands it to me as if we're in a relay race, and I'm off again.

The title of the movie is *Against the Wind*. It's Leo's original screenplay about the bloody Mau Mau uprising. Charlton Heston plays a British army officer who befriended a young Kenyan boy. The boy grows up to become Sidney Poitier, leader of the Mau Mau. Heston's job is to hunt him down and kill him. Ernest Borgnine, as a Boer mercenary, is Heston's top non-com.

I'm slogging my way back when I pass one of the exit doors. It opens and a young studio guide in a blazer with the Panorama logo stitched on his breast pocket leads three men and a woman inside. They look like Midwesterners, one man is carrying a Panama hat and the woman is wearing white gloves. Boy, are they ever in the wrong place.

"I'm sorry," I politely inform the guide, "this is a closed set." I've been made personally responsible by Leo for anyone penetrating our security.

"It's okay," the tour guide assures me. "I told the guard outside, these are personal guests of Mr. Mark Gunderson."

I repeat firmly. "Sorry. Closed set. No visitors."

The tour guide appraises me. I don't look all that impressive in my muddy work boots and sweat-stained Sorbonne T-shirt. He decides to show off for the personages he has in tow. "Please step aside, I have my instructions."

From across the soundstage I hear Leo bellowing over the bullhorn, "Day-vidddd!" No more time to waste. "Get the hell out of here!" I yell. For emphasis I lift the chop-top up into view.

It's an expensive replica of the head of Herbert Lom, one of the featured actors, who has been decapitated by the Mau Mau. Made of sculpted latex, woven hair, it's smeared with prop blood and looks real. I'm holding it by the hair and I shake it at the tourists, like a grotesque Halloween lantern. The woman covers her mouth in horror with her white-gloved hand and the tour guide propels them all out the door.

When I turn, I see Leo standing there. "Now that's what I call good old-fashioned Hollywood hospitality," he says with his hint of a smile.

He grabs the chop-top from me and goes to place it in the spot he wants it to be for the shot. Then he yells to Heston and Borgnine. "Let's go to work, boys."

For me it's not work. It's endlessly fascinating. I'm involved in my favorite activity, making a movie, this time with a big budget and top-drawer talent to talk to and learn from. But Leo rules by terror on the set. A monumental shit who knows precisely what he wants and tramples anyone who gets in his way. Temporarily misplacing a prop, forgetting one word of the script on camera, or spoiling a take by coughing are all causes for public humiliation. I only occasionally get lacerated in front of the crew. Hardly any of them ever heard of Teddy, so to them I'm not Teddy's Boy. They seem to think of me as Leo's Boy. Which makes me queasy.

Yesterday morning Bob Surtees, our veteran cinematographer, cozied up to me and asked, "What kind of mood is he in today?" As if I know. As if I have a clue as to what makes Leo tick. Or when he's going to explode.

I'm trying endlessly to figure out where I stand with Jana. We haven't really spoken since the night Leo hired me and I called her a "poor little rich girl." We're on the same lot and I see her almost every day. But apparently I'm invisible again. Early today she came to watch the filming a little and talk to Leo. I'm not more than a dozen feet away. Leo calls to me, "Can you get Jana a cup of coffee?"

I'm back in a flash, hold the cup out to her. "Light cream, one sugar." Just how she always liked it. See, I remember!

"Mm-hm," she mumbles and takes the cup. No eye contact. Turns her back on me. Well, she can't stay angry at me forever. Or can she?

A fter the chop-top incident, we're shooting at our usual snail's pace when two visitors arrive. The kind even Leo can't keep out. "Mind your manners, everybody," Leo announces loudly, "the big brass are here."

Barney Ott, the leader of the duo, is a pale, balding, sharp-featured man in his mid-fifties. He is dressed in his usual charcoal-black, three-piece Brooks Brothers uniform, complete with black, necktie. Like a mortician, at least that's what his detractors say. But only behind his back. He has an intimidating manner to go with his cobalt blue eyes.

A transplanted New Yorker, Ott is up from the ranks, went to work as an usher at Panorama's flagship theater on Broadway at the age of fifteen, rose to manage all their theaters on the eastern seaboard by the time he was twenty-seven. When he was thirty, the New York execs, who hold the real power in the corporation, sent him to Hollywood as their eyes and ears. Studio heads have come and gone over the years, but Ott is still here. A deep-dish company man whose lines of loyalty and communication go directly back to the money men in New York. Ott's title is vice president of operations, with a broad, purposely vague mandate. Labor negotiations are his specialty. He's also the well-connected Mr. Fix It for the studio's stars and hot directors when they get in trouble. Today his mission is to speed up operations.

We've been filming less than two weeks, but by projecting the pace of Leo the perfectionist, the studio production office estimates we're close to a month behind schedule. Directors on important pictures usually shoot four or five takes of a camera angle. Leo is in the habit of doing seventy or more before printing one—often from the first dozen. He also covers a scene from every conceivable angle—first group shots, then breaking down to smaller groups, then two shots, plus close-ups, often of varying sizes. Each new angle requires time for re-lighting and shooting. That's how the days mount up. Each day costs $35,000. So we're now a million bucks over budget, and hemorrhaging money as we lose more time every day, but Leo doesn't seem to give a shit. All he cares about is the quality of his movie. Joe Shannon has already been sniping in his column, calling the picture "Vardian's Folly."

Barney Ott starts out his visit by affably greeting Leo and then maneuvers him off to one side to talk quietly. In a moment, Leo is shouting. "You tell me, Barney! Do you want it good or do you want it Tuesday?"

"All depends *which* Tuesday we're talking about," Ott says reasonably. "We've got a problem, Leo, and I'm here to help you any way I can." He guides Leo out of sight behind a papier-mâché boulder.

While the crew continue to light the upcoming scene, Ott's associate sidles up to me. He's wearing a tweed jacket, open-collar cream-colored dress shirt, terrific tan. Jack Heritage is my height, broad shouldered and handsome as a movie actor, still in his forties with the broad upper body of a weight lifter. He met Ott during the labor riots in the late forties. Contract negotiations had collapsed and the blue-collar union workers at Panorama went on strike for higher wages after the wartime freeze on salaries. Labeling the union "a pack of Commies," Barney Ott imported dock workers from Long Beach who broke heads.

Police Lieutenant Jack Heritage led the flying wedge of Glendale cops who separated the warring parties by billyclubbing and arresting the strike leaders. The strike collapsed and a friendlier "house" union signed a status-quo contract. A few months later Heritage went to work for Ott as his second-incommand. His title is head of security. He still wears his police .38 in a shoulder holster under his jacket. Rumor has it he also still packs a blackjack "for old times sake."

"Hey, David, how's the Student Prince today? Learn any new secrets about the business from your Uncle Leo?" He chuckles to let me know he's only having some fun and not busting my balls. Neither of us is fooled. Heritage thinks I'm in on a pass and it annoys him.

"Is Barney here to shut us down?" I ask.

"C'mon, kid, we're all friends. Right?"

"Sure, Jack, everything's copacetic."

He glances at me to see if I'm being sarcastic. I am. He likes friction. Thugs usually do. He emits a baleful sigh:

"Ol' Leo, he's a genius, but know what's wrong with his pictures?" I shrug and he goes on. "Never has a broad in his movies you'd want to fuck. Winning prizes is terrific. But romance, that's what sells big."

"That's your definition of romance?"

"Absolutely." He gives me his Clark Gable grin. "What's yours?"

He tamps the perspiration on his brow with a handkerchief. "Wow, it's like a steam bath in here. When you were in Korea, was it hot like this?"

"I was there in the winter. We froze."

Leo and Barney Ott reappear from their confab behind the

boulder. I halfway expect to see the gory aftermath of a brawl, but they're both chuckling. Neither of them really meaning it.

"Okay, okay, Barney. For you anything."

"We're ready, Leo," cameraman Surtees calls.

Leo claps his hands for attention. "Listen up, folks! As a special favor to Mr. Ott, we're gonna really hump! Camera crew, you'll pan for Panorama! Actors will give double-time drahma for Pan-or-ah-ma! There will be no more shilly-shallying around here, lads!" He turns. "How's that, Barney?"

Ott isn't sure if Leo's rallying the crew or publicly mocking him. He decides to go with rallying. "Knew you'd pitch right in, Leo."

Leo moves closer to Ott. Only Heritage and I hear Leo add, "Next time Harry Rains has something to say to me, let him come say it himself."

"Hey, Harry's the boss. I can't tell him what to do," Ott says, then he and Heritage stroll out the exit door.

The rest of the morning whizzes by like a downhill nightmare. Leo is blistering butts, hammering the crew to move faster and faster, right up to the lunch break. While everyone escapes to air conditioning, Leo remains in the humid jungle, sitting next to the camera, slashing speeches out of the script, simplifying his shot list for the day. Trying to fend off the pressure from the front office.

I hotfoot it to the commissary to pick up Leo's lunch, his yogurt and berries, diet of the dyspeptic. As I'm waiting at the hostess' desk for my takeout order, I notice Jana and Markie Gunderson at a table inside the main room. Markie spots me, glowers and nudges Jana, who glances over and looks away.

Pauline, the unflappable commissary hostess, hands me Leo's lunch and I'm out the door and starting back when I hear Markie's voice behind me. He's followed me into the studio street. "Hey, Weaver!" He strides up like a pest exterminator intent on squashing a bug. "I'm pissed at you! Where do you get off terrorizing special guests I send to visit the set?"

"Take it up with Leo," I say. Can't take time for this, I've got a lunch to deliver.

I start to go on but he blocks me. Shoves my shoulder with the heel of his palm. He's almost as tall as I am, but it's not size that counts. "I'm talking to you, Weaver! Those people were important theater owners from the Midwest."

"Then send 'em over to where Fred Astaire's working, our set's closed."

"*Our* set! That's funny. You're just the slop boy around here and I'm an executive of this company, so when I authorize something—"

"Love to stay and chat, Markie, but I'm on a deadline."

I start to go again, but he blocks me again. "You stand still when I'm talking to you!" He gives me another heel of the palm shot in the shoulder. Harder now. My black rage is stirring.

"Don't do that," I say quietly, but he hears it as meek.

"Or what? You'll run crying to your Uncle Leo?" He reaches out to give my shoulder another jab. I'm finished with his bullshit! I let the Range reflexes kick in: I grip his hand, bending it sharply backwards. As I press he starts to go to his knees, his face white with the shock of pain. I feel great! Overdue payment on insults dating back to grade school.

"Boys, boys, am I still breakin' up schoolyard shenanigans between you two?" Rex Gunderson, Markie's father, has come up behind us with his entourage. He leaves them and ambles over. I release Markie's hand and he's rubbing his fingers to get the circulation going as his dad adds with a chuckle, "Bet the hassle's still about Miss Jana, am I right?"

"I was just showing Markie a Boy Scout hold, Mr. Gunderson."

He looks even more leathery than I remember, still clad in a safari jacket, jodhpurs and shin-high boots, like an imitation

Cecil B. DeMille. He began his career as an assistant to DeMi-
lle in silent-film days on *The Squaw Man*. Now DeMille's gone
Biblical and Rex Gunderson's still directing epic shoot-'em-ups.
But the last three have bombed.

"Heard you were back, Young Weaver." He holds out his
hand. Without thinking, I shake it. The hand that was instru-
mental in choking off Teddy's career. He squeezes hard, I squeeze
back; guess I pass the test, he nods approvingly and lets go.
"Sorry about your dad. We had our differences, but he was a
darn talented fella. Teddy and Leo wrote one of my biggest
hits."

"Yessir, if you'll excuse me, Mr. Gunderson," I hold up the
lunch bag. "I've got a starving director waiting for this."

"Better scoot then. Leo's gotta keep his strength up."

I trot off. Hating myself for even talking to that Blacklist-
ing bastard. I hope Teddy hasn't been watching.

Behind me I hear Rex Gunderson address his son in a with-
ering tone: "Boy, if you start a fight, be damn sure you know
how to finish it."

I can't resist a glance back. Markie is staring at the ground
with a whipped dog expression. All ri-i-i-i-ght!

For the rest of the day, Leo continues to crack the whip on
the crew. Spewing orders, insults, and threats. Like the sa-
distic drum beater on an ancient Roman attack ship setting a
vicious tempo for the slaves chained to their oars.

Markie Gunderson drops by in late afternoon, maybe just
to prove he can get on the set even if his guests can't. He chats
briefly with Leo and leaves. When there's a moment I ask Leo,
what that was all about.

"Studio's got a book they want me to consider as a possible
next project. So I guess they still love me."

"Sounds good."

"Well, the Gunderson kid says so."

"What do you think of him?"

"Shrewd bastard. So-so creatively, but sharp elbows. Knows how to play the studio game." He laughs. "You sizing up the competition?"

I wish. I'm not really even in the game yet.

The flogged crew performs valiantly and we not only complete the scenes scheduled for today, but also do an extra scene not scheduled. Barney Ott, take note! When we wrap, the crew look like survivors of a death march. A word of thanks from Leo would be nice, but he strides off the soundstage. I'm with him and climb behind the wheel of Leo's golf cart. Standing next to it, he surveys the crew staggering into the early evening gloom. They look at Leo. Napoleon is about to address his troops.

"Well, who knows, maybe I'll finally be able to get a decent day's work out of you assholes tomorrow!" he says.

Then he hops into the cart. "Go, David, *go!*" As we zip away, Leo smiles. "Wormed my way into a few hearts that time," he says.

I say nothing.

"What?" he challenges.

"No questions. That was the deal."

"Unless I invite you to ask one."

Okay. "Why do you do it?"

"Good question. Maybe to keep them on their toes. Or because I'm an insensitive prick. Or maybe I find that if everybody's scared to come near me, I avoid a lot of bullshit questions and can focus on what's important. Which possibility do you like?"

"I pick—all of the above."

His eyebrows rise. "Right answer," he says. Then he shifts gears. "What happened to you at lunch? You've been off your feed all afternoon."

So I tell him about my encounter with the Gundersons. I try to kiss it off in a sentence, but he wants details. He prods, so I give them to him. Leaving Jana's name out of it. But that's what it's about between me and Markie.

He's silent when I'm done. Staring ahead steely eyed. Then he mutters: "Humongous turds, father and son. They'll pay, David. We're gonna make 'em all pay."

I appreciate the sympathy. But when did it become "we"?

CHAPTER

15

DAVID

Way back during the frenzy of the first day of filming I noticed an island of calm. A tall, slump-shouldered man was seated close behind the camera in a chair marked KEELER BARNES. Early fifties, thick glasses, baggy brown suit, and brown snap-brim hat. Studious look on his craggy face as he worked *The London Times* crossword puzzle in ink. He rarely looked up while the activity swirled around him.

Not until Leo gave the camera crew a complicated design of moves. "And we'll cut to a closer angle at that point," Leo said. He darted a glance at Keeler Barnes and there was a telepathic communication between them. Barnes nodded almost imperceptibly, Leo went on giving instructions. Keeler caught me watching him.

"Trying to figure out how it's done, kid?" I nodded. "Okay, I taught Leo and your dad—no extra charge for members of the family."

Keeler is the film editor on *Against the Wind,* but they're usually tucked away in a windowless room gluing together snippets of celluloid, not sitting on the set. Leo prefers to have him here for those few times a day when he's in doubt. Some camera angles will cut together with invisible grace and some will jar the viewer. "I'm his insurance policy against making mistakes that will haunt him in the cutting room."

He worked on *Darkness Before Dawn,* a romantic thriller starring Henry Fonda and Margaret Sullavan, the first picture Weaver & Vardian produced, as well as wrote, before the war. And Keeler was with Leo since he started to direct while Teddy was away in the service. That would lead you to think this is a tight relationship, which it is—in the sense that Gilbert and Sullivan made beautiful music together, when they happened to be speaking.

Tonight is a good example. Leo and I join Keeler in a screening room to look at dailies, the prints of what was shot yesterday. Only the three of us. Leo forbids the crew to attend dailies, and he's even convinced the stars not to come. No dissension in the ranks that way, he says. On the first night I drove him over here, Leo invited me in. Ever since, I've been careful to listen and shut up.

As usual, Keeler is seated beside the center console that connects with the projectionist. Leo slumps wearily into the seat on the other side of the console. I'm in the row behind them, out of the line of fire.

"Okay," Leo says, "let's roll."

Keeler buzzes the projection room and the dailies come on. Leo murmurs which takes or portions of takes he prefers. Keeler jots notes. When dailies are over, Keeler instructs the projectionist to put on an entire sequence that's been assembled. This is where trouble often starts.

"Editing is the final rewrite," Leo has told me. "It's where the dream of what you wanted and the reality of what you've got come together—or try to."

That's the challenge of editing, I've come to realize. A scene can be assembled in many ways, favoring one character or another, making story points gracefully or clumsily. Leo justifies shooting so much film in order to give himself as many choices as possible. It's the cutter's job to dig through the haystack and assemble coherence and balance. Subject to the director's approval. That's where the battle lines are often drawn.

We saw a version of this scene a few nights ago. A heated discussion ensued then between Leo and Keeler. I thought it was going to become a fistfight.

"See, that works," Leo now enthuses, "just like I said it would!"

Keeler doesn't reply, but Leo's taking credit for an idea that Keeler suggested and Leo crapped on before. We go on. But the happy times are about to end.

"Why'd you do *that*?" Leo demands. Pointing at another part of the scene they'd argued about.

"Because you told me to, Leo."

"Did not."

"Yes, you did."

"No, I didn't!"

Keeler reaches beneath his seat. He swings a tape recorder onto the console and presses PLAY. Leo's unmistakable voice is heard giving Keeler the instructions he's now denying.

"Yes, you did," Keeler says flatly.

Without warning, Leo lunges and snatches the tape machine. He flings it as hard as he can against the wall. The tape recorder smashes and the voice stops.

"NO, I DIDN'T!" Leo roars.

Veins standing out in his neck, eyes bugging, he looks as if he's about to froth. I just stare at him. Nose to nose with Keeler—who suddenly bursts into laughter. Leo looks startled. Then he snorts, shakes his head, blinks, as if he's suddenly focusing on his operatic outburst. And he, too, begins to laugh. If you can call it laughter. They howl like a pair of banshees.

I think they're both crazy. This is some weird dance they do and the steps were designed long ago.

"Okay, okay," Leo gasps at last, "*who*ever had that dumb idea, change it back."

"Time for a drink?" Keeler says.

"Time for a coupla drinks," Leo agrees. "It's been a bitch of a day."

After sipping Glenlivet scotch in Leo's studio bungalow, and listening to Leo and Keeler match funny stories about the old days, we're walking to our cars. All the anger seems to be forgotten. It's Friday night, so the studio streets are deserted until Monday. Leo likes to park his Mercedes on the Western street only a few short blocks from the cutting rooms. Usually in front of the cowboy saloon set. Keeler and I keep going to the unpaved lot out in the boonies. But Keeler's car is in the shop today, and I've volunteered to drop him off at his house so he doesn't have to call a taxi.

So we're driving through the night streets in my car, a canary-yellow clunker with a zillion miles on it that I bought dirt cheap from a used car lot in Culver City. Keeler lives in the Echo Park area west of downtown L.A. Sleepy narrow avenues with clapboard houses where the Hollywood people first settled.

"You ever think of directing a movie?" I ask Keeler.

"Came real close once. Leo had a script we both liked but he didn't want to direct, so he convinced the studio boss at the time to give me a shot. In fact, he agreed to guarantee my work—if anything went wrong, he'd take over and do the job for scale, which was what they were going to pay me."

"So what happened?"

"Your pal McKenna—" I've told him about my adventures with the FBI "—he showed up in my cutting room and handed me a subpoena. I went before the Committee and refused to give names."

"You were Blacklisted?"

"Gray listed, black listed, white listed, I've done it all."

"I don't understand."

"Well, the gray list is before you're subpoenaed but you've been active in union politics and got a reputation as a Progressive, so some people are leery of hiring you. When HUAC calls and you take the Fifth, then it's real clear: you automatically make the Blacklist and the studio doors slam shut—my directing deal went up in smoke, and even with three Oscar nominations I couldn't get work as a fourth assistant film cutter. But all my friends were proud of me.

"And I had a new friend. McKenna. He'd call every month or so to find out how I was doing. That meant, 'Have you changed your mind and will you cooperate now?' So it was never closed—you had to be brave all over again every month."

That horrifies me. I'm filled with new loathing for McKenna. Then I realize Keeler has left out a part.

"But—what's the white list?"

"That's the real special one. Sure you want to hear about that?"

"If you want to tell me."

"Why not? Part of a bright lad's education. After I made the Blacklist, the only job I could get was a floorwalker in men's clothing at Bullock's Downtown, minimum wage, no commissions, no health benefits, and Nora, my wife, she's gone now, but when she got really sick and we were drowning in doctor bills, here's McKenna stopping by the store, just to buy some socks, he says, and asks, how's it going? And so, feeling desperate, the next week I testified again and gave HUAC some names and figured then I'd be able to go back to work in the industry. Pay for the fancy medicines Nora needed. That's what I sold out for." He looks haunted.

"But there was a joker. I found out that now I'd made the white list—all the Leftie friends who'd been so proud of me before now wouldn't talk to me, and to the assholes on the Right I was this scuzzy ex-Commie, so nobody would touch me. Only Leo. He put me back to work. Pushed it through over the studio's objections."

I've pulled up at Keeler's Spanish-style cottage. As he says "Thanks for the ride" and climbs out of the car, I call after him. "Hey, Keeler. That's the first good story I've heard about Leo lately."

He leans down to watch my face. "It was the least he could do. After all, Leo originally recruited me to join the Party— and then the reason I was Blacklisted was because Leo named me." Keeler gives me a wry smile. "Can't tell the players without a scorecard, can you, kid?"

He walks off toward his front door, while I white-knuckle clench the steering wheel so hard I think I might break it off. Leo, you asshole!

16

DAVID

After I leave Keeler I drive aimlessly through the night streets. I'm infuriated at the gut-wrenching journey Leo has inflicted on Keeler. Your patron, your betrayer, your redeemer. The man who ruined your family life has tossed you a bone and the price is an option on your soul. How much stress does it take to blow the circuits in your head? No wonder Keeler acts like a madman sometimes around Leo. How does he keep from killing him?

I'm flooded with trembling rage—for Keeler, for the crew that Leo abuses, for myself! Stopped at a red light, I pound the steering wheel viciously, wishing it was Leo. A cruel self-serving manipulating lying monster. Because he pats me on the head now and then I've started to like him again. But isn't he using me the same way as he does Keeler? Another of his victims he can publicly save? Am I just so desperate to find a surrogate father that I'm willing to lull *my* soul into submission? I wish to God I could talk to Teddy. If I concentrate hard enough, I can hear his voice.

C'mon, pal, can't just laze away your whole life," he said in Paris.

When I got back from Korea, Teddy took one look at me

and commenced to kick my ass. Despite my long hospital stay
in Tokyo, all I felt capable of doing was sitting and staring.
But Teddy got right on my case. Pretending he badly needed
my help as a writer again. Little by little I came out of my funk
and began to function again.

Teddy had become part of the Paris scene. Debonair in a
beret and his jacket over his shoulders without hands in the
sleeves, a bon vivant known at the hep sidewalk cafés on
the Left Bank near the seedy but charming little apartment
he rented. Money was easier because he'd built a black market reputation for "delivering quality merchandise at bargain
basement prices," he'd boom with laughter. Teddy still had
serious problems, but he hid them from me. His French visa
had long since lapsed, still no passport, and now the authori-
ties in Paris had tracked him down. The first I knew about
any of it was one afternoon when we were shaping a plot line
for a romantic comedy. "I have an appointment," he said.
"C'mon along and we'll keep working."

We went to one of the imitation Greek Temples overlooking the Seine that house the hordes of French bureaucrats.
After he registered at the front desk, we sat on a bench in a
corridor, spinning our story.

"Suppose the leading man is a jewel thief who's just been released from the Bastille and he orders a big meal in a bistro, but
discovers he can't pay for it because," Teddy said, "because—"

"—because," I jumped in, "he discovers that his wallet's
just been stolen." That's when Teddy's name was called.

We entered a small, tidy office. The dour old French clerk in
a musty three-piece suit barely looked up from the file he was
perusing. Waved us into chairs in front of his desk and began
to drone. In a moment I understood: this could be Teddy's last
gasp. He had filed the necessary papers to apply for political
asylum. Now the aged official shook his head, told him his
request had been rejected.

Teddy was rocked. If you didn't know him, you couldn't read that, but I could. End of the road. But the old guy hadn't dismissed us yet. He kept leafing through the file. I had no idea why the French government had a file on Teddy, until the man asked, "You were in the war, Monsieur Weaver?"

Teddy nodded.

The white-haired clerk now studied one particular sheet of paper. "And you were present during the liberation of Paris?" Teddy nodded again. "You were wounded then?"

Teddy shrugged. "A lot of people got shot that day."

Then the man haltingly translated a few paragraphs about a firefight near the Pere Lachaise Cemetery that day in 1944. Theodore Weaver was identified as one of the U.S. soldiers who saved the lives of two Maquis resistance fighters.

"One of those was the nephew of General Leclerc," the Frenchman mentioned. Teddy had never known that. The old bureaucrat ceremoniously brought out an ink pad and an official stamp. He slammed the stamp onto a booklet and handed Teddy an identity card granting him status as a permanent resident of France.

We strutted out of that office and when we were far enough away, Teddy stage-whispered to me, "Nepotism. Works every time."

Then he picked right up on the story we'd been working on. "Hey, suppose the jewel thief used to be in the Maquis, so even though he's a shady character we're rooting for him, and he finds out the person who picked his pocket is the girl he thought was lost to him forever. . . ."

I was so stoked. "Suppose her name is Jana."

He looked over at me with a smile. "Jana it is."

Jana. That's who I want to talk to more than anyone else. But I can't talk to Jana. Worse than the snubs, lately I've occasionally caught a flash of something in her eyes when she sees me. Fear. She's scared of me. Scared, I guess, that I'll start spouting at her again. But if I could talk to her, the way we used to, maybe I could make sense out of how I'm feeling.

I'm driving past the shuttered car agencies along Santa Monica Boulevard. Up ahead, I spot Dolores coffee shop, always open; okay, I'll stop for a cup of coffee. But as I'm parking I look down the street and notice the marquee of the Nuart Theater, a revival house. Colored lights and a fluttering banner announce MIDNITE SHOW TONITE! It's a prewar comedy written by Weaver & Vardian.

I glance at my watch: it's 12:10. I've missed the opening credits and maybe the first couple of scenes, but I know the picture almost by heart. It seems like just where I'm supposed to be.

The title tells it all: *The Chauffeur and the Debutante*. The idea is that the Mob is after a high-rolling New York gambler (played by John Garfield) for not paying his losing bets. He hides out by taking a job as the chauffeur for a swanky Park Avenue family.

I'm just in time to see the signature scene: Garfield, for the first time wearing the liveried "monkey suit," is about to drive Alexis Smith, the socialite daughter, in her limo. He's a guy who's never opened a door for a woman in his life, so he just climbs into the driver's seat. Alexis Smith stands pat at the rear door, tapping her toe. Garfield looks puzzled, then grins as he seems to understand. Without getting out, he leans behind him for the handle and throws the rear door open. "Hop in, honey," he says, and the audience laughs. They did then, and they do now.

Not that there are many people here. Maybe twenty-five

scattered around the dark theater, but you can tell they're enjoying the movie. At least at first, but after a while there are only two of us still cackling at all the jokes. Me and someone else on the other side of the theater. I wonder if that's because the picture's dated or if the rest of the movie buffs have fallen asleep.

The picture climaxes with a chase that winds up in a pastry shop where Garfield and Alexis are fighting off the Baddies, who are trying to kidnap her for ransom, and everybody starts flinging whipped cream pies. The conceit is that while the Heavies and the whole shop are soon covered in whipped cream, Garfield and Alexis, by bobbing and ducking, remain spotless until the cops arrive, and then Garfield catches one in the kisser. Alexis wipes the whipped cream off his face and kisses him. Fade out. The End.

There's only the sound of four hands clapping when the house lights come up. By then I know who it is. I can't see her at first, because other patrons are yawning and stretching as they rise. But then I spot Jana walking up the far aisle. Alone. She's not looking my way, so I don't know if she's seen me. I pick up my pace so that we reach the lobby at the same time. She's wearing Kate Hepburn tan slacks and penny loafers and a green sweater. She looks over in surprise. Not welcome surprise.

"Hey, what're you doin' here?" She plasters on a big nervous smile.

"Just passing by, needed a few laughs, so—"

She cuts me off. "Listen, I gotta go!"

She's ducking me again. Like at the studio. She darts into the ladies' room. Am I supposed to wait? I could use a pit stop myself, but if I do she may come out and assume I've left, so I stay in the lobby and pretend to study the old movie posters and hope for the best.

"Sorry," she says, emerging from the john, "you were saying?"

"Nothing special, just—feel like getting some coffee?"

Only a flicker of hesitation before she nods. "Okay, but—no cream pie for me."

We both chuckle a little more than the joke is worth. We walk down the boulevard toward Dolores café. Awkward as hell. Side by side, careful not to touch. Not talking the first half block or so. Then I say:

"Where's Markie?"

"How should I know? Home sleeping, I guess."

"I just thought that—"

"He doesn't like old movies. Unless his father made them."

We walk on a few more steps. I shouldn't have brought up Markie. Memory Lane should be safe ground, so I go into reminiscence mode. About when we were kids visiting the set watching that cream pie fight being shot.

"Remember how disappointed we were," I say, "when we discovered the pies were topped with shaving cream?"

I laugh, maybe it'll be contagious. It's not. She glares at me. "How'd you know I was here tonight?"

"I didn't. Until the second reel. I came in late."

"Then how'd you know?"

I do my basso imitation of Ezio Pinza in *South Pacific*: "'The sound of her laughter will ring in your dreams.'"

"Okay, okay," she acknowledges with a small smile, "so I still snort when I laugh."

"Like a barnyard critter. Hey, wasn't Julie funny?" Tonight's picture was the only full-scale comedy John Garfield ever did. Real name Julius Garfinkle. A warm, good-humored man, one of our close childhood "uncles." But my mention of his name casts a pall. Hounded by HUAC, he died at thirty-nine. A victim of the Blacklist.

"Poor Julie," she says. "He always had a bad heart."

Reflexively I correct her, "No, he had a *good* heart. That's why the bastards got him."

I mean it to sound rueful. She hears it as an accusation. Her face turns away as if she's been slapped. Me and my damn mouth! I really only want to talk about her. About us. She looks like she's going to turn on her heel and walk away, but we're at the entrance to Dolores and as she hesitates I pull open the door with a courtly gesture.

"Hop in, honey," I say. Giving it my best John Garfield-style Brooklynese. It works. She goes inside.

There are a scant few late-nighters hunched over coffee cups at the counter and we're off by ourselves in a booth. Jana wants only a cup of coffee. Realizing I haven't had anything to eat since breakfast, I order a chili burger and fries. But when it comes, I'm too nervous to dig in.

We keep talking about old times, trying to avoid anything about HUAC and Leo. That leaves what's happened to former schoolmates. Places where we used to hang out that have been torn down. In another second we'll be discussing the weather. It's painful. We can't stop chattering because silence will be even worse. Then we both dry up. She takes a sip of coffee. Her pinkie extended, the way it always was when we were kids. I'd tease her and we'd laugh. I poke at my food with the fork.

"Guess it's . . . kinda hard," I say finally, "getting together after almost a ten-year gap, there's so much we don't know about each other now. . . ."

She's staring down into her coffee cup.

I feel an aching in my chest. If Jana and I have lost our old connection, then I'm lost. With no one in the world I can really talk to. No one I can trust.

"Okay, look, I'll try to—"

"It's not you, David, it's me." Her hazel eyes come up and lock onto mine. There are tears welling. "I—feel like—I owe you an apology."

"Hell no, I'm the one who keeps bringing up all the old crap and—"

"And you should! The night you were at the house, you called me a spoiled little rich girl, and I got mad at you"—she waves me off before I can interrupt—"because it's true! We two were almost like a fairy-tale prince and princess, and then you got banished from the kingdom. You and your mom and dad—and we got to stay here and live the rich life that was supposed to be yours, too—it's such an ugly, horrible thing that's happened—and I can't even imagine what it was like for you—" Tears are rolling down her cheeks. But she doesn't take her gaze away.

"I wanted to believe what Leo told me, that he had to do what he did and that it was right, and for a while I did, but then—after I got into research, I got hold of everything that's been published and—I found out things. Disgraceful things. I can't judge him, David, he's my father, but it was Leo and the others—not me! *I'd never ever do anything in the world to hurt you!*"

She's too choked up to go on. Buries her face in her napkin to muffle the sobs as she cries. Without thinking, I slip out of my side of the booth and slide in beside her. Want to hold her, hug away the pain, but afraid even to touch her. She feels me next to her and she lowers the napkin, crumples it up, eyes still full of tears. "I've been wanting to tell you that for so long."

"I—I've been wanting to hear it—for so long." That's all I can manage to say. I hand her my napkin, she dabs at her face, blows her nose, and then leans her head against the back of the booth with closed eyes. I tentatively cover her hand with mine.

We sit there that way for a very long time in silence. But it's a good silence. I realize now how wrong I've been. I've assumed that these weeks of Jana's avoiding me were about her anger at my holding onto the past. But now I see that she wasn't mad at me. And it wasn't anger. It was shame. Survivor's guilt.

"Sh-h-h," I say—she's still trembling—"it'll be okay, we'll make it be okay. . . ."

We stroll back to where Jana's car is across from the darkened theater. She unlocks the driver's door, but doesn't open it yet.

"Just because I let Markie take me to some industry events he acts like we're going together. Comes and sits down at my table in the commissary. We're just friends. But at the studio everybody thinks we're an item."

"Fuckin' gossips," I say, "what do they know?"

"Yeah, what do they know?" she repeats. Then, tentatively: "On our next date, let's not talk about Leo or Teddy or any of that bad stuff. Okay? Let's see if we can do that? Just for *one* day?"

"Yeah. Okay. I'll try. But—" I trail off.

"But what?"

"This wasn't a date. A date is when someone brings you flowers and picks you up at your place and all that."

"So what do you call this?"

"A dream come true," I say.

"I missed you so much, David." Jana touches my cheek, then she gets into her car, turns on the engine, and pulls out.

I walk back to Dolores thinking this day sure ended a lot better than it started. I'm feeling great. Until the hackles on my neck rise; the survival instinct that kept me alive in Korea. I whirl around and scope out the deserted boulevard. A wino fast asleep in a doorway on the far side of the street. No one else in sight. So I continue on to my car, but all the way I have the distinct sensation that there's someone out there watching me. My guess is McKenna.

17

JANA

A little before nine the next morning the brisk desk clerk at the Chateau Marmont stops sorting the incoming mail as I walk up. I ask about David and he offers to ring his room and announce me. I tell him it's a surprise. He smiles knowingly and gives me the room number.

I go down the hall and knock on his door. There's no response. Could he have gone out for a run or something this early? No, anyone who works as hard as Leo works him during the week doesn't bound out of bed on Saturday morning. I thump on the blue door.

"Hey, you in there! Wake up time!"

I hear him tumble out of bed and stagger across the room. Throw open the door. Looking startled. He's in his pajama bottoms. Nice bod. Flat tummy. Good pecs. Even better than in my imaginings. The army builds men.

"Hey, Jana," he says. Knuckling sleep out of his eyes like when he was a kid. "What are you doing here?"

"We're having a real date. How's this?" I tick off the requirements. "Pick you up at your place—with flowers." I thrust a bouquet at him.

Grinning, he accepts it—and gives the flowers an exaggerated comic sniff. "Lilacs, my favorite."

"C'mon, get dressed," I laugh, "I'm taking you to lunch."

I follow him into the room, and as he dresses in the bathroom I'm left wondering what it would be like for us to jump back into that warm bed? Hey, hold the good thought. Don't want to rush things, or do I?

I drive out Sunset to the ocean and turn the Jaguar north on Pacific Coast Highway. "Yeah," I acknowledge, "the car was a twenty-first birthday present from Leo." Just above Big Rock on a straight stretch of PCH we hold hands for a while. Such a small thing, but electrifying. It's not a jolt. More of a tingling. I'm very aware of his hand's size, much larger than mine, the hard texture of his skin, no longer a boy's hand, the way his fingers wrap around mine, the slight sweatiness. All these years apart I thought I would never touch him again. Never share that closeness that made me feel like we were one person.

He notices the charm bracelet I'm wearing. It's gold with all kinds of doodads dangling. "Hey, that's cute. Something new?"

"It was a gift. Part of a bequest. From Wendy Travers." I show him that each of the charms represents one of the movies she wrote.

"You guys stayed pretty close."

"Like sisters. At first when she was killed, it was headlines, everyone was talking about it. Now there's nothing. Like she's already forgotten." His hand has tensed. "What?" I ask.

He takes a deep breath. Then he ventures onto thin ice. "Why did she come to Teddy's funeral?"

I hear his puzzlement and know I'm the only one who can answer his question. "Penitence," I say. "She hated herself for being part of what happened to Teddy."

He squeezes my hand. He understands. Maybe he forgives.

We're way past Malibu when I turn into Paradise Cove. It's a beach area worthy of its name. During summer vacations from school, when our dads were working, David's mom occasionally brought us out here. Far from the Hollywood scene, often we had the beach to ourselves.

I take a blanket out of the trunk, David hoists my goodie-laden picnic basket, and we trek along the ocean's edge until we find the right spot to spread out the feast. I turn on my portable radio. He uncorks the wine and proposes a toast to the future. I love the sound of that.

We've been talking nonstop. We both want to tell each other everything we've thought and felt since we were separated. Now he asks why I'm wearing a USC sweatshirt when last he heard I was bound for Northwestern?

"I had to come back when Leo got sick—so I finished up at USC. What you're really asking is, why am I still living at home?"

"You still read minds," he teases.

"Only certain minds," I say. "Leo's okay now, but . . . well, you know him. He comes on as this I-don't-need-anyone curmudgeon, but he's lonely and depressed a lot of the time. He's dated some women, but nothing lasted. So I keep him company, play hostess when he entertains people, which isn't very often. It's temporary."

I feel David's gaze, questioning how long "temporary" is.

"Don't give me that look," I say. "Tell me about Teddy in Europe. He got married again?"

David tells me about Helga Erikssen, the Danish actress Teddy met on one of his uncredited French pictures. "That happened while I was in Korea. Came back and I had a stepmother, but a keeper, a lovely, bright woman who made Teddy very happy. Except—"

He pauses. There's something in his voice. "Except what?"

"Teddy didn't have a passport, so he couldn't go with Helga when she worked outside of France. Otherwise he would have been on the plane with her when it crashed outside of Belgrade. No survivors."

I'm shocked. I squeeze his hand, but what I really want is to hug away another nightmare I wasn't even aware of. "That— that must have been—"

"Yeah, not a good time," he says.

After we finish brunch, we stroll barefooted in the surf, then the wind comes up. We retreat to the shelter of an embankment and wrap ourselves in the blanket like a sleeping bag for two. Laughing as we try to tuck in all the corners to keep the sand out—our faces close together, chattering happily, then kissing. As adults for the first time. I'm happier now than I've been in so long. Lost in the smell of his hair, the feel of his skin, the taste of him. Our hands groping excitedly under our clothing, rubbing and caressing; his fingers slip inside me, I tremble.

"Know what I want to do now?" he says in a husky voice.

We look deeply into each other's eyes.

"Me, too."

There's a small inn at Paradise Cove and we're in a room with the shutters closed but we can hear the crashing surf. Blending our bodies, knowing exactly the right moves as though we've been doing this for years. Forget about anyone else. I now know the meaning of the words "making love." We fall asleep entwined in each other.

In the middle of the night, after a breathtaking encore, I feel so at peace. We're laying there exploring each other with wandering fingers.

"I love your body," he says. "Even better than I imagined."

"Shoulda been around a few years back, there was a lot more to love. I was as big as the Goodyear blimp. They called it a chronic eating disorder."

"That's tough stuff. How'd you get over it?"

"Guess I knew I had to—because someone exactly like you might drop by."

My fingers pause on his back. There is a coarse knot of skin below his left shoulder blade.

"What's that scar?" I ask.

"Nothing. It's old."

"But from what?"

"Korea."

"You were—shot?"

"Shrapnel. From a mortar shell."

He doesn't say any more. But I have to know more. I prop myself up on my elbow, gaze at him in the shaft of light coming from the opening of the bathroom door, and ask:

"Did you kill anyone over there?"

"I was a medic. I didn't carry a weapon."

"Doctor David? How'd that happen?"

"Well, I volunteered for the Rangers and went through training with them. Then they wanted to throw me out because they discovered I was 'political.'"

"Because of Teddy."

"Yeah, but my company commander was a stand-up guy. Instead of giving me the boot, he gave me a Red Cross armband. So that's how I went to Korea. Carrying pressure bandages and sulfur packs instead of a machine gun. At least I could stay with the guys—they'd become my friends."

I touch his scar again. "Was this from the time you won the big medal?" He draws back.

"Nah, the medal thing—that was before." He shrugs it off. "Pulled a few of our wounded guys to safety under fire. This was from—later. Hey, you don't want to hear all that. It's all healed now."

"Is it?" I sense there's much more. I see a tic in his cheek that was not there before.

"I want to tell you everything," he says slowly. "Whenever I thought about us somehow getting together again, I promised myself—no secrets."

I nod. Agreeing. Encouraging. But scared of what he's about to say.

"We," he coughs a little, "me and my squad, we'd been through a lot, but we'd been lucky, only lost three guys. On this icy morning we were climbing a steep hill. In the snow. Near the Chinese border. Suddenly from the distance we heard the sound of bugles. That's how the Chinese announced themselves. We were strung out, one in front of the other. I was last as usual. That was part of my job. Bring up the rear. Patch up the wounded. When the mortar round came, it hit us an instant before the sound. Then I was all alone on that hillside."

I choke up. Fearing the answer, I ask, "Where were the others?"

"Gone." He coughs again. "Dead. Just bits and pieces. All around. Blood on the snow. Body parts." I'm staring at him. Reliving his horror. "I felt so—glad to be alive, and then—guilty. See, my job was to help them. But there was nothing, no one left." The tic in his cheek fires again. "All gone. Except for me—The Lone Ranger." His ironic smile comes out a wince. "I didn't even know I was hit until the other squad reached us."

"Oh God . . ." I feel a jab of pain in my chest. He reaches out to reassure *me*!

"Jana, that was a lifetime ago. End of my tour of duty. Only, the thing is . . ." I'm fighting back tears as he forces himself to continue ". . . I still don't know why I was the only one spared."

I put my face down on his chest, his heart is pounding in my ear. God, I'm so glad he came back. "I love you, David," I say.

18

DAVID

Early morning, and it's misty on the Panorama outdoor back lot. The cast and crew are gathered in front of a four-story-high block-wide blue sky back drop. A ridge has been built in the foreground. Not papier-mâché, because horses with riders are going to gallop up and down. We're about ready to shoot, but Leo is in his aluminum trailer loudly hassling with Barney Ott and Jack Heritage.

I assume it's the usual. Leo has been falling further and further behind schedule, so the suits are applying pressure. Keeler Barnes sets me straight, that's not it. He holds up *Film Bulletin*. Folded open to Joe Shannon's column, The Rumor Mill.

The lead item reads: "Don't let it get around, folks, but the Panorama poobahs may be fed up enough with the fiscal foolishness on *Against the Wind* to fire Leo Vardian."

"Is it true?" I ask.

Keeler shrugs. "Can never tell with that cocksucker Shannon, he loves to play with people's lives."

I know why I'm pissed at Shannon—I've told Keeler about the run-in at the commisary—but I'm surprised at Keeler's vehemence. Is it because his job may be in danger?

"Just scratches open an old wound," he tells me. "Film editors usually don't rate Shannon's columns, but years ago he made an exception for me. Juicy items like, 'There's an unco-operative HUAC witness named Keeler Barnes in the cutting room over at Panorama who ought to be fired to make room for a loyal American.' Garbage like that, until they canned me."

The door to Leo's trailer is thrown open. Ott and Heritage emerge, followed by Leo, his chest puffed out, sure sign he's on the warpath. Ott is clutching a rolled-up copy of *Film Bulletin* and waving it in the air. They've found a common enemy.

"Filthy Fifth Columnist! Scandal-mongering son of a bitch! Wait'll I get ahold of Shannon, I'll rip out his intestines and play jump rope with 'em!" Heritage vows.

"Leo, you focus on making your movie," Ott pats his shoulder. "We'll handle this."

They stride away, Ott barking marching orders to Heritage: "Call Shannon's publisher, tell him we demand a retraction! Or we're gonna stop advertising in that rag!"

Leo wanders over to Keeler and me.

"Think Shannon will print a retraction?" Keeler asks.

"Does he ever?" Leo spits on the ground. "What I think is, those two bastards"—looking after Ott and Heritage just leaving the soundstage—"I think they planted that lousy item themselves. Screw it. Gotta go to work."

Leo goes toward the camera where Heston and Poitier, in makeup and costume, are waiting for him.

"Why would the studio put something in the paper that hurts their own picture?" I ask Keeler. "Just to amp up pressure on Leo to go faster?"

"Plus, rule number one in Hollywood: cover your ass. If this picture turns into a full-blown disaster, they already publicly identified the fall guy."

I look over at Leo, who seems totally absorbed in rehearsing the scene with his actors. How can he simply shut it all out? Then a vehicle zooms to a stop behind us. Keeler glances over his shoulder.

"Lookie-lookie, a visitor from Olympus."

The Rolls-Royce parks in a red No Parking Zone in front of a fire hydrant. Harry Rains springs out, hurries past us with cursory nods, mumbling, "Hey, Keeler—David, howyadoin'?" His arms wrap Leo in a bear hug. Announcing so everyone can hear:

"Came as soon as I read that trash, Leo, I'm outraged."

Harry Rains's presence on our set is an event. He hasn't been here since our first day of shooting.

"I'm going to call Shannon myself and read him the riot act. We'll get this all straightened out."

"I'm doing the best I can here, Harry. You know that."

"Of course you are." He massages Leo's shoulder reassuringly and they step off to the side and whisper together for a moment. Then Harry goes back on the public record, giving Leo a full-voiced endorsement: "Keep up the good work!" He turns to face the entire troupe. "That goes for all of you—thanks for your fine efforts, Panorama really appreciates it!"

"Come back and see us anytime, Harry," Leo calls as Harry waves and strides back to his Rolls.

Keeler looks after him. "If I parked my car there for thirty seconds, the studio bulls would tow me off to Inglewood."

I shrug. "Harry's been doing that since he started to drive. Parking in the red, white, and yellow zones. Told me he used to get a mountain of tickets, but here's his motto." I mimic Harry, "'Gray spaces are for gray people.'"

Keeler laughs. "Well, what the hell, it's Harry's world."

While the AD positions the extras and the makeup and hair people do final touches on our stars, Leo strolls over to me. "C'mere a second," he says, guiding me off by ourselves. What have I done now?

He grips my shoulder and growls in my ear. "I know about
it. You and Jana."

I stiffen. Paradise Cove was nearly two weeks ago. Since then
Jana and I have been spending every possible moment together. During workdays that means casual contacts at the
studio—and many glorious evenings in my bed at the Chateau, noshing on corned beef sandwiches from Greenblatt's
Deli and each other. On weekends we take off, driving to La
Jolla or Ojai, seeking out-of-the-way places. A week after we
were together, I asked, "Would you be interested in marrying
me sometime?"

She wrinkled her brow and said, "Yeah, I could work that
into my schedule."

But nobody else in town knew about us. Until now.

The other night I brought up the subject. "Are we in hiding?"

She laughed at the idea and said we were just being private.
Did we want to become fodder for Louella's column: NEWSOME
TWOSOME, SECOND-GENERATION FILMLAND SWEETHEARTS? I
sensed there was more to it than that. Finally, she admitted it
was Leo.

"But it's not what you think. He'll like the idea, he likes
you, since you've been working for him he respects you, he's
told me so."

I pushed it. "But—?"

"He's so enmeshed in his movie, under so much pressure
right now, I just don't want to do anything to, y'know, add to
his load. We'll tell him when the time's right."

J ana told me at breakfast," Leo says; his grip on my shoulder
tightens. Is he going to swing at me? "I couldn't be happier."

He actually smiles. "It's what I always dreamed of. Congratulations, David."

He shakes my hand formally, as if closing an important deal. Then he stalks back to his camera and rolls the scene. Leaving me stunned. Mostly pleased that Jana had decided now was the time. And despite my garbled feelings about Leo, I'm pleased, too, at his warm reaction.

I'm off-duty for lunch because Leo is eating with his business manager at Ramon's, the Mexican joint across from the studio. Jana and I were planning to do takeout sandwiches on a deserted spot on a hill overlooking the back lot. Instead, we're dining in the commissary, out in plain sight. Who cares who sees us?

"So how come you decided to tell him now?"

"It suddenly felt so high school, sneaking around, like I was scared of my own father. I'm a grown woman."

I nod approvingly. "Right, he can't ground you."

"And I told you he'd love the idea."

"So now we can find an apartment near the studio." We've calculated that between our salaries we can swing it, maybe up off Laurel Canyon.

She frowns. There's a joker in the deck.

"He wants us to wait a little. Just until the picture's finished. We go on seeing each other the same way, he's given us his blessing."

"Except he gets to play Director with our lives." It seemed too easy.

"It's only a few weeks, David, and he was all shook up that I might move out immediately. Really rattled. 'Right in the middle of everything?' he kept saying. He suggested an alternative: if you want to move into Stone Canyon with us, he says you kinda grew up in that house—"

I'm about to go into orbit on that one.

"—Of course I told him no, but—David, it's only a few weeks."

I see how torn she feels, so I shrug. We poke at our salads and chat about other things we pretend we're interested in.

I mention that Leo went ape about the item in Shannon's column.

She says he'll get over it. "But I was sorta surprised Shannon went after Dad, considering all that Panorama has done for him."

"Such as?" I ask as we munch our jumbo-shrimp salads.

"The studio paid big money for Shannon's unpublished book."

"What's it about?"

"Some old-time vaudevillian. It's under wraps, but Harry Rains is talking about getting Metro to loan us Gene Kelly to star."

We go on to a favorite routine—making fun of the tiny size of my room at the Chateau. "How small is it?" jokes. Subtext, of course, is that's where we're going to be spending even more time for a while.

Our first night in the room I actually worried about her childhood claustrophobia: we'd discovered it as kids when we went exploring a cave on Malibu beach while our parents were busy drinking margaritas. We got wedged in the cave, she panicked and screamed. I had to pull her out.

But Jana loved my hotel room. "It's cozy," she decided.

As usual, now we avoid talking about the Blacklist, but sometimes it has a sneaky way of creeping into the conversation. Like the night we're kissing down the hallway of the Chateau and peeling off our clothes as soon as we got in the room and my passport fell out of the back pocket of my trousers.

She picked it up. Like it was an ancient artifact.

"You're still carrying that around?" she said.

"I'd feel naked without it." She idly flipped the pages of my passport. "You don't carry yours anymore?" I asked her. "You feel safe?"

"I do now." She tossed the passport on the bureau and hugged me. "Wish you did, too."

That's when I told her about McKenna's visit to deliver Teddy's passport. At the mention of his name she froze. "I remember him, let's not talk about him."

Instead we climbed into bed and made love and fell asleep in each other's arms.

Now I gaze across the commissary table at her. She can't fool me. She feels bad about the compromise she agreed to with Leo.

"Hey," I say, "it's only a few weeks. Like they say in San Quentin, I can do that much time standing on my head."

She leans across the table and kisses me in relief. What's unspoken, of course, is that we've already lost years.

When I get back to the set after lunch, one of the wranglers getting the horses ready says, "He's looking for you." Leo is inside the prop truck. Tommy Duarte, the prop man, is tying a silver ribbon around a large, fancy Tiffany's box.

"Here's the man we need," Leo greets me. "Got a delivery I want you to make. A special delivery. To Joe Shannon."

"Better use one of the studio messengers. There's bumpy history between me and Shannon," I remind him.

"No problem," Leo insists, "just hand him the present and come on back."

Driving crosstown, I can't understand why Leo is sending a glitzy gift to the columnist who enraged him this morning. Maybe there's someone in this town Leo is still scared of.

CHAPTER

19

McKENNA

I've been spending the morning gathering more testimonials to the good citizenship and sterling character of Harry Rains. Still no closer to latching onto a case that can rescue me from Tinsel Town. I've found out from a pal in D.C. that what I'm really vetting Harry for is an ambassadorial post. Funny, we're both bucking for big new government gigs—but so far my bet is on Harry.

I push the melancholy thoughts aside. Orders from headquarters. Do the job. I can't limit my canvassing about Harry Rains to film industry executives, supplicant agents, fellow lawyers, and former clients. Have to see if I can dig up at least a smidgen of dirt. So I've come to a place known as The Rumor Mill.

My first time here, but it's easy to find. Ramona Court is a middle-class residential street, close to the Carthay Circle Theatre. The address I'm looking for is one of the small Spanish-style houses that were stamped out cheaply once the War ended and building materials became available. The owner is Joe Shannon, gossip monger supreme. But that's not who I'm here to see.

"Two fags get off a bus . . ." Okie O'Connell greets me in the doorway, baring horse-face teeth in a Halloween grin.

"Heard that one," I say. I usually find Okie amusing, and I could use a good laugh today.

"How 'bout, a priest, a rabbi, and a sexagenarian get off a bus"—Okie O'Connell interrupts himself with a hee-haw bray—"ahh, never mind, cousin, that's too dumb."

He's tall, early fifties, huge farmer's hands and nervous how'm-I-doin' eyes. He used to be known as one of the funniest men in Hollywood. Now he's known for other things. Okie is working as Joe Shannon's leg man these days, scouting news items for the column. He leads the way inside the house. "Let me show you around. . . ."

There's not that much to see.

The editorial rooms and printing plant of *Film Bulletin,* which features The Rumor Mill column, are elsewhere in town, but Shannon works out of here. It's not his home, this is his office space.

A frumpy secretary is answering the ever-ringing phones: "Sorry, Joe's not here, he'll have to call you back." Above the filing cabinets there's a wall of photos: Joe Shannon matching smiles with top stars and slinky starlets, plus Shannon shaking hands with moguls Darryl Zanuck, L. B. Mayer, Harry Rains, and Walt Disney. Places of honor given to autographed pictures of Dwight Eisenhower, Richard Nixon, and Joe McCarthy.

"That's my desk in the corner," Okie points, "and Joey's letting me camp in back. So the column never really goes to bed. Like Vegas, we never close."

A room in back. A far cry from the snazzy Westwood bachelor pad where I first met Okie. He was a busy, third-tier talent, vaguely known to the public for comedy sidekick cowboy roles in Errol Flynn and Randolph Scott movies. Around Hollywood, Okie was also fondly known for rewriting hit tune lyrics into filthy limericks, which he sang at private celebrity roasts. "Okie knows everybody in town and everybody knows Okie," he crowed to me back then in his Tulsa twang.

In the old days he had been a treasure trove for me. When he appeared before the Committee, he testified that he was led astray by his worldly friends. He thought of the Communist Party as a social organization helping people find jobs. In 1950, when the tide turned, he switched sides. If testifying as a friendly witness was the only way to keep working, Okie would be the friendliest. He named a record-setting 164 he said he personally knew as Communists.

But his plan backfired. Okie expected the Leftists would despise him. "But the Right wingers had got on to me, that I don't really have much talent t'begin with," Okie lamented to me several years ago, with more than a little bitterness. Now he has surfaced again under the Red-battling banner of Joe Shannon.

We settle in the small backyard at a patio table under the sunlit but winter-barren branches of a plum tree. Okie hospitably pours iced tea.

"How's it going—being a legman?" I ask him.

"More fun than skinnin' a possum." He loves to lay on that country-boy shtick. "I roam 'round the studios, visit all the sets, flirt with all the purty gals, get invites to big parties and premieres, 'cuz everybody's too scared of Joey's column to tell me to fuck off." He sips his iced tea. "So what can I do today for the federal government, cousin?"

"Harry Rains. You know anything I should know?"

"Ol' Harry, now there's a dude I admire. Charged his clients a fortune in fees for advice that was really good for the studios: Give 'em names and keep the studio's skirts clean. Now ol' Harry's runnin' a studio hisself, ain't that a surprise?"

"What else should I know about Harry?"

"Why do you want to know?" The voice now comes from the doorway behind us.

I turn to see Joe Shannon. Dressed, as usual, like a fashion plate. All courtesy of freebies from Dick Carroll's haberdashery on Rodeo Drive, quid pro quo for the frequent plugs in Shannon's column. Shannon advances toward us. It's turning into a garden party.

"Is my pal Harry in trouble?"

"Not that I know of," I say easily. "How've you been, Joe?"

"Then why are you asking about him?"

"Just busy work. Harry's up for a citizenship award or something."

"Sounds like a nice item for the column."

"A little premature and I don't know the details."

"Okay, keep it a secret, I'll get the lowdown from Harry."

"They're real close, y'know," Okie says.

"I put Harry on the high road to success in Hollywood by introducing him to Frank Tavenner at HUAC. When Valerie had those difficulties. Remember, Mac?"

I definitely do. That one got swept under the rug. But we established a valuable working relationship with Harry. He could talk good sense to his clients.

Okie shoehorns back into the conversation. "Harry's gonna make a movie outta the book Joey's workin' on."

"That's not what Agent McKenna is interested in."

"Sorry, Joey, want some iced tea?" He pours a glass for Shannon and starts to pull out a chair for him.

"You're not my house boy, Okie, you're my legman. A journalist now, not a clown. So the questions I'm asking Mac you should've been asking. It's called being a reporter."

Okie looks scared. "I was just gettin' to that when you got here."

Shannon sits down, gives me his full attention.

"Your first time here. Did Okie give you the grand tour?"

Shannon gestures at the cottage. "The House of Lies, the Mansion of Mendacity, the Fortress of Fabrication, the Bastion of Bullshit, the place from whence all the news that's barely fit to print emanates."

Shannon is quoting his critics, but the self-deprecating name-calling is an inverse boast. His batting average on scoops is a tribute to his far-flung network of sources. His items usually turn out to be true. Insider news laced with waspish wit. "Read it here first," Shannon is fond of congratulating himself, "before the denials, and long before the confessions and excuses."

"So what's your book about?" I say.

"Jimmy Savo. The old knockabout comic dancer. Rise from Nowhereville to fame, then lost a leg to cancer, how he hit bottom, then struggled and overcame disability to dance again on Broadway with an artificial leg."

"Everybody loves a winner," I acknowledge.

"That's exackly what Harry says."

"Okie—?" Shannon warns. "Mac and I are talking."

"Yeah, right, I—" Inside the house the phone rings. "That might be for me," and he makes his escape.

Shannon sips the iced tea, wrinkles his nose, sets down the glass. "Too sweet, I keep telling Okie not to make it so sweet."

"Hard to get good help these days. But who else could you hire who'd piss off everybody by being your man-about-town?"

The corners of Shannon's mouth quiver slightly, his equivalent of a paroxysm of laughter. "Yes, there is that." He lights a cigarillo, then says, "If you want to know about Harry, Okie's not the one to talk to—I am."

I wait. The best way to get info from Shannon is to let him offer it.

"We grew up together. In Boyle Heights. Ran around like a pair of wild Indians, snatching apples from fruit stands, graduated to swiping hubcaps and selling them to raise bus fare to get to the beach. And look at us now."

Self-serving Memory Lane stuff, I think. More how-Harry-became-wonderful.

"Joe—!" Okie reappears, looking agitated.

"We're still talking," Shannon snaps.

"I know, I know, but—a package just arrived."

"Well, sign for it or whatever, and I'll see to it when we're done here."

"That's the thing, the kid says his orders are to put it in your hands personally. It's a big gift-wrapped Tiffany's box."

"From who?"

"Panorama Studio."

Shannon glances at me, another twitch of the lips, "This could be fun." He waves at Okie. "Have him bring it out."

Okie goes inside.

"Panorama and I are in the middle of a tiff," Shannon explains. "This must be a peace offering."

Okie comes out again, followed by a large, ornately beribboned box and the messenger carrying it nods at me. "Agent McKenna," David Weaver says, "do you work here now?"

"Just visiting."

Shannon, who has been intent on the gift box, now looks up at the messenger. His face clouds. "What the hell are *you* doing here?"

20

DAVID

When I rang the bell, Joe Shannon's cottage door was opened by a guy with a jack-o'-lantern smile. He didn't recognize me, but I remembered him from long-ago Sunday afternoon lawn parties. Okie O'Connell. Used to clown with us kids, plucking nickels magically from behind our ears. That was before Teddy began calling him The Bargain Basement Judas. My inner alarm went on high alert.

But I was prepped by Leo. Package from Panorama. Must make personal delivery.

O'Connell checked inside, then led me through the house. Apart from the movie-star photos, it looked like a scruffy mail-order business. Guess I was expecting to see blood and gore on the worn carpet. I was brought out to the backyard—where Shannon and McKenna were at a patio table. Felt like I'd walked into a meeting of the evil coven. O'Connell, Shannon, and McKenna: the snitch, the bitch, and the witch-hunter.

What the hell are *you* doing here?" Shannon shrills.

"Making a delivery," I say, as instructed. "Compliments of Leo Vardian."

Shannon stares past me at Okie. If looks could kill. "Why did you let *him* in?"

Okie is into panic mode. "What's wrong, Joey? Who's he?"

McKenna tells him. "Okie, meet David Weaver."

Behind me, I hear Okie mutter, "Teddy's boy?"

Shannon's gaze drills me. "So you're working for Leo now." He makes no move toward the Tiffany box.

"There's a card," McKenna says, plucking it off.

"Read it," Shannon says. His sub-zero eyes remain fixed on me.

McKenna rips the envelope, reads aloud: "Dear Joe, in case you run short, I'm enclosing material for your next column. Love and kisses, Leo."

He hands it to Shannon, who tosses it on the table. Then Shannon slides off the ribbon, tears the expensive wrapping, pops off the box lid. A plastic covering lifts off with the lid and we all lean forward to see, just as a pungent aroma fills the air. Okie, the ex-farmboy, is first to identify it:

"Omigod, road apples!" he exclaims.

"It's horse shit," Shannon yells, "you brought me a box of horse shit!"

I'm as surprised as he is, but a snicker escapes from me. In an instant, he's gone from cool to boil and I expect steam to hiss out of his ears as he comes nose-to-nose with me.

"You Commie cocksucker, how dare you march in here with that obscenity! This is a place of business, not a pigsty or wherever you live! Think it's funny, don't you! Hilarious, right? Well, Leo's going to pay for this, in blood, and you, too—better fly back to Europe and hide some more, you little son of a bitch, because you're dead in this town! I'll see to that—I'll drive you out just the way I did your Bolshevik bastard father and your Stalin-loving cunt mother—"

That's when I belt him. The black rage unleashed. Straight right fist into his jawbone and he reels back. Banging against the tree behind him. Shannon sways there, clutching his jaw with one hand, pointing a finger at me with the other.

"McKenna, you saw it, arrest this—this piece of filth!"

"On what charge?"

"That's your business, goddammit! Assault—assault and battery!"

McKenna doesn't move. Guess what I did is not a federal offense.

Shannon shrieks at Okie, who's frozen and staring. "Call the cops before the little gangster tries to run away. Do it now!"

McKenna rises, shoots a hold-on look at Okie, and gets between me and Shannon. "Maybe, Joe, just maybe, you don't want to do that."

"Don't you tell me what to do!"

"He's just a messenger." McKenna nods at me. "Your beef is with Leo. And if the cops come they'll ask him why he hit you. And he'll have to tell them—including what you called his mother. Just in time for the early editions."

It's like watching the Wolfman transform back into Lon Chaney, Jr. I can see Shannon visibly forcing himself away from the brink.

"Joey? Y'want me to make the call?" Okie asks.

"Just shut the hell up. Where were you when I needed you?" Then to McKenna, "Okay, I see it." Turns to me, "Take a hike, sonny boy."

Dismissing me. Screw him. I stand my ground. Until McKenna intercedes. Politely but curtly. "On your way, Mr. Weaver."

I meet Shannon's piercing eyes. "Any message for Leo?"

"I'll deliver that myself, in my own way."

I start walking away, with O'Connell trailing me like a sheepdog.

"Start packing, asshole," Shannon yells after me. "I'm calling Harry Rains. You won't be working there anymore, or anywhere else in the Industry!"

"Agent McKenna," I toss over my shoulder, "isn't maliciously conspiring to deprive a person of his livelihood a federal offense?"

"Bye, Mr. Weaver."

Okie is ushering me out, and behind me I hear Shannon tell McKenna, "How could Barney Ott let Vardian get so out of control?"

As we reach the front door, Okie whispers to me, "You made a bad enemy."

"Hey, I inherited a lot of those, you lying fink!" I go for my car and drive away. Shaking with fury, not only at Shannon, but also at Leo for using me as his stalking horse.

Leo crows happily, "So David punched out the asshole, Harry!"

There's a celebration in Leo's bungalow office on the Panorama lot and I'm the star. Actually it's a Leo Vardian Production—written and directed by the great joker himself. The audience is small and select but very enthusiastic. Leo is hosting Barney Ott, Jack Heritage, Keeler Barnes, and now Harry Rains, having heard word, has just come speeding over to hear the details in person.

Leo pours a flute of champagne for Harry while urging me to repeat my visit to Joe Shannon. If I neglect a detail Leo jumps in. He's infuriating me.

"Well, Leo, guess you're even now for that lousy item in his column," Harry says as he accepts the brimming glass of bubbly.

"The only even is one-up!" Leo bellows.

"Here's to you, kiddo." Harry raises his champagne in my direction. "Headline: 'Little David Smites Gossip Goliath.'"

"I'll drink to that," Keeler shouts.

"About time somebody crowned that queen," Heritage says.

"Risky, though," Harry Rains points out. "Sending David of all people. It's like waving a red flag in Shannon's face."

"Good lesson for Shannon," Leo says. "Don't screw around with a war hero. Right, David?"

"Harder than nails, that's me," I say flatly. Getting more pissed.

"But the lousy things that swish said about your folks," Keeler muses, "I would've given him a lot more than just a rap in the jaw. I'd've killed the sonuvabitch!"

Leo leaps to my defense. "I think David handled it absolutely right."

"Turned out to be quite a day," Ott holds out his glass for more champagne. "Considering how it started."

"Yeah, maybe we owe Shannon a vote of thanks," Heritage says. "He put a burr under your saddle, Leo. But you are a clutch hitter. Great work!"

"I'll definitely drink to *that*!" Harry Rains says.

What they're talking about is that, for a change, Leo finished the day's work on schedule. It suddenly occurs to me that maybe that's really what they're all celebrating.

I dart a look at Leo and I can see the same thought in his eyes. He glances at his watch.

"Well, sorry to give you guys the bum's rush, but it's back to the grindstone for us working stiffs. Gotta go look at dailies and spend some time in the cutting room."

"You guys happy with how it's coming together?" Ott asks. So casually.

"Gold," Keeler says. "Solid gold."

"Any chance we can get a peek at some cut footage?"

"Barney, I want to keep you a virgin 'til the first preview," Leo says, "so I can get a pure reaction from you." They both know that's what Leo's contract specifies. No second-guessing until then.

"A man could die of curiosity, waiting." Ott smiles.

"Boys, boys," Harry Rains intercedes, "let's be on our way. We don't want to distract the genius from his appointed rounds."

"Yeah, thanks for stopping by. Stay, finish the champagne. C'mon, guys." Leo gestures for Keeler and me to follow him.

"The kid gets to see the cut footage, but we don't, huh?" Heritage reflects.

"David is family," Leo tosses back.

"Family," Ott repeats. "That's what I want to be in my next lifetime."

And we're out the door. Leaving them behind.

As we walk to the screening room, Leo complains: "Party-poopers. Those three could spoil a wet dream."

I can't hold back any longer. "Leo, next time I become your designated hitter, let me in on the gag first."

Leo's eyes darken, as they always do at even the vaguest hint of criticism. So now he's definitely about to blast off. Keeler stands clear. Then Leo softens. "You're right. Sorry if I hung you out."

Keeler looks astonished. I am, too. I didn't know the word sorry was part of Leo's vocabulary.

Before Keeler can signal the projectionist to start dailies, Leo makes a phone call to Army Archerd, Shannon's competitor at *Variety*, and jovially briefs him.

"Here's a guy who's been dumping a load of horseshit on the town every morning," Leo concludes, "so I figured he'd appreciate a hot new supply."

Next morning the most discussed item in Archerd's column is:

". . . Gift season galloped off to an early start yesterday for Joe Shannon, on the receiving end of a box of unexpected bon-bons from his biggest fan, Leo Vardian. Ask Leo's assistant,

David Weaver, son of Teddy W., just how excited Joe was to be remembered. . . ."

The following morning Shannon runs an item in his own column:

". . . Memo to Leo Vardian: thanks for the forget-me-nots. Owe you one . . ."

I figure that's it and the Hollywood gossip mill will move on. Although I still recall the look in Shannon's eyes when he promised to respond in his own time and in his own way.

21

DAVID

We're back in the jungle. Hot and humid as ever. This morning we shot the scene where Ernie Borgnine dies in Chuck Heston's arms after a Mau Mau ambush. It brought tears to most of the crew, even the hard-case teamsters. Shows you what fine actors can do to bring life to a basically cornball moment. I see the gloating look on Leo's face as he calls "Cut!" And then, of course, he spoils it for everybody by screaming at Tommy the prop man, usually one of his pets, for some nonsensical oversight.

The next scene is the final shot in the movie. Not the last one on our schedule, we've still got weeks to go, the studio brass still constantly climbing all over Leo's ass about slipping further and further behind schedule. But this is going to be the fade-out image of the movie. Heston, standing bloody but unbowed, on the ridge of a rock escarpment. The camera will start close on his sweaty face, then pull up and up into a very wide downward view of his figure—a musket-like Sharps rifle clutched in Heston's triumphant upraised hand.

Bob Surtees, our cameraman, has won Oscars, which is why Leo hired him, but Leo insists on initially riding the camera alone and setting up each shot for him. Then he lets Surtees go to work. It's the cumbersome way Leo has of communicating his vision. Now he walks toward the bulky Mitchell camera fixed on a huge Chapman crane that will provide the sweep and height necessary.

"C'mon, David," he says, "take a ride with me."

Leo gets behind the camera, I take the focus puller's bucket seat beside him. Leo signals to the crane operator and we move slowly upward. Heston's stand-in is on the rock, holding up the rifle. Leo squints through the eyepiece, waving occasionally to the crane operator to go faster or slower, while he twirls the handles on the camera. A kid with his favorite toy.

Beneath my dangling feet the view spreads until we're nearly seventy feet high. I can see the entire soundstage below, our weird man-made jungle, all our equipment, the crew rushing around. From up here they look like a tribe of ants. Leo signals for us to stop in midair. He looks down with me.

"Behold," he intones, "my kingdom."

I laugh. "Is that what being a director feels like?"

"It's what being God feels like." He waves expansively.

"The great God Jehovah," I add, "the one given to smiting."

"You mean Tommy Props? This is our third picture together. He's used to my shit."

Like Keeler, I think. But this is the friendly Leo. We haven't talked about anything except work in days. Nothing personal. No time. And I realize that's why he's brought me up here.

"So how's it going with you and Jana?"

"Couldn't be better," I lie. Although she's spending most of her time at my place, she's still at Leo's beck and call on Stone Canyon.

"Glad to hear it," he says. "Thanks for being so understanding about letting her keep my home fires burning a little longer. Once we wrap up this sucker"—he gestures at his kingdom—"we can get on with real life."

We both know that's just chatter. *This* is Leo's real life.

"Are you guys figuring on a big wedding? I'll be glad to

foot the bills. Father of the bride and all that. We could do it at the house, if you like."

"Actually, we're talking about something sort of small."

"Whatever you say. I just thought it'd be fun to show off in front of the whole town. Hey, I could buy you a house instead. Wedding present."

How do I tell him? "I think we'll hold off until we can afford to buy one on our own."

"That's what I like about you, David, you work hard and smart for what you want. You've got a real future in this business. I can see it, man, after our next picture you'll be ready to be an associate producer and—"

"What do they do?"

He shrugs. "They associate with the producer, but at a much better salary."

"The Son-In-Law Also Rises?"

"There's no harm in accepting a helping hand along the way."

I'm not so sure of that. Leo gave me a job when I really needed it. But I don't want to owe him any more than I have to. Don't know if that's stubbornness, macho pride, or self-defense. But a career working for him? Like Keeler? Like Tommy Props?

"The sky could be the limit," Leo promises.

The AD calls us on the walkie-talkie. Heston is in full makeup and on his way into position on the top of the rock. Leo signals and the crane lowers. In a moment we're back on the ground.

CHAPTER

22

JANA

It's Saturday night, and David and I are in my car, and I'm driving to a party in Silver Lake, the artsy neighborhood up in the hills next to Hollywood. It's our first full-on public appearance as a couple at a social gathering. It's a birthday bash for Carol Snyder. She's turning thirty. She's petite, freckled, and funny, a buoyant upper who's recently become a studio pal.

She's a script girl, just winding up on the Fred Astaire musical. It's a super-responsible job, keeping a meticulous record of what happens in front of the camera. Good script girls are treasured by the top directors. Funny, no matter how old they are, nobody ever refers to them as script women.

I expect the crowd will be young below-the-line film workers, similar to us. Production people, camera, sound, and electrical crew members. Not the glamorous above-the-line types who inhabit my father's world. The "line" refers to the itemized studio budget for a movie. Stars, director, producer, and writer are listed above-the-line—where the big bucks go. Everyone else is below. It's the Hollywood caste system.

On the drive over, David and I are discussing the screenplay he's been writing. It is loosely based on Lew Ayres, the movie star who played the last soldier killed in World War I in *All Quiet on the Western Front*, the kid who reached out for a butterfly and was picked off by a sniper. When World War II started, Lew Ayres was drafted but declared himself a conscientious objector. It caused a big time scandal, all the stay-in-L.A. superpatriots called him a coward. But he became an Army medic, like David was in Korea. Ayres landed on some of the bloodiest South Pacific beachheads and came home to Hollywood with all sins forgiven.

Despite the violence of war, the screenplay is sweet, gentle, and decent. Just like David. I told him I loved it and gingerly gave him ideas for several minor improvements; he said they were great. Our first experience working together. He knows my dream is to direct. We decide that's what we'll do: he'll write 'em, I'll direct 'em. We'll produce 'em together. Weaver & Vardian Redux.

We park up the street from Carol's bungalow. It's a cozy little white two-bedroomer cantilevered over a steep canyon. The party is already in full swing. Parked cars jam the narrow winding street. People sip drinks and chitchat on the lawn. Rock 'n' roll blares from inside the house. Elvis mostly. I don't know that many of the guests, but recognize faces from around the lot. As we walk up, several heads turn to look our way. At me? Because I'm the daughter of a hot shit director? Jeez, I hope not.

Rowan Lundy, my boss in Research, greets us. He's forty-one, one of the elders tonight. Tightly trimmed mustache, a courtly, bookish man, in tweeds and horn-rimmed glasses, wearing the only necktie in sight. And it's a bowtie. He looks like the chaperone at the school dance.

"You're a celebrity," Rowan says, raising his glass of Cabernet in salute. But he's talking to David. They've met briefly at the office. He nods at the partygoers staring at us. "They're all stoked to see the guy who made the special delivery to Joe Shannon." Then he looks past us. "Hey, here's the birthday girl! You look like a Dale Evans impersonator."

Carol Snyder, our hostess, is definitely dressed like the queen of the cowgirls. Flat-topped Stetson, red checkered shirt, buckskin vest, denims, and alligator boots. A preview of her next gig. She'll be going to Durango soon to work on a Burt Lancaster oater. We hug and she shakes David's hand when I introduce him. I've been gushing to her for weeks about him. One of my few confidantes.

"Heard a lot of nice stuff about you," he says.

"Same here," she grins. I can see they instantly like each other. I relax a bit. I want this party to go smoothly for David.

While Carol greets other arrivals, we elbow our way inside to the crowded bar. An attractive frosted blonde who works in studio accounting is acting as bartender. We snag a couple of white wines and retreat to a corner near the entrance.

We're hardly settled before three unfamiliar guys plow through. I get a strong whiff of booze. The leader of the pack jostles me, spilling some of my drink.

"Hey, watch it!" David grumbles after them, but I tug at his sleeve. Assure him it's no problem.

But there's one developing. At the bar, the trio cut to the head of the line, demanding service. "Screw wine, got any beer?" the leader yells. They all have menacing scowls, tight-fitting black T-shirts, and thick necks.

The barmaid produces beers for them and the leader whispers something lewd in her ear. Angrily she pushes him away. He just laughs and the trio clink beer cans.

David murmurs, "Did Carol invite storm troopers?"

I shrug it off. They're probably just brawny cable pullers from another studio. Someone near us speculates they're party crashers. We go back out onto the lawn and get into a conversation with Charlie Hix, a young camera loader on Leo's movie. Suddenly there is a crashing sound from inside the house. We see Rowan tumble down the front steps. He's pursued by the leader of the gate crashers, who yells. "Gonna kill you, y'faggoty old fart!"

He overtakes Rowan and pushes him viciously. Rowan falls headlong and skids on the grass. His horn-rim glasses go flying. The gate crasher looms over Rowan. "Where do you get off? So hoity-toity, telling us we gotta leave! Who the fuck are you?" He jabs Rowan's side with his pointy boot.

Everyone is frozen. Except David. He walks over and scoops up Rowan's glasses.

"What the hell y'think you're doin'?" the gate crasher demands.

"Just cooling things down a little," David says.

The other two crashers close ranks behind their leader. I'm doubly scared now, for Rowan and David. But David ignores the trio and offers Rowan his glasses, then tugs him up onto his feet, dusts him off. Behind him the leader is red-faced with rage.

"He your girlfriend, butch? Gonna stand up for him, are ya? Do the fairy's fightin' for him?"

Frantically I look around, but nobody is about to help. Doesn't David see the danger? All three are going to jump him in a second. "David!" I cry out in warning and take a step forward, but it's too late.

The big one behind him locks David's arms, setting him up for the leader, who rushes in, aiming a huge fist at David's face—and then a remarkable thing happens. David flips the guy behind him forward in the air to collide with the oncoming leader. While the fallen assholes fall in a heap, David pushes Rowan out of the combat zone, just as the third gate crasher is about to blindside him. Sensing him, more than seeing him, David smashes an elbow back into the man's gut. And he goes down. But the other two are up again and converging like enraged bulls.

And at the vortex is David, face expressionless, his eyes appear almost glazed, intent only on the battle. Seeing nothing but his next move and three moves beyond that. It's like watching the stuntmen staging a barroom brawl. But this is bone-crunching reality. Someone is screaming. I realize it's me. Then I'm rendered silent by what I see. David's body starts to sway methodically, side-to-side like a metronome, as though he were stoking a fire within himself. I'm watching a dance. A dance of destruction. Choreographed to inflict pain. They repeatedly attack him, but David counters their blows, leverages their momentum against them. Everything moves so fast it's a blur. Arms and legs flailing and I expect to see limbs torn off and flying at us.

I started out terrified they'd hospitalize him, now I'm scared he may kill them. He slams the leader against the side of the porch and when the thuggish boor tries to get up his right leg folds. He starts to crumple, but David grabs the front of his T-shirt and holds him up as he draws back a fist, about to deliver a hammer blow, when I yell, "Dayviddd! *Enough!*"

Just then we all hear the sound of an approaching siren. Now everyone is on the move. The gate crashers hoist up their leader, whose leg won't support any weight, and half-carry him off. Car engines are starting, drivers gunning away, as Rowan steps up beside me. He's wearing his glasses again, but they're off-kilter. "You okay?" I ask. He nods. David joins us.

"Thanks," Rowan says.

"Did he break your glasses?"

"Just mangled one of the stems. It's bent all out of shape." He smiles at David. "But not as bad as that crasher."

David just nods. He's still a little out of breath, and still looks slightly glazed. I'm still upset and confused at what I've just seen. Who was that automaton, that killing machine I just saw in action? I don't even know that person.

David and I wait with Carol and Rowan until the cops arrive. It's routine for them, just another party in the hills that got wild. They jot down the particulars, including our names and addresses. No one has a clue as to who the intruders were.

Then I'm driving us back to the Chateau. We travel down the hill for a while in silence, until David softly asks: "Did I scare you before?"

We're still able to read each other. "Yeah, kinda—it reminded me of what happened to Wendy. I mean, I appreciate your helping Rowan. It was very brave of you. And that martial arts routine. Wow!" No response. So I add, "You're very good at that stuff."

"I was taught by the best."

"When it was happening, I—didn't know if you could see me or hear me—or anyone. It was as if you were in a world of your own. Where nothing could reach you."

"That's where you have to go. To make it." This is upsetting territory for him. He gropes for words. "I wasn't out of control, Jana. Not really. I wasn't. Oh, maybe for a second here and there, but—please, don't worry, see it used to be an issue, but I've got a handle on it." He squeezes my shoulder, but I keep my eyes on the dark road illuminated only by my headlights. "Hey, inside it's still the guy you grew up with. It's me. Honest."

I dart a glance at him, I see the little boy face I know so well. But I know if I don't keep gripping the wheel my hands will be shaking. I drive down the twisting road. Trying to understand what these last years have done to him. To both of us, I guess.

23

MCKENNA

I'm at my desk at home writing checks for the monthly bills, looking forward to a Sunday afternoon backyard barbecue with Kathleen and the boys at their house, when the phone rings. I hear my nephew Donnie's voice. But he sounds very shaky. He tells me this is the one phone call they're allowing him to make.

The main office of the Santa Monica police department, including the jail, is located behind City Hall. I'm alone, waiting in a holding area, as the air lock on the reinforced inner door hisses and slides open. A jailer brings Donnie out. My heart aches to see him. He looks so scared. No color at all in his cheeks.

When he sees me the lights go back on in his eyes. I see his urge is to run and grab my waist the way he used to do whenever I arrived at his house when he was little. Now he's a teenager and too old for that, and too frightened to make any sudden moves. But the jailer gently prods him forward. Donnie walks to me. He doesn't know what to do in these circumstances, so he just stops in front of me.

"Hey, Donnie," I say softly.

He looks up at me, glances back at the jailer. Then, awk-wardly, trying to act grown up, he holds out his hand as if to shake mine. I take his hand and use it to pull him close. I hug him tight and he hugs back.

"Let's go home," I say.

I didn't really want to go riding with them," he's telling me, "I just wanted to play basketball."

We're driving north in my Mustang over the Sepulveda Pass into the Valley. Donnie is telling his story as if it's a Shake-spearean tragedy, rather than a dumbass teenage caper, but I'm not about to let him off the hook. I've already heard it all from the station captain, who, as luck would have it, I'd previously worked with on a kidnapping case with a happy result. I'm silently pleased that Donnie's details match up with the cap-tain's account. I've always trusted him to tell me the truth and I want it to stay that way.

What they both agree on is that the Ford sedan that Don-nie and his two older pals, Glenn and Thom, were riding in belongs to Glenn's parents. This morning they let Glenn drive to the schoolyard to play ball and pick up groceries at the supermarket on the way back. Instead, he took Donnie and the other kid for a joyride that ended with the car up to its hubcaps in the sand on the Santa Monica beach. A lifeguard called a tow truck, a cop car happened by to watch and josh the kids. Until one of the cops noticed the half-drunk bottle of bourbon on the backseat floor.

"They're good guys," Donnie says about these two prize-winners he's been hanging out with, "despite what Mom says,"

"Yeah, great. Look where they got you."

"We were celebrating. Glenn just passed his driver's test.

And when I climbed in the car I thought we were only going a
few blocks."

"Doesn't your mom have a rule about you never riding
with new drivers?" He nods, shamefaced. "But you figured
she'd never know. That's not only bad judgment, but flat out
sneaky."

"I know, I'm real sorry."

"Where'd the booze come from?"

"Thom's dad's liquor cabinet. But I just pretended to be
swallowing, so they wouldn't think I was a geek."

"You swallowed enough for it to register on the Breatha-
lyzer."

"Didn't the cop say it was under the level of—"

"You're all under age, Donnie, *any*thing is too much. Particularly in a car. It's a crime called Driving Under the Influ-
ence."

He nods abjectly. "I know, I'll never do it again." Then he
asks, "Do we have to tell Mom?"

"We sure as hell do," I tell him.

Now we're in the manicured backyard of their small Sherman Oaks house. Kathleen's rose bushes are flourishing;
gardening is her way of blowing off steam that builds up on
her job. Usually I'm in charge of the Sunday barbecue. But
today, kid brother, Patrick, who's out of earshot, is doing the
honors. My sister, looking stern as the judges she faces all
week long as a public defender, and I are sitting on the back
steps, while Donnie tells his mother everything.

When he finishes, Donnie and I both wait for Kathleen's
reaction. She gazes at her elder son's misery, then finally says,
"Go help your brother with the barbecue. We'll talk later."

Slump-shouldered, he walks off. Kathleen is looking after

him, so I can't see her face. "I think he's real sorry. I gave him what-for on the ride here. Swears he'll never do it again."

She turns to look at me. I know *that* look. It's scary.

"Did you put up bail for him?" she asks. Keeping her voice low.

"Turns out, it wasn't necessary."

"Because?"

"The captain's an old pal. And Donnie wasn't driving, the kids all agreed on that."

"So you went to the Favor Bank and Donnie walks?"

"It's not a federal offense, Kath."

"It took a federal officer to get it swept under the rug."

I'm on the hot seat and I do not like it. Got to try and put the proper slant on this. "Would you rather have your son sitting behind bars?"

"You had no right to do what you did! He reached out for you, ahead of me, and I can see why. Uncle Brian's got clout, he'll fix it for me."

"C'mon, he's just a kid. Kids make mistakes."

"Hopefully they learn from their mistakes. What you taught him is, when the going gets tough, you'll weigh in with your heavy badge and make it all go away. That's not a lesson I want him to learn."

"Rather have him go through the lousy justice system instead?" That ought to shut her up, but her response is instantaneous:

"Yes, as his mother, that's exactly what I would have wanted. Actions have consequences. I don't want him to think there are shortcuts if you've got a G-man in the family."

"I think you're overreacting, Sis. You should have seen his face when the jailer brought him out. He was scared shitless."

"Good! He should be. You should have bailed him out and let it go at that. It's what I would have done. It's what I want you to do now. Call that pal of yours and tell him not to wipe it all off the police blotter. We'll guarantee bail and produce Donnie in court."

"Kath, aren't you being a little too severe—and maybe a bit vengeful just 'cuz he called me instead of you?"

"Keep it up, Brian, and you're not gonna get any barbecue today. This is very important to me."

"That'll mean Donnie has a police record and—"

"He's got a good lawyer. Me. He's never been in trouble before. So he'll get probation—"

"—and it'll be a blot on his record!"

"Until he's eighteen. Then juvie records are sealed. I think it's an important lesson."

"What lesson is that, exactly, I'd like to hear."

"To thine own self be true."

I snort. "Don't go quoting Shakespeare. What's that got to do with Donnie?"

"Everything!" She gestures over at Donnie. "He just said he knew better when those big boys talked him into getting in the car. But he didn't want to look bad in front of them. Then they started passing the booze around. Again, can't let himself look bad, so maybe just a little. He sold himself out, and you enabled him to wiggle away. In my book, that's a big deal."

I don't have an answer. I realize she's right. And she sees that she got through to me.

"It's an important life lesson," she says. "One we all have to learn sooner or later, right? C'mon, those burgers must be done by now."

Happily, we have a terrific barbecue. That's one of the things I love about my sister. When something's over, it's over. On the trip back to my place, I start thinking ahead to how my life can work if I manage to get the D.C. job. Got to stay close with her and the boys. Well, I can catch rides on the Military Air Transport Service and fly out here, and she and the kids can visit me back there. Won't that be a kick!

24

DAVID

It's Monday morning again, start of another work week. Yesterday Jana and I slept away most of the day, then we went to see a festival of Chaplin shorts at the Silent Movie Theater on Fairfax. It was good to laugh together and unwind. She went home to Stone Canyon last night, and now I'm rolling down to Schwab's for breakfast. I stop at the newsstand. Lead story in the *Times* reports U.S. citizenship has been returned to five thousand Japanese-Americans who lost it during World War II. Nineteen years after the internment camp gates opened at Manzanar. Better late than never. I buy the paper and the trades and take my usual counter stool.

Mary Hanlon, my favorite waitress, saw me coming and has already toasted a bagel. She delivers it with my coffee and a teasing grin:

"Morning, Casanova," she teases. I'm puzzled. "Joe Shannon's column." Mary points at my unopened *Film Bulletin*. I flip to the second page and this leaps out at me:

"... Ain't Love Grand Dept.: Leo ("The Fastest Director Alive") Vardian's daughter Jana is skulking around town with Leo's sleazy scut-boy, David Weaver, son of the late, unlamented Scumunist Teddy Weaver. What do the Young Lovers do for pillow talk? Probably reminisce about how her Daddy blew the whistle on his Daddy during Leo's behind-closed-doors executive session with HUAC nine years ago . . ."

So I sit there just staring. Even the dead aren't safe. Teddy's getting ripped apart again. Feels as if a javelin has been plunged into my chest. This is Shannon's revenge. Probably with a data assist from McKenna. Shannon is too cagy about libel laws to print this crap unless it's true. Snickering to the whole town what is agony to me. But Shannon is only the torturer. It was Leo! We had always blamed Okie and director Eddie Dmytryk, who both named Teddy in public session. But Leo came first. Teddy would have died before he betrayed Leo, but Leo sold Teddy out so he could make more movies! God damn Leo!

"Can I warm up that coffee for you?" Mary Hanlon asks. I shake my head. Drop some bucks on the counter and head for the pay phones. Dial the studio, ask for our set. The second AD answers.

"Steve," I say, "it's David. Won't be in today. Tell Leo . . . I'm sick." Partial truth. "No, tell Leo—I quit." That's better. "Wait, while you're at it, tell Leo—tell him he can go fuck himself! Unquote. Yeah, that's exactly what I want you to tell him!"

I slam down the phone. There goes the tic in my cheek. What do I do now? I know what I want to do. Go kick the shit out of Leo in front of the entire cast and crew. In front of the whole town. Thousands will cheer. It's an irresistible idea. So I jump into my car and zip toward the studio. I'm fuming. For me and for Jana. And most of all for Teddy and Ellie. I let you both down. Trusted Leo the asshole. Thought it had changed.

I make the turn off Glendale Boulevard and roll toward the main entrance into Panorama. There's a studio parking sticker

on my front bumper and the gate man usually waves and lifts
the steel arm. Not this time. He emerges from his booth.

"Sorry, David, you can't come on the lot."

"Who says?"

"You've been barred. Mr. Vardian's orders."

The black rage roars through me. *"Open the damn gate!"*

He orders me to back up and leave. I stomp out of my car,
leave it blocking the entrance lane. "I'm gonna call Harry
Rains, he'll clear me through!" I grab for the phone on the
gate man's desk and he grabs for me and we scuffle. He must
have pressed an alarm button, because suddenly, in addition
to the honking cars clogged behind mine, three more studio
guards are rushing up and yanking at me. I contain the demon enough to stop short of swinging at them and I let them
push me out. I'm sweating from the struggle at self-control.
Barely managed to stuff the pin back in the live hand grenade.

"Don't blame me," the gate man yells after me, "blame
Leo."

Good advice, but I'm already doing that.

I'm back at Schwab's drinking black coffee and brooding.
I've been phoning Jana constantly, but her office says she's
not there and they don't know where she is. I'm desperate to
talk to her. To someone I can trust. Keeler would be a possible, but he's trapped in Leo's orbit. Don't want to involve him.
Then I think of a person I can turn to. Maybe the only one. I
dig in my wallet and find the business card Peter Zacharias
handed me at Teddy's funeral. I haven't been in touch with
him since that day—and I know why. But today's the day I
reach out to him.

The big bus emblazoned TOUR THE MOVIELAND HOMES lurches to a halt in front of Grauman's Chinese Theatre. The guide is first off and says her cheerful " 'Bye now" to all the descending passengers. Last person off is the driver.

"Wondered when you'd show up," Zacharias says to me.

Dark eyes still needle sharp. But he looks even thinner, if possible, than at Teddy's grave site. I hear no rebuke for my silence during the past weeks. Just a big hug for my reappearance.

"I could say I was just passing by. . . ." I joke, hugging him tightly. He feels almost brittle.

"Who gives a damn why? You're here, that's what's important." Then he studies me. "You in a hurry, Duveed? Come for a ride, no charge, we can talk along the way. About what's bothering you."

I feel like I'm being tossed a life preserver.

Loaded with new tourists, the bus tools up the Strip. The guide is cooing into a microphone as she points out Ciro's and the Trocadero, and then we're in Beverly Hills. I'm seated in the rear, and as we travel all our heads whip back and forth like at a tennis match. "There's Dean Martin's stately Colonial mansion!" Zacharias turns a corner onto Baroda Drive. "Here's Gary Cooper's home; he named his independent production firm Baroda Productions" and we're gawking at the cattle-baron-size ranch house. Another turn and the bus pauses at Alan Ladd's imitation Spanish hacienda, "See the mailbox— it's an exact miniature copy of the house." It's like a world tour of architectural plagiarisms. We park at the vast estate formerly owned by the late silent-screen comedian Harold Lloyd, and everyone goes off to tour the spacious fountain-studded grounds and staggeringly huge house—except me and Zacharias.

We lean against the side of the bus and he offers me a Lucky Strike. I shake my head, he lights up, inhales, coughs, and spits. Just like Teddy used to do. "Okay, tell me, *boychik*."

Where do I start? "You want to hear the best or the worst?"

"Any way you like."

"Best is—Jana and I are together again." He nods approvingly. "And I have, well, I *had* a job in the business. Quit this morning, but—I've been working for Leo." It's an explanation and an apology for why I hadn't called Zacharias. It also feels like a confession that deserves punishment.

But he isn't administering punishment. "You've been busy," he says. Without rancor or reproach. "Save you some time, I still read the trades. I saw Shannon's column this morning."

"Then you know!" And I let it rip. How I came to take the job, hoping that Leo was on the level and wanting to make amends, I wanted to believe that, never knowing, never dreaming that—

Zacharias cuts me off. Mildly but firmly. "Sure you did."

He's broken my litany of righteous anger. "I did what?"

"You knew. You're behaving like Shannon's item about Leo was news to you."

"It was! I knew about the others, of course, but not about Teddy. Leo swore to Teddy just last year in Paris that he didn't give Teddy's name to the Committee."

"Did Teddy believe him?"

"Yeah, he did!" And I describe the meeting at the Ritz Bar.

Zacharias listens stone-faced. "How do y'know Teddy believed Leo?"

I'm getting steamed at Zacharias. "Because Teddy cried when he told me, that's how I know! The only time I ever saw Teddy cry!"

Zacharias reacts to my anger with sadness. "Took a lot to make that man weep. All the years we knew each other—the only time I saw Teddy cry was the day we liberated Dachau."

Now I'm confused. "So what are you saying?"

"Why do you think Teddy was crying in Paris?"

"Well," I'm a tad sarcastic, "maybe because Teddy had just found out his best friend and partner was dying and—"

"—and Leo was *still* lying to Teddy about what he'd done. Even then, one final betrayal." Zacharias takes a drag on his cigarette. "That woulda been enough to make me cry."

That rocks me. Zacharias goes on gently.

"C'mon, Duveed, you're a smart guy. So was Teddy. He could figure things out. Y'think the Committee would squeeze Leo to spill his guts about everyone he knew in the Party and forget to inquire about his own partner? Harry Rains was a smart lawyer, he cut a face-saving deal for Leo: Give us Teddy in executive session, you can leave him out in the public hearing. The Committee would do that. Leo was a prize."

I'm hit with a wave of self-loathing. "Guess I just didn't want to know. Feels like I sold out Teddy. Going to work for Leo."

"Hey, Duveed. You just wanted a job. You wanted to be with Jana. Those are not sins. Piling on with the jackals, like Leo did, helping them tear people you love to pieces—*that's* a sin."

Zacharias is granting me absolution. But I'm not ready to let myself off the hook. Then he asks, "You talk to Jana since this hit the fan?"

"Not yet." And I'm now filled with a new dread. "You think she knew?"

"Guess you're gonna have to ask her."

That's the scary truth. That's what I'm going to have to do. So much is going to depends on her answer. I've been intent on holding back no secrets. Has she? Feels like I'm teetering on the brink again.

25

DAVID

The tour bus drops us all off back at the Chinese Theatre. I ask Zacharias to have a drink with me, but he
has another run to make. We stand on the curb while I
speculate as to what makes Joe Shannon tick.

Zacharias lights another Lucky Strike and spits. "Seems
like this to me: Shannon doesn't want people to think of him
as a homo, which, of course, he is; no problem there as far as
I'm concerned, but he thinks he can mask that by wrapping
himself in Old Glory, and I understand that."

"You making excuses for him?"

"Me? I'm from the club that wishes a bolt of lightning zaps
him. And the sooner the better. He did a bang-up job on me
back when it was my turn to be a fish in the barrel. I'm just
saying I understand what he's all about." Zacharias puffs his
cigarette. "So you assume it's the FBI guy's been tailing you
who provided all the dirt to Shannon?"

"Who else? McKenna was sitting right there with him."

"Well, it wouldn't be the first or last time the Slim Jims
spoon-fed their pals in the press."

The next batch of tourists are starting to board the bus. We
hug again, Zacharias pounds my back. "Let's stay in touch
now, okay?"

I go down the street to have a drink by myself at Musso & Frank. Dark-paneled restaurant and bar. Low lighting, warm buzz of chatter. I take a corner stool at the bar, where an ancient bartender tells customers about the days when William Faulkner and F. Scott Fitzgerald used to get shitfaced here. I brood and talk to no one. Sip my scotch. Try phoning Jana at the studio again. No, she hasn't come back, they still don't know where she is.

So I move on to the next bar along Hollywood Boulevard. No conversation except to order more scotch. I'm wallowing in rage over Leo. Waiting for the booze to fuzz my head so I can stop thinking. Well, can't be done in this bar, they must be serving watered-down hooch. So I continue on. Drinking my way to Cahuenga and then over to Sunset. Searching for Blottoville.

I sway out of a saloon near Sunset and Gower, hey, when did it get to be nighttime? Suddenly I've got that feeling again: someone's watching me! So I bellow into the blackness, "Come out, McKenna, you bastard, come out where I can see you!"

Nobody emerges from the shadows, but I scare an elderly platinum blonde in tight toreador pants and spike heels who's walking her springer spaniel. Her dog barks and she crosses the street to avoid me.

So I hit another joint, and my anger flips back to Joe Shannon. The craven vulture. Without him blaring his phony patriotics and nastiness in that shitty column none of this would have happened. Nah, I reject that—it excuses the real mindfucker in all this: me! Ignoring what's in plain sight. Took Zacharias to force me to see. But I still feel as if going over to Shannon's place and kicking his ass would be a terrific idea! A public service! I chugalug the rest of my drink.

Then I stagger out and go looking for my car, but can't find it. Later on I wake up in my car, so I guess I did find it, and I'm parked near a saloon on Western Avenue and there's a grease stain on my jacket and the right shoulder is torn. The knuckles on my right hand are bruised, don't ask me why. I'm drunk as a skunk.

Exercising extreme caution, I drive up Fountain Avenue, where traffic is lighter than on the main drags and less likely to be patrolled by the cops. I make it into the parking lot under the Chateau. As I cross the deserted lobby, the nosy young night clerk at the desk hails me. The clock behind him reads 2:20 A.M.

"You've got messages." He hands me a sheaf of the little slips. They're pink. Same color as HUAC subpoenas. I flip through. Harry Rains's office called, Mr. Rains wants to see Mr. Weaver at his house at 8:30 for breakfast. Probably wants to ream me for upsetting Leo, the fork-tongued Judas. All the other messages are from Jana. I shove them in my jacket pocket, notice the flap is torn, too. Rigidly upright to impress the clerk with how sober I am, I wend toward my room.

In front of my door Jana is hunkered down, hugging her knees, fast asleep. I look down at her. She senses someone's there and stirs, lifts her head, blinks, and I smile and she smiles back, because for a moment we've both forgotten what's happened.

"Hey," I say. I hold out a hand, she takes it, pulls herself to her feet.

"I was so worried," she says. "Since I saw the item in the paper this morning. I called the set, they said you quit. The gate man told me they chased you away. So I went looking for you everywhere, down at our spot on the beach, Dolores coffee shop, everywhere and—"

"Well, now y'found me." I say with a sheepish grin. "Went for a bus ride with good ol' Zacharias."

"You're drunk," she says.

"Pretty much."

Jana takes the room key from my hand, unlocks the door, and guides me inside. Helps me out of my clothes, then propels me into the shower, puts it on full blast, and leaves me there a while. Then she turns off the water and dries me. Such gentleness in the way she touches me. Mustn't forget: we've got each other. Despite Leo.

While she rubs me with the thick warm towel, I mumble: "Good ol' Zacharias, Leo used to say he was maybe the best writer in Hollywood, he's driving a crappy tour bus now."

"It's a lie!" she answers my unspoken question. "Leo swore to me! He didn't give Teddy's name! He didn't do that to Teddy!"

"Yeah, he did. We always knew, jus' didn't wanna know. Tha's what Zacharias says."

She stares at me as if I've hit her between the eyes. Then she shepherds me into my bed and tucks me in. She lies down, still clothed, on top of the blanket, beside me. Later on, it's still dark, but I wake up with a jolt and she's still there. Her eyes are wide open, staring at the ceiling. She kisses my cheek and says, "Shhhhhh, go back to sleep," and so I do.

26

McKENNA

I'm fast asleep when my phone rings. Groggy, I hear Willie Pierson's voice. "Mac, sorry to rouse you."

"So why're you doin' it?" The luminous dial on my wristwatch on the nightstand reads 3:17 A.M.

"I'm at the office, got lobster shift. The police scanner's on—"

"Willie, is there a point to this?"

"I don't know for sure. But—there's been a fire. In that house you were telling me about. The one where that fairy gossip columnist got decked, and—they think somebody's dead."

"Who?"

"Didn't say on the scanner, but—thought you might want to know."

"Thanks, kid, I'll check it out in the morning."

I hang up, pull the quilt up to my ears, ready to go back to sleep. But the call stays in my head. Somebody's dead. Okie O'Connell sleeps there. Is he dead? Cop instinct kicks in. Maybe this won't keep until morning. I switch on the lamp and get dressed. The last thing I do is strap on my watch. It has a wide leather band to conceal the ugly scar on my wrist. A childhood forget-me-not from my stepfather.

When I turn my Mustang into Ramona Court, I'm stunned. It looks like a V-2 rocket scored a direct hit on Joe Shannon's cottage. It's a pile of charred beams and water-logged debris. No flames, but two fire engines on scene. Smoke still rising in the air as the firefighters coil their hoses. A pair of them are still poking through the wreckage with picks and shovels. Parked near the engines there is the usual clutter of cop cars, marked and unmarked. Residents of the street, in bathrobes and slippers, gawk behind the police barriers in the gloom.

I park and push through the neighbors and flash my ID for the blue uniform at the barrier. But my ID doesn't work its usual magic. The uniform on guard shakes his head, no one told him I was coming. I insist he let me through, but he's stonewalling. Then I hear a loud testy voice:

"McKenna, who the hell needs you?"

Ray Alcalay stomps up, his gold LAPD lieutenant's badge pinned to the lapel of a navy-blue blazer, gray slacks tucked into klutzy knee-high wading boots. Tall, barrel-chested guy. Since I saw him last he's graduated to shopping at the Big Man's Store. Used to be stocky, now he's expanded to portly. Few years older than me, maybe fifty, with a hawkish, squinty-eyed face like the Indian on the old nickel. With the extra weight he reminds me of someone else, but I can't make the connection yet. Alcalay is star homicide, so this is not an accidental death case.

"Hey, Ray," I say, "long time."

"He okay, Lieutenant?" the copper asks. "You said not to let anybody through."

"Nah, he's not okay. But let him through anyway."

In the movies, that's how big lugs talk when they really like each other. Not this time. Alcalay genuinely hates my guts. I don't blame him. I wish it was some other investigator out here tonight.

I slip inside the barrier and advance a few steps, but Alcalay blocks my way. "Okay, Agent McKenna, state your business."

"Just wanted to help out if I can. Heard the call on the
scanner and—"

"—decided to jump out of your jammies and rush here.
Whattaguy!"

"I knew the stiff real well, Okie was a weird guy, but—"

"Hey, don't tell me, tell him."

He gestures toward a police car a distance away where
Okie O'Connell, his snazzy but outdated Sy Devore suit rum-
pled but not smudged, is gabbing with two detectives. One of
them nudges Okie, who makes to rush over, but the detectives
keep him there. So he yells:

"Hey, Mac—you saw it! When that Weaver kid belted
Joey. Left him with a shiner, lookin' look like a Disney rac-
coon."

I turn to Alcalay in confusion. "So who got clipped?"

"Joe Shannon. Another friend of yours, right?"

"Shannon was a contact," I say carefully.

"You don't seem broken up to lose him."

"We shared common interests a few years back. But a
mean bastard."

"For instance?"

Now a chance to demonstrate my insider credentials. "This
place was Shannon's office." Alcalay shrugs, he knows that.
"But once I went to his house for a Christmas party, a show-
case near Jack Warner's in Beverly Hills. I hadn't been there
before, so Shannon took me around. We came to the den, you
could hardly get in, it was piled *that* high with holiday gifts
from the studios and the stars. He told me, 'See the power of
fear?'"

Alcalay smiles. Thin and cold. "Hey, McKenna, a lot of
people think that's what *you* do for a living."

I let that one go by. He pats my shoulder. "Well, thanks for the dishy anecdote and for stopping by and verifying Okie's tale about this guy Weaver clocking Shannon. See ya around."

He starts walking away. The fucker's dismissing me. I can't let him do that! Because, like a thunderbolt, I know, I just *know* this is the case I've been hoping for. So I start to follow him, but the blue uniform's got my arm, yanking me back toward the barrier. "C'mon, Ray, cut the shit!"

Alcalay stops and looks back. Rubber-gloved hands on his hips. "Whadayawant, Feeb?" That's sneering cop slang for FBI "Want me to invite you into my life so you can screw me over *again*?"

The uniform is smothering a grin.

"Let's just talk, huh?" I say. "Privately. Two minutes. C'mon, Ray, you can spare two minutes."

Alcalay mulls, then nods at the uniform to let me loose. Alcalay and I walk behind one of the fire engines. No one else near us. He tells me, "You've got no jurisdiction here, Mc-Kenna."

"Unless you invite me in to consult."

"I'd sooner bite my balls off." Again, there is a resemblance to someone else, but who? He glances at his watch. "Y'got two minutes. Go."

"It's simple. You need me. This is a Hollywood homicide. I know all these players, you don't. I can save you time, put you onto leads, keep you from going off on wild goose chases, I know what skeletons are hidden in which closet. We can work together."

He peers at me with loathing. "Like the last time?"

What happened then was a sexy supermodel-turned-actress disappeared. LAPD began investigating, but I strong-armed my way in—kidnapping is classic FBI territory, and there were headlines to be had. So we made Alcalay suck hind tit. Grabbed all the cop data and made errand boys out of them.

Until I got a whiff that it was a put-up job. Not a lovely damsel in distress, but a panicky bitch and her manager seeking media attention to juice up her career. I told D.C. the score and suggested we update LAPD. Instead, Hoover instructed me to tell them nothing and back off. Orders from headquarters. When the thing blew up the Bureau's skirts were clean and LAPD looked like a bunch of idiots.

"It won't be like the last time," I say.

"Or the time before that?" He means the Sammy Davis thing. "Go home and go back to sleep. You're not sliming your way in here." Taps his watch. "Time's up."

He's ready to go off again. "Ray, listen—" I grab his sleeve. He shakes me off like I'm a leper. "I'm asking you *please*. Man to man. You gotta let me in." I can hear the desperation in my voice. So can he.

He stares at me. Appraising. "Means that much to you?"

"Yeah, it does."

He considers, then reluctantly: "Okay, who knows, you might be useful. Stranger things have happened."

"Thanks," I say. "You won't regret it. I owe you one."

"But just one itsy-bit of Bureau bullshit and you're gone."

"Deal," I say. And I mean it.

We're walking toward what used to be the house. He's bringing me up to speed. "First thought was a malfunction of the floor furnace heating system, those sumbitches oughta be outlawed, looked like the pilot light blew out, fumes filled the place, somebody lit a cigarette, and boom."

"Yeah, but?"

"But that was before the fire guys found the remnants of a tote can of car gas. They figure the place was doused and then torched. With the owner and proprietor inside."

"Only Shannon?"

"So far as we know. And he was pretty crisp when they dug him out."

"Maybe it wasn't him."

"Save it for your TV show. It's him. Wearing the jewelry. And we already woke up his dentist, got hold of Shannon's records. We have to be sure on this one." Then he adds, "Shannon's head was crushed like an eggshell. Not from a falling beam. Blunt force trauma. Killer beat him with a hammer or something. Real vicious shit. Someome had a real hate on."

"Joe tended to inspire those kinds of feelings."

Okie falls in step with us. Arm around my shoulder. "Glad you're here, cousin."

Alcalay says, "We been asking Okie if Shannon had any enemies—"

"—and I said," Okie reports, "only enough to fill the Rose Bowl. But the Weaver kid, he's the latest member of the fan club."

Alcalay asks me, "You think this Weaver's a top possible?"

"I'd sure talk to him, but—the kid won that round, so why would he come back for more?"

Okie offers, "Well, maybe 'cuz Joey tore him a new one in the column yesterday. Kremlin-loving creep."

I offer Okie a bleak smile. "You auditioning for Joe's job?"

"Big boots to fill, but somebody's gonna have to do it." Pure Okie, the crafty survivor. "Hey, look, I'm not sayin' Teddy's boy done it—'cuz I keep telling the lieutenant that I think the real target was *me*! I mean, I sleep here, Joey don't, and then there's the sign!"

"What sign?"

Gesturing for Okie to stay here, Alcalay leads me to the evidence truck. He brings out a glassine envelope with an 8x10 piece of white cardboard inside. There's a smudge at the top of the card, but I'm struck by the two words block printed large in black ink:

THE INFORMER

The sign takes my breath away. I cough into my hand to conceal my excitement. My instinct has paid off. The sign escalates a tacky local murder into a sensational crime against the Blacklist. Guaranteed to rivet Hoover's attention. I'm thrilled I talked my way in.

"It was hanging on the mailbox at the curb," Alcalay says. "What's your slant?"

"Title of a classic movie. Dublin in the thirties during the Troubles. Big dumb lummox sells out a pal who's in the IRA They find out and kill him. Very Irish. Victor McLaglen won the Oscar," I say. "But that title left here has a brand new meaning."

"Shannon one of your local helpers?" Alcalay asks.

"We fed him information from time to time. And vice versa."

"So he gave back, huh? Like an informer."

Okie has edged closer. "Hey, that sign don't refer to Joey. That's me, tell him, Mac, that's *me*."

"He's the World Champion Snitch," I agree. "Okie, if you were the target how come you're still here? Why weren't you sleeping in there?"

"Just lucky, I guess, cousin. I was out at a screening on the Columbia lot of the new Liz Taylor picture. The one where the Spanish kids cannibalize *her* cousin. That gave the preview crowd a real appetite." He hee-haws. "Big studio party afterwards at the Vine Street Derby. I stayed late trolling for items."

"So you saw lots of people and lots of people saw you."

"Hey, if I'm lyin' I'm dyin'—I partied out and then came home and saw the blaze. The neighbors had already called it in." He waves dramatically at the burnout. "Everything I owned in the world, up in smoke, all my clothes 'cept what I'm wearing."

"Why was Joe here so late?" I say. "Doesn't he wrap up the column by early evening?"

"Polishing his book, he's been doin' that a couple nights a week. How come all the questions for me, Mac?"

"Just want to make sure you're in the clear."

"Appreciate the concern, cousin." A tight toothy smile.

"Hey, Lieutenant—!" one of the firemen calls from the debris.

"On my way," Alcalay yells back. "C'mon, McKenna."

We make our way to where the firefighter is pointing at a section of scorched floorboard with a soot-covered metal box bolted to it. It's a closet safe, combination dial on the door. "The box is melted around the edges," the firefighter says. "We can get a torch and try to pop it."

"Handle with care," I murmur to Alcalay.

"Just cut it loose," Alcalay says to the fireman, "load it on the evidence truck. We'll send it downtown to the Lab boys."

Alcalay and I step back as the fireman starts working with his bolt cutters. Okie O'Connell shouts from the sidelines. "That's Joey's goody box."

"What do you think's inside?" Alcalay yells back.

"Who knows? The dark and dirty about the high and mighty."

Softly, so our voices won't carry, Alcalay asks me, "What's your reading on O'Connell?"

"A good ol' boy with a heart full of venom."

"He's got an alibi."

"I've been to those after-the-screening bashes. Everybody's so into boozing and schmoozing that you could walk out and come back later and nobody'd notice. I'd keep him on the list."

"Think he'd knock off a guy just to inherit his gossip column?"

"In Hollywood? People have done worse for less."

"And this notion that he was the real target?"

"Possible. But keep in mind, Okie loves the limelight."

"No shit." Then, "Send over a recap on whatever you've got on Okie." Alcalay knows that the FBI doesn't share unexpurgated files with other law enforcement agencies.

"I'll throw in a rundown on this Weaver kid, too," I say. "You gonna keep a lid on that sign you found? Might be useful later. Hidden clue, guilty knowledge, whatever."

"Too late for that—a photographer from the *Times* got here when the sign was hanging on the mailbox."

Something stirs for me. "Mind if I take another look at it?"

"Be my guest," he says. "No extra charge."

As the two of us stroll back to the evidence truck he says, "You adding this up the same way I am? The tote can of gas left inside means—"

"—the hitter wants the world to know it was not an accident."

He reaches inside the truck and hands me the sign. This time I focus on the smudge at the top of the card, right under the fold of the glassine envelope. I shake the envelope and the card slips down a tad revealing a small notation in the same black ink. It reads: #2.

"Didn't notice that before," Alcalay says. "What the hell's it mean? Number Two—who's Number One?"

"Wendy Travers," I say automatically. Then I examine what I said. "The gal who was bushwacked by a night-stalker up on King's Road a couple of weeks ago."

"Oh yeah, Sheriff's Department case, drug crime, no leads, but what's that—"

"She was L. B. Mayer's favorite writer. He always called her Number One. It was a nickname that stuck. Everybody in the business always kidded her about it." Then I make the connection for myself: "Wendy was a cooperative witness for the Committee."

"Another informer, huh?" Alcalay stares at me. "So you think Shannon may be the second scalp and she was first— and the asshole wants us to keep his score straight?" He sighs unhappily. "Now it's definitely political. I hate political cases. So, among other possibles, we're definitely looking to the Hollywood Blacklist crowd."

"I can be a lot of help there," I say.

"Chance for you to earn your keep," Alcalay sneers.

He's not about to ease up. Suddenly it comes to me, the physical resemblance now that he's hefty, plus the bullying manner. Alcalay reminds me of Declan Collins. And I wonder if I really talked my way in, or was he playing me? He knew about the sign before I arrived. He had the upper hand, so could he have seized the chance to get back some of his own by making me grovel? Well, now I really do owe him one.

R acing to the office, I run several red lights on the deserted pre-dawn boulevards. When I hustle into the office the night crew are wrapping up. Pierson looks over in surprise.

"Sorta early for you, isn't it?"

"Couldn't sleep after you woke me up." No time for details now.

The row of cubicles is empty. I plop down at my desk and pound out a telex. An encoded Eyes Only recap of Joe Shannon's death and the connection I made to Wendy Travers murder. I send it directly into J. Edgar Hoover's office, attention: Clyde Tolson.

Then I stroll down the hall, get myself coffee from the new pot the night shift leaves for the day shift. I go back to my cubicle and wait. It doesn't take long. I expect Tolson, but when my phone rings it is Hoover himself, expressing sympathy for the demise of his "old friend Joe Shannon." Hoover compliments me for getting on the case so fast. Particularly when we don't have jurisdiction yet.

"I pulled a few strings and got invited in." Never mind the humiliation.

Then Hoover says, "I want to know if this was more than just a lover's tiff between a couple of homos." Nothing like slandering a dead friend, but I voice a brisk Yessir. "But the linkup you established to the death of that screenwriter woman who was a friendly witness makes this of extreme interest to us."

Hoover's message is clear. If someone is rubbing out people for cooperating with us, the FBI can't let that go by. It's bad for our business.

Hoover muses, "If you had to venture a guess, who do you think might have done it?"

"Mr. Hoover, it's so early in the investigation—"

"Of course, Brian, but—we lawmen often have hunches."

Flattered by his confidence in my prowess, and wanting to keep the direct contact with my supreme leader going, I say: "There are so many possibilities, sir, even—"

I hesitate, but Hoover nudges: "Yes?"

So I give him the slice of raw meat he's after: "There's the possible involvement of the son of a Blacklisted writer. Wendy Travers came to his father's funeral recently. And the kid had a fistfight with Shannon just the other day." I can feel Hoover's pleasure through the line. "I was there at the time," I add, feeding Hoover's assumption I'm on top of all Hollywood activities of interest to the Bureau.

"A Red kid. Wouldn't that be nice," Hoover says.

"Of course, that's just very preliminary."

"Of course. I'm depending on you, Brian. You know these people."

The call is over. I finish my coffee, ill at ease at having

pointed a finger in David Weaver's direction. Doesn't feel like the kid's style, but who knows? I'm sure Hoover recognizes it as just cop chatter. The important thing is my hunch was right: I'm in the game again and I'm going to make it work out. It's my ticket onto the A-team in Washington.

27

JANA

After David falls asleep in his room at the Chateau, I lie there beside him on the bed, still dressed, and my eyes never close, I can't stop thinking about what Zacharias told him. That we all knew but didn't want to know. It's a mantra pounding in my head. Leading me off the edge of my world. Just before dawn, I can't stand it any longer. Have to go home. Have to see my father. So I get up silently, leave David a note saying I love him and we'll talk more later, then I tiptoe out and drive to Stone Canyon. Dad's Mercedes is in front. From the driveway I hear the typewriter clattering in the study. It stops as I come down the hall.

Dad opens his door looking as haggard as I feel. My reflex instinct is to offer him sympathy and concern, but I recognize that's been central to the problem. And I'm always easing his pain.

"Hi"—he runs his hand through his hair—"didn't realize it was daylight already. I've been chained to this damn desk all night." He glances at his watch. "Got to go meet Keefer in the cutting room soon."

Then he peers at me. The director deciding how to play this scene.

"You were with David tonight?" I don't say anything. "I've been trying to reach you all day. Were you ducking me?"

Good opening gambit. He's the injured party.

"Anyway . . . you know David quit me. Just phoned in, left a message, didn't even bother to come in and talk to me first . . ." He trails off.

"So he could explain?" He nods. "Or so *you* could explain."

He gauges me, deciding which tactic will work best. I've seen him do that with lots of people. I hate it when he does it to me. Then he sighs wearily. Embracing victim mode.

"Hey, it's okay, only a matter of simple courtesy. After all I've done for him, I thought he'd be man enough to at least come see me face-to-face."

"He said you had him barred from the lot."

"I don't know where he got that idea."

"Probably from the studio cops at the gate," I say.

He cocks his head. "Why are we standing out here in the hall, come inside and we'll talk."

He holds open the door to the study. I go in, but before he can get to the power spot behind his desk I sit on the couch. So he'll have to take the club chair facing me. No barriers to protect either of us. But I keep my hands clasped in my lap because they're trembling.

He detours, playing for time. Stops at the counter below the bookcase and picks up a bulging 11x14 Panorama envelope. "Want to hear a joke? Studio was supposed to send over a new project for me to consider. Irwin Shaw's latest." He holds up the envelope. "From your pal Markie Gunderson's office, they sent the wrong manuscript. It's Joe Shannon's piece-of-crap excuse for a novel. Funny, huh?"

I don't respond. It's not what we must talk about. He sits down in the club chair. It's as if the bell has rung for Round Two.

"Okay," he says, "you read some bullshit written by that malevolent, nancy-pansy bastard who stirs up old shit to fill his garbage pail of a gossip column. I'm sorry you and David

had to get dragged into it. Joe Shannon despises me because—"

I interrupt him. "Is it true?"

"Is what true?"

"Did you give the Committee Teddy's name?" *Please,* Daddy,
say no. Say it's all a mistake, say you never could have done
that.

"Shannon's twisting what happened. When I was up there
on the stand in front of that Flying Circus in Washington, with
the lights and cameras and crowds, it was like facing Robespi-
erre's mob, they—"

"I know what you said at the public hearings in Washington, I read your testimony."

"All you read is six to eight paragraphs in the *Times* that are
supposed to sum up a man's life. You were still only a kid who
couldn't really understand all the ramifications."

I can't believe he's doing this. I feel like the essence of my
life is on the line, my belief in the basic decency of my father—
and he's double-talking me. "I've read your complete public
testimony. In the Congressional Record."

That slows him for only an instant. Start of Round Three.
"Then you know I never mentioned Teddy. Honey, we went
over all this years ago."

"Actually, we didn't. You came back from Washington so
wounded that I didn't have the heart to ask you much of anything. I just accepted what you told me."

"Because it was the truth, Jana."

"The whole truth and nothing but the truth?"

"What is this? Am I back on the stand?" He gets up and
stomps to the desk for his corncob pipe. Regrouping. I can see
every ploy clearly. Now he turns back to me. Going on the of-
fensive. Trying for a knockout. "What do you *really* want to
know?"

"Why you did what you did. Why did you cooperate with

those people? I used to hear you talking about the Committee—you despised what they were doing, what they stood for."

"Look, I stayed up a lot of nights grappling with the decision, but despite my loathing for the Committee, I finally came to realize that in a crucial way they had become right—the world had changed, the Russians had the atom bomb, they were out to dominate the globe, destroy our country, the Commies had taken over China, we were at war in Korea, and my own personal views on morality seemed suddenly irrelevant."

More bullshit. Adrenaline surges through me. "So in the name of national security you gave HUAC the names of five screenwriters, three character actors, a film editor, an acting coach, and a guy who wrote jokes for Abbott and Costello. They were not espionage agents, Daddy, they were your friends."

"And they had the chance to clear their names by doing what I did!" More angry at me than I've ever seen him. "Would you rather have had a life like David's? Kicked around from country to country, never finished his education, haunted by the disgrace of his father. Did you want *that*?"

"I would have been willing, instead of—" But he won't let me finish.

"Well, I had to think for both of us. I chose to protect you from the chaos, maybe that was my mistake as a father—"

"No! Don't say you did it for me! Don't you dare put that on me! You own that one completely!" It's the first time I've ever shouted at him.

His hand flies up as if to smack me, but he catches himself. The wind goes out of him. He slumps back into the club chair and gazes at the carpet. His voice flat and exhausted. *King Lear,* Act III.

"When we went to Washington, Harry Rains told me, 'Leo, it's like being at the dentist, only hurts when you're in the chair. Then you can put it all behind you.' But Harry was wrong. It keeps on hurting."

It's always about *his* pain. I just wait.

"After Washington, they called me a stoolie. A rat. All my so-called friends, who let the right-wing reactionaries marginalize them. Drive them out of the industry. Well, I chose another course."

Another cue for me. I let that one go by, too. So he shifts gears.

"Let me ask you, who else would've made the movies I did since then? Controversial, political, critical. Dealing with racial tensions, juvenile delinquency, hypocritical hate mongers, greedy power brokers. I help audiences and critics see what's wrong with America. With the world. I'm playing the studio's game in order to reach the people."

An old self-patting rant. Not what I want to hear now. I'm terrified to ask for the rest, but I have to.

"Tell me what happened *before* you went to Washington."

He clenches the empty pipe in his teeth and stares at me.

"What happened in L.A. during the private executive session? Those records are sealed for fifty years. Unless someone leaks it sooner." As he fiddles with his pipe, I see that *his* hands are shaking. Part of me also desperately wants to stop, but I can't. We've gone too far. "You can't make me wait fifty years. Did they ask you about Teddy in executive session?"

"Look, of course they did, he was my best friend, he was my partner, we did everything together, everyone in Hollywood knew that—"

"So you did. You gave him up. So you could survive." I hate myself for saying those words.

"They already knew about Teddy!" he shouts as if in expiation.

"But not from you."

"I agreed to cooperate with them only on condition that I didn't have to name him publicly. Harry said they'd never go along with that, I was risking a contempt citation and a jail sentence, but I stuck to it—"

"How brave of you!" The sarcasm leaps out of me.

"Jana, I know you're upset, but be careful what you're saying now."

"Or what? What could you possibly do that would hurt me more than I'm hurt now?"

"I never turned my back on Teddy, never! Some of those under-the-table writing assignments he got in Europe, I sent them his way, he never knew that, I don't want any credit for doing that but—"

"Yes, you do, you always want credit. Like the *Variety* ad you took, *anonymously*, as a memorial tribute to Teddy. But you kept the photo on the shelf"—I point at it—"so David would notice it when he came to see you. So he'd agree to work for you."

"If you knew that, why didn't you speak up at the time?"

"Because I wanted him to come back, too!"

"Then what was the harm?"

"Do you think any of that makes up for what you did to Teddy?"

"Honey, it's all ancient history dug up by a vicious scumbag. None of this would have ever come up except for Shannon! He'll burn in hell! But—it doesn't have anything to do with us!"

"It does! You betrayed Teddy and let me believe a lie all these years."

"What good would it have done to tell you, Jana?" He rubs his eyes. "I was—afraid you'd hate me—as much as I hated myself."

Yet another cue for me to feel sorry for him. "Zacharias says we didn't want to look at what really happened."

"Is he the one who's poisoning your minds against me? You and David? Zacharias is a bitter, self-righteous blowhard crackpot who—"

"He was one of the people you named."

"Jana, I was fighting for my life, and yours, too! It was ugly and unfair and unavoidable and I dealt with it the best way I could. I saved myself, I saved you. Teddy could have saved himself, and Ellie and David, too, he could have done the same thing!"

"No, he couldn't! Don't you see?"

"Well, that was their choice, his and Ellie's."

I feel a sense of horror growing within me. "Ellie was like my mother!"

"And I'm your father!"

I take a deep scalding breath and force myself to ask the question I dread the most. The question that haunted me all through the night.

"Did Ellie's name come up in the executive session?"

He hesitates. Then, as if expecting a blow, he says, "I—I made them agree not to subpoena her. And they didn't. See, I protected her."

My chest feels like glass and it's shattering. *He named her.* "Daddy, she killed herself!"

"I know—I know." His eyes mist. He blinks rapidly and succeeds in fighting back tears.

I don't know what else to say to him. So I rise, unsteady on my feet, but standing. When I can manage words they are shaky.

"I'm moving out. I can't live in your house anymore."

Then I leave the room and stumble down the hallway. He calls out once. "Don't go, Jana, please . . . you're all I've got."

There it is. In one awful sentence. Banal, pathetic, needing, claiming, repentant, hoping, grasping, forlorn, finally naked and—and so unforgivable. I know if I go back to see him I'll never leave. So I pretend I didn't hear and go to my bedroom, take the suitcase out of my closet, and begin to pack. There is a big crash down the hall. My instant reaction is that he has fallen down. But there are more crashes and bangs and glass breaking and I know what's happening.

The noises stop after a few minutes, and the front door slams followed by the sound of his car pulling away. I carry my closed suitcase down the hallway, stop to look inside the study. He has trashed the room. The desk has been overturned, lamps strewn on the floor. The head of his Oscar statuette is broken off and the robot-like gold-plated body is lying in the mess, along with the photo of Teddy. Its glass frame is shattered.

I go out the front door, load my suitcase in the car, and drive down the road with tears distorting my view. I backhand at my eyes, then turn the wheel sharply when I reach the Hotel Bel-Air. David, I need David! I jump out and tell the parking attendant I've got to make an urgent call and race into the lobby to a pay phone. I dial the Chateau, the switchboard operator rings his room, rings and rings, and says there's no answer. Now I recall David has a breakfast meeting. I've never yearned for him more.

As I walk out of the lobby, a headline on the newspaper vending machine rocks me. The early edition of the *L.A. Examiner* blares:

GOSSIP COLUMNIST DIES IN FIRE; POLICE SEEK BLACKLIST KILLER

I see a photo of Joe Shannon. My father's ranting words about Shannon just minutes ago replay in my head: *"He'll burn in hell!"* If my father's been at the house for hours rewriting, how could he have seen the newspaper? Or maybe he didn't have to. Thinking of him as the possible killer fills me with a new dread.

BOOK TWO

THE HUNT FOR
THE BLACKLIST KILLER

28

DAVID

When I wake up, I feel a stabbing pain behind my eyes even before I open them. I sit up in bed and my head feels like a string of fireworks exploding behind my frontal lobe. Then the hangover pain grows even worse as I remember last night. Only bits and pieces—the Hollywood drinking tour, but spotty on the details. Starting off at Musso's bar, ending up miles and drinks later. What happened in between? Who cares? Just trying to drown the scorching truth about Leo's betrayal of Teddy. Jana waiting on my doorstep. Scared she knew all along, but she didn't! She took the news as hard as I did. I remember we talked until I passed out.

I look around my room. Jana is gone, I see a note on the other pillow: Love you, call me after breakfast. It's next to the message slip from last night summoning me to Harry Rains' house at eight thirty. I check the clock. Oh, jeez. It's already almost eight o'clock. Can I still make it? Should I go?

Harry must have heard I quit and Leo barred me from the lot. Harry hears everything. Guess he wants to guilt me for botching the wonderful opportunity he gave me. But he could do that on the phone. Why the breakfast invitation? I can't think with this pounding headache. What the hell. Teddy's motto. Always take the meeting.

I gobble a handful of aspirins, shave, and while I'm putting on my clothes I notice Teddy's passport lying on the dresser. The posthumous gift from McKenna. I open it and see Teddy's smiling face. I gaze at it for an instant, then I close it and set forth. Moving as fast as my pulsating head will allow. Through the lobby, detour to grab a cup of steaming black coffee from the breakfast room and scoop up a free copy of the L.A. Times at the desk. Fold it under my arm, find my car, climb in, and toss the paper on the passenger seat. It flips open and below the fold on the front page I see the face of Joe Shannon and the report of his death. Good. One less asshole in the world.

But as I quickly read the story it hits me with the impact of a Wilshire Boulevard bus. This victim is a guy I've had two public clashes with since I came back to L.A. Anyone who reads the trades knows that. Or Agent McKenna can fill them in. So why the hell did Joe Shannon's demise have to happen on a night when my recollection of my own whereabouts is foggy?

As I drive into Beverly Hills I sip the black coffee, which helps to penetrate the haze. I piece together what I can recall about my bar-hopping exploits. Fill in some of the blanks, but by no means all. I've got a patchy memory of where I went and what I did. Between Musso's and that dive on Western there are gaps strewn all along the way. Don't remember anyone I talked to. If a cop comes knocking on my door asking questions, I'll be shit out of luck. No real alibi. That's a very scary thought. Do I need a lawyer? Well, I'm on my way to see one—Harry.

I turn into Rexford Drive and pull up in front of his palace only five minutes late. I see a Mexican maid unloading groceries from a seven-year-old brown Nash Rambler at what I assume is the kitchen door. I focus on my bruised knuckles on the steering wheel and a terribly sobering bit of last night floats to the surface. Between the boozing and the wandering that became staggering, I remember thinking it would be a terrific idea to drop in on Shannon and beat the living shit out of him.

Maybe that's just what I did.

The white-coated, portly, elderly Negro butler guides me to the breakfast room. "Miz Valerie," he announces, "Mr. Weaver's here."

Valerie Nolan Rains is alone at the table. She's a ray of sunshine befitting the scene beyond her. An emerald lawn slopes down to an Olympic-size pool with cabanas and the tennis court just beyond the pool. The sprinklers are on and the early morning sun dances and fractures in the spray. It's the glossy way the cinematographer would light it for her TV series.

"Hi, cookie." She greets me and pats the chair beside her. There are three table settings, but the third seat is empty. She pours coffee for me from a carafe. Very welcoming. But Harry still could be furious at me and she just doesn't know it.

She's wearing no makeup other than light lipstick, her hair pulled back and tied simply with a scarf that matches the gold-and-silver-flecked designer robe. She looks fabulous. Valerie must be in her fifties. Even in the morning light she could pass for forty.

"Harry's been on the phone for almost an hour, he'll be here soon. At least that's what he keeps promising on the intercom."

"Is it about that?" I ask. The *L.A. Times,* folded to the Shannon story, is next to her coffee cup.

"I suppose so," she says. "Barney Ott woke us up at the crack of dawn with the news." It doesn't seem to mean much to her, but I'm having difficulty thinking of anything else. Last night's blackouts. With the rage rising within me. Hating Shannon as much as Leo. Did I go over there? How could I forget something like that? Could I have killed him and not remember it?

"Such a commotion over Joe Shannon," she says dismissively, "I can't imagine why. A very unkind man. In fact, a total prick."

That takes me so completely by surprise that I nervously laugh. Valerie *never* curses.

She laughs, too, hearing herself. "I mean, he was. Really. Even if he is dead." Then she reaches out to touch my hand. "What he wrote yesterday. About you and Jana. Disgraceful."

"It was the part about Teddy that hurt the worst. You knew what Leo did, didn't you."

"Harry was Leo's lawyer." She sighs heavily. "Such a hideous period. You had to be there."

"I was." Does she think that kids can't feel pain and fear?

"There were so many layers, like the box within the box within the box. You were too young to understand it all."

"Well, I've spent all the years since trying to figure it out."

She squeezes my hand. "Don't let it ruin the friendship between you and Jana. That would be awful—if it went on for another generation."

"We're trying not to. It's difficult."

"And it's so sad. Teddy and Leo were like peas in a pod—to force one of them to turn on the other—"

I cut her off. "Are you asking me to feel sorry for Leo?"

"Everyone did something they regret in that awful time."

"Teddy didn't! You didn't!"

She looks at me. "I—"

Before she can continue, the butler enters again, trailing the phone on a lengthy cord. "It's Mr. Rains," he says. She takes it. "Yes, Harry, uh-huh, yes, fine." She hangs up, tells me, "He wants you to join him downstairs in the gym. Why don't you take your coffee with you?"

I rise and lean over to kiss her on the cheek, and she hugs me with surprising strength. From all those rounds of singles with Dinah Shore out on the tennis court, I guess. "Don't be a stranger, David."

The butler shows me to the workout room. It's like a miniature outpost of Vic Tanny's gym. Shiny exercise machines, free weights, and punching bags. Harry the ex-Golden Glover. He looks trim, still a light heavyweight. He is in workout clothes on the treadmill, reading glasses perched on the tip of his nose, perusing the folded sports section of the morning paper as he marches to nowhere.

"Hey, here's my unemployed protégé, howyadoin?"

"Doing just fine, Harry." He's not pissed at me. So why am I here?

"You look like hell. Had a big night?"

"What I remember of it."

Harry laughs. "Ah, to be young again." The treadmill dings its conclusion and slows to a stop.

"What do you think about the Joe Shannon thing?" I ask. Testing the water. Looking for an entry into my fear. Harry could advise me. But he's into waxing philosophical:

"Live by the sword, die by the sword. Y'can't keep jabbing folks forever like Joe did without getting jabbed back." He sighs heavily. "But y'hadda know him when we were kids. Always covering each other's ass. Getting into and out of stupid scrapes together."

Harry towels off the sweat as he reminisces. "This one time, we were being chased by a pair of cops, can't even remember what we'd done, swiped something, I guess. But I got over a fence, Joe didn't. They caught him, sent him to juvie camp at

Boys Republic and he never mentioned my name—good thing, too, because later on a police record could've disqualified me from becoming a lawyer."

"So he saved you by not giving your name," I say bitterly, "and he lived to terrorize other people who also refused to give names."

"Hey, that's something, isn't it? Never looked at it that way."

"You think someone we know killed him?"

"Hate to think so, but could be. Guess the police will figure it out."

Harry pulls on leather gloves and starts punching the heavy bag dangling on a chain from the ceiling. Putting his weight behind each shot.

"Let's talk about you, kiddo. You quit Leo, he told me, I understand why—"

Everyone understands everything, I think. So how come it's all so screwed up?

"—but I thought you knew all that old stuff and had come to terms with it. Leo said you've done a great job for him, he's sorry to lose you."

"He'll get over it."

"Yeah, well, now the question is, what's next on your agenda?"

"Haven't worked that part out yet."

"Open to another offer?" He stops hitting the bag to see my reaction.

I'm stunned. "Thought this was going to be the classy kiss-off."

"Nah, I don't give up so easy." He resumes beating on the heavy bag. "There's a job available. Unit publicist. Working on a little Western we're just starting on the back lot."

I can't believe he's giving me another chance, but: "What's a unit publicist?"

"Like a newspaper reporter covering the shooting. You conduct press interviews, if you can get 'em. Work with the still photographer on the set. Write up material for a press book they use when we release the picture. The guys in publicity can fill you in on the specifics. C'mon, you can practice your typing. Learn another facet of the business. Whaddaya-say?"

"Won't Leo go through the roof when he hears you're giving me another shot?"

"Leo runs his set. I run the studio. Look, call me a good-hearted schmuck, but I still feel a debt to Teddy. He was a dear friend, plus he steered legal business my way when I needed a start. And Valerie said she'd kick my *tuchis* if I didn't help you some more." He stops hitting the bag. "Hey, if you don't wanna do it—"

"Best offer I've got," I say, touched that he's willing to go to bat for me again. "Also the only offer. Thanks, Harry."

This I sense is not the time to tell him about my fear. It's enough that he's giving the son of an ex-Commie another job, without reminding him that when the cops start looking around for Shannon haters, I'll be on the A-list of candidates. Maybe that's where I belong.

Harry says, "There's only one proviso about this job."

Isn't there always. "What's that?"

"Regarding Leo. You gotta promise to steer clear of him."

Is that all? I'm relieved. "No problem there. As far as I'm concerned, he's dead."

"Then we've got a deal."

"When do I start?"

"You could check in this afternoon. They're expecting you." He knew this is how our meeting would conclude. "Don't worry, Slugger, you're cleared through the gate and I got you back your parking space."

For a moment Harry's generosity has made me forget about

Shannon. But as I walk out of the house, it's gnawing at me again. The fear is back.

When I come out, I see Valerie pruning the roses. As if she's been waiting for me. I wave and she walks over, carrying her flower basket and gardening shears.

"Did you take the new job?"

I nod. Thank her. She shrugs that off. I see Valerie's got something else on her mind.

"What did you mean before, when I said everyone has something to regret about the HUAC days—and you said I didn't?"

"Well, I heard that that they wanted you to testify, back during your first marriage, and Harry talked them out of it, because the stress might endanger your pregnancy and—"

"And I lost the baby. Probably because of the stress."

"Anyway, Harry got you off the hook."

"That's more or less what happened, but not exactly in that order. I did testify in Executive Session—"

An echo of Leo Vardian.

"—and I gave them names, and afterwards I was so sick that I miscarried. Harry did arrange it so that I never had to testify in public. But it took more than talk—it took money. Twenty-five thousand dollars worth. A payoff to someone at the Committee. The deal was brokered by Harry's childhood chum, Joe Shannon. Wasn't that cute?" She laughs harshly. "I wanted to take it off my taxes as a business deduction. But Harry convinced me not to. 'Don't poke the bear,' he said."

"Always protecting you," I say.

"That's one of the best parts about being a star, David. The whole system is geared to protecting you."

"How come you're telling me this?"

"Because—I don't deserve for you to think about me in the

same breath as Teddy and the others who stood up to those witch hunters. I'm not worth their spit."

I look at her and see the agony in her magnificent violet eyes, and I'm struck by a realization about the Blacklist that I never wanted to even consider until now. Even the winners were losers.

As I drive away, I'm thinking about that. No one got away unscathed. The Blacklist scarred everyone it touched. Even Harry couldn't protect her from that. And then Joe Shannon crowds my mind again. The questions to which I have no answer: What happened last night? While I was drunk, did the black rage demon get loose?

29

McKENNA

My first stop this morning is the LAPD police lab. I'm ten minutes early, but Alcalay greets me like I've kept him waiting:

"Slept in, did ya? Letting the rest of us do all the work."

I let that zinger go by. Actually, I grabbed a quick two hours sleep on a couch in the Bureau office's lounge. Then shaved, washed up, took a fresh shirt out of my bottom desk drawer. Gathered a packet of material for Alcalay—lists of Blacklistees still alive and in the area, a rundown on Teddy and David Weaver, plus Okie O'Connell, as promised, and Keeler Barnes as a bonus. I also threw in a set of the funeral photos I had shot the other day.

I'm just in time for the grand opening by the lab techies of Joe Shannon's metal strongbox. Inside there is an assortment of scorched and half-burned documents, all covered with a patina of light ash. The rubber-gloved techies extract the items with tweezers, inserting each of them in its own transparent glassine evidence wrapper and handing them one by one to Alcalay. I'm allowed to look over his shoulder.

I see Shannon's birth certificate and passport. A handful of baseball cards, probably from when Shannon was a boy. Personally autographed by Babe Ruth, Lou Gehrig, Joe DiMaggio, worth money in mint condition, which these no longer are. A couple of love letters from Shannon's ex-college roommate—I recognize the name on the return address.

"He's a state senator now in Sacramento."

"Blackmail material?" Alcalay suggests.

"Or nostalgia. Anyway, the senator is an ultra-active anti-Communist. He doesn't fit the Blacklist profile."

"We'll check him out anyway to be sure," he says

Alcalay and I examine a Panorama Studio stock certificate for 5,000 shares of common stock. "How much is that worth?" Alcalay asks. About a hundred-fifty grand, I tell him. There's also some hate mail from irate movie stars over slams in his columns over the years. And a charred letter of commendation on FBI letterhead personally signed by J. Edgar Hoover for unspecified acts of good citizenship performed by Joseph P. Shannon.

There's also a thin metal chain with what looks like a military dog tag. The face part of the ID tag has melted onto the wall of the safe, so the markings are obliterated. "Probably Shannon's Army dogtag," Alcalay speculates, "I've got mine in a drawer at home."

"Shannon was in the navy," I say.

"Well, whatever." Alcalay turns to the head techie, "Think you can do something with that?" The techie says they'll give it a try.

I'm disappointed. "What happened to the drop-dead, tell-all dirt Shannon was supposed to have on everybody and their brother?"

"Maybe only a rumor that was good for business." Alcalay chuckles. "Who knows, maybe there's nothing much in Hoover's files either. Wouldn't that be a pleasant surprise to a lot of people in D.C. and elsewhere who lose sleep over what he may have on them?"

I let that one go by, too.

"Last night," Alcalay recalls, "you said Shannon lived real high. Where did his money come from?"

"Well, his column is syndicated and he wrote stuff for the fan mags. Rumor was that included *Confidential,* the scandal sheet. But not under his own name, of course. They pay well."

"Still doesn't sound like it covers a hefty mortgage in Jack Warner's neighborhood. And where'd he get the bucks for the Panorama shares?"

"Okay," I agree, "blackmail's a good possibility, it could fit with the Blacklist. Maybe Shannon was selling stay-out-of-jail passes to Lefties who wanted to duck the Committee."

"Did he have that kind of clout?"

"At a certain point in time. How about that 'Informer' sign, had a chance to run it yet?"

Alcalay shrugs. Dead end. "Ordinary piece of cardboard, the kind comes from the laundry with your shirts, and the ink's from a marking pen every dime store and drugstore stocks. The string that the sign was hanging from is a brand new shoelace. No prints on anything."

I pick up the glassine envelope containing the letter of commendation signed by J. Edgar Hoover. "Can I borrow this?"

"For how long?"

"How about forever?"

"What have you done for me lately?"

I take out the bulging packet I brought from my office and describe the contents to Alcalay. He holds the packet in one hand, Hoover's letter in the other. He pretends to weigh one against the other.

"Seems like a fair exchange to me." He hands me Hoover's letter and I tuck it away in my briefcase. Keeping Hoover's name out of the investigation and out of the newspapers should be worth a large attaboy.

As Alcalay walks me out to the parking lot, he gives me an update on progress. There's not much. The Shannon autopsy verified the cause of death as hard trauma bludgeoning. "He was dead before the smoke and fire got to him."

"Bludgeoning," I say. "Like Wendy Travers."

I mention that, as we agreed last night, I've been in touch with Jerry Borison at the Beverly Hills cop shop. Alcalay and I have hit into a piece of luck: the *L.A. Times* printed their photo of "The Informer" sign, but cropped off the #2 marking. So I played it cool when I talked to Borison, as if I was just following up on what happened to a friend. "The connection to Wendy is still our secret," I tell Alcalay.

"So what do they have?" he asks.

"Basically zip. They're doing the usual, circulating descriptions of the stolen jewelry, monitoring missing credit cards. And how about us so far?"

"Only new thing was, we couldn't find Shannon's wallet."

I suggest it burned up in the fire. Alcalay says there would be traces, scorched leather, melted plastic, ashes from paper money, something.

"His watch was there, what's left of it, an expensive piece—but no wallet," Alcalay repeats. We both understand. The mugging element is another similarity to Wendy's murder.

"Okay," he says. "Figure Shannon is fresh meat, so we'll pound that one first, then see if we can warm up the Travers trail. I'll divvy your list of Shannon haters among my troops and we'll fan out."

"If you need more manpower, I probably can get you some."

He shakes his head. "One Fat Boy in this is plenty enough." Using another cop term for FBI agents. "Where you going to be?"

"Panorama Studio," I say. "Collecting alibis."

"Don't forget about that Weaver kid."

Alcalay and Hoover have something in common: they both seem to have sparked to the idea of David Weaver. It makes me uneasy. Too soon to be zeroing in on a target. I don't want to feel like we're starting with an answer and then tailoring the evidence to fit. Which used to happen a lot when I was a DA in Chicago. I've still got an open mind about the Weaver kid. Or is that just a pang of guilt because I blurted his name to Hoover for a pat on the back?

T here's really no reason to assume Joe Shannon's untimely death has anything to do with Panorama." Barney Ott is making sounds like a studio press release.

I'm in Ott's spacious corner office in the executive building. Décor befitting an eastern banker. Dark wood and recessed lighting, cushy black leather club chairs. We've been joined by his colleague Jack Heritage and their boss, Harry Rains. Heritage is playing cat's cradle with a long rubber band intertwined between the fingers of his hands, but listening intently.

"Except," I mention, "you guys have been having a nasty public ruckus with Shannon for the last week or so."

"You don't kill a columnist for printing a couple of lousy items," Harry says. "Though sometimes you might feel like you want to."

They all chuckle about that. I push another button. "How about Leo Vardian? I hear he was screaming on his set last week that he'd like to exterminate Shannon." I already worked a couple of studio sources before I came over.

Ott takes it in stride. "Leo's a very temperamental artist, they get emotional sometimes. But quick as it comes, it blows over." Acting as if I just fell off the turnip truck.

"Want to talk to someone, you might try that Weaver kid,"

Heritage suggests. "He's the one who actually mixed it up with Joe."

"I was there," I say.

"Hey, that wasn't the first time they went at each other," Heritage adds, adeptly manipulating the cat's cradle.

"Meaning what?"

Heritage looks at me. "A hassle in the commissary blue room couple of weeks ago. Weaver and Shannon squared off pretty good, I thought the kid was gonna belt him. Right, Harry? Happened at your table."

"No big thing," Harry says. "C'mon, David's okay."

I nod at Heritage, point taken. But is he being helpful to me—or trying to shift attention away from Leo?

Although I don't ask them for alibis, they each manage to work one into the conversation. Harry was home in bed with wife Valerie. Ott was up late, alone, reading Winston Churchill's wartime memoirs. "Hitler loses," I say as a spoiler, and Ott makes a smile. Heritage was in bed with a hot young lady. "I'm too discreet to mention who—unless I really have to."

"Look, Mac," Harry says, "anything we can do for you . . ."

Ott offers, "You want to see anyone on the lot, I can have Jack take you right over."

"Thanks, but I get better results when I surprise 'em." They all nod sagely. Respecting my work methods. Supposedly.

As I walk across the lot, I think: It's well known in the industry that Panorama is desperately hungry for a box office hit. The kind that Leo Vardian has provided in the past. They're pumping huge bucks into Leo's movie, so despite Harry's joke, would they eliminate a columnist who endangers all that? Long shot. But possible. Or they might be sitting on a bigger secret I haven't yet come across.

———

W here were you between the hours of . . ." Leo Vardian
      intones in a portentous *March of Time* basso voice. Then
he laughs. "I've written this corny scene so many times."

Leo and I are standing on an outdoor steel catwalk on the
second floor of the editing building. Next to the open entrance
to the cutting room where the editors are working on his
movie. The staccato sounds of gunfire spill out intermittently.

"Let's do it anyway, Leo, just for fun," I say. "From eleven
last night 'til about two a.m.?"

"I was right here. 'Til then and later."

Leo looks ragged, like a man who has been working day
and night.

"Who else was here?" I ask.

"Just Keeler and me." He yells over the gunfire into the editing room. *"Right, Keeler?"*

Keeler Barnes sticks his head out the door. *"What?"*

"Just telling our pal McKenna that we went real late last
night. Worked here until our eyeballs were falling out."

"Uh-huh," Keeler says, "that we did. And here we are back
for some more. No Biz Like Show Biz."

"So you guys can alibi each other," I say.

"Why do I need an alibi?" Keeler demands.

"As I recall, Joe Shannon was on your case pretty heavy in
the old days."

"Was he? I forget." Keeler disappears back into the editing
room.

I turn back to Leo. "You've got a long history of friction
with Shannon—right up to yesterday."

"Hated the man's guts. Is that what you mean?"

"Yeah, but I don't like to put words in your mouth."

"Sure you do." Leo gives me his thinnest smile. "That's
your job."

The relationship, if you can call it that, between me and
Leo Vardian has always been thorny. I served him a subpoena

and also participated in the behind-the-scenes meetings at which the details and parameters for his HUAC appearance were negotiated. Mostly centered on which names Leo would name. Always the stickiest part.

After his HUAC testimony, I'd occasionally run into him at industry events. Invariably, Leo cut me dead. Not unexpected. It was more palatable to blame the FBI than himself.

Then one late night after a post-premiere party at Romanoff's, Leo and I were the last ones left at the bar. Both drunk enough to share a nightcap and Leo was rather friendly. Also no surprise to me. After a passage of time several cooperative witnesses seemed to find it easier to relate to me. Like old soldiers who fought in the same war, although not on the same side. For better or worse, we had shared a moment of history.

We were shnockered enough for me to casually ask Leo if he had any thoughts as to why some witnesses refused to cooperate when their destruction was guaranteed? My perennial question. Perhaps Leo had the answer.

"That's all in the book," Leo said.

"What book is that?"

"The one I'm never going to write." Leo clinked glasses with me as if it was a toast. Since then, we've chatted briefly when we've met, but neither of us ever brought up the Blacklist again. But now Shannon's murder has put it back in the spotlight.

Our conversation outside the editing room is interrupted by a phone call summoning Leo. While we walk back to the soundstage, I say, "Question for you about your former comrades, Leo. Want to venture a guess as to who burned down Joe Shannon?"

No sooner are the words out of my mouth than I recognize them as an echo of Hoover's invitation to me to speculate.

"Don't have the vaguest," Leo says cheerfully. "But soon as

you find out, let me know—I want to nominate the guy for an Oscar for distinguished service to the motion picture industry."

The studio guard holds open the soundstage door and Leo disappears. I note that he wasn't surprised when I turned up. I'd bet a dime Harry Rains dialed him ahead of my arrival.

My take on Leo: his alibi is questionable. A flicker of hesitation on Keeler's face when Leo tossed the ball to him. Check studio guardhouse records, see if the time they both left the lot last night was logged. Keeler could be a ticking bomb from the old days. Leo has that going for him plus new stuff. Shannon had been attacking not only Leo, but his daughter. An enraged lion defending his young. Yeah, possible. Wouldn't that be interesting. Leo making headlines for me again.

30

DAVID

Jana and I are having an early lunch in the commissary. Leo never eats here. We're off at a rear table. As soon as we meet I want to tell her about my terror over what I may have done last night. But when I see her shaking almost like an addict in withdrawal, I just sit her down and let her talk.

And as close to word-for-word as she can recall, she tells me about her confrontation and break with Leo. Her tears fall intermittently. I try to wrap my arm around her to ease her pain, but she waves me off. I see the enormous effort it's taking for her to hold it together.

So I just listen, and then she gets to Leo's ghastly confession that he bartered not only my father's name, but also my mother's. The tic in my cheek fires up. Jana reaches out her hand and gently covers the twitching muscle. I press her hand to my face, and close my eyes, and we sit there. For a very long moment. A brand new bloody wound, after all this time. Zacharias would say it's just another truth we were hiding from. It still inflicts a pain beyond pain.

"I feel—shell-shocked, you know?" she says.

"I know . . . ," I say. Then, as if doing triage among the wounded, I whisper, "But—are *we* okay?"

"We're fine. Definitely. Eternally."

That's what I'm longing to hear. "Want to move in with me? I'd love that," I suggest.

"Thanks, but not yet. I need some time to think."

Jana's already made arrangements with her pal Carol to house-sit while she's on location in Durango for two months.

"I'm going to see a shrink," she says. "A woman named Sarah Mandelker over on Camden Drive. Rowan says she's real good. You went to one, didn't you, David?"

I tell her that I had two of them. One in Tokyo at the Army hospital. Then later another in Rome. Once France gave Teddy his permanent resident card, we shuttled between Paris, London, and Rome, like fruit pickers going wherever the work was.

"Did the shrinks help?" Jana asks.

I explain that the Army doctor kept saying what happened to my buddies in Korea wasn't my fault. He kept after me to say I agreed. So I did because I knew then he would discharge me. The one in Rome was smarter. I couldn't just pretend to see the light with him. He was very good.

"What'd he tell you?" she persists.

"They don't tell you, they let you figure it all out for yourself."

"So what did you figure out?" she asks.

"That I was massively angry. Of course I knew that before I walked in. I was itching to smash someone, my problem was I couldn't locate exactly the right person to blame."

But maybe last night I finally did. I desperately need to talk to her about Joe Shannon. But she's still focused on what I got out of therapy.

"Well, just that after losing my home, my friends, my mom, my girlfriend, and after Teddy's banishment—after all that, I was entitled to be monumentally enraged. I got it. But . . . thing is, when I finished treatment, I was angrier than when I began." I shrug. "But at least I didn't feel guilty about being so furious."

Until now. Now I'm feeling guilty and fighting panic. I play with the sugar cubes on the table. Building an igloo, knocking it down, working up to the biggie:

"My shrink said I was still looking to hold someone responsible. God, bad luck, HUAC, bully kids in Mexico, my personal karma, or the Red Chinese army—all strong candidates for the blame game. So I recognized that was what I was doing. Didn't mean I could stop doing it. But I can modulate it. The shrink calls it anger control. Thought I was getting good at it, until—"

I push the sugar cubes aside. "Jana, I keep thinking about Joe Shannon."

She leaps in. "Me, too!" She's as upset as I am. But she's worried about Leo. That maybe Leo killed Shannon. "He was trying to call me yesterday. After Shannon printed that garbage about us. He left messages everywhere. But I kept ducking his calls."

I say, "It's not Leo's style, and besides I can't see Leo taking time away from his picture to do it."

That makes her smile a little. So to keep her spirits up, I offer the one bit of good news I have. About the new job Harry has arranged for me. "Starting this afternoon. I'm gonna be a unit publicist." Then I can't help blurting, "If I haven't been arrested by then."

She's startled. "Arrested? For what?"

"For not being able to remember half of what I did last night and coming home all banged up—on the same night Shannon got killed."

"But you only met him, what, *twice*?"

"Public cluster fucks, both times. Plus the cops might look at me as a second-generation Shannon-hater." I stare at my bruised knuckles. And tell her the whole thing. "Suppose I lost it last night—I keep remembering how much I wanted to go over there and rack up Shannon. Suppose I did."

"No! You didn't kill that man," she says. But I can see she's worried. The memory of my battle with the storm troopers.

"How can you be that certain, honey, even I don't know for sure—"

"David, you could *never* do that!"

I see how much she wants to believe that. So do I.

After Jana goes back to the research department, I find the publicity building and check in. Trying to move on. Act normal. I'm sharing an office with a veteran flack, Art Sarno, a friendly little guy. He starts briefing me on what's expected of a unit publicist, but I'm distracted. Still stuck on what Jana and I talked about.

"Hey." Sarno smiles. "Lot of stuff, but not that tough, we'll go over it all later. Your picture started shooting this morning on the Western street. Why don't you just mosey on over and meet everyone. I'll stop by to see you in a while—there's a trade paper reporter covering the lot today and I'll bring him by your set and introduce you."

As I go out the door, Sarno tosses after me: "You gotta be a little careful with Sterling Hayden"—he's the star of the quickie cowboy picture—"he hates publicists."

So, as instructed, I mosey over, and as it happens, the first person I run into is Sterling Hayden. He's climbing out of a studio limo that's dropped him near the catering truck and dressing room trailers. A shock of blond hair and the physique of a Viking god. He's a giant, maybe the biggest man in Hollywood this side of John Wayne.

When I introduce myself, Hayden shakes a fist as big as a catcher's mitt in my face and demands: "So you're the punk who punched out Joe Shannon?" I nod, with some concern. He breaks into a huge smile. "Put 'er there, pardner!"

He grabs my hand and pumps. A firm, but not crushing

handshake. The man is aware of his power. "Joe Shannon lived a charmed life," he says, "bloody wonder somebody didn't cancel his subscription a long time ago." Then he squints at me. "I went to Washington in forty-seven with your father to protest the Committee. Teddy was a stand-up guy. Gotta get some makeup on, kid, but we'll talk later."

He walks off as I silently thank Teddy for another gift. Then I continue down the street. It's the usual movieland version of a cow town: general store, saloon, bank, white steeple church, even a rough-hewn gallows next to the stable and the blacksmith's shop. Leo's Mercedes has been evicted from its usual parking spot in front of the saloon.

The scene they're shooting inside the saloon is a golden oldie: the crooked banker drinking whiskey with his ruthless gunslinger and cooking up trouble for the nesters. The usual B-movie array of characters for a low-budget Western is assembled. Mustachioed bartenders servicing the rowdy crowd of gamblers, dance-hall girls, cowboys, and farmers, while a piano player tinkles away in the background. The director yells "Cut and print" and a cadaverous-looking man in a frock coat and a fur trapper's hat calls out to me from behind a Lincolnesque set of whiskers:

"Duveed, whaddayadoin here?" I'm startled to see it's Zacharias.

"What are *you* doing here?"

"Earning a dishonest day's wages," he says. "After you left last night, this casting gal came out of the show at Grauman's Chinese and spotted me standing next to my bus. She told me my face has oodles of character. So here I am. For a three-day job. Then it's back to the bus. Can ya guess who I'm playing?"

"Not Honest Abe."

"Nah, I'm the town mortician. Whenever the baddie bushwacks a farmer, I come rolling over with a coffin. A running gag. Great way to make my reentry into the Hollywood scene, huh?"

I tell him why I'm on the set, and joke about being here until they come and arrest me, because it's still giving me the jitters. "No problem," he says. "You lie and I'll swear to it. Just tell 'em you were with me all night."

Not a bad idea. Just then, the assistant director yells, "Positions, please," so Zacharias has to move off. I see Art Sarno at the swinging saloon doors waving me to come outside.

"Brought you that trade paper guy," Sarno says as we walk to the catering truck. "He's an asshole, always coming on to the starlets, but Harry Rains treats him like a VIP, gives him access to all the sets." The guy's back is toward us, he's snagging a chocolate donut to go with his free cup of coffee. "Oke, I want y'to meet—"

Okie O'Connell turns toward us with the gap-toothed smile that curdles at the sight of me. "Y'didn't tell me this sonuvabitch is here!"

"Guess you two know each other," Sarno says sardonically.

"All too well," I say. Mildly. Don't want to lose this job before I hardly have it. But Okie plows ahead, face turning purple:

"This peckerwood killed my best buddy!"

The crew people near the catering truck and surrounding trailers are all staring at us. Better show than the one they're shooting inside the saloon.

"You murderin' Commie piece a shit!" Okie rages on. "Tell 'em all what you did to Joe Shannon!"

"I don't know what the hell you're talking about," I shout back at him.

At which point Sterling Hayden, who has emerged from the makeup trailer, takes in the situation. While Okie rants,

Hayden steps between us. He winks at me, and flings his enormous arm around Okie's shoulders.

"Easy does it, pardner," he says to Okie, "been waiting for you to come around and tell me a joke, got a good one I haven't heard?"

Okie allows Hayden to propel him away, still glaring back at me. Art Sarno tosses me a "don't worry" gesture and accompanies them. They enter Hayden's dressing room trailer and close the door. The second assistant director has emerged from the saloon to yell, "Hey guys! Keep it down!" Everybody goes back to whatever they were doing, but as they disperse I see someone familiar. Looks like he's been here during the entire episode.

"Afternoon, Mr. Weaver," Agent McKenna says. "Is there some place quiet where we can talk?"

Well, here's my shadow. Why am I not surprised that *he's* my inquisitor.

Trying to play it cool, I suggest we first get a cup of coffee from the catering truck. The good host, but as I pour my cup I notice McKenna studying my bruised knuckles.

"Got into a fracas recently?" he asks.

"Is that a federal offense?"

"Depends. Could be."

I should be deferential and polite, I know that, but just the sight of this man enrages me.

"Bet you're here to talk about Joe Shannon," I challenge. Let's get this show on the road. "So how does the death of a gossipmonger qualify as an FBI case?"

"We're lending the LAPD a hand."

"Got nothing better to do with your time?"

"Look, kid—"

Hey, maybe I scored a little point with that one. "Don't call me kid."

"—I've got a busy day. So how about if I ask the questions, you give the answers, and then I'll be out of your hair."

"Yeah, sure, I'll be—cooperative." He doesn't take the bait. "Okay, let's go over there."

We go sit on the steps of the gallows. And we start. He takes notes, without comment. When he comes to where I was last night, I'm tempted to use the alibi Zacharias volunteered. But then I think, don't do it, this turd is trained to detect lies. So I tell it straight.

At last McKenna says, "Is that it?"

"You tell me." Don't know if I've helped my cause or ruined my life. He flips back the pages in his notebook to where he started jotting.

"Let me see if I've got it straight—you were upset because of the cracks Joe Shannon made in his column at you *and* your girlfriend *and* your father—so you went barhopping around Hollywood all night, getting bombed out of your mind, you didn't talk to anyone, except busy bartenders. There's a point, maybe more than one, at which you blacked out, don't know for how long, woke up somewhere else, with skinned knuckles and your jacket ripped, but have no memory of how that happened. No witnesses to any of this that you know of."

"You're my alibi, Agent McKenna." Let him know I'm on to him.

"How's that again?"

"Weren't you following me around town last night—the way you've been doing lately?"

Unless he's a better actor than Spencer Tracy, he's genuinely surprised. "Why would I be doing that?"

"A family tradition. You hounded my father, now you want to keep up the franchise with me."

He stares at me. "That make sense to you, Mr. Weaver?"

Suddenly it doesn't. It's a jarring realization. I've been operating on a stupid assumption. But I'm certain *some*body's been
following me. The tingly feeling outside Dolores coffee shop,
and I remember shouting McKenna's name into the darkness
last night. Or am I losing it?

"Got to tell you," he closes his notebook, "I think the account of your whereabouts last night is about the worst alibi
I've ever heard."

"Sorry to let you down." I know, I know, more sass from
me. But it's like he's asking for it. I lean in to him. "Look, I
didn't kill Joe Shannon!"

"How do you know? You don't remember jackshit, Mr.
Weaver. You definitely had motive, definitely had opportunity."

Screw him. I hold out my wrists. "Want to cuff me? Am I
under arrest?"

"Just trying to understand you. You sure don't make it easy."

The bell inside the saloon signals the end of the shot. A production assistant down near the catering truck yells, "Anyone
here named McKenna? Phone call!"

McKenna excuses himself and walks down the street. I
don't know if I've been dismissed or we're going to resume. So
I slowly trail after McKenna. As I pass the saloon, Zacharias
comes out.

"How'd that go?" he asks.

"I think he thinks I did it."

"Cops make everybody feel like that. It's how they get their
jollies."

They're calling for the next shot, so Zacharias has to go
back. He pats my shoulder encouragingly and walks off. Now
what do I do? McKenna is near the catering truck picking up
the phone. What I want to do while he's looking the other way
is race to the airport and catch the first plane to Argentina
or some country where they don't extradite. But that feels

premature. So I drift to the catering truck, pour myself a coffee refill, and wait nearby for McKenna to finish his call. Looks like he's enjoying it. Maybe they found fingerprints on Shannon's neck. Good news. Unless they're mine.

31

McKENNA

It's Alcalay calling. "How's it goin' at your end?" He asks so pleasantly I hardly recognize him. But I can do pleasant, too.

"I'm collecting a bushel basket of alibis," I tell him. "Everybody claims they were home sleeping. Except the Weaver kid. He was on the town but doesn't remember exactly where or with who. Got blitzed."

"Think he went knocking on Joe Shannon's door?"

"Too soon to say." Alcalay still hasn't told me why he's calling. "What's new at your end?"

"Well, we checked out Shannon's ex-roommate, the one who wrote the love letters we found in the safe."

"The state senator."

"Got a platinum alibi. He's in Singapore on a junket. He was feature speaker at a banquet at the time of the fire."

That's still not worth Alcalay tracking me down here. I wait for him to get to it.

"Listen," he says, "that military dog tag from the safe—we got lucky. It was melted by the heat of the fire, but the lab guys found the lettering had imprinted on the safe wall. You were right, it's a navy tag—"

"—belonging to able-bodied Seaman Joseph P. Shannon." I'm getting impatient.

"Not even close. Name on the ID tag is Yeoman Third Class Axel Atherton, serial number NA19583298, blood type O, date of birth 6/29/26."

"Who the hell is he? And what was Shannon doing with his dog tag?"

"The Bureau could help us on that," he says.

How nice. So now we're the *Bureau,* not the Feebs or the Fat Boys. Alcalay needs something. It must be eating him up. "Any way we can help, Ray," I say affably.

"I figure the Navy Department can give you a rundown. Atherton might still be in the service, or maybe they've got a forwarding address. But when we make that kind of query it usually winds up on the bottom of some pile. Thought if you make the pitch it'll move faster."

"Absolutely. We're on the same team." I'm twisting the knife. "I'll shoot in an expedited request to the Navy Department and the Pentagon. We'll also run this guy through the Bureau's data bank." Flip open my notebook, click my ballpoint pen. "The sailor's name is Alex Atherton, A-T-H-E-R-T-O-N?"

"*Axel* Atherton. A-X-E-L."

"Axel Atherton," I repeat.

"The Birthday Boy," a voice says behind me. I turn and see Okie O'Connell strolling by with Sterling Hayden. I give Okie a wait-a-second motion. "Talk to you later," I say to Alcalay and hang up.

I nod at Hayden. "Sterling. Long time."

"Not long enough, McKenna." He does an about-face and strides off. After all we did for him. Go screw yourself! But Okie's my man of the moment.

"Why'd you say, the Birthday Boy?"

"Huh? Oh. Well, y'know how Joey always ran a line in the column, wishin' folks he liked in the industry a happy birthday?"

"Uh-huh, so what's that got to do with—"

"Most of 'em were headliners, plus some old-timers who'd been forgotten, but I could always decipher who they all were—'cept for Axel Atherton. The mystery man. His name'd pop up in the column like clockwork every year, and damned if I could place him."

"Sure about the name?"

"Y'know me. I'm real good on names." A reminder of his record-setting score for HUAC.

"Ever ask Shannon about it?"

"Yeah, he just laughed and told me to mind my own ever-lovin' business. How do you know ol' Axel?"

I grin. "Mind your own ever-lovin' business." Okie laughs. "You inheriting Joe's column?" I ask him.

"Looks like it, cousin. At least on a trial basis. But I gotta show the publisher I can do an A-one job." He looks past me, spots Weaver at the coffee stand. "Hey, punk, there'll be a little somethin' in the paper about you tomorrow!"

The other studio press agent tugs Okie away and off the Western street as I consider if Weaver was close enough to hear any of my phone call. Well, who cares? Got nothing to do with him.

I start back over to Weaver. Could squeeze some more, but I have what I wanted from him. More or less. I pride myself on being able to read people, but this guy's got me puzzled. Everybody else I talk to about Shannon is on eggshells, while Weaver is into this whole-truth-and-nothing-but-the-truth shtick—no matter how bad it makes him look.

I'm tempted to believe him, maybe partly because I prematurely dropped his name to Hoover, but mostly it feels like only a masochistic idiot would make up such a cockamamie excuse for an alibi. Unless it's a crafty maneuver. The best offense is absolutely no defense?

I didn't ask him anything about Wendy Travers yet. I don't

want to tip our hand—also I've already checked with the Chateau Marmont and found out that on the night of her killing Weaver ordered room service and signed for it at eleven o'clock. He probably ate his food and went to sleep. But Wendy was killed about midnight on a street corner only about a mile or so away from the Chateau. On that basis, he still merits a spot on the list.

So as I reach him now, I say: "Thanks for the coffee. I'll be in touch."

I can see he takes that as a threat. The way things are going, he ought to. But I'll get Alcalay to have his troops cruise the Hollywood bars tonight and check out Weaver's story about last night.

As I walk off across the lot, I'm still feeling peeved at the frosty reception I got from Sterling Hayden. He, of all people, should be kissing my ass. Saved his life. Of course it was a two-way deal. We needed him as much as he needed us.

Hayden was the biggest star to admit to Party membership since Larry Parks, an Oscar nominee for playing Al Jolson, and a radical union organizer for the Screen Actors Guild. The Parks case had turned into a colossal screwup. The Committee had to strong-arm Parks into giving names. When finally he spilled his guts on the stand in front of the media, HUAC thanked him and sent him on his way to continue his career. Even superpatriot John Wayne said Parks had sinned, confessed, and now should be forgiven. But powerful gossip columnist Hedda Hopper was not in a forgiving mood. The deal Parks had made with HUAC was not good enough for her. Larry Parks was Blacklisted and his career over.

Even worse, the credibility of the FBI and HUAC was endangered. If we couldn't deliver amnesty for cooperative witnesses, we were out of business. Everyone we talked to would just tell us to fuck off and take the Fifth Amendment.

That's where Sterling Hayden came in.

Not only a movie star, also a war hero. Served with the OSS in Europe, smuggled guns across the Adriatic to Tito's forces in Yugoslavia. He won the Silver Star. Because of his admiration for Tito he joined the Party when he came back to Hollywood. He was a member for a couple of years until the Cold War heated up. Long enough to earn a subpoena.

Some coordinated arm-twisting by his agent, his lawyer, and his shrink—along with me—helped him find Jesus and the American Way. Hayden testified and recanted his membership and named names and went back to making movies. We had our inspirational example for those who followed him to the stand: give the Committee what they want and you can keep working.

True, as he grew older and more grizzled, the work was mostly in B pictures. What the hell, that wasn't our fault. We kept our part of the bargain, so why's he being so pissy now?

I'm on my way to see Rex Gunderson, that old bastard always knows the inside political scoop. En route to his office, I run into Jana Vardian. No eye contact. Strange on a studio lot where everyone looks you right in the eye, usually with a smile. Never know who can help you up whatever ladder you're climbing. Guess Jana is an exception to that rule—at least for me.

But I have a ready greeting. "Looking for your boyfriend?"

"What?" Thought she'd get by me with just a vague nod of recognition. We've met casually a number of times over the years. Before and after Leo testified.

"David Weaver," I say, "I just left him on the Western street."

"Oh, thanks." She can't get away from me fast enough. Well, scare 'em when they're young and you've got 'em forever. But I envy the Weaver kid the light that glowed in her eyes when I said his name. Young love.

I've only been in love once. When I was working in Detroit. Back then, in 1946, Detroit was known as the bank robbery capital of the country. It was my second posting as an agent. Most bank hitters snatch and run, but others tried to shoot it out, grabbing hostages as leverage. I developed a reputation as the first man through the door in all the stickiest situations. Every case was a potential explosion, but I felt indestructible. I was on a permanent adrenaline high. That brings me back to the subject of being in love.

Her name was Ashley Bowman. We met at the office Christmas party at a rooftop restaurant overlooking the lake. I came alone, the nurse I was dating had to work that night. I cruised the party, drinking and gabbing with the guys. Then I caught sight of a woman with shoulder-length honey-blond hair, wearing a black sheath dress, no jewelry except a strand of pearls. Classy. Alone on the terrace. I shouldered my way over in time to light her cigarette. When she turned her face upward to murmur thanks, I was looking at the boss's wife. I'd seen her once when she visited the office.

The smart move at that point would have been to put distance between us before her husband or anyone else noticed. But I was so stoked with testosterone from yesterday's bank job that I lingered a moment to flirt.

"What a party!" I smiled. "Like we're on a Caribbean cruise ship."

"Bound for the Bahamas," she played along.

"I prefer the Virgin Islands." I was that drunk.

"How did I know you were going to say that?"

I felt sheepish, don't know what I would have said next, but Rudy appeared. Rudy Bowman, Special Agent in Charge of the Detroit office. Rich kid from Harvard Law, a lanky know-it-all desk jockey, who taught criminology at Michigan Law, my alma mater. He snaked a husbandly arm around her waist, "Having a good time, Mac?"

"Agent McKenna was just telling me what his Christmas wish is."

"What's that?" he asked me.

"Peace on earth," I said.

"Then we'd be out of work," he said. We all laughed and he guided her away. That should have been the end of it, but I learned where she lived. After only a little hesitation, I staked out the house, followed her to the Farmer Jack supermarket, and pushed a cart around until I ran into her.

"Hey, do you come here often?" I hailed her.

"I thought people only said that in pick-up bars."

"Shows you the kind of company I've been keeping. Got time for a cup of coffee?"

She hesitated, then said, "Only if you can stop talking in one-liners."

That's probably when I started to fall in love with her. "I'll try," I said. And the affair began. The best six months of my life.

Ashley Bowman was everything I wanted in a woman. Gorgeous, smart, funny, incredibly hot in the sack. The high risk was an extra turn-on. The connection between us was astonishing. Both of us came from hardscrabble childhoods and never wanted to go back. She didn't talk much about Rudy, except to say that he was the big mistake of her life. They'd been married seven years and he had been cheating on her from the get-go.

"Have you ever been unfaithful to him?"

"Never." I believed her. "Until now."

Mostly we met at small inns or motels way out in Windsor

or Auburn Hills. We were magic together. Adored slow dancing to Sinatra's romantic ballads, scarfing extra-gooey pizza,
jogging by the lake. Hated the Detroit Tigers, rooted for the
underdog White Sox. Best of all, we would spend hours locked
in each other's arms, and she began dreaming of a future for
us. Ignoring the complications posed by her marriage and her
six-year-old son, Kim.

"Do you really think it's possible?" she would wonder.

"Why not?" I would blue-sky imagine with her. "All it
takes is two people who love each other."

And then our secret was discovered. Not by Rudy Bowman. By J. Edgar Hoover.

I was ordered back to D.C. for an "orientation seminar."
When I checked in at Bureau Central, I was referred to the
Director's office. Hoover and Clyde Tolson were looking grim.
Tolson led off:

"We heard about your intramural sexual escapade, Mc-
Kenna."

How did they hear? Well, there were rumors Hoover had
spies in all the Bureau stations. I braced myself for the drubbing
I deserved. Disgraceful conduct unworthy of a federal agent.
Losing the job I loved. Turn in your badge and your gun!

Instead, J. Edgar Hoover giggled.

It was a high-pitched squeak of a sound. "You really put the
horns on Rudy Bowman, didn't you?" Hoover said. Christ,
was that a question or an accusation? So I said nothing, but he
went on. "Cuckolded that posturing fool. Never did care much
for the man. An acceptable administrator, but basically a bean
counter, not field officer material. Not like you, Brian."

I was dazed. They know the worst and I'm going to get
away with it.

Hoover went on. "You've amassed quite a record in Detroit.

Apart from your boudoir activities. So we've decided to move you up. To the main arena. We're sending you to California. You'll be tracking subversives who have been conspiring to pollute the motion-picture screens and capture the minds of innocent Americans."

I wasn't sure what he meant, but it sounded great. High-profile cases. Glamour duty. A big step upward in the Bureau. With the potential for even more advancement. I thanked them. They both solemnly shook my hand.

I went back to Detroit and asked Ashley to marry me. "We can make the dream real," I said. First, of course, she'd have to go to Reno and get a divorce, then join me in L.A.

She cried. Not for happy. Out of fear.

"Rudy's father is rich and very powerful," she reminded me, "and Rudy's warned me that if I ever try to leave him he'll spend whatever it costs to take Kim away from me."

I said we'd get a terrific lawyer, we'd fight him, we'd—

Nothing I said could get her past that terror.

So I went off to L.A. alone, feeling as if I was leaving my heart behind. The pace of my job out here didn't leave time for another woman, at least that's what I told myself. The truth was, I was still crazy in love with Ashley. For a while we talked on the phone regularly. Then it tapered off to a call on my birthday or anniversaries of special occasions, like the summer solstice, when we had snuck away on our first full weekend together. But now she was too scared to allow me to send her flowers or call her. Her phone calls dwindled and finally stopped.

I began to drink after that. Nothing I couldn't control, and only on my own time. Tanqueray gin martinis, the kind Ashley and I loved. Flaked out in my apartment and getting bombed listening to Sinatra croon *I'll Never Smile Again*. Sloppy drunk. Winging into wild schemes to get her back. Maybe there was a way to leverage my clout in the Bureau against the power of Rudy and his father. Then waking into dawn's futility. Hungover, realizing it was just an aching delusion. After a while, the urge to drink lessened. I became resigned to my loss. But it still hurt whenever I thought of her.

After the HUAC days were over and I was on my "Special Assignment" status, I dated some women who worked in the Federal Building and even a few starlets. Nothing ever amounted to anything. Nothing to compare with the feelings I'd had for Ashley.

32

DAVID

After McKenna slithers off the Western street, I'm talking to Zacharias as Jana rushes onto the set. She warmly greets Zacharias and he hugs her. I'm glad to see that. He's known us both since we were kids.

"Hey," I say, "what's happening?" She seems bursting with excitement.

"Don't get mad, but—your screenplay. I slipped it to the studio, not as an official submission, but as a favor, and—they're interested in it! You have a meeting. Four o'clock today."

"Great! Who'm I meeting with?"

She takes a deep breath before answering. "Markie Gunderson."

Oh God. "Not exactly the president of my fan club."

"He's a pro, David; this isn't personal, it's business."

I put on a hopeful smile. But Zacharias adds a caution: "In Hollywood, business is always personal."

It's 4:21 and I'm cooling my heels in Markie's outer office. The wrinkled, henna-rinsed secretary looks old enough to have started taking dictation with a quill. She's lying into the busy phones on behalf of her boss: "Sorry, he's in a story conference." Truth is he's not here. She has offered me coffee, tea, soft drinks, trade papers, and magazines. I flip through the latest issue of *TIME*. Charles Van Doren confesses to a Congressional Committee that he won $129,000 on a quiz show because the producers gave him the answers in advance. A fable for our time.

"Ah, here's Mr. Gunderson now," the secretary announces.

Markie, sporty in a Panorama jacket windbreaker over a denim shirt, black workpants, and black boots, sweeps past me. "Any calls, Evelyn?" She hands him the message sheet. As he scans it he asks her, "You pick up my dry cleaning?" She says she did, he continues into his inner office, tossing behind him: "Come on in, Davey."

It's not a corner office, so Markie still has something to aspire to. The wall decor is movie posters, old hits directed by his father, but also non-Panorama classics like *Citizen Kane, Casablanca,* and *The Wizard of Oz.* I'm carrying my clipboard, which has a small battery-powered light for taking notes in the darkness of a screening room. A gift from my former mentor, Leo.

Markie gestures me into one of the small chairs facing him. He digs in his script pile. Comes up with the copy of my script that I'd given to Jana. Places it in the center of his desk, pats it. Approvingly?

"Read your piece—I know it's a first draft, but I'm impressed. Apparently talent does run in the genes. You write very well."

"Thanks. Glad you like it."

"It's Lew Ayres, right?"

"A combination of him and other people. That's why I didn't use his name. But, yeah, a movie actor who stars in an anti-war picture and then becomes a conscientious objector during World War II and everybody comes down on him like a ton of bricks like they did on Ayres—"

"That part was marvelous," Markie jumps in, "how they all thought he was a coward—at the time even my dad did, but then Ayres went on to vindicate himself and save so many lives under fire as a medic. It's an inspiring story."

I'm getting stoked. He gets it. He really likes it.

"Of course, it needs some work," he says.

"I guess everything does," I say.

He looks to see if I'm being facetious. I'm not. "Tell me what you feel it needs."

Markie leans back in his swivel chair, gazes at the ceiling. "The movie audience always has certain expectations. That's why I'm glad you fictionalized it to some extent. It gives us wiggle room. To fulfill the audience's desires."

"Which are?" Where is this going?

He holds a pencil in front of him with both hands, as if it's a field marshal's baton. "I once heard a very interesting discussion between my dad and Duke Wayne—about a script Duke had rejected at another studio. My dad asked him why, and Duke said, 'My fans always wait for me to strike a blow.'" Markie looks at me meaningfully. "Your hero never strikes a blow."

"He's—a pacifist."

"Of course he is. So was Gary Cooper in *Sergeant York,* but that didn't stop him from making his peace with God and finally killing and capturing half the kraut army. York won the Congressional Medal of Honor."

"And Cooper got the Academy Award," I add.

"Precisely!"

"So you're suggesting that my hero—"

He leans forward, selling. "Suppose he finds his best friend in the platoon, a loveable Brooklyn kid who he's encouraged to be brave, suppose he finds the kid's body in the jungle— butchered by the Japs. And when the Japs attack again your guy picks up the dead kid's machine gun and—"

"But that totally destroys the point of the whole script!" I blurt.

"Davey, you've got something with possibilities here. Don't go artsy-fartsy on it. *Battleground* was a big hit because our GI's won the Battle of the Bulge, not lost it."

This is getting nuts. "I'm not writing about a loser—my guy is a hero. He just doesn't believe in killing people."

Markie drops his pencil onto the desk with a clunk.

"Look, my job at Panorama is to help create tomorrow's box office winners. We like movies where the hero kills people. Warriors prevail. They defend what's right. You were a Ranger. Decorated in combat. Write what you know."

"I understand what you're suggesting, but—I can't do it."

He sighs. A big dramatic sigh. "I knew this wouldn't work. I told Jana."

"Told her what?"

"You're not a pro, Davey. Knew you couldn't accept input. It's a very arrogant and shortsighted attitude."

"Hey, sorry I wasted your valuable time." I want to charge over the desk and shake the smugness out of him.

"No problem," Markie says. "If Jana wants me to read something, I read it."

"No matter how big a piece of shit it is."

He smiles. Glad he got to me. "That's not what I said. But if that's what you heard . . ."

I rise quickly and lean over toward him, he flinches, but I'm just reaching for my script. I grab it and go to the door. As I open it, he calls to the outer office, "Evelyn, get me the coverage on the new Norman Mailer book. Need it immediately."

She says she'll rush to the file room and adds: "Your dad wants you to call him." Evelyn walks out with me. Darting a glance at my angry face.

"I knew your father," she says as we go down the corridor. "A lovely gentleman with a bizarre sense of humor." I tell her

I agree and ask why she said that. "He always referred to the executives here as the Tsar's Cossacks."

Then I realize I've left my clipboard next to the chair in Markie's office. I excuse myself and double back to get it. As I enter the outer office, I can hear Markie through the half-open inner door. He's on the phone:

". . . under the circumstances, Agent McKenna, I feel it's my duty to mention that Weaver is a hair-trigger personality, highly trained to kill by the Army, who—"

My impulse is to storm in there and shove the phone up his ass, but that would only prove his point. So I tiptoe out. I can get my clipboard back later.

33

MᴄKENNA

I'm on the phone in the gatehouse at the front entrance to the studio. The guard flagged me down as I was about to drive off the lot after a time-wasting visit with Rex Gunderson, who was uncharacteristically mellow. Not a bad word about anyone. He thinks Leo Vardian is a fine director, David Weaver an enterprising young man, and has nothing but kind thoughts about the Panorama honchos. Sad about the passing of Joe Shannon, a fighting anti-Communist: "We shall not see his like again."

Now I'm wasting more time talking to his son.

I've only met Mark a few times. I'm listening to him yammer on the phone like we're asshole buddies. Inviting me at his dad's suggestion to a memorial service for Joe Shannon here at the studio tomorrow morning. But that's not really why he had me flagged down. He's got a contribution to make.

"I don't know if you're aware of the recent altercation between Joe Shannon and David Weaver."

"I was there."

"Oh, really? Well . . . under the circumstances, Agent Mc-Kenna, I feel it's my duty to mention that Weaver is a hair-trigger personality, highly trained to kill by the Army, who—"

"Thanks for the tip, Mark, but we already know all about his military background."

"Just trying to help out. Hope you understand."

Sure I understand. I saw Jana Vardian accompanied by Mark at Teddy Weaver's funeral. Now she's with David. All's fair in love and war in Hollywood and the difference between the two is sometimes inseparable. Unless. Could be a twofer: maybe Rex Gunderson was so mellow because he's appointed Mark as his designated hitter.

"Well, appreciate you and your dad thinking of me, Mark. See you at the service."

I hang up and I'm climbing back into my car when another uniformed studio guard, aboard his spiffy little golf cart, brakes up. He's cutting off my exit lane.

"Agent McKenna, we need you over in the Visitors Parking Lot."

"What for?" Who do you have to fuck to get out of this place?

"The reporter guy, Mr. O'Connell, he's demanding your presence, sir. Says it's very important."

I rev my motor. "Tell Okie to call me at the office." I've had enough of his nonsense for now.

The studio guard doesn't budge. "'scuse me, sir, but Mr. O'Connell's, well, he's sort of flipping out. I really think you should follow me over there." The grim look on his face convinces me.

Okie drives a seven-year-old bronze T-Bird and it's parked in the subterranean Visitors lot. I see two more guards standing there with Okie, who's carrying on like an Italian fish peddler, arms waving, eyes bulging, fingers pointing. As I get out of my car Okie rushes toward me:

"Y'didn't believe me, didja, Mac? I told ya! I kept tellin' ya! But everybody thinks ol' Okie is fulla shit! Well, I'm not and now y'know!"

"Okie, calm down or we're going to drop a net over you. *Quietly* tell me what you're talking about."

"I'm talkin' about *that*!"

He leads me to the front of his car and indicates the square of blank cardboard tucked under the wiper blade on the driver's side. I don't get it for a second, so Okie makes it clear:

"Gotta get in the car for the view!" He yanks open the door, I slip in behind the wheel. Through the glass facing the driver is a message in the same black-inked block lettering I've seen before:

THE SINGING FOOL
YOU WERE LUCKY LAST TIME

I'm staring at it as Okie jabbers in my ear. "See, *I'm* the target! It wasn't Joey! Y'have ta protect me! The killer's out there tryin' t'get me!"

In his hysterical state, Okie doesn't realize that the killer isn't "out there." He's inside. Right here. On the Panorama lot. Only a couple of short blocks from the Western set where the Weaver kid works.

M r. Weaver, this is Lieutenant Alcalay of the Los Angeles Police."

After I make the introduction, I sit back and watch. Barney Ott has lent us his elegant office. Leo Vardian has been here and gone, so has Keeler Barnes. Zacharias is next door in Heritage's office with another detective. But this is what Alcalay has been itching for: his chance to evaluate his prime suspect.

"Hey, David. You mind me calling you David?" Alcalay starts with cop bonhomie. "Where do you park your car on the lot?"

It's not what the kid expects to be asked. "I've got a space way out on the backlot."

"But your car's in the Visitors lot now. How come?"

"Well, it's closer to where I was going and there was an empty spot." Weaver looks at me, puzzled.

"You like old movies, David?" Alcalay has jumped to another subject to keep him off balance. Thinks he's playing him like a trout.

So Weaver asks Alcalay, why does he care about his taste in movies? A reasonable response. Except cops don't appreciate people who answer questions with questions.

"Well," the big cop pussyfoots in, "I just thought, since your dad wrote lots of the old movies you'd probably be real familiar with them."

"You mean like *The Informer*?" Weaver asks. "I saw the photo in the *Times* of that sign they found at Joe Shannon's house."

That's a mistake, kid, I think, don't take the bait. I don't like Alcalay's interrogation technique. It's too Mickey Mouse. Reminds me of Declan Collins's smart-ass style of bullying conversation. Laying cute little booby traps. I doubt it will work with Weaver. He's too smart. I find you can get more being straightforward. By listening carefully to the answers, and particularly watching body language. But it's not Alcalay's way.

"Would you call Shannon an informer?" he asks mildly.

"Would you?" Alcalay doesn't answer, of course. So Weaver has to go on. "I'd call him a Red baiter. Self-appointed political hit man. Making America safe for Americans—even if it kills 'em."

"Some would say you sound bitter."

"Some would be right."

The kid's worried, but it's coming out snotty. I can see Alcalay loves the arrogance. It fortifies his theory.

"I hear you had a run-in this afternoon with Okie O'Connell." He's springing another subject.

Weaver shrugs. "No big deal."

"Rough day for old Okie," Alcalay muses. "Leo Vardian barred him from his set. Then he comes to where you are and you go after him like a Rottweiler."

"Hey! It was the other way around! He came after me." Weaver looks to me to support him. When I don't, he prods. "You can jump in anywhere you like, Agent McKenna. Don't be bashful."

He doesn't understand the pecking order. This is Alcalay's play. I say nothing. I see the hate in Weaver's eyes. I wonder what he sees in mine?

"O'Connell fingered your dad to the Committee," Alcalay says.

"He ratted out everyone from Malibu to Burbank," Weaver snaps.

"You were in Korea, weren't you?" Weaver nods. "And they gave you a medical discharge."

Weaver tenses. Surprised Alcalay knows details of his history. "Yeah, got banged up a little."

"Let's go back to the old movies for a second. I love the musicals. Ever see any Al Jolson pictures?"

Weaver seems mystified. "Saw a revival of *The Jazz Singer* at the Academy Theater when I was a kid, but what's—"

Alcalay cuts him off. "Do you know another Jolson picture called *The Singing Fool*?"

"Never heard of that one." Then a lightbulb goes on in his head. But will the kid have enough sense to keep his mouth shut?

"You found another sign, didn't you?" he says. "In the parking lot?" Amazingly, Weaver laughs. Is it a teasing boast or just pride that he's deciphered Alcalay's fragmented style of questioning.

Alcalay's face reddens—not embarrassment at getting caught being cutesy, but anger. So he runs with it: "Why would you say that?" and Weaver says "Just a wild guess" and I can see Alcalay thinks he's a liar but that doesn't give him enough to take action, so after a moment Alcalay looks at me and I sigh.

Weaver breaks the silence. "Hey, is Okie dead?"

Alcalay leans back and levels a Who-do-you-think-you're-fuckin'with? glare. Then finally he waves dismissively. "We'll be in touch."

I remember saying the same thing to Weaver earlier today. Only now it's looking much worse. I feel sort of sorry for him, but maybe that's mixed up with my annoyance at having to defer to Alcalay.

After Weaver leaves and the door closes, Alcalay says, "That kid's either a weirdo or he's got the biggest pair in town."

"It's just his manner."

"Yeah? Tell it to the judge—or the DA first." He ticks off points. "Trained by the Rangers on the Seventy-Seven Best Ways To Kill A Man. Treated for psychiatric disorder by the Army. That was in your handy-dandy info packet. Locally, lately, Weaver punched out Shannon for trashing the memories of his dear departed parents. Then Shannon stings Daddy again publicly in his gossip column, just like he used to in the old days. Not to mention smearing Weaver's girlfriend. So I'd say revenge certainly is a possible motive. Then there's O'Connell—who informed on Weaver's father. Today there's a near fistfight between the two of them. And then O'Connell finds the threat on his windshield, real close to where Weaver's car is parked. Oh yeah, and as you discovered, he lives a hop-and-a-skip away from where Wendy Travers got waxed. How'm I doin'?"

"Not nearly enough," I say.

"Hey, who's side are you on?"

"I didn't know we were choosing up sides yet." Alcalay fumes, but I go on. "He pisses me off, too, Ray." Remembering my conversation with Weaver in the hallway at the Chateau. "But what's the big rush? We're just getting started. Lots of possibilities."

"I'm getting a lot of pressure on this from downtown."

Or does he just see a career opportunity? Like I do? Ouch. But hold on, I'm the one plunking for a complete and thorough investigation, not a hurry-up-wrap-it-up job. So to get him back on the straight and narrow, I try sympathizing with Alcalay, one pro to another.

"This is a hot potato for both of us, Ray. But we've got to do it right. Can't lock someone up just because you don't like 'em."

Alcalay thinks about that. Then reluctantly, but snidely acknowledges, "Yeah, if I locked up everyone I didn't like, I'd have clapped you in irons long ago."

Probably that's as close as I'm going to get to a thank-you from Alcalay for keeping him from going off half-cocked.

It's almost 7:00 P.M. by the time Alcalay and I are finished and I return to where I left my car in the underground Visitors lot. There are two cars still there, mine, and David Weaver's several slots away. I get behind my wheel but don't turn on the motor yet. I sit there in the darkness reviewing. Then I hear footsteps and Weaver comes down the ramp carrying a script and a bunch of papers. He doesn't notice me until he's unlocking his car door, then he squints in my direction. I roll my window down and give him a small wave.

Slowly he walks over. "Working late?" I say.

"Looks like we both are." Standing next to my car window,

he glances at his watch. "But still enough time for me to go out and kill someone else."

I give him a weary smile. "C'mon, Mr. Weaver, give it a rest."

"Hard to relax around you." Then he gestures at my car, "If I didn't know better I might think you're following me."

"But now you know better." I point at the script and papers under his arm. "Homework?"

"Yeah, I'm trying to figure out my new job. How's your job going?"

"Word of advice? Stop doing what you're doing."

"What am I doing?"

"Cracking jokes and playing the smart-ass." For an instant I think his guard lowers. We're just two guys talking. Then suspicion floods back into his eyes.

"That's the good cop talking, huh? Would have been nice to hear from you when your pal was trying to mind-fuck me in the office."

I can't explain to him that I'm sucking hind tit in this case. And he wouldn't believe it anyway. I'm supposed to be the all-powerful FBI.

"Well, have a good night," I say as I start my motor. He nods curtly and starts toward his car, but then I call after him: "Mr. Weaver, can I ask you one more question?"

He turns back toward me. "Gee, I thought you'd gone off duty. But always one more. Sure, go for it."

"Why did you laugh?" He knows exactly what I'm refer-ring to, but I spell it out to be clear. "When Alcalay was ques-tioning you—and you figured out that there'd been another threat sign left here on Okie's car. You laughed."

He's far enough away from my car so that his face is mostly in the shadows and I can't see his eyes. But I sense he's verging on providing a straight response. Then he shrugs.

"You wouldn't believe it." Finality in his voice.

I'm annoyed. "So it's for you to know and for me to find out?"

"Do your best, Agent McKenna."

He turns and walks away.

I'm annoyed. We're back to Square One. I just gave him a chance to open up a little. Some people never learn. I put my car in gear and drive away. But I'm still wondering what he might have said.

I stop by my office and use a secure line to call Clyde Tolson in D.C. While I wait for the switchboard to find him, I thumb through my incoming box. Routine garbage. Finally Tolson comes on. I brief him on the day's events. When I'm done, he asks, "So this young Red, what's his name—?"

Tolson hasn't forgotten. But I'm forced to say, "Weaver, David Weaver."

"Interesting that all roads seem to keep leading to him."

"Well, the supervising homicide lieutenant on the case and I were talking about that—and it seems almost too pat. I mean, if Weaver's our man, it's kind of a stupid way for him to go. On his own doorstep, so to speak."

"Criminals aren't all as smart as they are in the movies."

Throwing Hollywood in my face. "Of course, sir, we're looking intently at everyone who might be involved."

"In your thoroughness, don't ignore the obvious, Brian. Keep us fully apprised on all developments."

I think he's about to hang up, but he clears his throat. "Received that document," he's talking about the letter of commendation from Hoover to Shannon. "As always, you handled it with discretion." So there's my attaboy. Big fuckin' deal. It's wrapped in a keep-up-the-good-work with an implied "or else."

Now the call ends. Leaving me double depressed. Feeling like a kiss ass and a non-team player. I haven't decided if

Weaver is a viable suspect, but everyone else seems ready to slap him in the slammer. I check my watch. It's late. But I dial anyway. Kathleen sounds sleepy, but she wakes up fast and listens until I've filled her in.

"Wow, lots of movement on your big case," she observes, "just what you wanted." She waits for me to say something. I wait her out, so she adds: "Definitely sounds like Tolson and Hoover have found their favorite entry in the sweepstakes."

"We're only getting started, Kath."

"Yeah, but the suggestion of a top-echelon superior, like Tolson, speaking for Hoover himself, can't be ignored."

I kiss it off. "Prioritizing leads is a basic procedure, pushing Weaver's name up in the batting order doesn't constitute a premature rush to judgment. So nothing to be upset about."

"Who's upset?" she asks innocently.

"I just follow the facts, wherever they go."

"You and Jimmy Cagney." Definitely razzing me.

"If the facts happen to land on Weaver, then so be it. Either way, I'll have done my duty. Right?"

"Uh-huh. But." She lets the word hang out there. For me to pick up.

"But—I kinda regret inserting David Weaver into their thinking so early—"

"—just to score brownie points," she adds. "Funny," she begins, then stops herself.

"What's funny?"

"This is probably how a lot of those people felt when you shoved them into the HUAC hot seat. Once you give up a name, you can't take it back."

Guess that's what's bothering me and why I called her so late.

"Yeah, I'm feeling out of sync, Kath. Off on the wrong foot, but I don't want to overcompensate in either direction. I mean, Weaver could be the guy. We just don't know enough yet."

I realize that I'm not arguing with her. I'm arguing with my-self. And somehow I seem to be on the losing end. It doesn't feel good. So I determine to just bear down harder on the facts. Let the chips fall where they may. I'm just the impartial tool of justice.

CHAPTER

34

DAVID

It's back. My dream, the one that repeats periodically in the dead of night like a bad TV rerun. But it really happened when I was fifteen. I think of it as my rite of passage into the real world.

Slouched. Backseat of a car. A winding country road. Steep, one-lane. Pitch blackness surrounds us. Scrunched between my dad and my mom, who's leaning forward to talk to the friendly Negro lady up front. I call her Aunt Viola. Her husband, Uncle Frank, a State Assemblyman from Harlem, is driving, we're in their Packard. Bumper to bumper traffic as far as you can see. Through what seems like a narrow black tunnel punctuated only by headlights. I'm drowsing, but I hear Uncle Frank remarking on what a marvelous day it's been. The picnic in the meadow. The singing that followed. Paul Robeson. Pete Seeger. Woody Guthrie. "Wonder what's holding us up?" Teddy says.

Then we hear shouting up ahead. Men's voices. Lots of them. Edge closer. Voices louder. Coming from the night hills. I'm wide awake. Not scared. Not yet. Then we hear the sounds of glass shattering. Screams begin. We're still inching forward. The voices float in through the open windows. "Commie bastards!" "Dirty kikes!" "Fuckin' niggers!" "We'll kill you all!"

Suddenly a state trooper's face. Glaring in at us. Eerily illuminated. His back to the steep hills. Teddy calls to him. "What's happening, Officer?"

The trooper yells at us, "Pick it up, keep moving!"

"We can't go any faster," Teddy starts to say, "the road's—" That's as far as Teddy gets: the state trooper smashes his nightstick down on the roof of our car.

"Keep moving, dammit!"

"Roll up the windows," Teddy yells to us. Our car creeps forward. State troopers loom up out of the darkness. Stationed at intervals. Urging the gridlocked traffic to keep going. Then rocks and bricks begin to fly. Thrown from where the voices are. The steep embankments on both sides. We're caught in the eye of the storm now. I want to leap out. Run away. Teddy pushes me and my mother down onto the floorboard. He tries to cover our bodies with his body. A crash shudders our car. Windshield shattering. I raise my head. Uncle Frank still at the wheel. Shoulders showered with glass fragments. Like glistening dandruff. Eyes protected by his glasses. But blood trickling down from his brow. There's screaming. Right here. Inside our car. It's Aunt Viola. "Oh God, Frank, can you see?" She pulls out a hanky, dabs at him.

Teddy pushing me down again, seeking safety where there is none. My hands go flat on the floorboard. I feel dozens of pinpricks. Glass all over. Piercing the palms of my hands. I lift my head again.

We're like a duck in a shooting gallery. On a conveyer belt. Moving through the gauntlet of catcalling, invisible rock-throwers. And we can't escape. From the curses—"White Niggers!" "Gonna string Robeson up!" "Nigger-Loving Commies!" "Howdoyalikethis?!" The hailstorm goes on and on.

A huge rock crashes onto our hood. I shrink down. But

then, can't stop myself. Have to peek up again. Police aren't doing anything to stop the guys on the hillsides. They're protecting them! Teddy continuously tugging me down. I wriggle and resist. If only I can see the face of one of those bastards. But all I see is the occasional contorted face of a state trooper. I stare at each one. Usually in this dream they're strangers. Made familiar by all the times I've relived these moments. But tonight, there are special cameo appearances: One of the cops waving us on is Alcalay. A trooper looms briefly out of the darkness and it's McKenna, and when I peer hard into the inky hills I glimpse Markie Gunderson aiming a rock at my head, and as he throws it, I shriek and—

—and sit bolt upright in my bed. At the Chateau. Jana beside me. Her hand on my arm. Looking as terrified as I feel.

"Sweetie, it's okay. It's okay. You're all right." I look at her, still dazed. She sits up beside me. "What were you dreaming about?" she asks.

"Peekskill," I say.

I was there. That was my experience. Years later, after Korea and after a night sweat repeat of the dream in our Paris apartment—I went to the offices of the *Herald-Tribune* and checked their back files to fill in the background details:

On September 4, 1949, there was an all-star concert in a rented meadow three miles outside of Peekskill, New York. Its year-round residents were mostly blue-collar people and their families. But the population exploded during the hot summer months with nearly 30,000 second-home owners and vacation renters from New York City. Many Jewish, most left-leaning, some Communists. For the prior three years, the annual concert had been held without incident.

Once again, Paul Robeson was the featured performer. He was the most famous Negro in America. Twice named an All-American football star at Rutgers, he followed with a career on the concert stages of the world, on phonograph records, and sang "Ol' Man River" in the Hollywood version of *Show Boat*. But it was his international role as a social activist pressing for equality in civil rights that during the Cold War made him controversial to the point of being incendiary.

Attendance at the Peekskill concert was later officially estimated at about 20,000 concert-goers inside the grounds and 8,000 protesters outside. Platoons of police on hand, including 900 state troopers, plus a helicopter overhead and four ambulances on call. But despite jeering at the arrivals—"You'll get in, but you won't get out!"—the concert went off smoothly. Many attributed the peaceful afternoon to 1,500 volunteers, drawn from the ranks of the Fur and Leather Workers' Union, the Teachers' Union, the United Electrical Workers, and some New York Longshoremen. They linked arms to protect the perimeter of the meadow. During the concert there were no speeches, only music. When Robeson finally appeared he was surrounded by fifteen volunteers to shield him from possible sniper bullets. Several protesters with rifles already had been removed from the neighboring hillside.

Trouble erupted after the concert. Police funneled all the cars through one exit that fed into a traffic jam on the dark one-lane mountain road. As the caravan crept along they had to run a crossfire of rock throwers. Cars and buses were overturned. 215 concert-goers, including women and children, were injured, 145 hospitalized, some with serious eye damage.

New York Governor Thomas E. Dewey ordered an investigation. A grand jury exonerated the state troopers. Dewey described those attending the concert as "followers of Red totalitarianism" and the victims were blamed for the violence.

Jana turns on the nightstand lamp. "I didn't know you were still dreaming about it." She first heard me talk about Peekskill after our family came home to California. She knew it had haunted me long afterwards.

"Comes and goes." I lean back against the headboard, breathing as if I've run the hundred yard dash. "Hasn't happened in a while. I know it's a stress symptom. Had it in Mexico after Mom died. Joe McCarthy was in it then. Throwing rocks. When I was in Korea, and the Chinese had us nearly surrounded, General MacArthur was directing Peekskill traffic."

We both know why I'm having this dream again tonight. With guest appearances by McKenna and Markie and Alcalay.

Earlier, when I had first burst into my room at the Chateau, Jana hadn't heard about the ruckus over Okie. She thought my excitement was about the meeting with Markie, but I minimized: "Markie says the script needs work." Tell her about that later—instead I brought her up to speed about *The Singing Fool*. Then I proclaimed the discovery I'd made during my interrogation by Alcalay "It made me laugh out loud with relief."

His clumsy questions had tipped me to the sign left on Okie's car. "Maybe I'm sketchy about what I did last night because I was too drunk, but I'm cold sober today. And I sure as hell know I didn't leave a sign for Okie!"

She picked up on it instantly. "So someone else must have done the Shannon sign, not you! And his murder! David! You can stop suspecting yourself."

"Yeah! My rage demon didn't get out of the cage while I wasn't looking."

I kissed her and whirled her around the room. We were caught up in this thankful news until I mentioned that I almost told McKenna about my discovery during our chat in the parking lot. "But then I thought, he'll never believe me—all he'd hear was that I've been suspecting myself. Probably take it as a half-assed confession. But I almost told him—"

At the mention of McKenna's name, the color drained from her face. "God, how I hate that man! He makes me feel crawly and ashamed! After your family went to Mexico, they'd come over to the house to work on Leo every night. McKenna and Harry Rains. They'd close the door to his study. I'd crouch on the landing above to eavesdrop. I couldn't hear much of what they said. But their tones—McKenna so silky, Leo screaming curses at him, calling McKenna every vile word you ever heard, Harry smoothing and calming, then McKenna persuading again, Leo screaming some more. Night after night. I was so proud of my father for standing up to them. Refusing what they wanted him to do. And then—Leo went to Washington and named names. McKenna had finally broken him!"

I was not about to defend McKenna. But I thought Jana was blaming the wrong guy. McKenna and Harry Rains pressured him, but Leo did what he did for his own reasons.

Now, in the middle of the night, we're facing new realities. "Okay," Jana says, "of course you're not the one who killed Shannon—but who's doing all this and making it look like you are? And *why*? Why you? Who wants to hurt you? What's in it for them?"

My heart is still pounding. I can't think. "It's like Peekskill. Same feeling. As if I'm being ambushed. Can't go back, can't go forward, can't stand still. And there's a steamroller about to run over me."

She wraps her arms around me and kisses my cheek. "You forgot one thing. You're not alone. Not anymore. There are two of us." She kisses me again, on the lips. Then, with that chairman of the board authority she's always had, Jana says, "We're going to do something about this."

"Like what? Where do you even begin?"

"We'll think of something," she says.

I'm not so sure, but we curl our bodies like a pair of spoons. I can't fall asleep again, but in a few minutes I think she has, until she says in the darkness:

"How about the phone call?"

"Hm-m-m?"

"The one you told me about. McKenna on the Western street today. And that stuff you heard Okie telling him after?"

"Axel Atherton. The Birthday Boy."

"Yeah," she says, "that's something. Let's start there."

"Alcalay is much more interested in me."

"So—if they're ignoring a lead, all the more reason we check it out." She tries teasing me. "C'mon, David. Got anything better to do?"

She seems so upbeat. So I mumble, "Okay, let's do it. But how?"

"Leave that to me," she says. We cuddle even closer and somehow fall asleep again.

35

JANA

I get into work extra early the next morning. Anxious not to lose any time trying to track down the one slim lead David and I have.

Most of what we do in the Research Department is in preproduction—from gathering background material for writers to checking out accuracy in completed scripts. I've had many dealings with the Pentagon and the other armed services, so I know who to reach out to now.

"Axel Atherton," I tell Commander Hal Heffernan, my contact at the Navy Department in D.C.

"Why do you want to find him?"

"We're working on a WWII aircraft carrier story. The name popped up in the research." Who knows? Atherton might have been a sailor on a carrier.

Heffernan gets dozens of similar requests every week from accredited journalists and film studios. "Here I thought you were calling this morning to make *me* famous," he teases, then says he'll get back to me. He sounds like a Hollywood agent.

While we're waiting, trouble seems to pile on. Rowan mentions to me one afternoon that Alcalay was asking about a police report that David was involved in a brawl at a Hollywood Hills party. Rowan painted David as a hero, but Alcalay was only interested in the level of violence. Then a couple of mornings later, Ken, the friendly studio cop at the front gate, popped out of his booth to confide to me McKenna was nosing around about David's hassle here on the morning Leo barred David from the lot. "Gathering more proof that I'm a short-fuse psycho," David glooms when I tell him.

I've started treatment with psychotherapist Sarah Mandelker. Her office is in a brick-fronted medical building north of Wilshire on Camden Drive, the Freudian-Jungian plush gulch in Beverly Hills. I hope she can help. I resent paying someone to listen to me, but I don't know what else to do.

My first day, I arrive forty minutes late for my fifty-minute appointment. Spouting excuses amid tears. All the traffic lights were against me, forgot to take the address, went to the wrong building, had to find a phone book in the gas station, no parking on the street, couldn't find the entrance to the underground parking lot, I'm scared of elevators so I had to walk up all three flights and—

"Sounds like you were a little ambivalent about coming here." She offers me a Kleenex.

Dr. Mandelker is a short, plump woman in her early fifties with a kindly face. Chest rounded like a pouter pigeon, helmet of close-cut graying brown hair, legs skinny as a bird's. She's wearing a stylish Anne Klein pantsuit. What did I expect? Hospital greens like a brain surgeon? She tells me she has an open slot in an hour, suggests I get some air, maybe a cup of tea, and come back. But she'll have to charge me for both sessions.

"Part of the treatment?" Sarcasm feels like a useful dodge until I get my bearings in this scary new environment.

"You don't pay, you don't get well," she jokes.

But when I come back for my session, I concentrate on

that. The money. Panorama's medical plan will pay most of the cost, but if I come here several times a week that still leaves me with a deductible that will add an extra hundred dollars a week to my expenses, which I'm determined to cover on my own now. Not taking any more extras from my father. I stop babbling, confess that I don't really know how or where to start.

"I think you just did," she says.

Of course, I expected to be talking about my father, and at first I do. I tell her who he is but she's not impressed. Doesn't recognize the name. Thinks she may have seen one or two of his movies. "I prefer reading," she says. I like that.

Then I realize I've really come here to talk about myself. I have finally looked at who Leo is, now I'm left wondering, who am I?

"Good question," she says, "let's try to find out together."

After a few sessions, I feel Sarah's office is a sanctuary. Quiet, warm, tasteful, with no distracting decorations. Comfortable chairs for both of us. Facing each other across a coffee table with a box of tissues on it. Which I use a lot. Guess that's part of the treatment, too.

But I'm constantly torn three ways. Trying to come to terms in my mind with Leo, figuring out how and why I'm the way I am, and most of all the aching worry about David. We still haven't heard back from the Navy Department.

Sarah and I meet five days a week, same time each day. Late one afternoon she challenges me to do a verbal portrait of myself.

"In twenty-five words or less?" She shrugs. So I give it a shot. "I see—a pampered, isolated young woman with no real friends. I still haven't gotten over losing Wendy. So there's just Carol and a few other people on the lot."

"And David," she reminds me.

"Of course, David." I grope for a Kleenex. "But I feel like

the princess in the tower—someday my prince will come. Now at last he's here—and I'm scared the cops will take him away."

She thinks I'm being an alarmist. She says that's understandable under the circumstances. But that still leaves me so afraid for him.

The sessions are painfully hard, but I'm astonished at the progress I make in just a handful of meetings. Dredging up the pain of the high school civics class when the teacher discussed Communism and the kids whispered and snickered about me while the teacher pretended not to notice. Or was that just an excuse for me to cut myself off from everyone? Punishing myself. To prove my loyalty to Leo. It's all been bottled up so long. Now it's coming out. I could be finished here in no time. Then Sarah mentions that she's pleased, too, but she expects the hardest stuff is yet to come.

D avid never asks what we talk about and I don't volunteer much. He's been in treatment so he respects my privacy.

I've settled into Carol's house in Silver Lake. It's a total change after spacious Stone Canyon. Small, casual, and comfy. It's built on stilts overlooking a wide brush-filled canyon. Like floating on a cloud. Soon I'll be looking for a place like this for me—and David, too. We talk about that, when we're not worrying about the mess he's in.

At the studio, we spend as much time as possible together, but peeking around corners to avoid colliding with my father. So far so good. I haven't seen him since I moved out nearly two weeks ago. That pleases me and guilts me. I feel like a righteous person and a bad daughter.

This afternoon, when I get back from a trip to the museum collecting research on ancient Mesopotamia for a tits-and-sand epic, Rowan shouts down the hallway, "Jana, telex for you."

It's from the Navy Department. A one sentence telex. At first glance I'm disappointed. Or am I? Have to find David.

I take the shortest route toward the Western street. Going past the row of editing rooms, but that seems safe. I checked by phone and Leo is in his jungle. Rounding the corner I see Keeler's faded Buick parked with the trunk lid open. Several cartons in the trunk and Keeler coming down the metal steps with two more.

"Hey, Keeler, moving to bigger quarters? Too much film for one room, huh?"

But he's in no mood for joking.

"You just missed your father. He roared through here like a nuclear blast and fired me!"

"Oh, he'll change his mind, you know that."

"Not this time. I've got fifteen minutes to get off the lot or he's sending the security guards to drag me away."

I'm staggered. "Why? What happened?" This is one of my father's longest professional relationships.

"Seems I'm a betraying sonuvabitch who's out to butcher his movie! That's what he keeps screaming at me." Keeler stacks the boxes in the trunk, then turns to me. "Jana, I had no choice."

"I don't understand."

"Barney Ott and his arm-twister Heritage stormed into my room and ordered me to show them some footage. Ott said he'd fire me on the spot if I refused."

"So—?"

"So I work for them. Just like Leo does. It's their studio. So I let them see what they asked for. The edited version of the ending of the movie. They hated it. Now the studio's demanding Leo rewrite and reshoot or they'll pull the plug. I tried to tell him there's a way to recut what we have that will satisfy 'em, but there's no talking to him. He's like a maniac!"

"Didn't you explain to him why you—"

"He said I should have let them fire me. I owe him that much." Keeler scoffs, "Just like he was willing to fall on his sword to protect me. He gave the Committee my name. But that was only my *life* at stake, this is something important— his fuckin' movie!"

"I—I'm so sorry to have it end this way between the two of you." I hug him, he pats my back, apologizes for giving me such an earful. Then he slams the lid of the trunk.

"I'm actually glad it's finished between us. I'm so tired of being reminded how he saved me—after he screwed me over. It's like the national debt, you never pay it off."

He gets into his car and leans out the window. "Classic Hollywood! What have you done for me lately? You know I lied to the cops for him, Jana, backed up his bullshit story that we were here together working late the night that creep Shannon died. This is my thanks."

Keeler's car roars off. I'm left there with another of my father's lies. It could be the worst one. I'd just about convinced myself Leo was innocent of the Shannon thing. Now I'm flooded with fear again. Could my father be a murderer? He had reason to despise Shannon and he has no alibi. Then another thought. Neither apparently does Keeler.

I've just told David about Keeler getting fired—and withdrawing as Leo's alibi. We're drinking coffee at the catering truck on the Western street and he can see how shook up I am.

"It doesn't fit," he says. "Sure, Leo's a liar, but I still don't see him as a killer."

I desperately want to be reassured. He's still my father. And then I remember why I hurried over here. I hand David the telex from the Navy Department. He reads the single sentence. "Subject Axel Atherton, then stationed San Diego, deceased 11/17/45 in non-service-related event."

Before he can spiral down into disappointment, I ask him: "What sort of 'event' would that be?"

A glimmer flickers in his eyes. Not excitement. But a faint hope. We're probably clutching at straws, but what else do we have?

CHAPTER

36

McKENNA

It's been an irritating wheel-spinning morning. Alcalay phoned early with an invitation. He'd gotten a search warrant for David Weaver's car and insisted I accompany him to Panorama. Without notifying Weaver, we found his car in his assigned spot in the rear parking lot and went through it. We found a black marking pen under a bunch of maps in the glove compartment. Like the one that wrote the movie title signs.

"Terrific, I've got one in my car, too," I mocked Alcalay. But it sailed past him. He was too intent on gathering even a quasi-morsel of "proof."

I also mentioned a new thought. "Know something, Ray, without the sign about *The Informer* and the reference to number two, we might not have plugged into the Wendy Travers hit and the whole Blacklist slant on this case."

But he treated that point as a sidetracking distraction. He concentrated on wrapping Weaver's pen in an evidence bag, we both initialed it, and he took it back to his lab. He's like a dog with a bone.

But only about some things. Take Weaver's alibi, for example.

After my initial interview with Weaver, I'd told Alcalay the meager details he offered as to his whereabouts on the night of Shannon's murder. I suggested LAPD send out troops to either verify or disprove his alibi. Alcalay seemed lukewarm on the idea, so I again offered to provide Bureau manpower. Again he scoffed at "allowing in more Fat Boys."

He said, "I'll take care of it."

Couple of days later I asked, and Alcalay hadn't gotten around to it. Obviously his way of taking care of it. So that night I went saloon-hopping alone with a photo of David Weaver. I followed the sketchy route as Weaver had described it.

The bartender at Musso's scanned the photo and said he remembered David. "I told him he looked familiar, turns out he's Teddy Weaver's son." Yes, it was definitely that night, he recalled other people who were there at the same time.

Okay, that much checked out—David Weaver did start here. I worked my way down Hollywood Boulevard. It used to be a fashionable shopping street, with exclusive men's stores on one side of the boulevard and women's on the other. Now it's gone honky-tonk with hookers, street freaks, and runaways on the sidewalks, lots of liquor stores, magic shops, sleazy soft-porn and gross-out T-shirt emporiums. The anchor store is risqué Frederick's of Hollywood, featuring edible underwear. And a shitload of saloons, which I methodically visited.

In a pub near Cahuenga, a bartender thought maybe David had been in, but he couldn't be sure. No one in any of the joints south of Cahuenga down to Sunset sparked to the photo. Then Weaver's memory supposedly got hazy. But I canvassed saloons on Sunset for blocks in both directions. No results. So I hopped to Western Avenue, where Weaver recalled coming into focus again with his knuckles raw. I tried every bar down to Beverly Boulevard. Not one bartender or cocktail waitress could ID David Weaver.

So that's where it wound up. Still gaping holes in the alibi. With ample unaccounted time for him to have detoured over to rack up Shannon—as Weaver himself admitted he'd been seriously considering. I felt disappointed. Guess I was hoping to balance the ledger on Weaver after my early blurt to Hoover and also to show up Alcalay's slipshod methods.

I did mention my search to him the next day, thinking he'd be embarrassed.

Alcalay shrugged. "See, told you it was a waste of time. C'mon, a guy says he went on a toot but don't remember where or how. That's a horseshit alibi if I ever heard one."

Asshole.

Do I believe the kid is innocent? Well, at this point I refuse to even consider that question. I'm just being thorough and evenhanded. Like Sgt. Joe Friday says on *Dragnet,* "Just the facts, ma'am." But I wonder if my galloping around from one bar to another was also to counter Kathleen's criticism.

Now I'm back in my cubicle, checking accumulated mail. More routine crap. But there's a reply from the Navy Department to my query. Able Seaman Axel Atherton, while stationed in San Diego, died in 1945 of a non-service-related event. That's what I call an alibi. I'll fax it to Alcalay so he can toss it in the dead letter section of his Shannon file, as I'm going to do.

The phone rings. It's Tom Churillo in D.C. He's effusive. "You're doin' it, Mac! Found your comet! Just want to let you know it's looking great for me to bring you aboard. Hoover can't stop talking about your case, says he's so glad you're our man on the scene. I mean, he's carrying on like you're about to take down Machine Gun Kelly."

He tells me to keep up the good work. I don't tell him anything about my hassles with the locals. After the call, I sit there thinking I should be feeling better than I do. But I don't. Not yet.

I call my sister because I want to complain to someone about Alcalay and the stupid marking pen, and she's the only one I can think of. I'm looking for sympathy. But she lumps us together.

"What are you doing, Brian?" Kathleen asks,

She doesn't shout. That would be better. She sounds disappointed in me. She's at her desk in the public defender's office in Van Nuys.

"We had a warrant," I assure her. "Alcalay gussied up a request to toss the car. I was surprised a judge would sign it, but he did."

"But what are *you* doing?" she repeats. "What happened to innocent until proven guilty? What happened to the full-on investigation that was going to happen? Follow *all* the leads? Not just the ones with David Weaver's name on 'em."

I've told her quite a bit about Weaver. Some details I volunteered, the rest she pried out of me. Maybe that's what I wanted her to do. I've been using her as a sounding board. I remind her how I trudged around Hollywood a whole night trying to check out Weaver's alibi.

"Don't take a bow for that! It's what you're supposed to do. Instead of ganging up with the goon squad. Look, here's a kid who was banished from his own country, went through who-knows-what in Korea, he's buried his mother and now his father, he comes back here looking for his girl—and suddenly the full weight of The System is bearing down on him. Who's looking out for him? Suppose it was Donnie, this Weaver kid's not that much older than he is, would you think Donnie was getting a fair shake?"

"Hey, I'm just one cog in the wheel."

"That was Declan's rationale."

Throwing that bastard in my face? "What's *he* got to do with—"

"Remember what he always said? 'Kid, y'gotta go along to get along.' We didn't know what Declan meant back then. The corruption that he was justifying. That's not why you and I signed up for the jobs we have, Bri. We said we were going to make a difference."

"*What do you want from me, Kath?!*"

"To thine own self be true!" She hits me with that golden oldie again. "Just ask yourself now and then—how much is that big job in D.C. really worth to you?"

It's a jagged end to the call. After I hang up, I make busy work, but I'm furious. Imagine comparing me to Declan, that fuckin' travesty of a cop. But I can't duck her basic question. What ever happened to the super-cop I set out to be? Where's he gone?

My phone rings and I'm sure it's Kathleen with another sermon, but the hesitant voice on the line is one that I never expected to hear again and it instantly banishes the Shannon case.

"Brian," she says, "it's Ashley."

The stately old Biltmore Hotel faces Pershing Square in the bustling center of downtown L.A. only a mile or so from my office. The clubby, mahogany, old-money dining room is jammed for lunch today. I had to pull strings not only to get a table, but a good booth. I'm already sitting there—ten minutes before we're scheduled to meet. Ashley arrives seven minutes early. A good sign.

I don't spot her at first, but then all the hot-footing waiters and table-hopping conventioneers shift out of focus and melt away. All I see in delightful detail is her walking toward me. Almost in slow motion. Arms and hips swinging, those fabulous legs encased in silk; she's wearing a robin's egg blue suit that perfectly matches her eyes, ash blond hair shoulder

length, longer than I remembered. I realize that time had
hazed my memory of how beautiful she was, but here she is to
remind me.

I stand up in the aisle—she holds out both her hands, I
take them in mine. Cordial greeting, if anyone's looking. Like
good old friends. My cheek brushes against hers, inhaling the
familiar scent of Shalimar, feeling the rush of all the old feelings.

We sit down in the booth and for a long moment it's a
smiling contest to see who can send the warmest, wordless
greeting. I wave away the waiter with an order for two dry martinis, Tanqueray gin. She's pleased that I remembered. We start
talking as if a dozen years have not intervened.

A strange thing happens as we talk: I'm raptly tuned into
what she's saying, but I'm also outside looking in, gleaning
subtext in her every utterance. At least I think I am. I hope I
am.

"I've never been in Southern California before and you're
the only one I know here," she tells me lightly with lots of
dimple. She's on her way back to Detroit from a vacation in
Hawaii with some girlfriends. She landed in San Francisco to
visit her son. "So I thought I'd stop by and say hello."

What I hear is she came hundreds of miles out of her way
to see me. And she definitely likes what she sees. I'm entranced
with the way her lips move as she speaks.

"I'm very proud of my son," she tells me. Kim spent last
summer in Mississippi registering black voters. Now he's a
social worker in Haight-Ashbury.

What I hear is that she's no longer worried about him. That
obstacle to our being together is gone. Her face is still flawless.
Her skin almost luminous.

"Rudy hates how Kim turned out," she tells me, "calls him
a brainless beatnik."

What I hear is that the marriage has endured but not improved. She puts a cigarette between her lips and I light it. As I did the first time we spoke at that long-ago party.

"Rudy inherited a lot of money when his father died," she tells me. He retired from the Bureau and started a security company. Big corporate clients in a tri-state area now, he travels a lot on business.

What I hear is that Rudy is still cheating on her. I'm aching to touch her.

"What about you?" she asks. "Has L.A. worked out for you?"

"Let's just say I've enjoyed about as much of it as I can stand."

She laughs. That throaty chuckle. "That's how I feel about Detroit."

What I hear are words that send my pulse racing. The waiter is approaching us with his pad.

"Are you hungry?" I ask her.

"Not for anything they have on the menu."

For a second I think I only heard that inside my head. But she really said it.

We don't have far to go. She has a corner suite on the seventh floor that costs more per night than I earn in a month. A great view of the city, if that's what you're interested in. We've got the drapes drawn in the bedroom and we're swimming in each other. The first time is a frenzy of groping, pounding, gasping, racing to a mutual climax. Desperate to confirm we're together again. Then we lie there spent and content, fingertips exploring each other, reestablishing the closeness we once had. Is everything the way we recall it? Is it really you?

When we make love again, it's tender and unhurried. A pair of synchronized dancers. Pacing, delaying, quietly reveling as if it can go on endlessly, and at the end she's smiling as tears slip down her face.

"Something wrong?" I say.

She shakes her head. "Just—happy." But the tears splay across her cheeks.

I wipe the tears away with the heel of my hand and kiss her gently. Feeling such gratitude that she's come back to me. Until this moment I haven't realized how shut down I've become.

The exquisitely tiled tub in the spacious bathroom is almost as big as a pond in the park. We're doing it in the water. Like primal creatures alone in the forest. Afterwards, still embracing, with me still inside her, water up to our shoulders, she murmurs, "Wish this could go on forever."

"Why can't it?" I ask.

"I'm booked on a red-eye flight tonight."

"Cancel. There are lots of planes."

She tells me she's hostessing a party tomorrow night at the mansion in Detroit for a bunch of Rudy's big clients. That's their arrangement. He leaves her alone. In return, she makes the necessary public appearances. She has unlimited use of the credit cards, neither of them asks the other questions. They're at home together as little as possible. He does whatever he does elsewhere, and so does she.

What I hear are the barren dimensions of her life. Like an echo of my own. "Don't go back," I whisper in her ear.

"A deal's a deal," she says as she rolls off me. We're shoulder to shoulder in the water now and she stares off.

She tells me she maintains a full social schedule, charity luncheons, golf and tennis foursomes at the country club with the girls, no fooling around at home, saving those activities for the cabana boys in Cancun or Belize or the Bahamas. She tells me she drinks far too much, her vacation visit in Hawaii was spent drying out, again, at a rehab clinic.

"None of that matters," I say. "Not now."

She just stares off.

"We missed our chance before, Ashley, but—"

She interrupts. "Not *we,* Brian, *I* missed our chance." Ashley climbs out of the tub and wraps a bath sheet around her as if it's a suit of armor. "I've got to go back. It's too late for me to start over."

What I hear is what I absolutely refuse to accept: finality and mournful resignation. It tears at my guts. No. I can't lose her again.

I'm talking as fast as I can. There isn't much time left. We're walking down the airport corridor toward her departure gate. I've got to convince her. She's just scared, bruised by the years; I can make her reach out for this chance, I know I can.

I tell her about the major investigation I'm working on now, how that's going to get me a big promotion, a top job in Washington, D.C. That beats small-minded Detroit and phony-bullshit L.A., right? Just think about it, Ashley, even if Rudy cuts you off without a penny I'll be making real money then, we can be happy there together, it can be like today always.

Before she walks through the doorway onto the plane she turns and we embrace and I kiss her for a long moment to let her know this is only the beginning, our new beginning, our forever is starting now. When our faces part I gaze into her eyes.

"Give us a chance, Ashley. Just think about it, okay?"

"Okay," she says. Do I see a flicker of hope? "Let's talk on the phone," she says. "See how things work out."

Then she's gone. I stand at the wall of glass staring off into the night as the plane taxis away. It can't end like this. I must find the way to get her back. It's all intertwined with this fuckin' case. My whole life can come together if it works out right.

37

DAVID

Atherton, Axel Atherton, yeah, sure, I remember, just a run-of-the-mill unsolved homicide. I'm surprised Hollywood is interested in that tired old tale. Feisty Ron Gorman is a retired San Diego detective sergeant. Now he's a bartender at the Tip Toe Inn, a cop saloon in the Gaslight District of the laid-back beach city. He's looking curiously at the two of us.

Jana and I have driven to San Diego after she checked the 1945 newspaper files of *The San Diego Union*. First looking up the date of Atherton's death, according to the Navy Department report. No mention in the paper for 11/17/45 or several days after. Then a week later, a small story on page eleven stating that the dead man found two days before buried in the scrub brush near the Mexican border had been identified as a U.S. sailor assigned to the San Diego Naval Station. Axel Atherton.

Sarge Gorman, who is polishing the bar top in the near-deserted afternoon quiet, was mentioned in the newspaper reports as lead investigator back then.

Jana tells him that, as research for a possible Panorama movie, we're interested in any details that didn't make it into the newspaper. He's proud of his memory and it's surprisingly good. Atherton was struck repeatedly by a blunt instrument. Massive head injuries. Stripped naked, the civvies clothes he was wearing and all identifying items gone. "Never did find 'em," Gorman recalls. "Coyotes had uncovered the shallow grave. A Boy Scout troop on a hike found what was left. Police lab founds semen stains on Atherton's crotch, so we figured it was the usual."

"The usual what?" Jana probes. Gorman clearly likes to talk to pretty Jana. It's like I'm not here.

"The usual weekend in those days. It used to be kind of wild around here, particularly on payday at the naval base. So a sailor gets picked up by a hooker, gets ambushed by her pimp, gets rolled for the greenbacks in his pocket. If he's real unlucky he gets killed."

Jana asks Gorman if they worked up a time line. They did, but it didn't go much of anywhere. Atherton and a sailor buddy went into town together. Hit a few saloons. The buddy drank too much, got the upchucks, took off back to the base. Last thing he saw was Atherton and an off-duty marine from Camp Pendleton buying drinks for a busty blonde in a crowded bar. End of time line.

"When we broke the bad news to the buddy, he was real shook up. They'd met in boot camp and were working together on the post newspaper. Guy blamed himself, said if he hadn't got sick, the other kid would still be alive."

"What was the buddy's name?" I ask.

Sarge Gorman looks over as if he's just discovered my presence. "What'd you say, Phil?" Somehow he got the idea my name is Phil and I've given up correcting him.

"Who was the buddy who started out touring the bars with Atherton?"

"Name was Shannon," he says. "Joe Shannon."

The only other lead we have in San Diego is at Camp Pendleton, the vast training center north of the city. Denny Pettigrew is a Chief Petty Officer now in charge of purchasing engine parts. Years ago he was part of the unit Axel Atherton and Joe Shannon were in. He was quoted in the old newspaper articles as saying Atherton didn't have an enemy in the world.

We are in his office in a warehouse on the base. Pendleton reminds me of Fort Benning, but instead of Rangers and paratroopers there are platoons of marines and sailors executing sharp formation turns on the parade ground outside Pettigrew's windows. I watch them and think, Shannon and Atherton once marched together out there.

Pettigrew is a chesty navy lifer in crisp fatigues who is giving us monosyllabic answers to our questions, until we assure him that the movie we're researching will change all the names and be totally fictionalized, probably even where it takes place. He relaxes.

"Good," he says, "I wouldn't want Atherton's memory to get smeared."

Jana and I exchange a glance. "But you think the cops were right?" I ask. "That Atherton got mugged and murdered?"

"Sure, something like that. Sailors looking for a good time are always a juicy target for lowlifes."

We ask him to describe Atherton. He recalls a friendly farm boy from Minnesota. Swedish descent, tall, skinny, good worker. From the time he disappeared, Joe Shannon kept saying Atherton never would have gone AWOL. When they heard his body had been found in the desert, Shannon wept.

"Never would've expected that," Pettigrew says. "Usually, he was a cold-ass."

"So he and Axel were close friends?"

"Shannon treated Axel like a kid brother, and Axel looked up to him like he was God."

We ask about Atherton's dogtag. Was he wearing it for sure when he left the base? Pettigrew says sometimes sailors on a weekend pass took off the tags or their wedding rings, trying to pass for civilians without any ties.

"Never fooled anyone, if you ask me. You can always spot a serviceman."

Time to ask the big question we've let slide, and Jana does: "Was Axel a homosexual?"

Pettigrew flares. "How the hell should I know? You said you weren't out to smear him!"

"We're not," she soothes. "We're just trying to figure out what happened."

"Know what navy policy is on homos?" he asks. Jana shakes her head. "There is none, because there are none. But if they ever found one, he'd be subject immediately to dishonorable discharge. That answer your question?"

We're driving north along the ocean on 101 heading back to L.A. and reviewing. Doesn't feel like a helluva lot and we're not sure how—or if—any of it fits in. According to Gorman, Atherton died of massive head injuries from a blunt instrument. The same way Joe Shannon was killed. Not that it was the same killer, but interesting. So now the question we're taking away is the one we came with: how did Axel Atherton's dog tag wind up in Shannon's safe? We float possibilities: Shannon took it off the body after he and the marine from the bar killed Axel. But that collides with the close bond between the two men. Or maybe Axel left the dog tag behind in his footlocker and Shannon claimed it as a keepsake.

"Imagine that," I say, "Joe Shannon, a closet romantic."

On one level, it's been a good day: Jana and I working

closely together. Even if all we accomplished was a welcome distraction from my fear that McKenna and Alcalay are homing in on me.

It's after six o' clock when we creep through the worst of the downtown L.A. traffic. We have to stop at the studio because I left my car there. While I'm on the lot I drop in at the publicity office to see if there are any messages. Everyone's gone home except Art Sarno, who's going to work the door at a press preview tonight in the studio screening room.

"You're gonna love this." He gives a Cheshire grin. "Supposed to be a deep dark secret, but we're always the first to know everything anyway."

"Yeah, why do they bother?"

"So get this. Your ex-uncle Leo. He's gone renegade, jumped the reservation. You know how the studio's been leaning on him to slash his script to make up time—and also reshoot the ending of his epic."

"Or they'll fire him and let another director. Yak-yak-yak. What else is new?"

"Well, Leo found a way to finesse the argument. He's absconded with the entire original sound track."

"What do you mean—absconded?"

"Okay, swiped. Stolen. Made off with it in the dark of night." Sarno laughs. "Told Barney Ott he'll destroy it if they interfere with him any more. So unless they want to dub the whole movie like they do those Italian masterpieces where the actors flap their lips but the sound never seems right—looks like Leo's got them by the gonads."

"The moguls must be bouncing off the walls."

"Well, Leo's made 'em an offer—forget about firing him, let him finish the picture his own way and at his own pace. And afterwards he'll be glad to bring back the soundtrack. So that's where it stands—he's still shooting tomorrow."

Leo, I realize, is nuts. Playing hardball with hard guys. It strikes me as a very dangerous game. Godzilla Meets Godzilla. Leo's arrogance versus Barney Ott's ruthlessness. Who knows where that contest might end? But the possibility Leo could finally get his ass kicked tickles me. "Quite a show," I tell Sarno, "and it looks like we've got front row seats to watch."

That's how it stays for the next two days. Mexican stand-off. Ott keeps shouting, Leo keeps shooting. Surprisingly, none of it gets in the papers.

Then Thursday, on the way back from lunch, Jana and I have an unexpected encounter. As we approach the research department, we come upon Leo leaning against the wall near the entrance reading *The New Yorker*. Must be on a break from the set while they're setting up the next shot. He spots us.

"Jana, can we talk a minute?" He pretends I'm on another planet. He didn't shave today, maybe not even yesterday. Looks like he's given up sleeping.

Jana says, "We don't have anything to say to each other."

"Of course we do. You've left a lot of your things at the house."

"I'll come by to pick them up."

"When?"

"When you're not there." She starts to move past him to go into her building. He grabs her arm. "This—this whatever it is, it's got to stop. I want you to move back home."

"That's not possible." She tries to pull loose, his grip tightens. "Let go of me, please," she says. I feel myself tensing, adrenaline pumping.

"You're my daughter and you can't just walk out like that. I'm all alone over there—"

"You're hurting me."

"And you're hurting both of us!" He's louder, squeezing

harder, I see the pain in her face. "No more of this childish damn nonsense, you're—"

"Take your hand off her, Leo!" I warn him.

"Stay out of it," she says to me. "I can handle this."

But he's still gripping her. "Let go of her, dammit!"

He lets loose of her and whirls to face me. I catch a whiff. He usually doesn't drink during the day. Vein throbbing in his temple. "You bastard, why the hell did you ever have to come back into our lives?"

"You think *I'm* the problem?" I shout at him.

"Don't blame David," she says. Drawing his attention back to her. "This is between you and me and what you did!"

"He's poisoned your mind against me!" Leo shrieks. People on the street have stopped to watch. "Don't you see what's he's done? We were fine, we were happy, until he—"

"It's always someone else," I shout, "never you! Poor Leo, always the victim, always—"

"Gonna hit me?" he challenges. And I long to. But Leo is seven inches shorter than I am and a generation older. "C'mon, soldier boy," he's daring me, "let's see what you've got. Give me your best shot!" Rolling his magazine tight like a cop's nightstick. "Do it, pussy," double-daring me, "let's go!"

Jana steps between us. "Stop it! Both of you!"

"I just don't want him hurting you any more, he—"

"I told you I could handle it, David!"

She strides away from both of us into the building. Slams the door behind her. Leo and I stand there a moment glaring at each other, then he grumbles, "Fuck this, I've got a movie to make," and he leaves. Still clutching his coiled magazine like a club to fend off the assassins.

I watch Leo strut away. Hating his guts—him and his fuckin' movie! Then there's movement behind me. I turn and see Jack Heritage, aboard his studio golf cart, gliding out from the shady side of the executive building. On an afternoon spin or is he the stalker I've been sensing these weeks? Finally emerging from the shadows? How long has he been lurking and watching today?

He comes closer. I'm ready for him. But he doesn't stop. Just gives me a casual two-finger salute. "Hi, Chief," he says as he passes. And follows slowly after Leo.

Big Brother is on Leo's tail. Better him than me.

38

M C K E N N A

I t's after midnight when I speed up to Panorama's main entrance, but the gate man raises the barrier as I approach.
I'm expected. He starts to give directions, but I tell him I
know the way. I roll between the sleeping soundstages and
park at the police barrier posted at the head of the Western
street. Next to a LAPD cruiser and three unmarked Crown
Vics, including Alcalay's. He tracked me down by phone less
than half an hour ago.

"We've got another one," he announced then.

The night street is washed bright by the white glare of a
giant klieg light. I see an ambulance parked down at the gallows, several men clustered there. I spot Alcalay's stocky figure. The trapdoor is open and a lifelike dummy dangles below
the platform. I know from Alcalay's call it's not a dummy.

It's Leo Vardian.

I walk toward the gallows.

Nearby two LAPD uniforms chat quietly with a studio security captain. One of the uniforms looks over at me. I hold
my badge in the air and he goes back to his conversation.
Barney Ott and Jack Heritage are loitering in front of the cowboy saloon where Leo's Mercedes is parked. They're watching
the forensics team dust the car and scrape bloodstains off the
wooden walkway. Heritage notices me and nudges Ott.

Ott steps out to somberly greet me. "Panorama's lost a good friend."

"You guys got here real fast," I say.

"We were still on the lot. Working late."

"Stick around. We'll talk." I continue on.

Two of the men at the gallows are paramedics waiting beside their ambulance with a wheeled stretcher. I join Alcalay, who's standing by himself observing Hiro Kobata, L.A.'s medical examiner. He is a cadaverously thin ancient in a baggy suit, crumpled white shirt, no tie. Looks like he tumbled out of bed. He is perched on a small ladder checking the body. There are streaks of blood running down Leo's forehead, his face purple and mottled, eyes bugged, thick tongue lolling grotesquely. Guess that's why they put hoods on them at hangings. For us, not them.

"Been waiting for you to get here, Mac," Alcalay says.

For Alcalay that's a rousing welcome. He's using my nickname. My bullshit antenna goes way up. I came here with a big bone to pick, but he doesn't know that yet.

"Whatcha make of this?" He nods at the body.

I match the tough talk. "Leo wasn't the worst guy I met out here."

My gaze remains riveted on Leo's face. A hard man to like, and the petty tyrant persona he'd basked in during recent years made it harder. But he didn't deserve this kind of an ending. I think of how rough this is going to be on Jana Vardian.

Up on the ladder, the M.E. glances over and sees me.

"Doctor K," I greet him.

"Ah, G-Man arrives, now we're cooking." He turns his attention back to the body.

I recall the last time I was here. Sitting on the steps of the gallows. Sipping coffee and doing Q&A with David Weaver.

It's as if Alcalay reads my mind.

"Well," he says, buddy-to-buddy, "if you're ready to shed a

tear for the deceased, then guess who went nose-to-nose in a
public shouting match on the lot this afternoon? Vardian and
the Weaver kid. Damn near turned into a punch-out. The girlfriend had to referee."

"According to informed sources?"

"Same ones you're always quoting." He indicates Ott and
Heritage, gazing at us from over at the saloon entrance.

"The eyes and ears of this nasty little world," I say. "How
coincidental they're working late tonight of all nights."

"Kinda missing the major point, aren't ya, pardner?"

He's pushing the Weaver agenda hard. I expected that. He
wants me to click my heels in the air. Like he's ready to do. So
he's keeping a cork on his usual anger. That's okay, I've got
enough of my own to spare.

As Kobata pivots the body, the klieg light splashes across
Leo's chest and I see the sign hanging around his neck. Hand-
written in black letters like the other two. This one reads:

BROTHER RAT

I translate for Alcalay. "Another movie from the thirties,
Ronnie Reagan and Eddie Albert playing cadets at a military
academy."

"This case is a real Hollywood education."

Then Alcalay briefs me. Body discovered at 10:32 P.M. by
studio cop on his rounds. Figure Vardian was coming for his
car. He usually parked there. And that's where the attack occurred. Bludgeon marks on the head. Like Shannon and
Wendy Travers. Attack weapon a claw hammer, found on the
ground in front of the saloon set. The kind used by construction workers on the lot. No sign of resistance. So Vardian was
either jumped or more likely knew his killer. Unconscious body
dragged over from the saloon. There's a bloody trail from there
to here. Alcalay points out a sandbag at the M.E.'s feet below

the open trapdoor. Used to yank the noose down to the ground, where it was wrapped around Leo's neck. Then the body was hoisted to finish the job. Took a strong person to do all that.

"So looks like we got a shot at wrapping this up tonight," Alcalay concludes.

That's when I lose it. "Know something? As a cop you're a joke! You're also a lying piece of shit!"

Alcalay doesn't flare, instead he gives a soft raise of the eyebrows and the hint of a smile. I want to belt him in the face. "Wow," he murmurs, "sticks and stones. Let's step into my private office."

He grips my arm to guide me around to the far side of the ambulance. I shake off his hand, but stomp ahead and when we're out of sight of the others I turn on him, glaring.

"Okay, he says, "you've got a wild hair up your ass, so let me hear. But keep it low, we don't want to scare the neighbors."

"Don't tell me what to do!" But I keep it down. I don't need an audience while I rip him a new one. "Let me tell you what an investigator does. He investigates! He doesn't fake it, go through the motions, cut corners, ignore leads—"

He cuts me off. "For instance?"

"You let me think you were checking out Weaver's alibi for the Shannon hit, but—"

"Old stuff. What else?"

I get right in his face. "You want new? I got brand new. Just spent yesterday and today humping around town grilling a half dozen Blacklisted guys—all names on the list I gave you. Checking their alibis. Basic grunt cop work. Know what I found out? Two of the six were never contacted by any of your troops. But why bother, right? You made up your mind from the get-go that it was Weaver, so screw anything that doesn't point at him. That's your grand strategy. I can't decide if you're inept, corrupt, or just don't give a shit! Hell, I don't know if the kid is innocent or guilty, but—"

"Neither do I." That stops me. Until he adds: "But it sure seems like he's our guy, don'tcha agree?"

"There y'go! We're not the jury, we're—"

"I know, we're investigators. And you're smarter than I am. But that doesn't make me dumb. I'm just building on your good work. You dug out the slant about his going mental in the Army. You found out about the beef Weaver had in the commissary with Shannon. You found the link to Wendy Travers plus the proximity. You saw him lose it in Shannon's backyard. You were here when he and O'Connell squared off. And tonight, after fighting with Vardian, who happens to be the guy who fingered his father for your Committee—"

I cut him off. "So he decides to kill his sweetheart's daddy? And Weaver picks the perfect place to do it—on the street where he himself works? So no one would suspect him? Do you really buy that?"

"I got no trouble with it. Maybe this hit wasn't planned—suppose the two of them just ran into each other here. And they picked up their fight from this afternoon. Or maybe it was planned, we've established the kid's a bit of a nutcase. Doing it here only has to make sense to him. Maybe he thinks it's poetic justice or some crap like that."

He shrugs. The old philosopher.

"Look," he says, "I know what you're saying—that I'm stacking the deck against Weaver."

"Sure as hell smells like it to me!"

"Well, despite what you say, I take my job seriously. I'm not running this show the way you would? Well, I'm in charge and you're not. It's my responsibility to allocate resources to get the best results. Told you before, I didn't think Weaver's booze tour alibi was even worth listening to. Now, about your independent check of six Blacklisted guys—did they have decent alibis?"

"Yeah, they all did, but you couldn't know that because—"

"Because I'm a shitheel. I'm sorry we missed contacting those two guys, don't know how that happened. But we did check out twenty-seven others. All kosher. So, sue me, I concentrated efforts on the hot lead—that's Weaver. That's how we turned up a police report on a party brawl up in Silver Lake a few Saturday nights ago. Weaver faced off with a trio of crashers—and he creamed 'em all. Kid's a juggernaut, huh?"

"*That's* what you've been investigating? You've still got nothing. Just character material. All circumstantial stuff. Not one piece of hard evidence!"

"Hey, I've gotten convictions on circumstantial evidence—and so have you. C'mon, McKenna, be straight with me. What's really eating you?"

"The whole damn situation stinks! Every time anything happens, there's a trail of bread crumbs leading the same way—back to the Weaver kid. That's what spooks me. If he really is our guy, how can he be doing such a lousy a job covering his tracks?"

"Who knows? Suppose he's one of those weird 'Stop me before I kill again' freaks. A kid who's crying out for someone to put him out of his misery. How do I know? I'm not a shrink, I'm a cop! And so are you! Our job is to bag the bad guys. Period."

"And you're perfectly okay with that?" I feel like I'm arguing with Declan. We start out with the answers, and the questions don't matter. But now Alcalay leans in on me.

"Don't make me the heavy, McKenna. Like I'm ramming something through. Pulling a fast one."

"*Aren't you?*" I feel the vein throbbing in my forehead.

Alcalay looks disgusted. "We're in the same business, whether you like it or not. We're sanitation workers. Garbage men. We keep the streets clean. That's what our bosses—and the public, the *nice* people—all want us to do. We hope we're doing it right. They just prefer we do it fast."

I don't know what to say to him. Because these thoughts also have been swirling in my head. Contradictory. Ambivalent. Worst of all, expedient. Ashley's face flashes. I push it aside.

"I just follow the clues," Alcalay says. "Go where they take me."

Now he sounds like me. "Doesn't it bother you? Just a little? Doesn't it seem too neat? Too easy?"

"Hey, why can't it be easy for once?" He looks me in the eye. "So just tell me what you would do now if you were me?"

Before I can come up with an answer, we hear Kobata calling Alcalay. They're ready to take the body down from the gallows. Alcalay goes off, I trail a few steps, enough so I can see the paramedics lower the body onto their gurney. Before they draw the blanket over his face, I catch another glimpse of Leo's bug eyes. When I was a kid I saw a dumb B movie in a fleabag theater in the Loop. It was about a photographer who invented a camera that could take a picture of the final image in a murder victim's eyes. Identifying your killer from the great beyond. Proof positive. If only it was that simple.

While they load Leo into the ambulance and Alcalay is talking with Kobata, I walk slowly to where Ott and Heritage are waiting and watching.

"The Weaver kid wouldn't happen to have been around the lot tonight, would he?" I wearily ask them.

"As a matter of fact," Heritage says, "the picture he's working on is shooting late on Stage Four. I already called over. He was there earlier and left. No one's sure exactly when."

Alcalay has come up behind me. "Does he have an office?"

When we get to the publicity building the lights are off and the front door is locked.

"Want to look inside?" Ott asks.

"I don't have a search warrant," Alcalay says.

"You don't need one. *Mi casa, es su casa.*" Ott nods at Heritage, who produces a master key. Both of them ready to grease the skids for David Weaver. Tidy up Panorama's mess.

We flick on the lights and locate Weaver's office. Ott and Heritage stand outside in the corridor as I go in and watch Alcalay search the desk. In the bottom drawer he finds a half-empty bottle of Dewar's scotch and tucked away in the back a hand-tooled Italian leather wallet. Alcalay takes it out carefully with a handkerchief. He flips it open and we both stare at it. Alcalay gives me a head tilt, indicating Ott and Heritage, who are rubbernecking from the doorway.

I turn to them. "Guys, you mind waiting outside the building?"

They shrug. I'm not sure if they saw what we saw, but they go. I shut the office door. We wait until their footsteps fade and hear the sound of the outer door closing. Then Alcalay flips the wallet open again on the desk. So we both can gaze at the driver's license with photo.

"Now we know where Shannon's missing wallet went to," he says. "Now this is what I call hard evidence, don't you?"

The itch I feel is still there. "Yeah, but—"

He laughs harshly. "Why did I know those were gonna be the first words out of your face?"

But I plow on. "Why would Weaver take away a prime piece of incriminating dynamite—and stash it here?"

Alcalay instantly dismisses that. "Kid's a certified psycho. Who knows what goes through that type of brain. Probably a ghoulish souvenir. Some killers collect scalps, he likes wallets. It fits with the purse and jewelry taken from Wendy Travers. C'mon, Mac, whaddayasay?"

I know he wants me on his side. My future is on the line with this case, but so is his. He's willing to share the glory, because he wants me to shoulder a big chunk of the responsibility. He needs the imprimatur of the Bureau, He's worried about going it alone.

Truth to tell, despite the hostility I feel for him, the cop side of me adds it up the way he does. The way Hoover and Tolson do from three thousand miles away. I look at Alcalay. He's waiting for an answer. So I give it to him.

"Okay, let's go for the Weaver kid."

Alcalay grabs the phone and calls in an all-points bulletin to be broadcast immediately for the arrest of David Weaver. May be armed, should be considered dangerous. It's official, no room left for questions or qualifiers. The machine is moving into high gear. David Weaver is going down.

Alcalay hangs up the phone and gazes at me. "Still fretting over why the wallet's here?" I nod. "Well, we can ask the kid when we see him."

He thinks that's funny. I wish I did. But then I feel a spike of relief. It's over. Hoover will be doing cartwheels. And then a series of snapshots appear in my head. My new big office in D.C. A beautiful apartment in Georgetown. With Ashley waiting for me there.

39

DAVID

Late this afternoon I phoned Jana from my soundstage to apologize for getting into that hassle with Leo. Let's go some place special for dinner. She said, "I'm bushed, David, just gonna head home to my place and hit the sack." She meant alone. "I'm just so tired of thinking about all this," she said, "I need a night off."

So I hung around the set a while, then grabbed a sandwich and went to see Jean Renoir's antiwar classic, *Grand Illusion*, at the Vagabond. It was powerful and depressing.

When the show lets out, I drive back to the Chateau and come up the back steps from the parking lot. As I enter my room I notice a pink message envelope that's been slipped under the door. From Jana! I'm sure of it. Probably a message to call her, maybe come over to where she's house-sitting. I rip the envelope open.

It says:

> *David,*
> *Regret argument this afternoon. Know we can work out all problems between us. Man-to-man. Please come my house tonight whenever you get in. I'll be working very late but most anxious see you soonest and settle matters.*
> *Thanks,*
> *Uncle Leo.*

Uncle Leo? When did *he* come back into my life? The only invitation I'd expect from him is to face a firing squad. But he's talking about settling things. What's that mean? For Jana's sake I'd love to scale the heat down. If that's possible. I don't see how, but—I glance at my watch, it's only 11:20. What the hell? Why not?

When I pull up near the Vardian house on Stone Canyon I don't see any lights. I turn off my motor and sit there. I'm still wondering what in hell Leo and I are going to say to each other. Can a bridge really be built over this divide?

Looking across, I think maybe he is inside and the thick drapes are concealing the light. So I ring the bell. Then try knocking. Maybe he's around back. Fiddling with his movie in the private projection room. So I stroll up the side path to the rear. The underwater lights in the kidney-shaped pool are on, so are the sprinklers in the flower beds. I see a cabana next to the pool. Showers, sauna, steam room, and changing cubicles on one side. With a private screening room on the other. I knock, no response here either. Try the handle, it's locked. What do I do now? Leo must've been delayed at the studio. Should I wait? Be dopey not to. Drove all the way over in the middle of the night.

I see a lounge chair almost surrounded by foliage near the diving board. Good spot to observe the house and the projection room while waiting. I stretch out. I'm so tired and feel so alone. I close my eyes and drift off to the whisper of the sprinklers.

My eyes pop open! Staring into near-total darkness. Been asleep. Where am I and why? Oh yeah. Pool lights now off, sprinklers off. And I know what woke me up. Sounds. Footsteps and the murmur of a voice. Approaching on the side path I came up on. Preceded by a flashlight beam. Must be

Leo, but I hear other voices. Thought this was going to be a private meeting, just the two of us. Man-to-man.

Four figures appear from the path, dimly silhouetted by a heavy-duty flashlight and the sliver of moon above. They seem not to expect anyone to be around. So I stay still, I think I'm invisible unless they aim their light across the pool at me. They walk to the entrance to the projection room and the flashlight beam focuses on the door. A hand reaches for the handle, yanks, confirms it's locked.

"Your first challenge of the night, doctor," Barney Ott's voice says.

I hear chuckles from the man with the flashlight—now I can identify Jack Heritage. He illuminates one of the other two guys, who is dressed like a workman and snaps open a toolbox, takes out a pair of lock picks. The back of his shirt reads LESTER THE LOCKSMITH.

In a minute, with a flourish, he opens the door. It swings out. He reaches in and finds the light switch. I'm still beyond the illuminated area but I see them enter. The locksmith followed by Ott and Heritage. Keeler Barnes is trailing behind.

What the hell's he doing here? I thought Leo fired him. What are they all doing here? Something's wrong about all this and my instinct says get the hell out.

I hear Ott's voice from inside saying: "Check the projection booth, Keeler, maybe it'll be that easy."

Yeah, of course. They're looking for the stolen sound track! I hear shuffling sounds, a moment, then Keeler's voice says, "Not here."

"Then it's up to you, Lester," Ott says.

"Well, I'm not sure I can," the locksmith whines.

"Sure you can!" Heritage snaps. "You installed the fuckin' vault."

The vault. Jana had mentioned the studio built one for Leo

when they put in the projection room. For his wine collection and prints of his old movies. Perfect place to stash a stolen sound track. I hear Lester grumble that Mr. Vardian probably changed the combination and the vault's got a complicated time lock and—

Ott doesn't want any of that. "Open sesame. Get on it."

They all move into another section of the windowless room. I can't see any of them. My curiosity propels me closer. One peek before I take off. I manage to sneak up behind the open door so I can peer in through the slit made by the hinges.

The locksmith has a stethoscope pressed to the vault door while he slowly turns the dial and tries to hear the tumblers. Ott and Keeler sit in cushy projection room seats watching him work. Heritage hangs over Lester's shoulder to apply intimidation. Now Lester yanks the stethoscope out of his ears frustrated.

"No good, I'll have to drill."

"If you gotta, you gotta," Heritage says.

Lester digs for the equipment. I wonder where in hell these guys are getting their nerve from? Aren't they worried Leo will walk in on them and yell for the cops to book 'em all for breaking and entering? Maybe I ought to get to a phone and call it in, though it surprises me I'm thinking as if I'm still on Leo's team. I only have an instant to mull that, as Heritage is starting to light up a cigarette. Lester warns him. "No smoking in here, I've got flammable stuff."

"Take it outside, Jackie," Ott says.

So now Heritage is walking up the aisle heading straight toward me. I hug the wall behind the door as he emerges. Hold my breath. There's a flare as he lights his cigarette, tosses the match on the ground. I hear him puffing and smell the aroma. I wait for him to finish and go back inside, so I can tiptoe away and go home. All this is getting way too complicated.

Ott calls, "Hey, Jack, we've got it open."

"Be right there," Heritage calls back. I see the half-smoked cigarette when it hits the Spanish tiled deck. Heritage's foot reaches into view to step on it—but the damn butt rolls. So he takes another step to get it, moving closer to me. He grinds his heel on the butt and when he looks up he sees me.

"What're *you* doin' here?" As if I'm the last person in the world he expected.

"Could ask you the same, why're—"

I stop because he's whipped a short-barreled police .38 out of the shoulder holster beneath his jacket. On pure reflex, I leap in and chop the heel of my hand across his wrist. The gun goes flying and we clinch. As we tussle Heritage gropes into his back pocket and confirms the rumor that he still carries a blackjack. He swings at me and misses my head. But with his follow through he smashes the blackjack into the left side of my rib cage. A really solid shot, but I have no time to register pain. I grab his arm now, twist it behind him and manage to heave him into the pool. He screams "Barney!" as he goes in with a great splash.

Ott calls, "Hey, what's happening out there?" I slam the screening room door shut and shove a big potted plant over to block it. And I race for the pathway to the street.

A glance back as I reach the corner of the house shows me that Ott has burst out of the projection room and Heritage is climbing out of the pool. Keeler is in the doorway, staring over at me. "Get the gun," Heritage yells to Ott.

I keep going up the pathway and now I hear pursuing footsteps. But I'm into my car and rolling away by the time Ott and Heritage appear. "You can run but you can't hide, you little cocksucker, we'll getcha!" Heritage screams after me, while Ott races for his Cadillac in the driveway near the front door.

I floor the accelerator and fly down the road and round the curve and yank the wheel and screech into the dark deserted overflow parking lot of the Hotel Bel-Air. Cut motor and lights. Then I stare through the foliage at the road. The Cadillac speeds by and keeps going. Soon as it disappears, I rev up and pull out, go back the way I just came. I know a series of back roads deep in the canyon that wind up and over the mountain into the San Fernando Valley.

I'm elated to have lost them and stunned that crazy Jack Heritage really seemed ready to kill me. I can't believe they're this vicious over a fuckin' petty studio squabble. What's going on? But by now the adrenaline high is wearing off and the pain hits me. The sharp ache in my rib cage reminds me I haven't gotten away unscathed. All I want to do now is go home and swallow a bunch of painkillers and sleep it off. But the Chateau would be the next place they come looking for me.

So I have to go somewhere safe.

Hollywood is calling it a night. The neon signs just went out on the movie marquees and most of the storefronts along the brassy boulevard are already darkened.

The tour bus with a MOVIELAND BY NIGHT banner on it rolls up to Grauman's Chinese right on time from its last run. The tourists, the guide and driver, debark. For a few moments the bus door stays unattended, and no one notices as I slip on board, clutching my side, swaying down the empty aisle, and collapse into a seat at the rear. My throbbing ribs scream with pain. I hope I don't pass out.

My eyes droop shut, but I fight it. I force my eyes open in time to see the driver return to the bus reading a newspaper. Zacharias climbs into the driver's seat. Levers the front door closed, turns on the motor, adjusts the rear view mirror, and his hand freezes. I give a small wave and he turns to stare back at me. He walks down the long aisle. When he reaches me he doesn't like what he sees.

"Hey, what the hell happened?"

"Don't ask me." I try for a snicker. It comes out a wheeze.

"But I gotta ask you, Duveed!" Zacharias unfolds the newspaper to display the front page of the bulldog edition of the *L.A. Times*. The war-declared-size headline shouts:

HOLLYWOOD DIRECTOR SLAIN
POLICE HUNT BLACKLIST KILLER

Featured beneath it there is a studio portrait of Leo next to a lousy photo from my Army ID card. I look squinty-eyed and mean. Perfect casting for the role of a demented killer. Then the blackness of the night envelops me.

McKENNA

Alcalay and I are searching David Weaver's tiny room at the Chateau Marmont and finding nothing. Well, actually a lot, just not evidence. There are His and Hers toiletries in the bathroom medicine cabinet. Some of Jana's clothes in the closet and a smattering of her undies and tops in a dresser drawer. An Olivetti portable typewriter on the table with a half-used ream of paper and a script about World War II. Everything neat and tidy, maybe the chambermaid's doing, but no stacks of disarray.

"Give me your reading on the room," Alcalay asks.

"She spends a lot of time here, but not all. He's working on a script. Not bad. No sign that he's about to fly the coop. No sign of a disturbed, deranged occupant."

"Don't start on that again."

We look around. Where's left to search? Then I notice that the empty wastebasket has a small pink message envelope clinging to the side. I open the flap, show it to Alcalay. The envelope is empty.

"Let's go talk to the guy at the front desk," I suggest.

The frazzled young night clerk listens attentively. He's already called the manager, who's on his way over, and the clerk has his orders: Do whatever is necessary to get the cops out of the building as soon as possible.

"Yeah, there was a call for David Weaver at eleven o'clock," the clerk tells us. "When I came on duty it was the first call I logged. David's room didn't answer, but the guy said it was important, so I had the bellman stick the message under his door."

"You wouldn't happen to have a copy of it."

"Sure do. We write 'em on a carbon pad." Alcalay and I both read the message from "Uncle Leo."

"Logged in at 11:01." Alcalay points at the time entry. "Which makes it the neatest trick since Harry Houdini—Vardian was leaving a phone message a half hour after his body was discovered."

"You think David called in the message himself?"

"Sure. More fancy tap dancing," Alcalay says. "I'm onto this guy's style now. Probably trying to concoct another weird alibi."

"Lieutenant Alcalay?" the clerk interrupts. "Call for you. You can pick it up on the house phone."

"Alcalay," he says into the phone. "Hey, Barney, how'd you find me? You oughta be a detective—what? You *saw* David Weaver? Where the hell are you?"

It's chilly inside the temperature-controlled vault where Alcalay is but I can see he is simmering. The vault is a ten-by-twelve room with fitted shelves on two sides for the rows of theater-size film cans. From my aisle seat nearby in the screening room I can see they are prints from the Weaver & Vardian days up through those pictures Leo did alone. On the far inside wall there are floor-to-ceiling racks laden with vintage wines.

A mousy-looking fortyish corporate type in dark-framed glasses, charcoal-gray suit, white shirt with French cuffs, and an old-school tie is busy checking the contents and making notations on a clipboard. Alcalay is ignoring him, focusing instead on Barney Ott, who's leaning comfortably against the open steel door.

"Are you saying you caught David Weaver cracking this safe?" Alcalay growls.

"No," Ott says, "actually *we* were in process of opening the vault—"

"Which can be interpreted as one felony or two," Alcalay cuts in. "Breaking and entering—at a crime scene under investigation."

"Didn't see any crime-scene tape," Jack Heritage says. Then he sneezes. He looks like a beached sea otter, slouched unhappily in an aisle seat. Wearing a beach robe from the cabana with Leo's initials on it over his soaked suit, his hair all tousled.

I'm in the row right behind Heritage. Hating his guts. No crime-scene tape! Another Declan Collins. The same kind of arrogant turd.

"Hey, ex-copper," Alcalay snaps at Heritage. "You know better, you knew we were working our way over here." Alcalay gestures expansively with his arm to indicate the entire estate. The guy inside the vault with the clipboard cautions him:

"Careful, Lieutenant, don't knock any of the wine bottles off the rack, some of them are quite expensive."

"Who the hell are *you* anyway?"

"I'm Eli Nugent. From Panorama's legal staff."

"And what're you doing with that damn clipboard?"

"Taking inventory. It may be necessary for probate."

"Point is," Ott resumes, "we had our locksmith working on the vault when Weaver snuck up on us and without provocation attacked Jack."

"Bastard came out of nowhere. Slugged me and shoved me into the pool." Heritage sneezes again. He blots his nose with the sleeve of Leo's robe.

"And then Weaver just ran off into the night?" Alcalay is skeptical.

"We tried to pursue but he got away," Ott says.

Alcalay steps out of the vault to confront him. "Before we get into why *you* were here," Alcalay says, "any idea why Weaver was here?" Obviously Alcalay doesn't feel like sharing the information about the phone message left at the Chateau.

"Well," Ott says, "I assume after he killed Leo, the kid knew the coast was clear, so he came here to rob the place."

"No sign of a break-in," I point out, "except for the little burglary job you guys did here." I think I know what they were after: I've heard scuttlebutt about Leo snatching his movie's sound track as a negotiating pawn. But before I can go there, Eli Nugent, the fussy little studio lawyer, emerges from the vault and clears his throat:

"Pardon me, officers, but I must object to any intimations that my colleagues have broken the law."

"Thanks for your unbiased opinion, counsellor." Alcalay is delighted to have someone engage with him. "We'll have to see if the DA's office agrees."

"Yeah, you do that." Jack Heritage snickers and again blows his nose on the robe's sleeve.

"And I'll have you in a cage downtown until we clear this up, cowboy!" Alcalay snarls.

Eli Nugent moves between them. "Mr. Heritage is indulging in a bit of sarcasm. Possibly because of the trauma he's sustained tonight. But the fact is that he and Mr. Ott—"

"And who else was here?" Alcalay's got his notebook out. "I need the names of all witnesses—or perpetrators—present."

Eli Nugent responds. "The name of the locksmith is Lester Morell. His firm is located in Culver City. Also present was film editor Keeler Barnes, who—"

I jump in. "I thought Leo fired him."

Barney Ott shrugs. "Old news. Leo fired him, I rehired him. As Panorama's new supervising film editor. Overdue recognition for a talented man."

"What did Leo say when he heard that?" I ask.

"Didn't get around to telling him. But he would have read it in the trades tomorrow." I raise an eyebrow. "Hey, McKenna, directors don't run the studio. Harry and I do."

"Why'd they leave? Keeler and the locksmith?" Alcalay asks

"I sent 'em home," says Ott. "They weren't needed here anymore."

"*You* decided that," Alcalay bristles.

"You're welcome to talk to them, of course, but after we sighted David Weaver we thought the most urgent thing was to notify you and—"

"Second most urgent thing," I correct him. "Opening the vault was top priority, right?" Ott says nothing. "Find what you were looking for?"

"Yeah, as a matter of fact I did."

So he got the sound track. "The show must go on, huh, Barney?"

"That's what they say," Barney Ott meets my gaze. Unblinking. Making me wonder: Would these guys actually kill Leo for a sound track? Maybe. But that wouldn't explain Joe Shannon.

Eli Nugent cuts off my speculation. "There was material here of a time-sensitive nature that Mr. Ott thought might be in the vault."

"Studio property," Ott says.

"Stolen from *private* property." Alcalay gestures at the vault.

"Now that's rather harsh, Lieutenant." Eli Nugent steps in. "When the studio, at its expense, built the cabana, the projection room *and* vault, Mr. Vardian sold his interest in the house and overall property to Panorama. He rented back the premises on a lifetime basis for one dollar per year."

He offers documents for Alcalay's perusal.

"We like our talented people, like Leo, to be happy," Ott says.

"So Mr. Ott and Mr. Heritage were here tonight as duly authorized representatives of the titleholders," Eli Nugent affirms. "And therefore cannot be accused in any way of unlawfully entering the premises."

"We own the place," Jack Heritage says with a fuck-you smile.

But that smile transforms into another sneeze and I don't bother to say "God bless you" while Alcalay looks like he's ready to cart the whole conniving bunch of them away. I'm so tired of all this Hollywood horseshit I'm ready to help him try. But of course we can't. They own the place.

After leaving Stone Canyon, Alcalay and I split up to cover other ground. He goes looking for Keeler Barnes and Lester the Locksmith, while I take the touchy but potentially more productive assignment of notifying next of kin. Assuming Jana Vardian hasn't heard yet.

I get her current address from the studio switchboard. When I reach the bungalow in Silver Lake, the street is dark. I thought a TV crew might have found her first, but it's quiet.

I've had only glancing encounters with Jana in recent years, mostly at Hollywood screenings or social functions where she accompanied Leo. The few words we exchanged on the studio back lot recently are as close as we've ever come to a private conversation. I ring the doorbell. Wait, ring again. In a moment the lamp outside the front door switches on and I hear her muffled voice. "Who's there?"

"It's Brian McKenna."

Chain being unlatched and the door swings open. Jana looks sleep-rumpled, barefoot, wearing a terrycloth bathrobe.

She looks at me and says nothing, but an awful dread comes into her eyes, realizing I'm the bearer of news that she does not want to receive. I've seen that look too many times.

"We have to talk. Can I come in, Jana?"

"Is it David?" she whispers, clutching at the collar of her robe.

Clearly, as far as she's concerned, the bogeyman has arrived. I'm uncomfortable causing that reaction, but I know how strategically valuable it can be. Like it or not, it's part of the job. She steps aside so I can enter and I close the door behind us.

41

JANA

Ring. Loud knock. I'm jolted awake. Grab a robe. Stagger to the front door. Who's there? Oh, God. Yank it open. McKenna on the doorstep. Been trailing David for weeks, concocting evidence. I want to punch him, fall down and scream. What the hell's he want? Somber as an undertaker. Suddenly my heart's in my throat.

"Can I come in, Jana?"

Somebody's dead. Must be. Another one.

Please God. Don't let it be David.

Invite him in. Sit down. Hold my breath. He tells me. My father. Killed. Dangling like a side of beef. "No!" I scream, again and again. Then a flash of relief. David's alive! And I'm swamped by shame. It smashes into me. Tears pour. Can't stop, though I hate showing emotion to this manipulative creep. Daddy's dead. Impossible. He survived the Blacklist. Survived cancer. Seemed immortal. But he's gone.

Just like that. Gone.

I pretend to listen to the details. Not hearing McKenna. Who cares? Dead is dead. It can't just be over like this! Not yet, when there's no chance to make it better. Never another hug. Another smile. But one thing for certain. My father loved me. Always. How he loved me! And not just in the great glowing moments.

But I have to stop. Suck it up. No more tears. Still gasping. I try to tune in. What is Slim Jim selling? Snake oil, as usual. Under the smarmy sympathy. The hidden agenda. He's after David. Hunting David. Can't be. David would never . . . could never . . . could he? And that's when it hits me. Why McKenna really is here. To get me to help him catch David.

"Jana, is there a possibility in your mind that David may have done this terrible thing?"

So that confirms it. He's nailed me. Because how can I be sure? Not totally. There's a side to David that—

Phone rings. Stare at it. Don't want to answer. Have to talk to David! But not like this. Not with McKenna here.

"Probably just a reporter," McKenna says.

As if he doesn't care if I answer it. Really urging me to pick it up. Help him. No. I won't consort with the enemy. That what I'm doing? Like father, like daughter? I reach for the phone. Slowly. Please don't let it be David. Press the receiver tightly to my ear. Containing all incoming sound. Trying not to betray the identity of my caller. Say hello.

"It's me . . . did I wake you?" David's voice is odd. Thick. Slurry.

"No, I was up," I say. McKenna staring at me.

"You heard, huh?" David reads me. "Jana, I'm . . . so sorry. No matter what Leo did, he was your father and—"

I'm crying again. No, I'm caterwauling. I can't control it. There's a sound. A high pitched keen. It's coming from me. David's trying to talk to me. I hear only a few words here and there. ". . . honey, I know." ". . . be okay . . ." My hysteria blots him out. I want to speak, I have to speak. Finally through the floodgates I form the words that I must ask:

"Did you kill my daddy?" I'm shocked at my little-girl tone.

"No, of course not, how could you even—"

"Sorry, I didn't mean it, I—"

Behind me McKenna insists, "Let me talk to him!" David

asks, "Who's there with you?" McKenna yanks the phone from me.

"David, this is Agent McKenna. Come in, kid, make it easy on everyone, you—" McKenna blinks. Then lowers the phone. "He hung up."

McKenna turns to me. He wants David. But he's got me. And that's when he turns up the heat. Like he did to my father. Warning me. For my own good. Threatening in that velvet way. Working my hopes and fears. Offering me only one possibility.

"You have to help us bring him in, Jana."

Never. Never. Never. My arms are crossed and wrapped tightly around me, clutching my own shoulders, trying to block out his words while I hold on for dear life.

42

DAVID

I fling the phone down as if it's molten lava. "McKenna's there," I yelp.

"Of course he is," Zacharias says, "he's everywhere."

We're in a motel in the Valley. I cannot recall how we got here. I'm back into trying to fill in mental blanks. I recall being in the rear of Zacharias' tour bus. His showing me the newspaper with my picture. Guess I've read the story because I know what it says: Leo's dead! I still can't believe it. And they're blaming me. Hunting for me. I remember Zacharias dropping the bus off at a big car barn. When the coast was clear, Zacharias toting me to his car. Then I must have passed out again.

I woke up a few minutes ago, still aching but not as much as before. Zacharias in a chair next to the bed, where I've been conked out. My ribs all taped up. Band-Aids on bruises. Did we stop at a pharmacy somewhere? There's a bottle of prescription painkillers with Zacharias' name on it next to the phone. Must have taken some because my tongue is thick and my pronunciation fuzzy.

The first words out of me when I opened my eyes and the room swirled into focus were:

"I've gotta call Jana."

Now I can check that one off my list. She's in the hands of

the enemy. I feel new panic: what's she telling McKenna? I know how he scares her, but she wouldn't help him—how can I even think that? It's horrendous, losing her dad like that, of course she's hysterical.

"They've got her," I say to Zacharias. "Working on her right now. Convincing her the way to avenge Leo is to let them use her as bait to get me. She'll resist, but the assholes will keep working on her, that's their technique, they—"

"Cut it out," Zacharias says sharply. "You love her?" I nod. "Then believe in her. Don't doubt her."

"But suppose—"

"Fuck *suppose*! That's their game. Divide and conquer. Turn us against each other, so we'll do the job on ourselves that they want done. Don't let it happen, kid. Close ranks. Stick together." He stares at me. Gauging if his words are penetrating. "You get it?"

I nod. Ashamed that I doubted Jana even for an instant.

Then the enormity of Leo's death sweeps over me. The bad memories superseded by the loss of my Uncle Leo. I flash on how once he performed a miracle for me. On my tenth birthday party at the Stone Canyon house. We had received a War Department telegram a week before. Dad had been wounded in the liberation of Paris, but he was going to be okay. My mom and Jana and I were faking joy, when we really felt relief plus sadness that Teddy wasn't with us today. By pulling Pentagon strings, Leo arranged for a phone call to go through during the party to a field hospital in France so my dad could wish me a happy birthday.

"That was a gift," Zacharias agrees.

Then Zacharias fills me in on defense strategy. "They know we're friends, I figure they'll come to my place. So I checked you in here. Under my name. Paid cash, no credit card record. So you can lay low."

"You taped me up?" I touch the ribs gingerly. Wince. Even the merest pressure lights me up.

"Yeah, too tight?"

"It's fine. The Army will give you a job as a medic anytime. How many of these did I take?" I point at the pill bottle.

Zacharias holds up two fingers. "You were hurting pretty bad. Babbling a lot of stuff about tonight. Up at Leo's house."

"Uh-huh. So what do we do now?"

"I was hoping you had a few ideas."

"Maybe I do. Could be Ott and Heritage, they've been on Leo's case real heavy lately. Or maybe—" I hesitate.

"Y'got my attention, Duveed."

"The face I saw tonight. With that look when he spotted me. At Leo's house with those assholes. Helping them recover the movie sound track. Making himself a hero to the studio."

"Keeler Barnes?"

"He's always had this love-hate thing going with Leo. Mostly hate, though. Keeler blames his wife's death on the Blacklist—and Leo for naming him. Keeler also had it in for Joe Shannon."

Zacharias looks thoughtful. My eyes feel heavy again. Then he says, "Maybe you got something. But the question is, What can we do about it?"

"That's the part I haven't worked out yet," I admit. "Is it getting darker in here?"

"Only for people who took two pills," Zacharias says. "Close your eyes, kid, get a little more rest. I'll be right here."

When I open my eyes again, he's in the chair watching me sadly while eating soup from a Denny's coffee shop take-out container.

"Chicken soup," he says, "want some?"

"Couldn't hurt," I say. It's an old Yiddish punch line.

So he's spooning soup. Into me. My ribs glad I don't have to do any chewing.

Zacharias says, "You ever wonder if I was what they said I was? A dirty rotten Commie?"

"None of my business," I say.

"That's what I said to HUAC, but I'll tell you. I joined the Party early and stayed late. Long after Teddy and most of the others quit. I hung in until Khrushchev made that speech in Moscow. Spilling the beans, revealing all the gory details of the Stalin regime. Turns out my hero, Uncle Joe, was a mass murderer, slaughtered as many people as Hitler did. For a while I felt like a world-class putz."

"That's a heavy load."

"I finally made peace with myself. Stalin fooled me, for decades. But the things the Party advocated in this country, they were the right things. And we made some headway. Got anti-lynching laws, collective bargaining, enabled more blacks to vote, all that. So I decided I was wrong about Stalin, but not about me. When you get a chance to do something good, you gotta grab it, no matter what kind of label is on it."

I know there's a subtext here, he's telling me something important, but I'm not clear what it is.

"Not to worry, Duveed," he says. "I've still got a coupla tricks up my sleeve. You'll be okay. I guarantee it." I doze off again before I can ask him how he can be so sure.

43

MCKENNA

Alcalay and I are in Tiny Naylor's in West L.A. Only a scattering of customers in the franchise coffee shop. It's almost 4:00 A.M. We're pounding caffeine and reviewing where we are. I don't know about him, but I'm exhausted.

Alcalay tracked down Lester the Locksmith, who stated that all he saw removed from the vault were the missing reels of sound track, which Keeler Barnes identified and took away. And then Keeler confirmed to Alcalay that he stopped off at the studio and the sound track is again under Panorama lock and key. Has no idea where David Weaver might be.

I mention going past Zacharias' apartment in Sherman Oaks. No one home. I stuck one of my cards in the doorjamb. Wrote on the back for him to call me ASAP.

"So where y'think he's at?"

"Who knows?" I say. "Zacharias could be hiding the Weaver kid in the trunk of his car and tear-assing to the Mexican border. Or maybe he propositioned one of his tourist ladies tonight and got lucky, he used to be quite a pussy hound."

Earlier, after I left Jana, I reached Alcalay by phone and he assigned an unmarked cop car to watch her house. Now he tells me he woke up a judge to authorize a wiretap on her home phone.

"And her work phone at the studio?" I ask.

Alcalay nods, he did that, too. "Know something, I'm glad I let you into the case. Gave you a lot of shit, tried to run over a lot of what you said, but you hung in there like a real pro and played it straight up." Clearly he thinks the case is solved and the rest is just mechanics. "We're almost done, so why are you looking so gloomy?"

"You know. I just don't like loose ends."

"Then you're in the wrong fuckin' business." Alcalay drains the last of his coffee. I think I liked him better when he disliked me.

It's all over but the shouting," Clyde Tolson gloats on the secure phone line. It's still predawn in L.A. and this is the second time I've called the deputy director at home tonight. The first was to alert him to Leo Vardian's murder.

"There are still some nagging inconsistencies," I mention.

"Naturally, but I'm sure they'll clarify as you fellas button it up. My compliments, this has been very well managed. The berserk son of a Commie who fled a HUAC subpoena runs amok. That'll go a long way to convincing some of the doubters that the Red Menace is still to be reckoned with. Good work."

Then Tolson shares with me as if I'm already part of the top tier. "Timing could not be better, Brian. You and the L.A. police will run this Weaver terrorist to ground just in time for Congressional consideration of our annual budget. So be very watchful, please. We don't want this apple cart upset, you understand?"

I know this isn't the moment to ask him about the job heading up the countrywide bank robbery unit. That's not how the game is played. Bureau protocol, unwritten but understood by all us long-timers, dictates that I wait for them to introduce it. Giving me the opportunity to pretend surprise and express gratitude.

Tolson, like Alcalay, is assuming only insignificant details remain. That catching the Weaver kid is simply a matter of hours. I don't contradict him, but I'm not at all sure. After all, here's a guy who's been trained by the Army Rangers to evade capture in hostile territory.

44

DAVID

The early morning sun is seeping around the edges of the drawn drapes when I wake up in the motel room in the Valley and find Zacharias is gone. On the nightstand I see a note: "Duveed, It's going to be okay. Love ya, kid." Signed with a flourished "Z" that reminds me of Zorro, defender of the downtrodden.

I call a taxi, and when it arrives I tell him to take me to Las Palmas and Franklin in Hollywood. That's near where I dimly remember parking my car last night before I staggered the few blocks to Zacharias' bus.

I spot my dusty jalopy on Las Palmas above Hollywood Boulevard. I don't just walk up to it. First I lurk in the doorway of a nearby apartment house and scan for signs of a stakeout. I'm about to stride forward when a uniformed meter maid comes rolling down the street. Blond and busty, marking tires with her chalk stick. She stops at my car. Climbs out with her pad, looks at my license plate. I hold my breath. That makes the ribs throb, so I let the breath out. There must be an APB out for my car. But she writes a parking ticket routinely, stuffs it under my windshield wiper, and rolls on.

I stay put until she turns the corner. Then I stroll forward, reach for the ticket, and I feel teased by a shard of elusive memory. Something I want to recall, but it's just out of reach. No time to ponder it now. I pocket the ticket, jump in the car, and take off. No bells, no whistles, no sirens. No one follows. Okay, at least I've got wheels again.

Driving south through the morning traffic, I don sunglasses and my New York Yankees ballcap, turn up my collar. Now I'm anonymous. I hope. I have to do the same thing for my car.

The long-term parking lot at L.A. airport is jammed, but I don't need a space. I roll to the farthest aisle, stop just long enough to hop out with a screwdriver, swap license plates with one of the cars, and drive off. Hoping the owner of that parked car doesn't return for days.

Next stop is Earl Scheib's car emporium on Lincoln in Santa Monica that boasts a bargain basement $59.95 paint job. What color do I want? "Make it black." Like the heart of whoever is setting me up for this gigantic fall. They drive my yellow Ford into the car washing section. Soon it'll be disguised as a miniature hearse.

I watch the process through the splatter-protecting glass for a while. Then I get self-conscious. Standing in one place long enough for someone to notice me, maybe even someone just reading the *L.A. Times* with my face displayed, doesn't seem like a good idea. So I take a stroll.

My mind is racing, of course. Mostly in circles. I'm cut off from the person I need the most. Jana. I ache to see her, at least talk to her. But they'll expect me to contact her again, so what can I do? Have to steer clear. At a time when she needs me more than ever.

As soon as my car is finished, I can do something—I can start surreptitiously watching Keeler, see where that leads and if I can get him alone, I'll—what? In the light of morning I'm starting to poke holes in my brilliant solution. Having seen

Leo and Keeler go at each other, I can buy that Keeler might have run into Leo last night and bad led to worst. A spontaneous eruption. But a premeditated, intricate scheme? Designed to ensnare me? I don't see Keeler doing that. Not the Keeler I know. Barney Ott and Jack Heritage on the other hand—

Hey, is that guy I just passed on the street looking at me funny? I hurry around the corner, glancing back over my shoulder. I'm in front of the public library on Santa Monica Boulevard and duck inside. Quickly conceal myself in the stacks where I can peek at the entrance. The guy hasn't followed me in. So I'm still okay. Then I notice an early afternoon edition of today's *Mirror-News* on the newspaper rack. I take it to an inconspicuous table in the far corner. I'm still leading the news. Search on for Blacklist murderer. Revenge seen as motive. Hate-filled ex-GI described as highly trained killer. Sure sounds like there's a monster on the loose.

My head's throbbing and so are my ribs. I've got Zacharias' pills. Wash one down at the water fountain. Still too soon for the car to be finished. I return to my table. Spot an interesting sidebar story in the paper:

PANORAMA STUDIO PRODUCTION CHIEF HARRY RAINS ANNOUNCED TODAY THAT RENOWNED FILMMAKER REX GUNDERSON WILL TAKE OVER AS DIRECTOR OF THE LATE LEO VARDIAN'S FILM *AGAINST THE WIND* AND COMPLETE IT FOR THE STUDIO.

Leo will do somersaults in his grave. But how's that for a motive? Rex's career has ground to a standstill. Suddenly he's back in the game—finishing off a major movie, probably get co-director credit, and the studio will owe him a big favor. Like approving a new movie for him. Resuscitating his career. So could it be Rex? Or maybe it's all a present for Dad from

Markie? Or more manipulation by Barney Ott? Shit, it could all be just stupid conjecture. If it's Ott and Heritage who did all the dirty deeds, and then contrived to lure me over to Leo's house last night, why did Heritage seem so startled to see me there?

While I'm putting the newspaper back in the library rack, I notice today's edition of *Film Bulletin*. I thumb through it, nothing about Leo's death. Guess they went to press too early. But there's an announcement on page two next to this morning's Rumor Mill column that Okie O'Connell has been designated as Joe Shannon's replacement. Could that really have been enough for Okie to cook up this murderous mishmash—along with the demeaning way I saw Shannon treat him. Yeah, that could be. Suppose Okie killed Shannon, then started leaving the Blacklist signs, including the one threatening himself, and then tossed in Leo to complete the misdirection. Yeah. Okie is vicious enough, but then is he smart enough?

As I'm putting today's *Film Bulletin* back in the rack and thinking about Okie, another fleeting thought surfaces. A bit of research I've been meaning to do. I ask the librarian if they have back copies of *Film Bulletin*.

"Going back to 1938," she says.

"Can I see last year's volume?"

She gets 1958 for me. I take it to my table and start checking Shannon's columns. Looking for those Happy Birthday listings. I heard Okie tell McKenna that Shannon never forgot to mention "the mystery man," Axel Atherton, who was born, according to the Navy records Jana got for us, on June 29. I find lots of June salutations, but no mention of Atherton. So I check May and July. Still no Atherton. What the hell. Just one more dead end. But then a new idea hits me: Axel Atherton died on November 17.

So I thumb to mid-November and there it is in the middle

of Shannon's column the way Okie said: Atherton's name
sandwiched in between birthday greetings to choreographer
Busby Berkeley and comedian Harpo Marx.

For a long time I just stare at it. Then I get the volumes for
1956 and 1957. Axel Atherton made the B-day roundup both
those years, too, always in mid-November. I close the volumes. Thoroughly confused. Joe Shannon was methodically
offering greetings year after year not on the occasion of Axel
Atherton's birth but on the anniversary of his death. As if it
was some kind of message. Like a reminder to someone who's
still alive.

45

M C K E N N A

He looks like he's in a blissful sleep. The muscles on his hawkish face are relaxed, a man at peace. Lying on his bed, fully clothed, in his own apartment. He's oblivious to being the center of activity.

The forensic crew and the coroner's people do their dance, working with the agility and coordination that comes from a lot of grim shared experience. I watch them dust the open-topped prescription drug containers on the nightstand for prints. The containers are all empty. The techie has already done the water pitcher and glass beside them. Propped against the lamp is the business card I left in the doorjamb of Peter Zacharias' apartment late last night.

"Who found him?" I ask.

"Cleaning lady," Alcalay says. "She came at ten. This was her regular morning. She called the Sherman Oaks cops."

The apartment house is on a sycamore-tree-lined side street off Van Nuys north of Ventura. It's a tired-looking double-deck block of a dozen two-bedrooms. Stucco exterior is cracking and repatched, there's a small pool and a hot tub with water a brackish color. It's a place for struggling young couples and old pensioners. The neighbors are all hanging out their windows watching the action.

Zacharias' apartment is on the upper floor. It's neatly kept, lots of books on cinder block shelves. Mostly political theory stuff, plus a weathered assortment of the usual suspects like Steinbeck, Hemingway, Faulkner, Joyce, and Tolstoy. The books all look like they've been read. A few museum Impressionist posters, several photos. Zacharias and a smiling attractive woman in front of the Eiffel Tower. Another of Zacharias and Teddy Weaver in swimsuits on a beach grinning at the camera with a young David Weaver standing between them.

"Did Zacharias leave a message or something?"

"Hell," Alcalay says, "he left a manifesto."

Alcalay leads me to a corner of Zacharias' bedroom. A battered old manual Royal typewriter is on the small desk. Next to it is a sheet of paper in a glassine evidence envelope. I lift it up and read.

> *To Whom It May Concern,*
> *I've always wanted to start off a script with those words and I finally got my chance. I wish to confess that I, and only I, am the person the newspapers have lately been referring to as The Blacklist Killer. Specifically, I willfully, with premeditation and pleasure, murdered Joe Shannon and Leo Vardian. Each, in my estimation, deserved to die as punishment for the injuries they had caused to myself, also to many others I knew and held dear, as well as the damage they brought to the core principles of this country. Using the label they casually but brutally attached to others, they were truly un-American.*
> *   I went to Joe Shannon's cottage, which is listed in the public phone book, struck him with a paperweight I found on a desk and set fire to the building with the tin of gas I had brought with me. The night of Leo Vardian's death, I penetrated the Panorama*

Studio lot by mingling with the members of the iron gang as they entered the side gate reporting to work. Then I hid on the Western street, and when Vardian came for his parked car I killed him.

While seeking revenge and a measure of justice for the crimes I deem they had committed, I cannot now allow anyone else to be smeared or punished for what I alone did. I am willing to be judged for my deeds, which were mine and mine alone. May God have mercy on my soul.
Peter Zacharias

I put the letter down. "Whaddaya think?" Alcalay asks. He's watching me as if I'm in a police lineup.

"First reaction," I say, "is that sews it up. We can call off the hunt for David Weaver—"

Alcalay explodes. "Dammit, I knew you were gonna back-slide and go soft again, I—"

Just like that I'm back on this guy's bad list. But I override Alcalay: "My second reaction is—most of the details in this confession Zacharias could've picked up from the press plus scuttlebutt around the studio—"

Alcalay gets it and likes it. "Yeah! Except for Shannon's missing wallet! We kept that away from the media—so it's not in the confession. All r-i-i-i-ight! What else?"

"Well, even more important, a bag of bones like Zacharias couldn't drag Leo down the street, under the gallows, and into that noose."

"Exactly!" Then Alcalay looks sheepish. "You were yanking my chain."

"Not hard to do. So you figure Zacharias killed himself to get Weaver off the hook?"

"They were buddies."

"Ray, if you get in trouble, don't look to me for a favor like this."

"Suppose you had nothing to lose."

Now I see he's holding a hole card. "Okay, what else've you got?"

"The doctor who wrote those prescriptions for Zacharias. Talked to him on the phone and he said the pills were high-octane painkillers. Designed to ease his last weeks. Zacharias was dying of cancer."

I look sadly at the body on the bed. The paramedics are preparing to zip Zacharias into a body bag. "Poor bastard. He was a war hero."

"Well, my bet is that the two war heroes did it together."

Bottom line is the APB on David Weaver stays in effect. He's still our target.

Better and better," Clyde Tolson exults long distance from D.C. I'm talking to him quietly from a phone line I've stretched off to a far corner of Zacharias' living room. Tolson savors the exquisite symmetry. "An old vicious Bolshevik combining forces in a plot with a Red Diaper Brat to undermine the fabric of America."

Then he's into projecting the successful future.

"After the arrest, assuming this Weaver person is taken alive, well, even he isn't—we'll want you to fly back here for a press conference. Director Hoover will personally preside. You'll detail the background and he'll place it in the larger context. Lingering conspiracy. Threat to the nation. That sort of thing. This is a big one for us. And"—Tolson shines the golden light on me—"once we get you back here, Brian, we're not going to let go of you. We need you here with us at Central on a permanent basis. I think you know what I'm talking about."

"Yes, sir." I sure as hell do.

"Stay on it, boy."

That's it. I have been officially anointed. The good soldier gets his reward. For following orders from headquarters. That's how it works. Go along to get along. See? It all worked out. That's what I keep repeating to myself as I watch the paramedics wheel the gurney with Zacharias aboard it into the street.

46

JANA

I wish so much that I had Wendy to talk to right now, but of course that's impossible, so this is second best:

I'm in my familiar chair in Dr. Sarah Mandelker's office. It doesn't seem like a sanctuary this afternoon. I'm tense as a clenched fist. I know how I must look. Didn't dare peek in the mirror or I wouldn't have left the house. But the reaction of a woman I passed in the lobby on my way up here told me. I look like someone who's been crying all night. Eyes raw and swollen.

"So very sorry about your loss, Jana," she says. "I wasn't sure you'd show up."

"Neither was I. Not that there was much choice. Couldn't bring myself to go to the studio, couldn't stand staying at the house with reporters constantly calling. Definitely not ready to go back to Stone Canyon. So here I am. Thought if I canceled on such short notice, you'd still charge me." It's my lame attempt at a joke.

She gives me a wan smile. Then gently homes in.

"You've been through such a lot just since yesterday. I assume you want to talk about it."

"It'll take more than fifty minutes to tell."

"Let's see how far we get. What's the first thing on your mind?"

I don't dare tell her the truth. McKenna cautioned me not to tell anyone. Okay, okay. Skip that part.

"My father. I forgot how much I loved him. Everything we've been talking about here the last few weeks, it all seems so trivial now. I feel like a spoiled nasty child, who's been groaning and complaining about Daddy. I mean, sure, he did some very bad things, but he didn't deserve what's happened to him! And"—that damn McKenna—"and more bad things keep coming so fast I don't know what to do!"

My cheeks are burning. I'm crying again. Groping for a tissue. And.

"I just want my Daddy! I want him to come fix everything! That's how it always was. Whenever I had a problem, I always ran to him. Daddy, take care of it! He could do that—he was so powerful, he could make problems be gone, but now—*he's* gone. So that leaves just me. And David. David needs me. But . . . I don't know what to do."

Sarah waits. Then, softly. "Do you believe the things they're saying about David on the news?"

"No, of course not! They're making him the fall guy, but—" Need another tissue. "In a way I blame myself—for all this."

"That's interesting. How'd you arrive at that?"

"Because I wanted so much for David to come back to L.A. It's as if I willed it. If he'd stayed in Europe . . . then maybe none of this would have happened."

"You really think you have that much control?"

I laugh through my snuffling. "Me? I can't even stop crying. I'm falling apart. Don't know what to expect. I can't rely on myself anymore."

"To do what?"

"Anything! I used to think I was one tough cookie. Snubs. Insults. Public humiliations. Handle the worst anyone can dish out. Without crumbling. Straight talker. Knows right from wrong. Acts accordingly. But that was nonsense, because—look at me, I'm coming unglued."

"What's that feel like?"

I don't know what's safe to say. I'm too near the third rail. But I've got to tell her something. "It's just so . . . horribly sad. The way they have of forcing people to do things . . . they hurt you . . . take things away . . . spoil 'em . . . they broke Leo . . . they destroyed Ellie and Teddy . . . and maybe now David."

"Who can do that? Who's 'they'?"

The fear rises into my throat. "You know who they are, they're—" I suddenly focus on the pad in her lap, the pen in her hand. "Are you writing all this down?"

"Our sessions are private and privileged, you know that."

"Yeah, there was another Hollywood psychoanalyst, not too many years ago, who told his patients he operated that way, but he was slipping tips to the FBI and the Committee on the side."

Wow. Did I just say that? How could I accuse her like that?

"Jana, you must be feeling very vulnerable now. I certainly understand your fears, so tell me only as much as you feel comfortable with."

Okay. Why else did I come today? Here goes. Off the high board.

"McKenna. An FBI agent. He's been lurking on the fringes of our lives for the last ten years. He hounded both our families. Made Teddy and Ellie leave the country, then talked Leo into giving names. Convinced him to be a Good Citizen. Spill his guts and abandon everything he ever believed in. Whenever McKenna is around, it's like a visit from the Angel of Death." Deep breath. And. "He dropped in to see me last night. Brought the news about my father. Broke it to me so gently. Then the hook went in. He didn't really give a shit about my losing my father. He was really only there to get me to help him catch David."

I stop. My chest is heaving.

"Oh, he dressed it up in a bunch of compassionate verbiage: If you love David then the best thing for David is to give himself up. If he's innocent, then the truth will emerge."

"Did McKenna threaten you?"

"Not exactly. Just pointed out the advantages. And disadvantages. He told me that if I knew anything and withheld it—or did anything at all to help David, if I have any contact with him and don't report it, then I can be arrested and tried as an accomplice. Here's my card, he says, call me any time, but you must call!"

"Sounds very threatening."

"He said I could be in big trouble if I—I told anyone what he said." I almost choke on the words. As if McKenna will leap out of the closet now with handcuffs.

"Thank you for trusting me," she says.

"He—he really scared me. I mean, I'm terrified of going to jail! I couldn't handle that. Locked up in a cell."

"Your claustrophobia. Does McKenna know about that?"

"Who knows what he knows."

We're both silent for a long moment, then she says, "Last week you told me that when Leo was writing a screenplay he always asked himself: What is each major character most afraid of?"

"Uh-huh."

"What do you think Leo was most afraid of?"

I don't hesitate. "That they wouldn't let him make movies anymore."

"How about you, Jana? What are *you* most afraid of?"

"I told you, going to prison, being sealed up in a tiny hole."

"I sense there's something else."

Mandelker the mind reader. Got me. Finally. But I still have to sneak up on it. I can't just say it outright.

"See, this is how it is: David's out there somewhere. Mc-
Kenna and the police know he'll try to reach me, they must be
watching, tapping my phone. David's smart, he knows that,
too. So David can't get to me, and I can't get to him and he's—
all alone." I feel the tears building again. "But—maybe he's
safer that way."

"How do you mean?"

It rips my guts out just to put it into words. "Character is
destiny. That's what writers always say. So suppose I have
a—a character flaw. A genetic thing. Like father, like daughter.
So the absolute worst would be if—history repeated itself
and—I betrayed David."

"But—would you ever do that?"

"What I keep thinking is, there were people who resisted all
the HUAC pressure and McKenna didn't waste time on them.
But he saw something in Leo that told him, here's one I can get
to. Turned out he was right." I stare at Sarah Mandelker, feeling so scared and ashamed. "So maybe he's right about me."

Now the tears come in torrents. We sit together. At the end
of the session she asks, "See you tomorrow?" I nod and she
hugs me as if I'm a woebegone child. It brings back memories
of Ellie. I'm glad I came here today. Sarah listens. She really
listens. She hears me. No matter what ghastly things I tell her.

As usual I walk down the flights of stairs into the parking
garage. Thinking of my David. Totally unsure of his future.
Or even his survival. The lighting is dim and there's hardly a
vacant space as I plod toward my car. When suddenly I feel
someone's presence.

I scan the area. No one in sight. But someone could be hiding between cars. Or behind a pillar. I'm midway from the
staircase to my car, don't know whether to go forward or go
back, could be a mugger, or maybe I'm just imagining someone's here, like David does, or, yes, maybe it's McKenna or
one of his minions.

"Come on out, whoever the hell you are!" I say as bravely as I can.

I hear footsteps off to the right. Shape of a man. Walking out of the darkness. Into the light.

"It's me, honey," David says.

I see him. Or am I dreaming? Thank God he's here. But I see he's been crying.

DAVID

A few hours earlier, I arrived back at Earl Scheib's as my car was emerging from the paint-drying booth. I drove away, not knowing where to go. I needed a safe place to think. Then I realized I was near one. Only a few blocks away.

I rolled onto the Santa Monica pier past the amusement rides and found a parking space at the far end where the amateur fishermen line the rail. Hardly any sportsmen here, these people fish for food. Wearing sunglasses, and with my Yankees cap pulled down, I blended in. I put my elbows on the rail, head in my hands, and stared down at the muddy water, hoping for some clear thoughts.

The key question, of course, is who's framing me and why. I start with Jack Heritage—and eliminate him because he looked surprised when he saw me at the Vardian house. Whoever lured me there wouldn't have looked surprised. Barney Ott is more likely casting for Machiavelli, so maybe Ott just neglected to bring his strong-arm crusher up to speed until necessary. Or. Or . . . what?

I'm in way over my head, that's what. I don't know what the hell I'm doing. I'm not Sherlock Holmes.

But suppose I look at it as if it's something I do know about: plotting a screenplay. Yeah, that seems less intimidating. Inside my head I hear Teddy's chuckle:

"Story conference!" he says. "This one's a mind-bender, huh, pal?"

"Usual life and death situation. Only this time it's *my* life."

"Relax. They ain't invented a story yet that Weaver & Weaver can't lick. What do we know for sure?"

I know I'm making up dialogue for Teddy, but working so closely these last few years I got to know how he thought and what he felt about almost every subject.

"Basically," I tell him, "my hero, namely me, is in the crapper. Someone went after me and got me good."

"You have to take the emotion out of it, pal. It's a distraction. Let's refer to you as The David Character. Okay?" Good idea. "So the first thing we know about The David Character is that he's an accident."

"How's that?"

"Well, if the objective was to frame him for a crime, then one murder would have been enough. So The David Character is not the core of this story. He just flew into town at the wrong moment. But just in time to become the patsy in somebody else's script."

"But the villain's gotta be someone he knows," I offer.

"Well, at least someone who knew enough about The David Character's background—and could keep track of him. Chart his schedule—on and off the job—and know when he didn't have a solid alibi."

"A clever operator," I say.

"Absolutely. So now we can assume there'll be no more Blacklist killings."

"Based on what?"

"The David Character is on the run and therefore not

available for further framing. So the killer can't take a chance now and claim another scalp—because his patsy might have an ironclad alibi."

"Yeah, so the last thing he wants is to distract the cops from The David Character."

"So what is the core of this story?" Teddy asks.

"Vengeful Blacklist murderer is bumping off HUAC blabbers."

"But," Teddy points out, "Shannon was a leader of the pitchfork brigade. He was a red baiter, not a HUAC snitch."

"So there goes the pattern. Unless—"

"Say it, pal!"

"—unless there's another motive besides the Blacklist." So how do I follow this trail? "You taught me that there are only five basic motives. Sex. Greed. Fear. Power. Revenge."

"Or combinations thereof," Teddy says.

It feels like we're cracking a movie story. Maybe time for a twist. One suddenly occurs to me. "If you count Okie, there have been three targets. But what if—the killer really was after only one?"

Teddy chortles. "And the other two were just window dressing. Okay, let's suppose the game was to hide the real target in a small crowd."

"With signposts helpfully supplied—to mislead."

Then Teddy suggests, "Let's focus on the odd-man out. Joe Shannon. The guy who doesn't fit. How about that deal down in San Diego. Anything there?"

"Well, according to Shannon's statement to the San Diego cop, Sarge Gorman, Atherton was drinking with an off-duty marine when Shannon felt sick and went back to the base."

"Yeah, but . . . again, what if?" Teddy speculates.

"Yeah. Suppose he wasn't really a marine. Just another guy

with a crewcut. Hitting on sailors." Sudden light bulb. "Or—
maybe there was no other guy—maybe there was only Shannon!" Teddy rejects that. "Why not?"

"I have no trouble thinking of Shannon as a killer—"

"Right!" Now I'm selling it. "Suppose it was a lovers' tiff
between two homosexuals that got way out of hand and
Shannon later tried to bury his mistake—"

"—and went to all the trouble of stripping the body naked,
taking the dog tag, hoping Atherton won't be identified"—I
think Teddy's buying my idea, but he continues—"and then
keeps the dog tag in his office safe all these years as a memento
that could implicate him in a murder."

"Okay, okay, you made your point. Dumb idea."

"Hey, we agreed a long time ago to say everything because
a dumb idea can lead to a smart idea."

"So what's the smart one?"

"Question: what possible use was Axel's dogtag to Shannon?"

"Blackmail?" I ask. "But Atherton died in 1945, way before the HUAC hearings began—"

"—which gives weight to the notion that the whole Blacklist thing is just a diversion." Teddy's pleased. "*Now* tell me a
story."

"Okay . . . There's an old murder in San Diego. Committed
by someone who's since come to Hollywood, and reads the
trade papers, so he's reminded every year by Shannon that he
can still expose him." I like that. "But we still have no idea
who's doing all this stuff."

"Don't we?"

A thought flashes into my head. It's too enormous for me
even to say.

"That's not the same as *knowing*," I say.

"Then check it out," he says.

"How do I do that?"

"You're smart. You're my boy. You'll find a way." I want to groan, feeling hopeless. But Teddy reminds me, "Good writers usually remember all the good lines of dialogue they hear."

Glumly, I trudge back to my car and reach into my pocket for the keys. But a slip of paper comes out with the keys. It drifts to the ground. I bend over for it. It's the parking ticket I had plucked from my windshield on Las Palmas this morning. The nagging thought I couldn't bring up makes it through now. A voice echoes inside my head—not Teddy's, but one most familiar:

"... I ran up a helluva score in parking tickets. Parked in the red zone, the white zone, the yellow zone ... gray people park in gray spaces."

And then another echo of the same voice:

"A buddy of mine was stationed in San Diego at the naval base. He convinced me to come down for a weekend and he'd help me forget my troubles. So I went down there and drowned my sorrows. Helluva weekend."

Teddy was right, as usual. Now I have an idea what to do next.

I find a pay phone outside the old merry-go-round at the entry to the pier. The hurdy-gurdy organ is playing a Strauss waltz in the background, and through the windows I can see the carousel turning and the kids lunging for the brass ring, just the way Jana and I used to.

The phone at the other end is answered on the third ring and I recognize the voice even before he identifies himself. "Tip Toe Inn, this is Sarge."

Sarge Gorman, the ex-cop turned bartender at the Gaslamp District saloon in San Diego.

"Hi, I'm the guy from Hollywood who was in to see you a few days back, we—"

"Oh, yeah, hiya, Phil. How's Jana?"

"She's fine. Wow. You remembered my name." Glad he held onto his misinformation, now that my real name is in the headlines.

"Years of training," he boasts. "Never forget a face or a name. So what's new in Movieland?"

"Same old. But I thought you might be able to do me a small favor."

"How small?"

"Well, you mentioned all your buddies who are still on the Job down there come into the bar—"

"What's this about, Phil?"

"Parking tickets," I say quickly.

He laughs. "You want me to fix a parking ticket? Getoutahere. Pay the two dollars like everybody else."

"No, no, it's not like that, it's—some more research. Might be connected to that old case we were talking about."

"The Atherton thing? What's that got to do with a parking ticket?"

"Maybe nothing, but—it could be more than one ticket, could be several. All in the San Diego area during the week of November fifteenth, 1945. Do they keep records from back that far?"

I hold through a long wait. "Sarge, you still there?"

"Yeah. Those records are still available. 'Cuz there was so much money attached to parking fines, the Department's been real careful to keep track. You want me to have somebody look that up?"

"Yeah, if you could, if that's not asking too much, I'd really appreciate it, I—"

"Then you better give me a name, huh?"

I take a deep breath. Maybe this talking with Teddy was all nonsense. Just a lot of imagining on my part. But if you're going to try to knock a king off his throne, you have to start somewhere. "Rains," I say. "Harry Rains."

DAVID

Now I see Jana in the dim lighting of the underground parking garage. I was banking that today of all days she would keep her shrink appointment. I step out from behind a car and she rushes into my arms. God, that feels good.

"You've been crying," I say to her.

"So have you." She touches my damp cheek.

"Just heard on the radio driving over here. Zacharias is dead—killed himself."

"Oh, Jeez. Why?"

"To save me—left a note, taking blame for everything—only now the cops think we did it together."

"When is this craziness ever going to end?"

"Maybe today," I say, "today could be the day."

She hugs me tight and I wince. "You're hurt," she says. "What happened?"

"Let's get out of here and I'll tell you all about it."

Jana crouches out of sight in the passenger seat beside me as we drive out. I had figured that even if she was followed, my repainted and replated jalopy would pass for just another patient's car. Looks like it worked. I go around a few street corners, and no one is on my tail.

"I had to take the chance," I tell her. "Had to see you."

We drive over to Roxbury Park on Olympic Boulevard, a grassy, tranquil place in the lower-rent district of Beverly Hills. I used to play shortstop on a Little League team here. Saturday mornings Jana would be in the bleachers with my mom cheering me. Feels like a million years ago.

We park in a secluded corner of the lot. After we talk about Leo's awful death, I fill her in about what's been happening to me. She looks so scared as she listens. Then even more scared as she tells me about McKenna's visit.

"He just won't stop, David."

I don't want to deal with that. Maybe later, but not now. So I hug her close until she stops shaking, then tell her I have a couple of ideas. "Are you up for hearing?"

She backhands away tears and nods, and I tell her how I added it up on the pier and why it seems to come out Harry Rains.

"But why would he kill the snitches?" she asks incredulously. "Harry wasn't Blacklisted, he was the industry's go-between. Talking his clients into cooperating."

"That's the curve ball," I say. "Suppose it all has nothing to do with the Blacklist. Suppose Harry had his own reason—to get Joe Shannon off his back. I think it's all connected to Axel Atherton."

And I tell her how Harry once mentioned to me that when he thought he had failed the bar exam, he despondently went looking for fun down in San Diego. Where his childhood pal, Joe Shannon, was stationed. Along with Axel Atherton. "I think Harry must have got into a hassle with Axel and killed him. Shannon helped cover it up—but Shannon was black-mailing Harry ever since."

Jana stares at me. Trying to digest it. I give her a little more. "Probably it's not the only time Shannon's been involved in blackmail. Valerie told me that Harry had to pay off someone on the Committee to quash a subpoena for her—and Shannon brokered the deal." Then I shift gears and hit her with another idea I've come up with.

"Tell me about the book Joe Shannon sold to the studio," I say.

"Well, the word is Panorama paid Shannon a small fortune for it."

"Have you read it?"

"Only coverage. Very brief. About five pages. I was curious, so I asked for the manuscript. Markie told me nobody could see it now. Being kept under wraps because of its unusual style and structure."

"So who has seen it?"

"Hardly anyone, I guess. It's unusual. Basically we bought it based on the insistence and enthusiasm of"—she hears herself—"Harry Rains."

I jump on that. "So it would fit. Harry found a way to make another payoff to Shannon, out of Panorama's pocket. And you mentioned talk about getting Gene Kelly to star. Maybe Shannon was pushing Harry to put the picture into production before he leaves to be Ambassador to Britain. And who knows if that would've been the last of it. Harry must have felt he would be on the hook forever."

Jana thinks for a long moment, then says, "Is this for real, David, or are we just wishing it into place?"

"Honestly? I don't know."

"You have no proof—you can't be sure that Harry was even in San Diego the weekend when Atherton was killed."

I glance at my watch. It's been a few hours. Maybe time enough. "Well, let's see if at least that much checks out."

W e go to a pay phone on the wall outside a Roxbury drugstore. I dial the number I've memorized. After all, my whole life feels as if it depends on it.

"Sarge," I say, "it's Phil from Hollywood. Don't know if it's too soon, but I wondered if you'd had a chance to check on that thing?"

"Yeah, matter of fact, I did."

I'm tilting the ear piece away from my head so Jana also can hear.

"This guy Harry Rains, whoever the hell he is, got four parking tickets over that weekend, one of them downtown. Not far, incidentally, from the bar where Atherton was last seen." Then: "Want to tell me what it's all about?"

"Just—research," I manage to mumble.

"Well, make of it what you will. I'm not a cop anymore, so I don't need answers, David. Give my condolences to Jana."

Jana stiffens beside me and I go numb.

"We have newspapers in San Diego, too," Sarge says.

"Then why'd you help me?" I ask slowly.

" 'Cuz you got me wondering—why someone being tracked by the LA. fuzz would be spending time chasing down details about an ancient murder instead of running far and fast." Then Sarge adds, "Besides, us cops down here have never gotten on particularly well with the L.A. bulls, they always treat us like we're hayseeds. Good luck, kid."

He hangs up before I can thank him. Jana and I stand there.

"Okay," she says. "Now we know Harry was down there that weekend, probably visiting his old pal from the neighborhood, Joe Shannon, but it still doesn't prove anything."

I say, "I've got some ideas on what to do next." She listens eagerly until I add, "That's why I had to see you. It can't work without your help"—a shadow of fear crosses her face—"and it's kind of risky for you."

She looks into my eyes. "What do you want me to do?"

49

JANA

The veteran security cop at Panorama's front entrance, who has known me forever, says, "Sorry for your loss, Jana," as he presses the button lifting the barrier.

I left David twenty minutes ago and drove straight here to begin my part. It's the first time I've been to the office since my father died. Was that only last night?

My parking space is waiting for me in front of Research. Getting a parking slot on the main lot, rather than in the boondocks, is a perk that doesn't come with my lowly job. But as Leo's daughter, I rated it. Now that he's gone, I wonder how long I'll get to keep it. Then I realize with a shock that I'm thinking of trivial things to distract myself from the horrendous matters at hand. Okay, I tell myself, whatever gets you through.

As I walk toward the entrance to my building, I notice a couple of studio workers strolling up the street. They seem to slow and stare at me as if they know: her father was murdered. I climb the stairs and make my way to my small office, my desk, my tiny island of continuity, my safe haven. But not anymore.

I sit down, take a slip of paper out of my pocket and place it squarely in the center of my desk blotter. It's the number of the pay phone where David is waiting. Then I swivel my chair to face the window. Usually when I'm working, hours can go by without my looking out. But today is different. I've got a full view of the imposing white three-floors-high executive building. The #1 parking slot in front is empty. No Rolls-Royce. So Harry Rains is not in his office.

I settle down with a research report about the siege at Khartoum in my lap and a red pencil in my hand and pretend to read, but my gaze is out the window.

Time passes. So slowly. I try to keep my mind a blank. But it's as if there are savage warriors pounding on my fortress walls trying to get in. I somehow force myself to ignore them. The smoggy violet sun is starting to set over the Panorama lot, but it's still a fireball.

I'm jarred back to the task at hand by the sight of the Rolls-Royce pulling in. Now I see Harry Rains get out and enter the executive building.

I reach for the phone and dial the number written on the slip of paper on the desk. David answers the pay phone on the first ring.

"He just came back," I say.

"Here we go," he says.

I hang up. My hand is shaking. I can't breathe.

50

DAVID

After receiving Jana's call, I wait a few minutes for Harry Rains to reach his office. Then I dial the studio and ask to be connected. His perky young secretary answers and wants to know who's calling.

"Tell him it's Teddy's boy."

"Teddy's boy?" It means nothing to her.

"He's expecting my call. Very urgent."

"Hold on, please," she says dubiously.

She goes off the line. Then Harry Rains is in my ear. Hushed and surprised. "David?"

Tone is going to be everything. I have to hit just the right tone or this won't work.

"Harry, I'm so scared." I don't have to be a great method actor to deliver that line.

"Where are you?"

"Some gas station on the west side, I don't know, it's— Harry what am I gonna do? Everybody's after me! You gotta help me."

"Take it easy, kid. What can I do?"

"Can you bring me some money so I can get away from—"

"They'll find you, David, no matter where you go."

"Then what should I do? Tell me! You're a lawyer and— you're my friend and—"

"Of course I am. No matter what."

"I didn't do any of those things!"

"Then that's what we're going to convince them of. You've got to give yourself up. We'll get you the best defense team in the country and—"

"They'll kill me first, the cops, they think I'm a mad murderer, they'll shoot me on sight, even before I can say a word!"

"Be cool, David, there is a way—I could meet you somewhere. Bring you in. They won't hurt you if I'm with you."

I'm agog. I can't believe this is happening. I got him to say the words I wanted to hear. Now it's my turn to make suggestions. I propose a time and a meeting place. He says he'll be there. Provide safekeeping while he surrenders me to the cops, then he'll have one of Hollywood's top criminal lawyers waiting at the station to meet us, it's going to be fine.

"But you'll come to me alone, right?"

He promises me that he will. I hang up. Sweat is dripping down my face. I guess my tone was perfect. But so was his. Two bullshitters convincing each other. God, I hope so.

Okay, the way I calculate it there are now two possibilities: Harry will call the cops and meet me with them hiding around the corner ready to pounce; or he'll come alone without telling anyone and try to kill me thereby closing the case forever. No more questions asked. The bizarre thing is, I'm counting on the second possibility.

51

JANA

I 'm still at my desk looking out the window when Harry Rains hurries out and takes off in his Rolls-Royce.

So far, so good. I think.

Now it's time for me to go. The toughest assignment is still ahead and I'm trembling. I take a deep breath, steeling myself. Ready to go. But as I swivel away from the window, I'm looking at Barney Ott in the narrow opening to my office.

"Hey, Jana," he says. "I heard you were on the lot." The man hears everything. He advances to my desk. "Wanted to come by and tell you how terrible we all feel about Leo. He was a great man and a great filmmaker."

He says it with enormous sincerity. As if he's on stage at the Oscars about to present Leo with the Thalberg Award.

"Thanks, Barney," I mumble. Not able to meet his probing gaze. "Appreciate that." I rise, but Ott doesn't move, so I can't leave.

"Got a minute for an old friend?" He takes the chair in front of my desk and gestures me down.

" 'scuse me if I'm a bit presumptuous," he begins, "but with Leo gone, I feel like a Dutch uncle to you. I mean your father's not here to give you guidance at this point, and he was a good friend of mine, so I feel it's my responsibility to mention a couple things."

I'm checking the clock on the bookcase. Whatever advice he's about to deliver, I want him to hurry it up. So I nod.

"First thing is, I know how you feel about David Weaver. I respect that. It's something real special. Wish I could have had something like that in my life"—he grimaces wryly—"but that's another story."

Lord, is he about to tell me the soap opera of his life? Get on with it!

"But you have to face reality, Jana. The *Titanic* sank, you're in the lifeboat. And there's no room for David, that's the plain fact. If you try to save him, you'll both be lost. David has to go down, for what he did to your dad and Joe Shannon, and for the good of the town! A town that's been real good to you. Right now you have everybody's sympathy, you don't want to turn that to hate. Depending on what you do or don't do now, you could get locked up—if you aid a fugitive from justice. And at the very least, you'll be banished from this town."

I expect him to ask me if I know where David is. But he rises.

"That's all I wanted to say. I know you'll do the smart thing. You got a good future ahead. We'll always look out for you."

The man does know a good exit line. He leaves. I'm still frozen, until I hear his footsteps clumping down the stairs. Then I race down the hall, check the staircase—through the glass door below I can see the street. Nothing out of the ordinary. Coast is clear. I scoot down, push open the door and I'm outside—when I see Ott up the street leaning over the open driver's window of a green Lincoln. Talking to Jack Heritage.

For an instant my eyes meet Barney's, then he turns away to continue chatting with his henchman. Making believe he's not aware of me, but through the windshield Jack Heritage is watching me.

I feel blocked. I can't get into my car and drive off. Not

with them following me. Got to lose them first. So I walk
briskly away. Past my parking space. Don't know where I'm
going. Just intent on seeing whether they're tailing me. I glance
back. The Lincoln, both of them in the front seat, is creeping
after me.

So I keep on walking. Frantically trying to think of a way
to shake them off. I stop at a kiosk covered with flyer an-
nouncements of studio activities, touch one as if I'm reading
it, dart another glance back. The car has stopped, waiting for
me to go on. So I do. Down past dressing room row, the cozy
apartments for the top stars at Panorama. Small nameplates
on the front door of each. I see one that says MR. HESTON.
He knows me. I can go in the front door, run through and out
the rear door onto another street. I grab the front door handle
and—it's locked. Of course, his director was killed last night,
so they're not shooting today.

I turn back to the street. The Lincoln is gone. I breathe
easier and start back for my car and then, up ahead, the hood
of the Lincoln noses out from around a corner. Enough so we
all see each other. Like a game of cat and mouse. I pivot and
hurry off. I come to a heavy door on the wall of the soundstage I'm passing. I yank at it. That's locked, too.

Now I'm into the back lot, on the rows of phony movie
streets. The Western street, where my father was lynched. Behind me I see the Lincoln stop and they both get out. They're
following me on foot now. Go faster! Here's the machine shop
where the sets are constructed. The carpenters are hard at work
and don't pay me any attention. Toss another look and see Ott
and Heritage picking up speed, I've walked into a dead end—
and then I see the answer right there in front of me.

A leftover from when David and I as children romped over
every inch of the studio. Back in the rear of the machine shop
there's a narrow space between the closely stacked walls of
old sets. Our secret passage! Dark and mysterious. Perfect. I

slip inside and move forward. I can hear running steps, so I plunge around a bend in the path, if you can call it a path, it's really just a meager space left when they leaned all these tall flats together. I hear voices behind me. I stop. Totally still. Listening.

"Where'd the little bitch go?" I hear Jack Heritage say.

"Gotta be around here somewhere," Barney Ott says. "Let's keep looking."

So I can't go back. Have to go forward. In the darkness, just a glimmer of sunlight filters down from between the tops of the giant walls. It's like groping blindfolded through a maze made of rotting wood with occasional nails jutting out. They are tearing at my clothes and scratching my out-thrust hands. Knowing that the passage comes out two studio streets over is what keeps me going, but I imagine that the walls are getting closer and closer. The space between the stacks seem to be getting narrower, then I realize maybe it's not that the sets have slumped together. It's me, I'm bigger now, no longer the small child I was the last time I came this way. I suddenly feel nauseous and recognize the symptoms: my claustrophobic response. Cold sweat. Shaking. I want to go back to where it was wider, but there isn't even room to turn around, so I have to keep moving ahead. For David to have any chance I have to make it through this, but what if it gets even narrower and I'm stuck in here and even if I scream, who can hear me? My escape route could turn into my tomb. I'll have failed David, it's all over and—then there's daylight ahead. I have to crouch and scrunch sideways like a scuttling creature and force myself through the last few yards but then I'm outside again. In a deserted outdoor storage area. Old rusting vehicles and a motley assortment of discarded props. Ott and Heritage probably don't even know this area exists.

I look at my watch. Still time. Barely. But I can't risk going back for my car. So I tidy myself up and hurry to one of the rear gates used for deliveries. The guard is a stranger who just glances at me as I walk off the lot.

I know there's a small hotel about four blocks away, and that's where I go. A taxi is parked by the entrance. The driver reading a newspaper. I pull open his rear door and climb in, yanking the door shut. The driver folds his paper and looks at me in the rearview mirror:

"Where to, Miss?"

And suddenly this strikes me as the most frightening question I've ever heard. I'm still quaking from my escape and from all the threats that McKenna and Barney Ott have been raining down on me.

"C'mon, Miss, we can't just sit here—where are you goin'?"

My heart is telling me one thing, my head another. David needs me now. But what I want to do is run away and hide. Because what I'm supposed to do now is infinitely harder than what I have just gone through.

52

McKENNA

It's near quitting time, so the office is emptying. I'll go, too, in a few minutes. The Weaver kid is out there somewhere. And that's the sum total of what we know. Undoubtedly on the run. But every hour he remains on the loose diminishes the prospects of our nabbing him.

It's getting dark outside. Downtown L.A. turns into a ghost town after the office workers go home. I've still got my jacket off, shirtsleeves rolled, as I thumb through pointless memos that have piled up. A few items for the files, the rest for the wastebasket or the shredder. Then I notice a brief report from an FBI agent in San Diego. After the Navy Department advised that the sailor, whose dog tag we found in Joe Shannon's lockbox, had died in the San Diego jurisdiction, I'd bucked a pro forma request down there for follow-up.

The report that's come back is boring and less than one full page. But a sentence at the bottom catches my eye.

AN INTERVIEW WITH CHIEF PETTY OFFICER DENNIS PETTIGREW INDICATED THAT TWO HOLLYWOOD FILM RESEARCHERS, JANA VARDIAN AND DAVID WEAVER, HAVE VISITED HIM RECENTLY SEEKING SIMILAR B.G. INFO ON SUBJECT ATHERTON.

I check the date on the report, received by teletype three days ago, before Leo was murdered. So what was David Weaver, the alleged Blacklist Killer, doing down there? Was it a going-through-the-motions charade for Jana Vardian's benefit? To assure her of his basic innocence? Why else?

Atherton. One of those messy loose ends.

Both Alcalay and I had explored the idea that something in Shannon's lockbox could have been blackmail material. But no signs of forced entry, so everything was still there. Obviously a metal box won't burn, and the documents inside were scorched but identifiable and explainable. Nothing unusual, except for the dog tag. So we discarded that early on. Not as if we had found fingerprints on the dog tag.

And then it hits me. The long-ago FBI classroom lecture about fingerprints. "Hollywood crime films lead us to think of fingerprints as the perfect piece of evidence, the indelible individual proof of guilt. The unique formation of swirls and loops can be that. But be aware that fingerprints are extremely fragile. They are essentially sweat, mixed with body oils. Exposed to extreme temperatures, the water component will evaporate, leaving an organic grainy residue that is easily dispersed."

So if Shannon's killer was out to destroy fingerprints on the dog tag—he didn't need to crack the goodie box, all he had to do was douse it in gasoline and cook it away. Could that be why the place was torched?

I could call in this new development to Clyde Tolson. And definitely anticipate his reaction:

"Focus, Brian, focus! This idea is irrelevant. Our case is solved, all we have to do is catch the traitorous culprit—and we know his name."

Yeah. Focus. There are always several of these unanswered questions in every case. Always! Push them aside. This is a flight of fancy I cannot afford. David Weaver is the prize of the decade. When he goes down, I go up. It's that simple.

I mark the San Diego report "File Only" and place it in my outbox, then there's a knock on the doorjamb. It's Willie Pierson.

"Got that answer you wanted. Joe Shannon's nifty house up in Beverly Hills is owned by All-Star Realty Investments, Inc."

"So who are they?"

"A subsidiary of Panorama Studio. Shannon was living there on a lifetime dollar-a-year lease."

I stare at him. "We own the place." Just like Leo's house. Now Shannon's place. Also owned by Panorama. A payoff. For what?

"Something wrong?" Willie says.

I shrug, not knowing what to do with this new bit of information. "Thanks, Willie."

He goes off. I sit there holding the sheaf of bullshit papers, pretending to see them, resisting the thoughts forming in my head. But, hey, how about just for argument's sake? The gift house to Leo was a perk to a big money-making director to keep him happy and on the lot. But why would Panorama be so interested in keeping Shannon happy? Or quiet?

The practical voice in my head shouts, What the hell's that got to do with David Weaver? Nothing, that's what!

So who am I arguing with? Which part of myself?

There's a small pile of messages in the corner of the desk from Kathleen pleading with mounting urgency for me to call her back. I know what she wants to say. Always the public defender, she's on the other side of the fence, she doesn't understand how the system really works. The stampede in Weaver's direction is unstoppable. Too late for discussion.

Well, I can hide from Kathleen, but not from what she has already said: How much do you really want this job in Washington?

I feel an itchy-burning sensation on my wrist. My right

hand has been directly under the heat of the desk lamp. I un-
strap my watchband and rub the irritated scar tissue beneath.
I started wearing a wide leather band years and years ago to
avoid questions or assumptions. Is the scar from a suicide attempt or a childhood accident? Which is worse: horror or pity?
Of course, I was too ashamed to ever mention being tortured
by my stepfather. Better to conceal. But now, with the wristwatch off, I stare at the scar.

Declan Collins. I've tried never to think about him. Until
lately, Kathleen and I rarely spoke his name. He's our sick secret. Declan sprawled on an icy pavement. Both of us crying.
As we abandoned him. She cited him recently as a reproach
and a warning. Declan had his price. Have I found mine? He
took his payment in cash. I'm about to take mine in power. A
chance to spend my last years with the Bureau in dignity doing meaningful work. Go out the way I came in. That's worth
a lot to me.

Enough digressions. I strap on my watch, slip into my jacket,
about to leave in search of a stiff drink on my way home, when
the phone rings. Maybe it's Alcalay and all the doubts and
temptations will be over.

But it's another cop. Jerry Borison at the Beverly Hills cop
shop. On the q.t. we notified him a while back of the connection between Wendy Travers' death and the Blacklist killer.
But that whole aspect of the investigation has been a dry
hole, kind of neglected really, while everything concentrated
on Shannon's murder and now Leo's.

"Well, we got our man," Borison tells me proudly.

I can't believe it. "You got David Weaver?"

"No, but we got the guy who whacked Wendy."

Stunned, I listen to his report. A man walked into a pawn
shop on Pico Boulevard and tried to hock a necklace. The
pawn shop operator recognized the piece from the insurance
photos the Bev-Hills bulls had circulated of the jewelry snatched

from Wendy Travers' body. He called the cops, they arrested Henry Joseph Vitale, a druggie previously convicted for car burglary. "We went to his house and found Wendy's missing credit cards. We're charging him in the morning. Knew you'd wanna know."

I hang up and sit there pole-axed. Now where the hell are we? My big first assumption, my brilliant deduction, linking Shannon's death to Wendy's—it's suddenly become the ultimate loose end. And it's completely unraveled. I suck in a chestful of air, my head spinning as I struggle to make sense of all this.

And the phone rings again.

I assume it's Borison with a detail he forgot to mention, but it's only the Bureau receptionist announcing a visitor who has no appointment. I say it's okay. Could be I'm about to catch a break. I sure could use one.

And Jana Vardian enters.

Looking scuffed and scared. Behaving as if she's tiptoed into the snake pit. I gesture and she sits down opposite me. I wait. Until.

"I've—been thinking a lot about what you said."

I nod encouragingly.

"You said I could, I mean *should* contact you whenever . . ."

"That's right, Jana." Wait again. Then I decide to cut through. "Do you know where David Weaver is?"

The pause is heartbreaking. I can see it in her eyes. Her fear. Of me? Of something or someone else? Of herself? Finally she swallows and answers:

"I—I know where he's going to be."

McKENNA

The sky is dark enough for the show to start on the big outdoor screen at the drive-in theater on Olympic near Bundy Drive.

"Th-that's all, folks!" Porky Pig stutters his signature closing line in the cartoon. I'm parked in my Mustang surrounded by families and amorous twosomes. I'm alone. I climb out of my car and go to the snack stand. It's nippy weather, a cold wind blowing in from the beach.

The snack stand is jammed with flirting teenagers and harried parents with tots in tow. I buy a large black coffee and a donut. Then I stroll slowly around the small building—flat-roofed, whitewashed walls—and I take special note of the large trash Dumpster with its lid closed near the rear door.

I amble on and casually walk behind the sixty-foot-high screen. The ground underfoot is unpaved but hard packed. Okay, that's good. I return to my car, settle behind the wheel. Everything seems in order. Jana has clued me in, but I've brought along a surprise or two of my own. Covering all bases.

I sip my coffee and watch the drive-in's main feature, Billy Wilder's *Some Like It Hot*. I've seen it before, it's still funny. Wish I was in a laughing mood.

My main feature will go on later.

DAVID

I'm leaning back in the darkness against the sea wall on a deserted stretch of beach between Santa Monica and Venice. Music wafts down from the ancient ballroom up above. Not Elvis' revolutionary riffs. Old timey stuff. Big-band arrangements of Glenn Miller's and Artie Shaw's greatest hits. Once upon a time they held marathon contests up there. Dance until you drop, last couple standing wins the big prize. Can't make it without the right partner.

Jana taught me to dance. I didn't think it was possible. "I've got *three* left feet," I told her when we were still sub-teens. But she insisted. "Yes, you can, David, we can do *any*thing together." So we did. With her in my arms I could feel the music and make all the right moves.

After my phone conversation with Harry Rains, I went shopping. To a hardware store to buy a bolt cutter. To RadioShack for a battery-powered tape recorder with an extra-long microphone wire. Then I went looking for some insurance for tonight. I assume Harry will come loaded for bear. Simpler for him that way: dead men don't blab, quibble, or deny. But my trying to buy a gun was not an option. By now I had to assume that all the gun shops had been alerted, so I'd be busted before I even finished filling out the paperwork.

But the Army-Navy store on Third Street has a sale on Commando knives. Ugly mothers, dull black tempered steel, slanted saber-tooth edge, slides in easy and rips out hard. That will level the playing field if necessary. Anyway, in a bout between an ex-Golden Glover and an ex-Ranger, I'm confident that Rangers rule.

So this is the calm before battle. I feel ready. One way or another it's going to be over soon. There is a bright full moon. A hunter's moon. The wind is picking up, urging the ocean into small sharp waves that smack emphatically against the shoreline. From above I hear the band begin to play "Dancing in the Dark." I glance at my watch. I get up and dust off the beach sand. Time to go to work.

McKENNA

It's the final scene of the movie. The speedboat races away from shore. Tony Curtis has snared Marilyn Monroe, but Jack Lemmon has wound up with Joe E. Brown, who wants to marry him—even when Lemmon, who's still in drag, whips off his blond wig and confesses he's a man. "Nobody's perfect," Joe E. Brown says forgivingly. Was there ever a more profound line?

Then the entire parking lot springs to life. Car engines and headlights turn on, drivers begin to exit. It rapidly becomes a traffic snarl. I maneuver into a line that will bring me past the sixty-foot screen. When I get there I veer off and glide behind it as if seeking a shortcut, hoping no one follows me. No one does. I switch off my engine and lights and sit there in the darkness. Wondering how tonight will end.

It takes a while for all the cars to leave, then I wait some more. I hear doors slamming and faint talking, sounds of the place closing down. After a while, a few more cars leaving. Probably the last workers. Silence. I get out of the car and edge forward to peer around the corner of the screen. No vehicles and no people in sight. The night light is shining above the locked entry door to the shuttered snack bar.

I get a black tote bag from the car. It's custom-made, as long as a duffel bag with a zipper running down the spine. Tote it to the rear door of the snack bar. Place the bag on the closed lid of the Dumpster. Hoist myself and the bag up onto the roof. Carry the bag across the flat roof, zip it open, take out a blanket, spread it on the tar paper and squat on it.

Then I bring out an array of metal pieces that all fit together like a shoulder-fired bazooka. Under the right circumstances, this device can cause even more damage. One of the
latest inventions from the FBI's resourceful gadgeteers. They've
named it The Shotgun. Assembled it looks like a Buck Rogers'
space ray gun. I've been fooling with it around the office since
it arrived. Who'd have thought it would come in so handy so
soon?

I lie prone, bring the shotgun to my shoulder, and look
down the barrel. Through the telescopic sight, I scan the entire expanse below. The night light over the front door of the
snack bar casts long eerie shadows. But nothing down there
except rows and rows of sound speakers hanging on their
hitching posts. No, more like whipping posts. Waiting for the
whipping boy.

DAVID

From the side street across Olympic Boulevard I stare through
the windshield of my jalopy as the last worker emerges from
the main gate of the drive-in. He snaps the padlock shut on the
chain. Sealing up the place for the night. He thinks.

I let him roll out of sight down the boulevard before I drive
across and stop at the gate. Hop out with my new bolt cutter
and in a moment the joint is open again. I push the gate wide
enough for me to drive through, then I get out and close the
gate, but not completely. A private invitation for my expected
guest.

I park about dead center inside the drive-in. Open my
trunk. The tape recorder with its two reels is in there. Cued
up. I've already attached the extra-long microphone cord and
I run it under the car, bring the mike up at the speaker post.
With a roll of black electrician's tape, I fix the mike to the

back of the drive-in speaker. Then put the speaker back on its
hook. I look at it. Invisible? Well, good enough in this dim
light. Gotta be.

Then I walk back to the trunk of my car. I press the RE-
CORD button on the tape machine. The red light goes on and
the reels start slowly turning. Good for two hours. Should be
way plenty. I lower the trunk lid. Gingerly leaving it a few
millimeters open. Don't want to risk severing the mike wire.

I go to lean against the driver's door, facing the entrance to
the drive-in. I bend over to pull up the thick GI socks I bought
at the Army-Navy store. The holster with the Commando knife
is strapped to the lower part of my right leg, concealed by the
sock. I straighten up. Feeling prepared as I can be for whatever comes. Same feeling I used to have in Korea. Shaky and
scared during the briefing sessions, but icy cool when the action began. I hold my hand out in front of me. Rock solid.
Nerves of steel. Never needed them more than tonight.

MCKENNA

Through the telescopic sight, I've been watching David Weaver's preparations. Thinking all the while, I can take him out at
this instant, no questions asked. Never mind that bullshit movie
mythology, about how you have to yell, "Freeze, sucker," and
never fire unless fired upon first.

Here's Weaver, the most wanted fugitive in America, and
there are no witnesses. Easy shot. Easy for me, anyway. The
upside is fame and advancement. And happily ever after with
Ashley. Weaver's life ends. My life begins again. There is no
downside. Or is there? How about the promise I made to Jana
Vardian: that if worse comes to worst, I'll take him alive. But
the FBI team who gunned down Public Enemy number one

John Dillinger in Chicago in the thirties didn't ask permission from his informant girlfriend. Cops lie sometimes to get at the truth. But what's the truth here and now?

The winter wind from the ocean has turned sharp and raw, but beads of sweat are running down my face. My body recognizing my turmoil. I know what Hoover and Tolson would prefer. Bird in the hand. Officially declared a predator. Open season. Actually he's the Golden Goose. Shoot him and the verdict is in and final. Wrap up the Commie bastard this instant. That would be the Bureau position.

So why not do it? My finger tightens on the trigger, taking up the slack, testing how it feels. Weaver's at my mercy, so why do I feel like I'm the one who's under siege? Being attacked by the assumptions of a lifetime. I've never been much for navel-gazing, I avoid cosmic questions like, What's it all about? Core values? The kind politicians shout about when they're conning for votes, or preachers threaten you with to get you to increase your donations instead of thinking for yourself? That's not me. So who am I? Really?

My teeth are chattering. But despite the chilling wind, my face and hair are soaked in perspiration. I ease off the trigger and reach into the tote bag for a hand towel. I mop up the salty sweat dripping into my eyes and refocus the telescopic sight on Weaver. I'm bathed in a new river of sweat.

So that's the question of the night. Who the fuck am I really? Am I defined solely by my job? What else? Well, I'm a good brother, good uncle. Does that make me a good person? Or am I just a walking-talking jumble of personal likes and dislikes? An amalgam of the foods and clothes and cars and women and teams and tunes I happen to prefer? Is that all there is to me? Because tonight it's Bedrock City. I must decide. Ass on the line.

I stare down the barrel, framing him in the crosshairs. I

wonder what Weaver's thinking right now. My finger's on the trigger but—I ease off again. Where's the harm in waiting a little longer? Just to see what, if anything, happens?

DAVID

"I'll be there, David!" Harry Rains had pledged. But suppose he ignores my call and just doesn't show up. Assumes the cops will get me sooner or later, so why run the risk? Don't tip your hand, don't get involved.

Maybe that's it. He should be here already. I glance at my watch, twelve minutes late, he's *not* taking the bait. Where does that leave me? Up shit's creek, no paddle. Then the glare of headlights hits my face even before I hear the motor and the sound of tires crunching across the gravel. I squint into the approaching brights. I can't identify the vehicle until it parks across from my jalopy.

Harry Rains steps out of the Nash Rambler. I recognize it as the runabout house car I saw at the Rains mansion when the maid was unloading groceries. Of course, the Rolls is too conspicuous. I wonder how many nights this car has been tailing me these past weeks.

He has a big, reassuring smile.

"Howyadoin', kiddo?"

Arms outstretched, he strides over and wraps me in a warm *abrazo*. Despite myself, I hug back, hungering for kindness. Maybe I'm wrong about him. He's patting my back like I'm a baby in need of burping. No, I'm not wrong. He's not patting, he's frisking. I stiffen slightly.

"I'm not armed," I lie.

"Good boy," he says, "the cops would love the excuse to plug you." But he takes my word, doesn't frisk as far as my ankles. Instead he stops with a final tap-tap to my side. I flinch.

"So Jack Heritage was right—he did ding you up a bit."

"I'll live," I say.

"Well, that's what we're here to talk about, David."

I lean against my front fender. Near the speaker post. Have to keep him close enough for clear recording.

"Is there a lawyer waiting for us at the police station?" I ask.

"Yeah, yeah, just like I said. And I brought a bunch of cash with me, in case they allow bail. Right here in the car." He turns away to the open window of the Rambler, reaches in. Instead of money he brings out a Colt Commander, 9 mm, nine rounds. Harry looks like he knows how to use it.

"Would you do me a favor, kiddo? Step away from that post you're hugging."

Oh God, I've given it away. But I try to bring it off. I glance at the speaker post as if I hadn't noticed it before. I shrug innocently, sidestep. He waves me back further, then carefully approaches, spots the tape, yanks on the wire. My microphone falls to the ground.

Harry sees that the wire runs beneath my car. I start to say something but Harry raises an index finger to his lips and whispers sh-h-h. Gestures with the Colt for me to precede him to the rear of my jalopy. He notices the slightly open trunk, flips up the lid. The tape recorder whirring away inside. He presses the Stop button. Red light goes off. The whirring ends. He smiles over at me.

"This why you invited me out here tonight?"

"Worth a try." There goes Plan A. But he doesn't know about the Commando knife, so I've still got the element of surprise working for me.

"That's what I admire about you writers," he says, "your ingenuity. I always wanted to write a real clever script like Teddy or Leo."

"I think you did, Harry." Follow the Ranger play book. Keep him talking. Find an opening.

"Well, I had a lot of help from you." He's mock grateful. "I want to thank you for unwittingly collaborating with me on my scenario. Making it so easy to set you up. Before you arrived on the scene, I had a good plot, but I had no villain. Then there you were. When Shannon mouthed off at you in front of everybody in the commissary, I knew my idea would work."

"One thing I don't understand—why Leo?" I take a small step toward him, as if I'm that anxious to hear his answer. He doesn't seem to notice.

"Leo was an added starter. Not part of the original scheme of things." See, he wants to tell me. Pride of authorship.

"Yeah, you already had gotten what you wanted. Joe Shannon. You dragged in all that HUAC garbage as a smoke-screen—"

"And then, as they say in the movies, Leo got too smart for his own good."

"He found out something?"

"By accident. That idiot secretary in Mark Gunderson's office sent the wrong manuscript to Leo. Joe Shannon's book."

That lady I met. Maybe no accident. She doesn't like Markie much. "Was it that terrible?"

"Worse," he grins. "As a writer you'd howl at the stupid scribbling."

"But you paid him a small fortune for it. You must have known that would come out sometime."

"After I was gone to the Court of St. James. Whoever took over at the studio would just stick it on the shelf. Chalk it up to his predecessor's bad artistic judgment. Happens all the time in Hollywood."

"*That's* what Leo had on you?" Doesn't sound like enough. I edge another half-step closer. Can't let this scheming fucker win. He's still into boasting.

"Well, that plus—Leo and Joe had a drunken conversation

at a party last year. Became a cockwaving contest. Leo boasted that the studio bought him his house—and Joe, never could keep his faggoty trap shut, Joe said the studio did the same for him."

"So Leo put one-and-one together and started threatening you—"

"To protect his precious movie! He was just guessing, of course, only I couldn't risk even a whisper of scandal at this point. He promised his silence. But Leo always was a pragmatist. He did give names to the Committee, right? So after I went to all the trouble of getting rid of Joe, I wasn't about to trade one blackmailer for another. Leo had to go. It also gave me the chance to sew you up tight as the Blacklist Killer."

Another realization hits me. "You gave Shannon that filthy item for his column about how Leo ratted out Teddy to the Committee. Knowing I'd go ballistic!"

"And there you were right on cue, trying to crash the studio gates to get at Leo. Picking a fight with him in the studio street."

Harry actually takes a half bow. The rage demon rouses within me. But I force the demon back in the box. Stay cool. Wait for the right moment.

"Shannon was bleeding you for decades, right?"

"Hey, Joe was like that. Always was. Since we were kids. Never knew when enough was enough."

"Where did Valerie fit into all this?"

He flares. I've pressed the wrong button.

"She doesn't know a thing! I'd never tell her! She thinks all you Bolsheviks are heroes!" He cocks the Colt. Gotta distract him!

"Wendy Travers's murder the night of your awards dinner, was that just part of your cover-up? To disguise getting rid of Shannon?"

Another wrong button. But this one produces tears in his

eyes. Gun hand shaking, he stresses, "I didn't kill her! Being on that corner that night was just her bad luck—"

I suddenly see it all. "And your good luck. You were having an affair with her."

"How do you know that?" he demands.

"Jana told me Wendy had a mysterious boyfriend. Mr. Wonderful. Was she pressuring you, too?"

"I loved that girl. But she wanted me to leave Valerie. She threatened to tell her about us. I didn't know what to do— then some crazy dope fiend solved that problem by murdering and robbing Wendy. I mourned. And waited a while. The cops weren't getting anywhere catching her killer. Word around town was they probably never would. So I saw a way to get rid of Shannon and blame both crimes on the Blacklist."

"Namely me." He nods and aims the gun. "Wait! How are you gonna explain tonight?"

"That's easy. Tonight I step out of the shadows into the limelight. My turn to be a hero. Hollywood Mogul Catches The Blacklist Killer. A mixed-up kid, who I loved like the son I never had. Only, poor guy went psycho. What could I do?"

Deliberately or unconsciously, he's toying with me. Moving a step away for every step I sneak in. Tigers circling each other. "Won't work," I say. "Too many dangling details."

"C'mon, David, give it a chance: Let's say I came here to talk you into surrendering, but you turned on me, tried to kill me. Fortunately I had a weapon, a gun I bought months ago after reporting a prowler. Good advance planning, huh? You fought me for the gun, it went off—what's the matter with that? A sad story. I'll do the eulogy at your funeral."

He raises the gun. Where's Plan B?

"I know about Axel Atherton."

That gives him pause. He squints at me. "What do you know?"

"That was Shannon's club over you. He knew you murdered Atherton, he had the dog tag. Your fingerprints were on it, right?"

"One drunken weekend, with a lot of reefer thrown in. I couldn't let my life be destroyed for that! I was just blowing off steam after the bar exam, drove down to see Joe, one thing led to another, got kinda wild and—"

"And Atherton was dead. Did he come on to you? He and Shannon were swishes, he must've assumed that you were too, so—"

"He was a fuckin' pervert! I was so drunk that—"

"—I-didn't-know-what-I-was-doing. That's what they all say. And afterwards, well, it had to be Atherton's fault. Because, after all, you were a *real* man. So you beat him to death to prove it. And Shannon helped you bury him in the desert. But not deep enough."

"Shut the fuck up!"

I have to face it. Plan B is not operative. I'm in this all by myself. Adrenaline pumping hard. Have to do something fast. "I'm not the only one who knows."

"You told Jana?' He laughs. "Who's going to believe her? The lovesick girlfriend who refuses to believe her boyfriend killed her father." He takes aim. "So long, kiddo, sorry you got caught in the crunch, but it was a big help to me."

I make my move. A tuck and roll and I go for a do-or-die dive at him, drawing the Commando knife out of its sheath as I come. But he's ready and he clubs me across the shoulder with the gun. When I go down he kicks me in the bad side of my ribs. Then steps on the knife and points the Colt at my head—I'm a goner, I'm finished, he wins—but then the voice of God speaks. Through a bullhorn.

"Rains! Harry Rains!" The metallic voice resonates across the vast emptiness of the drive-in. "Drop the gun!"

Gun still aimed at me, Harry looks around frantically.

"This is the FBI, Harry! Drop it or I'll drop you!"

Harry turns away from me, wildly searching for the source of the voice. Calling out as if imploring the heavens: "Mc-Kenna? That you? I caught him! Got David Weaver for you!"

"The gun on the ground! Now!"

Harry tosses the Colt away and steps back from me. I'd get up if I could but I'm hurting too bad. Then we're not alone. Sirens and flashing lights. Cop cars and even an ambulance. Roaring through the entrance gate of the drive-in. Everything but a brass band. That's what I register just before I pass out.

When I open my eyes, I'm choking. Gagging. Looking up at a paramedic. He's wafting an ammonia capsule under my nose. And Jana. Kneeling beside me. She came riding in with the troops. Plan B at work after all. The Cavalry have arrived. She's holding my hand. Gazing anxiously. Now she's smiling. So am I.

"Thought for a second you were going to miss the party," I say.

"Not if I had to walk through fire," she says.

The paramedic helps me sit up. We're surrounded. Squad cars. Cops in flak jackets. Alcalay is listening to Harry Rains, who's shouting persuasively, "The kid murdered 'em, Lieutenant, he confessed to me—I tried to talk him into giving himself up, but he tried to kill me!"

Then heads turn as McKenna appears. Marching across the emptiness of the drive-in from the snack bar. Carrying a black tote bag, with a small bullhorn sticking out of it. He has an Army walkie-talkie strapped to one shoulder that matches the one Alcalay is holding. Guess that's how McKenna cued Alcalay when to make his entrance. McKenna is also carrying a weird long-barreled weapon balanced on his other shoulder.

"Brian!" Harry Rains shouts at the sight of him. "You tell them, I captured the Blacklist Killer for you, right?" Harry standing beside me. Pointing an accusing finger down at me.

"It's not me, McKenna, he's the one!" I yell back. Oh God. He's a big shot and I'm a nobody. They're going to believe him.

McKenna stops. Facing us both. Drops the tote bag. And aims his weird weapon right at me. Hand on the trigger. He pulls the trigger. And suddenly Harry's voice speaks from the small player on McKenna's belt:

"—after I went to all the trouble getting rid of Joe, I wasn't about to trade one blackmailer for another. So Leo had to go—"

McKenna releases the trigger. Harry's voice stops.

"Whaddaya call that gizmo?" Alcalay asks.

"The Shotgun Mike," McKenna says. "Can record what a person says up to three hundred yards away."

I'm looking at Harry, who seems to shrink. "Then you heard—?"

"Everything." McKenna nods at Alcalay, who cuffs Harry Rains and leads him away.

McKenna kneels beside me. "You okay?"

"Cut it kinda close, didn't you?"

He shrugs. "I got caught up in the conversation. But I figured you could take care of yourself." Then, "Can I ask you something, Mr. Weaver?"

"Slim Jim. The Man Of A Million Questions."

"When you sent Jana to see me, to tell me you were going to be here and what you were going to try to do—how did you know you could trust me?"

He really wants an answer. So I tell him. "Because of the

passport. You brought me Teddy's passport. And you didn't have to."

He has the oddest look on his face. "Glad I was worthy of your confidence," he finally says.

54

McKENNA

This is Big Sky country. Not like the painted backdrops on the studio back lots. The real thing. Montana. Even though I've been here nearly two years, I'm still in awe of the spectacular vistas. After the unreality of Los Angeles, I found sanity here. Snow in the winters, incredible bloomings in the spring and summer, dazzling changing colors in the fall. Not too many people, most of them easy to understand.

I came here on a whim. Answered an advertisement in a *Peace Officer* magazine. Sheriff Wanted. The township of Whitefish was seeking someone to fill out the term of an ailing lawman. I sent off a résumé. I was here six weeks later, figuring it was sort of a paid vacation and then I'd move on. But I liked it and ran in the next election and won.

Of course I invited Ashley—pleaded is a better word—to join me. But she cried and repeated what she'd said in L.A. "I can't start over." Meaning, I guess, in a tiny town in Montana. Even with me. Living the mansion life can become an unbreakable habit. Maybe I read her wrong from the start.

Basically, my career with the Bureau ended with the Blacklist Killer case. As I'd known it would.

The FBI took national bows, of course, because of my central role in the resolution of the case. But from that night when I phoned Clyde Tolson from the drive-in theater and gave him the news, I knew I was finished. Even before that, actually. When I was laying prone on the snack bar rooftop and I didn't bring down David Weaver. I knew then. Soon drumbeats from D.C. informed me Mr. Hoover had been disappointed. Despite the private thanks he received from the White House for saving them the embarrassment that would have come if Harry Rains' ambassadorial appointment had already been announced, he nonetheless was wistful about losing the scenario he really preferred: Commie Kid Killing Anti-Reds. Mr. Hoover did not take well to disappointment.

I was still in L.A. for the trial. The recording I'd made of the confrontation between Harry Rains and David Weaver was the crucial evidence. Kind of completing a circle. The FBI lab guys had been inspired to invent the shotgun mike in emulation of the fishing-pole sound booms used on movie sets. So a Hollywood-originated tool had enabled me to bring down a Hollywood mogul. Harry Rains was convicted on two counts of premeditated murder and sent to the San Quentin death house, where he has reportedly hung up curtains and settled in for years of appeals. I may grow old and die before he does.

Some things have changed in Hollywood since I left. Dalton Trumbo, Blacklisted for many years, got screen credit as writer of both *Exodus* and *Spartacus*. The often-threatened American Legion picket lines never appeared. Both pictures were box office successes. So apparently the Blacklist era was over. Or at least badly dented. On the TV front, ratings slipped and *The FBI* series went off the air.

I don't get down to L.A. much, but I talk to Kathleen and my nephews a couple of times a week and they come up to visit several times a year. They love it as much as I do. I've lost touch with almost all the other people I knew in Hollywood. But not all.

David Weaver phoned me after an item ran in *Variety* that

I was resigning and going north to Montana. He wished me well. Thought that was the last I'd hear from him, but he called me in Whitefish a month later. Just to chat. We've been talking every few weeks ever since. David and Jana are doing fine. They're married now.

Ironically, Leo provided her dowry. His movie, *Against The Wind*, was finished off in style by Rex Gunderson and was nominated for a Best Picture Oscar. It lost to *Ben-Hur*, but the picture made oodles of money and both Gundersons hogged the credit. Mark was promoted to head of development for the low-to-medium-budget unit. Jana guilted him into pushing David's script through into production. She was associate producer and, of course, Rex directed. It'll be released at Christmas, but advance word is so good that Mark is already taking bows for his boldness in making a movie about a pacifist. He's promising to let her direct the new screenplay David's writing. Hollywood promises, so who knows? But sometimes dreams come true.

They came up for a visit last summer. Called it a second honeymoon. Did some fishing and hiking. Not much else to do around here. The best thing was, I could see Jana isn't scared of me anymore. That night when David sent her to see me, she was terrified I would betray them both. She described what they had put together about Harry Rains and what David's plan was—to try to get him to confess on tape and then we could move in for the arrest. I didn't mention that I had backup insurance. The shotgun mike. I got Alcalay to marshal his troops, but agree to hold them back until I gave the signal. Afterwards, I was too ashamed to mention to the kids the temptations I wrestled with on that roof. They're grateful to me. But I owe David and Jana so much. They helped me discover who I am.

Being sheriff means rescuing stranded motorists caught in the winter snows, or breaking up a barroom brawl, usually by locking up both combatants and kicking them loose in the morning. That's what passes for major crime.

Lately I've been courting, as they call it around these parts, a lovely, independent woman named Lorraine Korwin, who teaches Civics and American History at the high school. Marriage is a possibility, although she teases me that the idea of the Sheriff and the School Marm seems too much like the plot of an old cowboy movie.

Occasionally, I tell her about the days in Hollywood, usually just funny stories. Recently I opened up enough to tell her more about my HUAC experiences and the question that had haunted me back then: "If I'd been in their place, those people I was trying to convince to turn on one another in order to save themselves, what would I have done?"

My school marm asked, "Did you ever find out?"

"Yeah. One night in a drive-in theater, I remembered why I first wanted to be a G-Man."

ADDENDUM

I remember the first time I saw the word: Blacklist.

I was barely a teenager, living in the far reaches of Brooklyn, New York. A rough neighborhood. One spring morning I was walking to my junior high school—the most distinguished graduates were Danny Kaye, the comedian, and Anthony Esposito, the gangster, who went to the electric chair when I was in sixth grade.

Already I was in love with the movies. They provided an escape into other worlds. By the time I was twelve, I also had found my way into Manhattan (a subway ride cost only a nickel) and become an autograph hunter. Another escape. Standing at the stage door for "A Streetcar Named Desire" to get Marlon Brando's signature or outside the "21" Club to thrust my autograph book at Burt Lancaster (never imagining that in a handful of years I would be working on movies with each of them).

Anyway, I'm a teenager walking to school and my eye was caught by the front page of the New York *Daily News*, then the largest circulation paper in the nation. The face of Larry Parks, one of my favorite actors, filled half the page. After a "B" picture career, he had shot to stardom (as they say) playing the Oscar-nominated title role in *The Jolson Story*. It was unusual to see a movie star on the front page of the *Daily News*, space usually reserved for ballplayers, presidents, and axe murderers.

It wasn't a very interesting photo. Parks looked upset, but all he was doing was sitting at a table talking into a microphone. I bought the paper and read the story and discovered that Larry Parks had admitted before the House UnAmerican Activities Committee (HUAC) in Washington, D.C., to having been at one time, years before, a member of the Communist Party. I didn't understand exactly the significance of all that. But I figured if Larry Parks was in Washington, maybe he'd come to New York and I might get his autograph.

That didn't happen, but I followed the news stories and a day later John Wayne was quoted as saying that Larry Parks had made a clean breast of his past, apologized for what he'd done, and apparently that was that. Except it wasn't. The next day Hedda Hopper, in her nationally syndicated gossip column. said John Wayne was wrong and what Larry Parks had done could never be forgiven. Turns out, she was right. Parks' acting career was over. Additional news stories explained that although he was deemed a "friendly witness" by HUAC, nevertheless he now had been "blacklisted." That was the first time I saw the word. The newspaper explained that meant he could not make movies any more.

The next time I saw Larry Parks was in real life a dozen years later. I had moved to L.A. and initiated my own career in movieland (which is to say, I'd gotten a few lower rung jobs) and my parents had followed me west. They rented an apartment in Santa Monica and while I was visiting them one day, their landlord stopped by to collect the rent. It was Larry Parks, who had gone into the real estate business. I told him how much I'd enjoyed his performances. He said thanks, but seemed almost embarrassed to be reminded of those days. I never did get his autograph.

HUAC had ended its forays into filmland by the late 1950s, but more than the memories lingered on. The effects were pervasive. Just review the blandness of the general run of movies made during those years—even as apolitical (but socially conscious) a picture as *The Blackboard Jungle* was denounced as Commie propaganda; its director, Richard Brooks (I worked with him later, too), was accused of being anti-American. Those few movies that dealt with the blacklist spoke in code: *High Noon*, it was whispered, was really about McCarthyism, disguised as a Western; *The Invasion of the Bodysnatchers* masked it as a sci-fi thriller.

At that time I was a journalism major in college—City College of New York—and the name of Senator Joseph McCarthy (R-Wisc.) had become synonymous with the blacklist. Witnesses who refused, on whatever constitutional grounds, to answer his questions were deprived of their livelihoods. As editor of the student newspaper, I wrote an editorial protesting the firing of CCNY professors for long-forgotten political memberships. No proof seemed required that a math teacher, for example, had ever tried to sneak Marxist doctrine into his algebra equations before he was fired. However, the biggest fish caught in McCarthy's net was an Army captain who allegedly had been a Commie and now was a dentist stationed at Fort Monmouth, New Jersey. Then McCarthy overreached and went to war against the U.S. Army, accusing top-ranking officials of subversion and hinting at treason. During those hot summer days I was working as a copy boy at the Associated Press in Rockefeller Center. TV sets blared in the newsroom while the Army-McCarthy Hearings were in session. A bedrock Boston lawyer challenged the Senator: "At long last, sir, have you no decency?" Our teletype machines clacked the details of McCarthy's downfall to media all around the world. It was like a Frank Capra movie. Scary, emotional, finally a heart-warming but powerful happy ending. It's all over now. Safe to come out.

But it wasn't.

The blacklist still reigned. Hundreds of Americans had been

smeared as evil suspects in a dark Communist conspiracy. They lost their jobs; some lost their lives. Unimaginable betrayals occurred. Marriages were destroyed, as were treasured friendships. Brother had been turned against brother. Native born citizens had been forced to flee their country and go into exile.

Initially I came to L.A. seeking a job as a reporter and instead was hired as an apprentice publicist with one of the leading independent film production companies of the day. I shared an office with an affable young man who had less experience than I did—he had none—but was being paid more money. He explained to me the secret of his success. His father was a nationally known, fiercely right wing political columnist. One of the name partners of our company was a former Communist who had testified before HUAC as a "friendly" witness and named names. Hiring the columnist's son was further proof of his repentance. "They're all shit-scared of my Daddy," my roommate giggled.

In the years that followed, as I moved from studio to studio and network to network, advancing from publicist, to publicity director, to TV and film writer and eventually as producer-writer, showrunner, and now, as a novelist, I came into contact both professionally and socially with literally dozens of those who had been caught up in the maelstrom called the blacklist. I met survivors from all sides of the political spectrum. Those who gave names. Those who were named. Those who prospered, those whose lives were derailed or destroyed. I knew their wives and husbands and their children, who were of my generation. Some were willing to talk about it, some weren't.

In time, I knew two of the Hollywood Ten, who had gone to prison for Contempt of Congress for invoking the First Amendment and refusing to answer HUAC's questions about their personal beliefs. One of the two was the writer who eventually did more than any other single person to break the blacklist by dint of his talent, diligence and snarky sense of humor. The other was the only director in the group, who had served his jail sentence and then recanted before the Committee; after naming names he was allowed to work again. It was the only ticket to ride available in those days.

The parents of my best friend (and frequent writing partner) were blacklisted when he was a child. His mother killed herself and his father took him to Europe in order to survive economically. They couldn't come back for nearly ten years.

I knew Lillian Hellman, who famously lectured HUAC that she "will not cut my conscience to fit this year's fashions." She was blacklisted but managed to outlive HUAC and be restored to her position as one of America's most respected playwrights. I worked on two of the movies made from her stage triumphs and she encouraged me in my ambitions. "You want to write, then don't talk about it—do it." Decades later, I wrote about her and her relationship with Dashiell Hammett in an award winning teleplay, *Dash and Lilly* (which starred Sam Shepard and Judy Davis).

I spent a week in Utah with Elia Kazan, the superstar stage and film director. He was visiting the location where his wife, Barbara Loden, was starring with Burt Reynolds in a movie I'd written. Kazan was as magnetic a figure as I've ever encountered. We spent a lot of time together and talked about many things, but the blacklist was not one of them. I obliquely tried once, but he gave me his craggy I-see-where-you're-going smile and interrupted me halfway into the first sentence. "Hey, kid, I'm saving all that for my book." Eventually he did write his memoir and it is a fascinating document though it only partially explains how he brought himself to be a "friendly" witness testifying against the friends of his idealistic youth.

In 1963, I was in charge of publicity for a director-oriented company that was the major supplier of films for United Artists. The names on the lobby directory read like a roll call of the notable film-makers of that time: Billy Wilder, William Wyler, John Sturges, Blake Edwards, John Frankenheimer, Norman Jewison. One morning I was called to the offices of the great Fred Zinnemann (*High Noon, From Here To Eternity*). He was preparing a picture for the company based on James Michener's mammoth novel, *Hawaii* and had a press announcement he wanted me to release. We had just signed a screenwriter.

When I walked into the office, Zinnemann indicated the couch where a white haired man in a blue blazer with gold buttons, was seated. He had an almost military bearing, belied by sparkling inquisitive eyes enlarged behind black rimmed glasses, the face dominated by a Hussar's handlebar white mustachio.

"This is Dalton Trumbo," Zinnemann said.

The introduction was superfluous. I'd never met him, but by then Trumbo was a media figure. Once renowned as arguably the best and surely the best paid writer in Hollywood, later reviled as one of the Hollywood Ten who went to prison for defying HUAC, he emerged from jail as he always had been: fractious, gifted, funny, and determined not to be destroyed. He become almost a one-man black market, specializing in quality screenplays at bargain basement prices while laboring in uncredited anonymity.

But Hollywood enjoys nothing more than idle gossip. So after a while, word began to seep out. No specifics, of course. But rumors had it that many—if not most—of the best written new movies had either been written or rewritten by Trumbo. Mischievously, he never confirmed or denied when reporters called. Then the writing Oscar at the 1957 Academy Awards ceremony was won by *The Brave One*, a touching little film about a Mexican lad who sets out to save his childhood pet from the bull ring. The credited writer, Robert Rich, did not run up to the microphone. His absence was explained to the vast audience: Mr. Rich was at the hospital where his wife was about to give birth. By the next morning, the cat was pretty much out of the bag. There was no Mr. Rich (let alone a Mrs. Rich). The Oscar-winning screenplay had been written by Dalton Trumbo. This time his jocular evasions were ignored. Although official credit would not officially place his name on *The Brave One* until years later, the blacklist had become a laughing stock. Trumbo's Revenge, some called it.

The fissure in the facade of the blacklist became a chasm scant months later when producers Kirk Douglas and Otto Preminger gave screen credit to Trumbo for writing *Spartacus* and *Exodus*. Despite dire threats, when those films opened, no picket lines appeared at the theaters and both movies were financial successes. Trumbo was back. Once again the most in-demand and highest paid writer in town. Under his own name.

While he was adapting *Hawaii*, Trumbo and I would often lunch in the small, communal executive dining room on the Samuel Goldwyn lot. He was still keeping up his end of past agreements, still protecting the names of the producers who had hired him in the dark days, as well as the names of the films he had authored and the names of other writers who had risked their own careers by "fronting" many of those screenplays with their names and passing along the proceeds that kept Trumbo and his family afloat. But in other ways he was willing to discuss HUAC.

I can still recall him telling me that despite the general impression that he had stonewalled the Committee, he had actually offered them an opportunity to look into his innermost thoughts. "When I testified, I brought along a stack of scripts—every produced screenplay I had written—and invited them to comb through every page and cite specific instances of un-American propaganda." But HUAC didn't accept the offer. They were there to write headlines, not read scripts.

Time out for a little romance. Actually a Big Romance. In Hollywood there is a screenplay device known as the meet-cute. It's the unlikely coincidence that brings together the boy and the girl. So here is a classic that never made it onto the Silver Screen. Just into the history books.

Once upon a time there was an actress named Nancy Davis. Matter of fact, there were two actresses with the same name. One was a society deb with a promising career as an M-G-M contract player, while the other was a little known but apparently Leftish L.A. actress. Enough confusion for the society deb-cum-starlet to find herself on the blacklist. Frightened, she asked a friend for advice. The friend suggested Nancy contact her friend Ronald Reagan, who in addition to being a mid-range movie star and a stellar force in the Screen Actors Guild, also had pull with a powerful ad hoc organization that had taken upon itself (with the acquiescence of the moguls) the authority to evaluate the "Americanism" of people in the industry.

So Miss Davis met Mr. Reagan and he was successful in resolving Miss Davis' problem. She was removed from the blacklist. And a romance ensued. Some years later my wife and

I were in Washington attending a White House luncheon at which the president presented medals of distinction to various legendary figures in the arts. As I watched the First Lady gaze adoringly up at the President, I couldn't stop thinking this was the Ultimate Meet Cute: "When Ronnie Met Nancy."

That was one way to get off the Blacklist. Here's another, only sort of similar: It's the mid-Sixties. I'm a freelance TV writer, sitting in the living room of my West L.A. apartment with a new friend I met at a beach party in Malibu. Knew the name, now I know the man. Abram S. Ginnes. Everyone calls him Abe.

He wrote a number of the most memorable episodes of *Naked City*, a series that inspired me to try to write scripts. It was the show that always ended with the Narrator intoning, "There are eight million stories in the Naked City. This has been one of them." At the time we met, Abe was in Hollywood writing a big movie for United Artists. But he's recalling his years on the blacklist. "How did you finally manage to go back to work?" I ask him.

"Because of a secretary who was a bad speller. There was a separate blacklist in New York for television and whenever a producer wanted to hire a writer or an actor or a director, they had to submit the name for approval by one of the Madison Avenue advertising agencies that controlled TV. 'Red Channels,' a list compiled by an upstate New York supermarket owner who threatened to boycott food brands that sponsored shows employing any of those on the list, was the ad industry's Bible. So I'd been denied work that way for years, but then this one time there was a new secretary and she submitted 'Abe Guinness'—like Alec—not Abram S. Ginnes, like me. The name went through, I got the job, wrote the script, there were no protest letters, the sky didn't fall, no product boycott, and by accident, after eight years, I was back in business."

So eventually, gradually, things got better. As I was writing episodes for such mainstream network shows as *Mission: Impossible* and *Hawaii Five-O* and *I Spy*, I noticed new-old faces being cast. Survivors of the blacklist. Other actors had become directors, mostly on or off-Broadway, and one by one they were being allowed entry to the sound stages. The flood-gates never were thrown wide open, but the trickle became a flow. There was no day of armistice declared, there are people who to this day still refuse to speak to other people, but it was kind of over.

I was in the audience at the Writers Guild Awards the night Dalton Trumbo was given the Laurel Award for a lifetime of distinguished work. In his acceptance speech, he asked those gathered to evaluate the past in a new way. Saying that the experience had taught him that everyone touched by the black-list had been damaged in some measure because they all were forced to do things they would not have otherwise chosen to do. Looking back, he suggested, we might discover that "There were only victims."

A most generous comment from a great gentleman.

It took many years before I saw the events I had lived through and the people I had known as material for a novel. Of course, by then I had read shelves of non-fiction accounts. I chose to work in the realm of fiction. To only slightly para-phrase the words that ended those Abe Ginnes teleplays: There are hundreds and hundreds of stories in the naked city and in writing this novel, I have tried to tell some of them.

Lest we forget.

———

Two people deserve special mention for their contributions to *Blacklist*. Tobi Ludwig, my muse, my sounding board, and invaluable partner-in-crime. And Albert Zuckerman, an infinitely knowledgeable and creative man of letters and a super agent.

ABOUT THE AUTHOR

JERRY LUDWIG wrote the novel *Blacklist* after spending most of his creative career in Hollywood. He worked with and knew many of the people—on both ends of the political spectrum—who were caught up in the maelstrom of the Blacklist.

Earlier he dealt with a different aspect of those dark days: he wrote and produced *Dash and Lilly,* depicting the political and personal challenges faced by Dashiell Hammett and Lillian Hellman (portrayed by Sam Shepard and Judy Davis). The A&E TV film was nominated for nine Emmys, and his teleplay won the Writers Guild of America prize for Best TV Movie. He also has been nominated for the Golden Globe, the Humanitas Prize, and the Mystery Writers of America Edgar Award. His writing credits include *I Spy, Mission: Impossible, Hawaii Five-0, Columbo, Police Story, MacGyver,* and *Murder, She Wrote.* He now lives in Carmel, California, with his wife, Tobi, an artist.